SAVE
ME

SAVE ME

MONA KASTEN

TRANSLATED BY RACHEL WARD

Berkley Romance
NEW YORK

BERKLEY ROMANCE
Published by Berkley
An imprint of Penguin Random House LLC
1745 Broadway, New York, NY 10019
penguinrandomhouse.com

Book design by Daniel Brount

Amazon, Prime Video, and all related logos are trademarks of
Amazon.com, Inc., or its affiliates.

Library of Congress Cataloging-in-Publication Data

Names: Kasten, Mona, 1992- author. | Ward, Rachel, 1978- translator.
Title: Save me / Mona Kasten; translated by Rachel Ward.
Other titles: Save me. English
Description: First edition. | New York: Berkley Romance, 2025. | Series: Maxton Hall
Identifiers: LCCN 2024053333 (print) | LCCN 2024053334 (ebook) |
ISBN 9780593954201 (trade paperback) | ISBN 9780593954218 (epub)
Subjects: LCGFT: Romance fiction. | Novels.
Classification: LCC PT2711.A785 S3813 2025 (print) |
LCC PT2711.A785 (ebook) | DDC 833/.92—dc23/eng/20241220
LC record available at https://lccn.loc.gov/2024053333
LC ebook record available at https://lccn.loc.gov/2024053334

Originally published in German by Bastei Lübbe AG, Köln, 2018

First Berkley Romance Edition: July 2025

Printed in the United States of America
1st Printing

The authorized representative in the EU for product safety and compliance
is Penguin Random House Ireland, Morrison Chambers, 32 Nassau Street,
Dublin D02 YH68, Ireland. https://eu-contact.penguin.ie.

For Lucy

PLAYLIST

"Endlessness" by Gersey

"daydreams" by gnash (featuring julius)

"Lightness" by Death Cab for Cutie

"A Lack of Color" by Death Cab for Cutie

"Save Me" by BTS

"Slow Hands" by Niall Horan

"Cinder and Smoke" by Iron & Wine

"There's Nothing Holdin' Me Back" by Shawn Mendes

"Teenage Fever" by Drake

"Meet Me in the Hallway" by Harry Styles

Ruby

My life is divided into colors:

Green—*Important!*

Turquoise—*School*

Pink—*Maxton Hall Events Committee*

Purple—*Family*

Orange—*Diet and Exercise*

I've already completed purple (*take Ember's photos*), green (*buy new highlighters*), and turquoise (*ask Mrs. Wakefield for maths revision notes*) for today. Ticking something off on my to-do list is the best feeling in the world by miles. Sometimes, I even write down things I did ages ago, just so that I can cross them straight off again—although I use a subtle gray for that, so that I don't feel like so much of a cheat.

If you opened my bullet journal, you'd see at a glance that my daily life consists mainly of green, turquoise, and pink. But just over a week ago, at the start of the new school year, I added a new color:

Gold—*Oxford*

The first task I noted down with my new pen was "*pick up reference from Mr. Sutton.*"

I run my finger over the letters with their metallic shimmer.

Just one more year. One last year at Maxton Hall. I almost can't believe that it's finally here. In a little more than a year's time, I might be sitting in a politics seminar right now, being taught by the world's cleverest people.

It won't be long until I know whether my deepest wish will come true, and the mere thought makes everything within me tingle with excitement. Will I get in? Will I be able to study at *Oxford*?

I'd be the first in my family to go to university, and I know that I'm lucky that my parents gave more than a weary smile the first time I announced, at the age of seven, that I was going to go to Oxford, and later, that I wanted to study Philosophy, Politics, and Economics.

But even now—ten years later—the only thing that's changed is that my goal is now within touching distance. It still feels like a dream that I've even got this far. I keep catching myself in the fear of suddenly waking up and realizing that I'm still at my old school and not at Maxton Hall—one of England's most famous independent schools.

I glance at the clock over the classroom's heavy wooden door. Three minutes to go. We're meant to be working, but I finished the task last night, so all I have to do is to sit here and wait for this lesson to finally come to an end. I jiggle my leg impatiently, earning myself a dig in the ribs.

"Ow," I mutter; I'd jab my friend Lin back, but she's too quick and dodges out of the way. Her reflexes are incredible. Presumably because she's been having fencing lessons since primary school, so she needs to be able to strike like a cobra.

"Stop fidgeting," she whispers back, not taking her eyes off her paper. "You're making me edgy."

That makes me pause. Lin never gets nervous. Or if she does, you'd never tell, and she'd never admit it. But at that moment, I can actually spot a hint of worry in her eyes.

"Sorry. I can't help it." I run my fingers over the letters again. I've spent the last two years doing everything I can to not just keep up with the others, but to be better. To prove to everyone that I have a right to a place at Maxton Hall. And now that it's time to start filling in our university applications, the anxiety is almost killing me. I couldn't help it, even if I wanted to. I'm slightly reassured that Lin seems to feel the same.

"Have the posters arrived, by the way?" Lin asks. She squints over at me, and a strand of her shoulder-length black hair falls into her face. She brushes it back impatiently.

I shake my head. "Not yet. Should be here this afternoon."

"OK. Shall we put them up tomorrow after maths, then?"

I point to the bright pink entry in my bullet journal, and Lin nods in satisfaction. I glance back up at the clock. It's a real effort to stop my legs from jiggling again. Instead, I start to put my pens away, as subtly as possible. All their nibs have to point in the same direction, so it takes me a while.

I don't put the gold pen away though; I slip it solemnly through the thin elastic band around my planner. I twist the lid so it's facing the front. Only now does it feel right.

When the bell finally goes, Lin jumps up out of her chair faster than I'd have thought humanly possible. I raise my eyebrows at her.

"Don't give me that look," she says, slipping her bag over her shoulder. "You started it!"

I don't reply, just put the rest of my stuff away with a grin.

Lin and I are the first to leave the room. We hurry across the west wing of Maxton Hall and take the next left.

I spent my first weeks here getting constantly lost in this huge building and ended up late to class more than once. I was so embarrassed about it, but the teachers kept on reassuring me that most new arrivals at Maxton Hall do the same. The school is like a castle. There are five floors; south, west, and east wings; and three other buildings for subjects like music and IT. There are countless corridors and shortcuts to get lost in, and you can't be certain that every staircase comes out on each floor, which is enough to drive you insane.

However confusing it was at first, I know the buildings like the back of my hand now. I'm pretty sure I could even find my way to Mr. Sutton's office blindfolded.

"I wish I'd got Sutton to write my reference too," Lin grumbles as we walk down the corridor. There are Venetian masks adorning the wall to our right—the work of last year's A-level art students. As always, I'm amazed by all the playful detail in them.

"Why's that?" I ask, making a mental note to ask the caretaker to put the masks away safely before the Back-to-School party at the weekend.

"Because he's liked us since we worked on the summer ball last year, and he knows how dedicated and hardworking we are. Plus, he's young and ambitious, and it's not that long since he was at Oxford himself. God, I could kick myself for not thinking of that."

I stroke Lin's arm. "Mrs. Marr was at Oxford too. Besides, I bet it looks better to get a recommendation from someone with more teaching experience than Mr. Sutton."

She eyes me skeptically. "Are you regretting asking him?"

I just shrug. At the end of last term, Mr. Sutton picked up on how desperate I am to get into Oxford and said he'd be happy for me to pick his brains, ask him anything I wanted to know. He didn't study PPE, but he was still able to give me heaps of insider information, which I devoured greedily and later noted down carefully in my journal.

"No," I reply in the end. "I'm sure he knows what to put in."

Once we reach the end of the corridor, Lin and I are heading in opposite directions. We agree to speak later and say a quick goodbye. I glance at my watch—1:25—and pick up the pace. I'm due to meet Mr. Sutton at half one, and I don't want to be late. I hurry past the tall Renaissance windows, through which the golden September light floods into the hallway, and squeeze past a group of students in the same royal-blue uniform as me.

Nobody takes any notice. That's how things are at Maxton Hall. Everyone wears the same uniform—blue-and-green tartan skirts for the girls, beige trousers for the boys, and tailor-made blazers for everyone—and yet there's no mistaking the fact that I don't really belong here. Everyone else comes to school with expensive designer bags, but my green backpack is so threadbare these days that I'm constantly expecting it to rip. I try not to let myself be intimidated or fazed by the fact that certain people here act like they own the entire school just because their families are rich. To them, I'm invisible, and I do everything I can to keep it that way. *Just keep your head down.* So far, so good.

Eyes lowered, I push past the others and take one last turn to the right. Mr. Sutton's door is the third on the left. There's a heavy wooden bench between his and the neighboring office, and I glance down at my watch again. Two minutes to spare.

I can't wait another second. Resolutely, I smooth out my skirt, straighten my blazer, and check that my tie is where it should be. Then I knock on the door.

No answer.

With a sigh, I sit down on the bench, looking both ways down the corridor. He might just be getting some lunch. Or tea. Or coffee. Which reminds me that I've drunk too much caffeine already today. I was antsy enough as it was, but Mum had made too much, and I didn't want to waste it. Now my hands tremble slightly as I take another look at my watch.

It's half past one. On the dot.

I look down the hallway again. Nobody in sight.

Maybe I didn't knock loud enough. Or—and the thought makes my pulse race—maybe I've made a mistake. Maybe I'm not meeting him until tomorrow. I tug frantically at the zip on my backpack and pull out my planner. But when I check, everything's correct. Right date, right time.

I close my bag up again and shake my head. I'm not normally this out of it, but the idea of not getting into Oxford only because I messed something up on my application is freaking me out.

I force myself to calm down. I stand up, walk back to the door, and give a firm knock.

This time I hear a sound. Like something being knocked to the floor. Cautiously, I open the door and peek into the room.

My heart skips a beat.

I did hear something.

Mr. Sutton is there.

But . . . he's not alone.

There's a woman sitting on his desk, kissing him passionately. He's standing between her legs with both hands around her thighs.

The next moment, he grips her tighter and pulls her to the edge of the desk. She groans softly into his mouth as their lips melt together once again, then buries her hands in his dark hair. I can hardly tell where one of them stops and the other begins.

I wish I could tear my eyes away from the two of them. But I can't. Not when he slips his hands farther under her skirt. Not when I hear his heavy breathing or her quiet sigh of "God, Graham."

By the time I've shaken off my state of shock, I've forgotten how to work my legs. I stumble into the room, knocking so hard into the door that it slams into the wall. Mr. Sutton and the woman leap apart. He whirls around and sees me in the doorway. I open my mouth to apologize, but the only sound that emerges is a dry choke.

"Ruby," Mr. Sutton says breathlessly. His hair is messed up, his top buttons are undone, and his face is flushed. He looks like a stranger, not like my teacher.

I feel a hellish heat flood my cheeks. "I . . . I'm sorry. I came to collect . . ."

Then the young woman turns around, and the rest of the sentence sticks in my throat. My mouth drops open and my whole body runs ice-cold. I stare at the girl. Her turquoise-blue eyes are at least as wide as mine. She jerks her head away and fixes her eyes on her expensive heels, stares at the floor, then looks helplessly up at Mr. Sutton—or *Graham*, as she just sighed.

I know her. Specifically, I know her red-blond, perfectly waved ponytail that bobs around in front of me in history.

Which *Mr. Sutton* teaches.

The girl who's been here making out with her teacher is Lydia Beaufort.

I feel dizzy. And like I'm about to be sick.

I stare at the two of them and try desperately to delete the last few minutes from my memory—but it's impossible. I know that, and Mr. Sutton and Lydia know it too, as I can tell from their shocked faces. I take a step back; Mr. Sutton comes toward me, his hand outstretched. I stumble again, just about keeping myself upright.

"Ruby . . ." he begins, but the roaring in my ears is louder than ever.

I turn on my heel and run. Behind me, I can hear Mr. Sutton saying my name, considerably louder this time.

But I just keep running. And running.

James

Someone's pounding a jackhammer into my skull.

That's the first thing I notice as I slowly wake up. The second is the warm naked body lying half on and half off mine.

I glance to one side, but all I can make out is a mane of honey-blond hair. I don't remember leaving Wren's party with anyone. To be honest, I don't even remember leaving the party at all. I shut my eyes again and try to summon up images of last night, but all that comes to mind are a few disjointed scraps: Me, drunk on a table. Wren's loud laughter as I fall off and land on the floor at his feet. Alistair's warning gaze as I dance right up close with his big sister, pressing hard into her arse.

Oh, fuck.

Cautiously, I lift my hand and stroke the hair off the girl's face.

Double fuck.

Alistair's going to kill me.

I sit bolt upright. A stabbing pain shoots through my head, and for a moment everything goes black. Beside me, Elaine mumbles something incomprehensible and rolls onto her other side. At the same time, I realize that the jackhammer is actually my phone, buzzing on the bedside table. I ignore it and hunt for my clothes off the floor. I find one shoe close to the bed and the other right next to the door, beneath my black trousers and belt. My shirt is on the brown leather chair. I pull it on, but when I go to do it up, I discover that a couple of the buttons are missing. I groan, seriously hoping that Alistair isn't still around. I don't need him seeing either the wrecked shirt or the red scratches that Elaine's bright pink fingernails left on my chest.

My phone starts to buzz again. I glance at the screen and see my dad's name. Great. It's almost two on a school day, my head feels like it's about to explode, and I've almost certainly had sex with Elaine Ellington. The last thing I need right now is my dad's voice in my ear. I reject the call.

What I do need is a shower. And clean clothes. I slip out of Wren's guest bedroom and shut the door behind me as quietly as possible. On my way downstairs, I encounter the wreckage of last night—a bra and various other items of clothing are hanging over the banisters, and the hallway is scattered with cups, glasses, and plates of uneaten food. The stench of booze and smoke hangs in the air. Nobody could miss the fact that a party was going on here until just a couple of hours ago.

I find Cyril and Keshav in the sitting room. Cyril's dozing on Wren's parents' expensive white sofa and Kesh is sitting in an armchair by the fireplace. A girl is cuddled in his lap; her hands are buried in his long, black hair; and she's kissing him passionately. When Kesh breaks away from her for a moment and spots me, he throws his head back and laughs. I flick him the finger in passing.

The huge French windows are wide-open into the Fitzgeralds' garden. I step out and wince. The sunlight isn't particularly bright, but it feels like a stab in the temples all the same. I glance around cautiously. Out here looks no better than in the house. Worse, if anything.

I find Wren and Alistair on pool loungers. Each of them has his hands linked behind his head, and their eyes are hidden behind shades. I hesitate for a second, then stroll over to them.

"Beaufort," says Wren cheerfully, pushing his sunglasses up into his curly black hair. He's grinning, but I can see how pale his skin looks despite the tan. He must be about as hungover as me. "Have a good night?"

"Can't quite remember," I answer, venturing a look in Alistair's direction.

"Fuck you, Beaufort," he says, not looking at me. His hair shines golden in the afternoon sun. "I told you to keep your hands off my sister."

I'd been expecting that. Unimpressed, I raise an eyebrow. "I didn't force her into bed. Don't act like she can't make her own decisions about who she wants to shag."

Alistair pulls a face and mumbles incomprehensibly.

I hope he's going to cool it and not hold this against me forever, because it's not like I can turn back time. And I'm not in the mood to justify myself to my mates. I spend enough time doing that at home.

"Just don't break her heart," Alistair says after a while, looking at me through the mirrored lenses of his aviator glasses. I can't see his eyes, but I know they're more resigned than angry.

"Elaine has known James since she was five," Wren points out. "She knows exactly what he's like."

Wren's right. Elaine and I both knew what we were getting into last night. However little I can remember, I can still hear her breathless voice in my ear: *This is only happening once, James. Only once.*

Alistair doesn't want to admit it, but his sister is out for just as much fun in life as I am.

"If your parents find out, they'll be announcing your engagement any moment," Wren adds wryly, after a while.

I scowl. My parents have wanted to marry me off to Elaine Ellington for years—or any other daughter of a rich family with a huge inheritance. But I'm eighteen, and I've got far better things to do than waste time worrying about who or what will come along after my A levels.

Alistair snorts equally disdainfully. He doesn't seem too keen on the idea of me as the newest member of his family either. I press a hand to my chest with mock sorrow. "That almost sounds like you don't want me for a brother-in-law."

Now he pushes the shades up into his curly hair and glares at me through dark eyes. He pushes himself up from the lounger as slowly as a big cat. He might be slim, but he's strong and quick, and I know it. I've experienced it often enough in training.

The way he looks at me, I know what he has in mind.

"Watch it, Alistair," I growl, taking a step back.

It happens faster than I can blink. Suddenly we're face-to-face. "I told you to watch it too," he retorts. "Not that you took any notice."

The next moment, he shoves me hard in the chest. I stumble back, straight into the pool. The landing smacks the air out of my lungs, and for a moment, I'm totally disoriented. The water rushes in my ears, and underwater, the pounding headache is all the worse.

But I don't swim up right away. I let my body go limp and hold myself still, face down. I stare at the tiles on the bottom of the pool, which I can only vaguely make out from here, and count the seconds in my head. For a moment, I shut my eyes. It's almost peaceful. After thirty seconds, I'm starting to run out of air, and the pressure on my chest is increasing. I let one last, dramatic bubble of air rise to the surface, wait some more, and then . . .

Alistair jumps into the pool and grabs me. He drags me to the surface, and as I open my eyes and look into his shocked face, I have to laugh out loud, even as I'm gasping for air.

"Beaufort!" he yells in disbelief, lunging for me. His fist connects with my side—bloody hell, he packs a punch—and he tries to get me in a headlock. Seeing that he's smaller than me, that doesn't turn out the way he planned. We wrestle for a moment in the water, then I get a grip on him. I pick him up easily and throw him as far as I can. Wren's laughter sounds in my ear as Alistair sinks with a loud splash. As he resurfaces, he stares at me for a moment, so angrily that I burst out laughing again. Like all the Ellingtons, Alistair has the face of an angel. However hard he tries to look menacing, his hazel eyes, blond curls, and fucking perfect features make it impossible.

"You are such a wanker," he says, spraying water at me.

I wipe my hand over my face. "Sorry, mate."

"OK," he replies, but splashes me again. I spread my arms out and let him. Eventually he stops, and as I look at him, he shakes his head.

Now I know we're cool again.

"James?" says a familiar voice.

I whirl around. My twin sister is standing on the edge of the pool, blocking out the sun. She wasn't at the party yesterday, and for a moment, I think she's here to make my life hell for skipping school with the lads. But then I look properly and shiver: Her shoulders are slumped, and her arms hang listlessly at her sides. She won't meet my eyes, just stares at her feet.

I swim over to her as fast as I can and clamber out of the pool. Regardless of how wet I am, I take her forearms and force her to lift her head and look at me. My stomach flips. Lydia's face is red and swollen. She's been crying.

"What's wrong?" I ask, holding her a bit tighter. She goes to turn away, but I won't let her. I grip her chin so she can't avoid my eyes.

Hers are swimming with tears. My throat goes dry.

"James," she whispers hoarsely. "I'm in deep shit."

Ruby

"Right here is perfect," says Ember, stopping between the gorse and the apple tree.

There are apples all over our little garden, which need picking up. But even though our parents have been nagging about it for days, *pick up apples* isn't in my diary, in purple, until Thursday.

I know perfectly well that the moment Ember and I bring the baskets into the house, a fight is going to break out between Mum and Dad over who gets more. Like every year, Mum's planning to bake cakes, pies, and turnovers, and set them out as tasters in the bakery, while Dad wants to make hundreds of jars of crazy-flavored jam. Unlike Mum, he doesn't have so many willing taste-testers at the Mexican restaurant where he works. Unfortunately, this means that Ember and I will probably have to stand in as guinea pigs. If it were a new tortilla recipe, that would be great, but not when we're talking apple, cardamom, and chili jam.

"What d'you think?"

Ember strikes a practiced pose. I'm constantly surprised by how good she is at this. Her stance is relaxed, and she gives her head a quick shake to make her long light brown curls tumble just a little more wildly. When she smiles, her green eyes positively sparkle, and I wonder how it's possible to be this wide-awake so soon after getting up. I haven't even managed to comb my hair yet, and my straight fringe is sure to be sticking up toward the sky. My eyes may be the same color as Ember's, but they're certainly not sparkling. They're so tired and dry that I have to keep blinking in an effort to stop them from stinging.

It's only just gone seven and I spent half the night lying awake, fixating on what I saw yesterday afternoon. When Ember came into my room an hour ago, it felt like I'd only just fallen asleep.

"You look great," I say, raising the little digital camera. Ember gives me a nod and I take three photos, after which she changes her pose, turns aside, and throws me—or rather the camera—a look back over her shoulder. The dress she's wearing today has a black Peter Pan collar and a striking blue design. She nicked it off Mum and altered it slightly, to give it a waist.

Ember's been overweight for as long as I can remember, and she regularly struggles to find fitted clothes that work for her shape. Sadly, the market isn't exactly flooded with them, and she constantly has to improvise. Her first sewing machine was a thirteenth-birthday present from our parents, and since then, she's sewed her own clothes, the way she likes them.

These days, Ember knows exactly what suits her. She's got a great eye for street style. Today, she's teamed her dress with a denim jacket and white trainers with silver heels, which she painted herself.

A couple of days ago, I was flicking through a fashion magazine and spotted a jacket that looked like it had been made out of bin bags. I wrinkled my nose and hastily turned the page, but now that I think about it, I'm pretty sure Ember would rock that jacket like a supermodel.

That's a lot to do with how self-confident she is, both on camera and in real life.

It hasn't always been like that though. I still remember the days when she hid in her bedroom, heartbroken over being bullied at school. Ember seemed small and vulnerable back then, but over time, she's learned to accept her body and ignore what anyone else says about her.

Ember has no problem describing herself as "fat." "It's just an adjective," she says anytime anyone's surprised by her choice of words. "Like 'slim' or 'thin.' It's only a word, and not a negative one."

It was a long road for Ember to learn that, which is why she started her blog. She wanted to help other people in a similar situation to accept themselves. For more than a year, Ember has been telling the world that she considers herself beautiful the way she is, and her impassioned posts on the subject of plus-size fashion have built up a whole community with her as the pioneer and inspiration.

Mum, Dad, and I have learned loads from her too—not least because she keeps sharing articles with us—and we're so proud of what she's achieved.

"I think one of those should be good," I say, once I've photographed her third pose. Ember comes straight over and takes the camera from me. She clicks through the images, wrinkling her nose critically. But one of the ones where she's looking back over her shoulder makes her smile.

"I'll go with this one." She plants a kiss on my cheek. "Thanks."

We walk back through the garden to the house together, trying to step between the windfall apples. "When are you putting the post up?"

"Monday afternoon, I thought." She gives me a sideways glance. "Think you'll have time to check it over this evening?"

Not really. After school, I have to stick up the posters for the party at the weekend, and then I have to work on my history essay. And I have to come up with a way to get my reference without ever having to speak to Mr. Sutton again. Just the thought of yesterday—Lydia Beaufort on his desk and him between her legs—makes me feel nauseous again. The sounds they were making . . .

I try to shake the memory out of my head, but that only makes Ember stare at me in surprise.

"No problem," I say hastily, pushing past her into the living room. I can't look Ember in the eye. If she spots the bags under my eyes, she'll know that something's wrong, and if there's one thing I don't need right now, it's her asking questions.

Not when I can't get Mr. Sutton's muffled groans out of my head, however hard I try.

"Morning, love."

Mum's voice makes me jump, and I hastily try to get my face under control, to look normal. Or whatever you look like if you didn't just catch a teacher kissing a pupil.

Mum comes over and gives me a kiss on the cheek. "Are you OK? You look tired."

Seems like I need to work on my looking-normal face.

"Yeah, just need caffeine," I mumble, letting her guide me over to the breakfast table. She pours me a coffee and strokes my hair before setting the coffee down on the table in front of me. Meanwhile, Ember goes to show Dad the photo I took of her. He immediately puts down the paper and leans over the screen. He smiles, deepening the slight lines around his mouth. "Very pretty."

"Recognize the dress, darling?" Mum asks. She leans over him from behind, putting her hand on his shoulder.

Dad brings the camera closer, and his eyes look thoughtful behind his reading glasses. "Is that . . . Is that the dress you wore on our tenth anniversary?" He looks at Mum over his shoulder, and she nods. Mum and Ember have the same basic body shape, so at the start of Ember's adventures with the sewing machine, she had a few clothes available to experiment on. In the beginning, it made Mum sad if Ember messed up and pretty much destroyed the dress, but that hardly ever happens now. These days, she's thrilled by everything that Ember can conjure up out of her old dresses and tops.

"I gave it a waist and a collar," says Ember. She sits at the table and pours cornflakes into one of the bowls that Mum's got out for us.

A smile spreads over Dad's face. "It's turned out really well," he says, taking Mum's hand. He pulls her down until their faces are level and then gives her a tender kiss.

Ember and I look at each other, and I know she's thinking the same as me: *yuck*. Our parents are so in love that it can make you a tiny bit sick. But we bear it with dignity. And when I think about what happened to Lin's family, I know how lucky I am that mine is still together. All the more so as we had to work hard for the strong connection that binds us.

"Let me know when your post is online," Mum says once she's sat down next to Dad. "I want to read it right away."

"OK," Ember replies through a mouthful, gobbling it down because we'll have to hurry to catch the bus.

"You will check it first though, won't you?" Dad asks me.

Even after a year and more, Dad's still dubious about Ember's blog. He doesn't like the internet, especially when it's his daughter putting pictures and stuff about herself out there. It took Ember a long time to convince him that a plus-size fashion blog is a good idea. But Ember's thrown so much heart and soul and bravery into *Bellbird* that Dad had no choice but to agree. His only condition is that I—her sensible big sister—proofread Ember's articles and check the photos before she posts them to make sure no details from our private lives end up on the internet. He doesn't need to worry. Ember is very careful and professional, and I admire her for what she and *Bellbird* have achieved in such a short time.

"Of course." I wash my own spoonful of cornflakes down with a large gulp of coffee. Now Ember's the one looking revolted, but I ignore her. "I'll be a bit late back today, just so you know."

"A lot on at school?" Mum asks.

If only she knew.

I wish I could tell Mum, Dad, and Ember what happened. I know I'd feel better for it. But I can't. Home and Maxton Hall are two separate worlds that don't belong together. And I swore to myself that I'd never mix them. So nobody at school knows anything about my family, and my family doesn't know about anything that happens at Maxton Hall. I set that boundary on my first day at the school, and it was the best decision I ever made. I know that Ember often gets irritated by how secretive I am, and Mum and Dad can't always hide their disappointment quickly enough when they ask me how my day was and I just answer "OK"—I feel so guilty when that happens. But home is my oasis of calm. The things that count here are family, loyalty, trust, and love. Whereas at Maxton Hall, all that matters is money. And

I'm scared that bringing that stuff back here would shatter our peace.

It's none of my business what Mr. Sutton and Lydia Beaufort get up to together, and I'd never rat on them. Nobody at Maxton Hall knows anything about my private life, but that only works because I stick firmly to the rule I set for myself: *Just keep your head down!* I've spent two years making myself invisible to most of the school and flying under their radar.

But if I told anyone about the thing with Mr. Sutton, or went to Mr. Lexington, the head, it would create a scandal. I can't risk that, not now that I'm so close to my goal.

Lydia Beaufort, her entire family, and especially her arsehole brother, are exactly the kind of people I want to keep at arm's length. The Beauforts run the oldest and grandest menswear company in the country. They've got their fingers in all kinds of pies, especially at Maxton Hall. They even designed the uniform.

No. No way am I messing with the Beauforts.

I'll just act like nothing ever happened.

I just smile at Mum and mumble, "Nothing much," but I know how fake it must look. So I'm grateful that she doesn't insist, just pours me more coffee without comment.

———

School's a nightmare. I'm terrified of bumping into Mr. Sutton or Lydia in the corridors between lessons, and I practically sprint from one classroom to the next. Lin gives me several funny looks, and I make an effort to pull myself together. The last thing I want is for her to start asking questions I can't answer. Especially seeing that I don't think she bought my story that I got the date wrong and that's why I haven't got my reference yet.

After our last class of the day, we go to the school office together to pick up the posters, which finally arrived in the post yesterday. I'd prefer to go to the dining hall first—my stomach was rumbling so loudly in maths that even the teacher turned to look at me—but Lin said we should save time by sticking a few up along the way.

We start in the school hall and attach our first poster to one of the huge pillars. Once I'm sure the sticky pads will hold, I take a step or two back and cross my arms. "What do you think?" I ask Lin.

"Perfect. Everyone will see it the minute they come through the doors." She turns to me and smiles. "They've turned out really smart, Ruby."

I study the looping black script announcing the Back-to-School party a while longer. Doug's done a great job on the graphics—the combination of the lettering, the subtle golden sparkles, and the silver background looks grand and glamorous, but modern enough for a school party.

Maxton Hall parties are legendary. At this school, we have them for everything—new academic year, end of term, foundation day, Halloween, Christmas, New Year, Mr. Lexington's birthday . . . Our budget on the events team is eye-watering. But, as Lexie keeps reminding us, money can't buy the image conveyed by successful events. In theory, the parties are for us students. But really, the main aim is to impress parents, donors, politicians, and anyone else with the money to support our school, to give their children the best start in life and a direct path to Oxbridge.

When I started here, I had to pick an extracurricular activity, and the events committee seemed the best choice. I love planning and organizing, and I can hide in the background without my classmates taking any notice of me. I didn't expect it to be this much fun though. Or that, two years later, I'd end up co-running the team with Lin.

She turns to me, a broad grin on her face. "Isn't the way nobody gets to boss us around this year the best feeling in the world?"

"I don't think I could have lasted another day under Elaine Ellington's rule without punching her," I reply, which makes Lin giggle. "Don't laugh. I'm serious."

"I'd have loved to have seen that."

"And I'd have loved to have done it."

Elaine was a terrible team leader—dictatorial, unfair, and lazy— but the truth is that I'd never have hurt her. I'm not the violent type, and besides, it would have broken my rule against attracting attention.

But it doesn't matter anymore. Elaine's done her A levels and left the school. And the fact that Lin and I were elected as her successors proves that the rest of the team hated her bossy style just as much as we did. It still hardly feels real though.

"Let's get these two up and then have something to eat," I suggest, and Lin nods.

Luckily, by the time we get to the dining hall, the queue's gone down. Most people are heading to their afternoon lessons or soaking up the sun on the grounds. There are plenty of empty tables, so we get a good spot by the windows.

Even so, I keep my eyes fixed on my lasagna as I carry my tray through the room to our table. I only dare look around once I've sat down with the rest of the posters on the chair beside me and my backpack on the floor. Lydia Beaufort is nowhere in sight.

Lin opens her planner on the table opposite me and studies it while sipping her orange juice. I can see Chinese pictograms, triangles, circles, and other symbols on the pages, and yet again I admire her system, which looks way cooler than the colors I work with. But then I remember the one time I asked Lin to explain what they all mean and what she uses them for; half an hour later, I'd given up even trying to understand.

"We forgot to put a sample poster in Lexie's pigeonhole," she murmurs, stroking her black hair behind her ear. "We'll have to do that after lunch."

"No problem," I say through a mouthful. I think there's tomato sauce on my chin, but I don't care. I'm starving, probably because all I've been able to eat since yesterday is a few cornflakes.

"I have to help Mum with an exhibition after school," Lin says, pointing to one of the Chinese words. Her mother recently opened an art gallery in London. It's going well, but Lin often has to help out, even on weekdays.

"If you need to head out early, I can put up the rest myself," I say, but she shakes her head.

"When we took this job, we agreed to split the work fairly. We do this together or not at all."

I smile at her. "OK."

At the start of term, I told Lin that I don't mind doing some of her share now and then. I like helping other people. Especially my friends—I don't have that many. And I know that her home situation isn't always easy and that she often has to take on more than she can really manage. Especially considering how much schoolwork we have this year. But Lin is just as ambitious, and just as stubborn, as I am—that's probably one of the reasons we get on so well.

It's almost a miracle that we found that out. When I started at Maxton Hall, she moved in very different circles. In those days, she'd spend her lunch breaks sitting with Elaine and her friends, and it would never even have occurred to me to speak to her, despite the fact that both of us being on the events team meant I'd clocked that she's just as keen on journaling as me.

But then Lin's father created a genuine scandal, and their family lost not only all their money but also their friends. Suddenly, Lin was alone at break times—I'm not sure whether people didn't want anything to do with her anymore or whether she was too ashamed to speak to them. But I do know what it feels like to suddenly lose all your friends. It was the same for me when I moved here from my old school in Gormsey. I felt overwhelmed—higher academic standards, the nonschool stuff, the fact that everyone here was so different from me—and at first I couldn't manage to keep in touch with people from home. My friends there made it pretty clear what they thought of that.

Looking back on it now, I realize that true friends don't just laugh at you for wanting to get involved with things at school. I used to laugh off names like "nerd" and "smartarse," but it wasn't really funny. And I know that it's not real friendship if they don't even try to understand what you're going through. They didn't ask even once how I was, or if they could do anything to help.

But back then, it really hurt to see those friendships break up like that, especially as nobody at Maxton Hall wanted anything to do with me either—or even noticed me. I'm not from a rich family. I have a six-year-old backpack, not a designer bag, and a secondhand laptop, not a gleaming MacBook. I don't go to the weekend parties that the cool kids spend the whole next week discussing— for most of my classmates, I simply don't exist. These days, I like it that way, but my first few weeks at Maxton were lonely, and I felt very isolated. Until I met Lin. Our experiences with our friends aren't the only thing we have in common. Lin also shares my two biggest hobbies: She loves organizing stuff, and she loves manga.

I have no idea if we'd have got to know each other without the business with her parents. But although I sometimes get the feeling she misses the days when she was a somebody here and hung around with people like the Ellingtons, I'm glad to have her.

"OK then. You go to Lexington and put up the posters in the library and the study center on the way. I'll do the rest, OK?"

I hold out my hand for a high five. For a moment, Lin looks like she wants to say something, but in the end, she smiles gratefully and claps my hand. "You're the best."

Someone pulls out the chair beside me and drops onto it. Lin turns pale. I frown as she stares, eyes wide, from me to the person sitting next to me, and then back to me again.

I turn very slowly—and find myself looking straight into a pair of turquoise-blue eyes.

Like everyone at this school, I know those eyes, but I've never seen them up close before. They belong to a striking face with dark brows, high cheekbones, and an arrogant, handsome mouth.

James Beaufort is sitting next to me.

Looking at me.

From close up, he looks even more dangerous than he does at a distance. He's one of the guys who act like this school belongs to them. And he looks like it does too. He's perfectly poised and self-assured, his tie is perfectly knotted and straight. The uniform is pretty ordinary, really, but on him, it looks amazing, like it was made to measure. Which is probably because his mother designed it. The only thing about him that isn't precise is his hair—unlike his sister, he prefers a messy style.

"Hey," he says.

Have I ever heard him speak before? Yelling across a lacrosse field or drunk at an event, yes. But not like this. His "hey" sounds friendly, and there's a spark in his eyes. He's acting like it's perfectly normal for him to sit next to me at lunch for a chat. But it's the first time we've ever exchanged words. And I'd rather keep it that way.

I look around cautiously and gulp hard. A few heads have turned our way. It feels as though the cloak of invisibility I've been wearing the whole of the last two years has slipped a little.

Not good, not good, not good.

"Hey, Lin. Mind if I borrow your friend a minute?" he asks, not breaking eye contact with me even once. His eyes are so intense I get shivers down my spine. It takes me a while to process what he said. The next moment, I turn to stare at Lin, trying to tell her without words that *I* would mind that, but she isn't looking at me, only James.

"Sure," she says, "no worries."

I just about have time to grab my bag off the floor before James Beaufort's hand is on my lower back as he steers me out of the dining hall. I speed up a touch to get away from his hand, but I can still feel the warmth of it, as if it had burned through my blazer onto my skin. He leads me past the huge staircase in the lobby and doesn't stop until we're well out of sight of anyone going in or out of the dining hall.

I can imagine what he's after. He hasn't even looked once at me in the last two years, so this must have something to do with his sister and Mr. Sutton.

It's only once I'm certain that no one can hear us that I turn to him.

"I think I know what you want from me."

His lips twist into a slight smile. "Do you, now?"

"Listen, Beaufort . . ."

"I'm afraid I'm going to have to stop you there, Robyn." He takes a step toward me. I don't flinch, just look at him, eyebrows raised. "You're going to forget whatever you saw yesterday immediately, got that? If I find out that you've uttered even a single word about it, I'll get you kicked out of this school."

He presses something into my hand. Dazed, I glance down and stiffen once I see what it is.

In my hand, there's a heavy bundle of banknotes. I gulp.

I've never held this much money before.

I look up. James's superior grin speaks volumes. It's clear that he knows exactly how much I could use the money. And that this isn't the first time he's bought someone's silence.

Everything in his eyes and his whole stance is so smug that I'm suddenly furious.

"Are you serious?" I ask through gritted teeth, holding up the money. I'm so angry, my hand is shaking.

Now he looks thoughtful. He reaches into the inside pocket of his blazer, pulls out a second wad, and holds it out to me. "I can't go higher than ten grand."

Stunned, I stare at the money, then back at his face.

"If you keep your mouth shut until the end of term, we can double it. Till the end of the year, we'll quadruple it."

His words echo in my head, over and over again, and the blood boils in my veins. Standing there like that, tossing ten grand at my feet and trying to keep me quiet. Like it's nothing. Like that's just what you do when you were born with a silver spoon in your mouth. Suddenly, one thing is very clear to me.

I can't stand James Beaufort.

More than that. I *loathe* him. Him and everything he stands for.

The way he lives—with no respect or fear of consequences. The name Beaufort makes you untouchable. Whatever you do, Daddy's money will somehow sort it out. While I've been working my arse off for the last two years just to have a chance at a place at Oxford, school for him is just a walk in the park.

It's not fair. And the longer I stare at him, the angrier I feel.

My fingers cramp around the notes in my hand. I bite my teeth together and rip off the thin paper band holding the bundle together.

James frowns. "What the . . ."

I jerk up my hand and throw the money in the air.

James meets my stoical expression with an iron glare; his only reaction is a throbbing muscle in his jaw.

As the notes slowly float to the ground, I turn and walk away.

Ruby

A strawberry-blond ponytail sways in front of my face. I focus all my rage on it.

This is all Lydia's fault! If she hadn't been making out with a teacher, I wouldn't have caught the two of them at it, and she wouldn't have been able to go running to her brother about me. Then I'd be able to focus on the lesson and wouldn't be getting worked up about the fact that he called me *Robyn*. Or that I actually threw five thousand pounds up in the air.

I bury my face in my hands. I can't believe I did that. Of course it was right not to take the money. But all the same—my mind has been racing since yesterday afternoon with all kinds of things I could have done with it. Our house, for instance. Since Dad's accident ten years ago, we've gradually been doing it up and making it wheelchair accessible, but there are still a few places that could do with improvement. And our car's been on its last legs for ages, when we're all dependent on it. Especially Dad. The forty grand that James offered me by the end of the year could have bought a brand-new people carrier.

I shake my head. No, I'd never take hush money from the Beauforts. I can't be bought.

I pull my journal out from under my history book and open it. Every bullet point for today has already been ticked off. The only thing that's still glittering mockingly at me is *pick up reference from Mr. Sutton.*

I grit my teeth and stare at the letters. I wish I could erase them—that and the memory of him and Lydia.

For the first time since the lesson started, I dare to peek over Lydia's head to the front. Mr. Sutton's standing at the whiteboard. He's wearing a checkered shirt and a dark gray cardigan, and the glasses he always has on in class. He has neat designer stubble, and I can see the dimples in his cheeks that the whole class swoons over.

Laughter rings out around me—he's cracked a joke.

One of the reasons I always used to like him so much.

Now I can't even look at him.

I don't get it—Mr. Sutton got into Oxford, did his degree, started work at one of the poshest schools in the country straight after graduating, and then the first thing he goes and does is get involved with a student? Why, for God's sake?

His eyes meet mine and immediately, his smile slips slightly. In front of me, Lydia stiffens. Her shoulders and neck go rigid, as if she's putting every ounce of strength she has into not turning around.

I lower my gaze so hastily to my planner that my hair flies across my face like a dark cloud. I spend the rest of the lesson hunched in that position.

When the bell finally rings, it feels like days have passed, not ninety minutes. I take as much time as I can. I gather up my stuff in slow motion and put it carefully away in my backpack. Then I do up the zip so slowly that I hear each individual tooth lock into place.

I don't stand up until everyone's footsteps and voices are gradually fading. Mr. Sutton seems miles away as he stuffs his papers into a folder. He looks tense, every scrap of humor that was on his face just now has vanished.

The only person still in the room with us is Lydia Beaufort. She's hanging around by the door, looking from me to Mr. Sutton and back again, her jaw tense.

My heart is pounding in my throat as I shoulder my backpack and walk to the front. I stop a good distance away from Mr. Sutton's desk and clear my throat. He looks at me. His golden-brown eyes are full of regret. His guilty conscience is tangible. His movements are jerky and robotic.

"Lydia, would you give us a minute?" he asks, not looking at her.

"But . . ."

"Please," he adds gently, his eyes drifting over to her for a second.

She nods, lips pressed together, and turns away. She shuts the classroom door quietly behind her.

Mr. Sutton turns back to me. He opens his mouth to say something, but I cut him off.

"I just wanted to pick up my UCAS reference," I say hastily.

He blinks, confused, and it takes him a moment to react. "I . . . Of course." He flips frantically through the folder that he just put his class notes away in. He doesn't seem to find what he's looking for, so he leans over, picks up his brown leather bag from the floor, and heaves it onto the desk. He opens it and digs around for a while. His hands are shaking, and I can see his cheeks starting to flush pink.

"Here's your copy," he mumbles as he finally pulls out a clear plastic folder with a sheet of paper inside it. "I was intending to talk it through with you first, but after . . ." He clears his throat. "I've already uploaded it because I didn't know if you'd still be collecting it."

I take it with stiff fingers. "Thanks."

He coughs again. The situation is getting worse by the second. "I wanted to tell you that I . . ."

"Don't." My voice is a hoarse croak. "Please . . . don't."

"Ruby . . ." Suddenly I recognize a second emotion alongside the regret in Mr. Sutton's eyes: fear. He's afraid of me. Or rather of what I might do with the knowledge I have of him and Lydia. "I only wanted to . . ."

"No," I say, and this time my voice is firmer. I lift my hands to ward it off. "I have no intention of telling anyone about it. Really, I don't. I . . . I just want to forget the whole thing."

He opens his mouth and shuts it again. His expression is equal parts surprise and doubt.

"It's none of my business," I continue. "Or anyone else's."

Between us there's a pause, during which Mr. Sutton eyes me so intently that I don't know where to look. It's as though he's trying to read my eyes to find out whether I'm serious. In the end, he says quietly: "You know that that means I'll still be your teacher."

Of course I do. And the idea of spending several hours a week in the same room as Lydia and Mr. Sutton is anything but appealing. But the alternative is going to the head, and my encounter with James Beaufort gave me a very clear foretaste of what that would mean for me.

Besides, I genuinely do believe that Mr. Sutton's private life has nothing to do with me.

"I just want to forget the whole thing," I say again.

He exhales slowly. "And you have no . . . conditions?" When he sees my outraged expression, he hastily adds: "You're on course to pass with flying colors anyway. You're one of the best in the class, you know that. All I meant was that . . . I . . ." He breaks off, groaning with frustration; his cheeks are red, his body language uncertain, and his eyes are almost despairing. He suddenly looks incredibly young, and, for the first time, I really clock how young he is—not that much older than us.

I try to smile, without much success. "I just want to get through my exams in peace, sir," I say, putting my copy of the reference in my bag.

He doesn't reply, and I walk to the classroom door. Then I look back over my shoulder. "Please don't give me any special treatment."

He stares at me like I'm a ghost—and not a friendly one. His eyes are suspicious, which is hardly surprising.

"Thanks for writing the reference."

I see him swallow hard. Then he nods again. I turn away and walk out of the classroom. Once I've shut the door, I lean my back against it, shut my eyes, and take several deep breaths.

Only then do I realize that I'm not alone. A soft sound makes my eyes fly open again.

James Beaufort is leaning against the wall opposite me. He's crossed his arms over his chest and has one foot against the wall. His eyes are on me—his expression is harder than yesterday; his mood seems darker. There's no more trace of the conspiratorial grin with which he tried to foist his money on me.

He pushes himself away from the wall and comes over. His

steps are slow and almost threatening. The moment seems to last ages. My heart starts to race. This is his kingdom. And I feel like an interloper.

He comes very close before he stops. He looks down at me without a word, and for a moment I forget how to breathe. Once I've got that under control again, I realize how nice he smells. Like star anise. Spicy and tangy, but pleasant. I'd like to bring my nose closer to him, but then I remember who I'm facing here.

James reaches into his inside pocket.

That frees me from my paralysis. I narrow my eyes and glare at him. "If you try to bribe me again, I'll shove your money down your throat."

His hand pauses a moment, then draws back. His eyes flicker darkly. "Cut this whole Mother Teresa bit out and tell me what you want from my family." His voice is velvety and deep—a strange contrast to his harsh words.

"I don't want anything from your family," I begin, glad to have the door at my back. "Apart from you to leave me alone, maybe. Besides, Mother Teresa would have taken the money and handed it out in the dining hall or given it to the needy on the streets or something. Love thy neighbor and all that, you know?"

James's face freezes. "Do you think that's funny?" he asks, the rage clear in his voice. He takes another step toward me, so close that the toes of his shoes are touching mine.

If he comes another millimeter closer, I'll kick him where it hurts—regardless of who at Maxton Hall knows my name after that. "I don't want any trouble with you, Beaufort," I say, keeping my voice calm. "Or your sister. And I really don't want your money. All I want is to get through the upper sixth."

"You really don't want the money," he says with an air of such disbelief that I can't help wondering what he and his family must have experienced in the past. Or who they've had to deal with.

None of my business, none of my business, none of my business!

"No, I don't want your money." Maybe if I repeat it a few more times while looking him straight in the eye, he'll believe me.

He watches me for what feels like an eternity, studying every inch of my face and reading my intentions. Then he lowers his gaze to my lips, then to my chin and neck, and then lower still. Centimeter by centimeter.

When he looks up again, understanding has dawned on his face. He steps back a bit. "I see." He sighs and then looks both ways down the corridor. "Where do you want it?"

I have no idea what he means. "What?"

"Where d'you want it?" He rubs the back of his head. "I think one of the tutor rooms over there is free. I've got a master key." He looks questioningly at me. "Do you get very loud? It's right next to Mrs. Wakefield's office, and she generally stays late."

I can only stare at him, wondering what the hell he means. "I don't have the least idea what you're on about."

He raises a mocking eyebrow. "Right. Listen, I'm familiar with the whole 'I don't want money' thing too." Then he grabs my hand and pulls me down the hall. Outside the room he mentioned, he pulls the key from his pocket and opens the door.

He's started loosening his tie with his free hand.

Where do you want it?

Once I realize what he meant by "it," I'm gasping with outrage. But he suddenly takes my hand and starts to pull me into the room. I grip on to the doorframe and tear my hand away.

"What the hell?" I snap.

"Let's start the negotiations over again," he replies. He glances at his watch. The strap is black and the casing is bronze, and it looks very stylish. And crazy expensive. "I've got training in a bit, so it would be good if we could get a move on."

He holds the door for me and nods into the room, untying his tie altogether and starting to unbutton his shirt too. My brain short-circuits as his chest comes into view and I get a glimpse of his muscles. My throat is dry as dust.

"Are you insane?" I croak, taking a step back before he can get to the last button.

He looks intently at me. "Don't act like you don't know how this works."

I snort. "You must be out of your mind if you think you can buy my silence with your body. Who do you actually think you are, you arrogant bastard?"

He blinks again and again. Opens his mouth and shuts it again. Then he shrugs his shoulders.

My cheeks are hot. I don't know whether I should be repulsed or ashamed. I think I'm feeling a bit of both. "What's wrong with you?" I mumble, shaking my head.

Now it's his turn to snort. "Everyone has a price, Robyn. What's yours?"

"My name's Ruby, for fuck's sake!" I snarl, clenching my fists. "Here's my price: Leave me the hell alone from now on. I seriously can't afford to be seen with you."

His eyes are spraying sparks. "*You* can't afford to be seen with *me*?"

The disbelief in his voice ought to make me angry, but by now I almost feel sorry for him. Almost.

"It's enough that you spoke to me in the dining hall. I don't want to be part of your world."

"My world," he repeats.

"You know . . . the parties, drugs, all that crap. I want nothing to do with it."

Suddenly, I hear footsteps. My heart skips a beat and then starts to race. I shove James into the room and slam the door behind us. I hold my breath, listening intently and hoping desperately that whoever is out there won't come in here.

Please no, please no, please no.

The steps grow louder, and I screw my eyes shut. They pause outside the door. Then they fade away again and disappear altogether. I breathe a sigh of relief.

"You're serious." James's tone is inscrutable, like his face.

"Yes," I say. "So kindly do your shirt up again."

He slowly complies with my request but doesn't take his eyes off me. Like he's searching for some back door that I might have left open somewhere. He doesn't seem to find one. "OK then."

The pressure on my chest eases abruptly. "Good. Great. So, I have to get home; my parents will be waiting." I gesture over my shoulder with my thumb. He doesn't speak, so I awkwardly raise my hand to wave goodbye. Then I turn to the door.

"Even so, I don't trust you." The sound of his dark voice sends goose bumps down my arms.

I press down the handle. "The feeling's mutual."

James

The mood in the changing room is tense, the air crackling with adrenaline. These few moments before our pep talk from the coach and finally getting onto the field are the best and the worst at the same time. In these few minutes, everything seems possible: victory and defeat, pride and shame, joyful triumph and unbearable frustration. This is the time when the team spirit is at its peak and we're at our most motivated.

From outside, I can hear the cheering spectators—our schoolmates and the opposing fans alike. It's hard to believe that six years ago, nobody at Maxton Hall gave a fuck about lacrosse. In those days, it was a loser sport, a dumping ground for those who were shit at rugby or football, and as a result, the team was shit too. A mishmash of adolescent beanpoles with spotty faces and gangly limbs that weren't fully under control.

I thought it would be a laugh to sign up. I was mainly hoping to seriously annoy my dad. I never expected to actually enjoy it. Or that within a week or two, I'd have ambitions to make something of the team. I convinced my mates to join in, told Lexie to hire a better coach or feel my dad's wrath, and got our top designer to work on our uniforms.

It was the first time in my life that I'd felt passionate about anything. And it paid off. Now, six years later, after many hours of training several nights a week, after all the blood, sweat, tears, and a few broken bones, we've won three championships and we're the school's poster team.

We've worked our arses off to get where we are now. And every time I look into the determined faces of my team before a match, I feel the same pride.

Like I do now.

But there's another emotion mixed in there today. Something so dark and painful that for the first time ever, I find it hard to pull the shoulder pads over my head.

This is the first game of my last year at the school.

After this season, I'm done. Lacrosse will have been nothing more than part of a slow, gruesome countdown that I can't stop. However hard I try.

"You all right?" Wren asks, bumping me with his shoulder.

I shove the thought back down. We're not at that point yet—I've got a whole year to do whatever I want. My grin is only half fake as I turn to him. "We'll show those Eastview wankers."

"McCormack is mine," Alistair chimes in, as if he'd been waiting for his cue. "I've got a score to settle with him."

"Alistair," Kesh says from my left. He rubs his nose, where it was broken last year. "Drop it, OK." His tone and the expressive way he looks at Alistair tell me this isn't the first time they've had this conversation.

But the only reply he gets is "No."

Last time we played them, McCormack—whose first name I

sadly share—waited for Kesh to take his helmet off and then intentionally whacked him in the face with his stick. The memory of the shock as Kesh was knocked to the ground is very vivid. The blood spraying from his nose onto his top. The moment when he lay there, unconscious.

McCormack was suspended for the next three matches, but the memory of Kesh's battered face brings the rage to a boil again—and Alistair clearly feels the same, as he's still staring Kesh down.

"Just don't do anything stupid," Kesh says, pulling on his blue shirt. Then he ties his hair back in a low, messy man-bun and shuts his locker.

"You know what he's like," mutters Wren, leaning on the locker, a wry grin on his face.

"I don't care if I'm out for the rest of the season. McCormack's going to pay." Alistair claps Kesh on the shoulder. "Be grateful I'm there to fight for you and your honor."

Before he can pull his hand away, Kesh grabs it and holds it there. He glances over his shoulder. "I mean it."

Alistair narrows his amber-colored eyes to slits. "So do I."

The two of them stare at each other a moment, and if the mood was tense earlier, now you could cut the air with a knife.

"Save your aggro for the game," I say, in a voice that makes it clear I'm speaking as their captain, not their friend. Two pairs of angry eyes are fixed on me, and I clap my hands before anyone can reply.

The team gathers in the center of the room. As I walk, I pull on my shirt with the number seventeen. It's so familiar, it's like the fabric is part of me. The dark feeling tries to force its way up again, but I fight it down with all my strength and focus instead on Mr.

Freeman, our coach, who is now walking over to us from his office. He's a tall, rangy man, with such long limbs you'd take him for a distance runner or an athlete. He pulls his blue cap over his hair, which has thinned and lightened over the years, straightens the peak, and puts his arms around me and Cyril, his co-captains.

He gazes around the room. "This might be your first season, or your last. Our aim is to win the title," he growls. "Anything else is failure. So get out there and beat the bastards."

The coach is a man of few words, but he doesn't need them. Those few sentences are enough to rouse up a rumble of agreement.

"We have to make this the best season Maxton Hall has ever seen," I add, a touch louder than the coach. "OK?"

The lads roar again, but it's not enough for Cyril. He holds his hand to his ear. "OK?"

This time, the yell is so loud, my ears ring—which was the desired effect.

Then we pull on our helmets and grab our sticks. As I walk out of the changing room and down the narrow tunnel, it feels like I'm underwater—the sounds from outside are muffled, like there's pressure on my ears. I hold tighter to my stick and lead my team out onto the field.

The stands are packed. Everyone cheers as we run out onto the field; the cheerleaders are dancing. Music blares from the loudspeakers, setting the ground shaking beneath my feet. Fresh air floods my lungs, and I feel more alive than I have for weeks.

The subs and coach head for the side of the field, while we walk out into the center and position ourselves opposite the other team, who all look just as motivated as us.

"This is going to be a great game," Cyril mutters beside me, which is just what I was thinking.

As we wait for the referee, I let my eyes roam over the stands. From here, about the only person I can make out is Lydia, who always sits right at the top with her friends, acting like she couldn't care less about the entire performance. I glance over to the edge of the field and check out the other team's subs, then their coach, who is wandering over to say hello to Freeman.

At this point, someone's brown hair catches my attention. A girl has gone over to them. She exchanges a few words and points to something in her hand. As the wind blows her hair off her face, I recognize her.

I seriously can't afford to be seen with you.

The memory of her words feels like a punch in the guts. Nobody has ever said anything like that to me before.

Generally, the opposite is the case. People are *desperate* to be seen with me. From the moment I started at this school, I've had people latching on to me, trying to get my attention. It goes with the name. Since my mother's family founded Beaufort's, the gentlemen's outfitters, a hundred and fifty years ago, building it up into a multibillion-pound empire, everyone in the country knows who we are. The name "Beaufort" means money. Influence. Power. And there are loads of people at Maxton Hall who think I could get them those things—or even a fraction of them—if they just butter me up enough.

I'd need more than the fingers of both hands to count how often I've partied all night with someone and then they've tried to slip me a design for a suit. How often people have got chatting to me just so they can ask for my parents' contact details. How often people have tried to worm their way into my group of friends just so they can get gossip on Lydia and me and sell it to the press. The picture of me doing a line of coke at Wren's sixteenth two years ago is just one example. And that's not counting everything Lydia's had to go through.

That's why I pick my friends very carefully. Wren, Alistair, Cyril, and Kesh have no interest in my money—they've got more than enough of their own. Alistair and Cyril are from seriously posh families, Wren's parents are filthy rich city traders, and Kesh's dad is a famous film director.

People *want* us to notice them.

Everyone but . . .

My eyes are fixed on Ruby. Her dark hair shines in the sunlight, tousled by the wind. She's battling against her fringe, smoothing it down with one hand, but it's pointless—two seconds later, it's blowing everywhere again. I'm pretty sure I'd never set eyes on her before the business with Lydia. Now I wonder how that was possible.

I seriously can't afford to be seen with you.

Everything about her raises my suspicions—especially her piercing green eyes. I want to walk over to her, to see if she looks at other people the way she looked at me, with fire and scorn.

That girl saw my sister making out with a teacher. What is she planning? Is she just biding her time? It wouldn't be the first time my family have hit the headlines.

Mortimer Beaufort's 20-Year-Old Lover

Cordelia Beaufort Battling Depression

Addict! Will Drugs Destroy James Beaufort?

Dad had dinner with a colleague, and the media turned it into an affair; my parents had a row, and suddenly my mum was massively depressed; and they made me into a junkie on the brink of overdose, in need of rescue. God knows what the hacks would write if they heard about Lydia and Sutton.

I keep watching Ruby. She digs a camera out of her backpack and takes a photo of the coaches as they shake hands again. I grip my stick so hard I hear my gloves squeaking. I can't make sense of Ruby and have no clue if she meant what she said or if she hides ice-cold calculation behind that façade.

My family's fate—and especially Lydia's—lies in that girl's hands, and I don't like that one bit.

I seriously can't afford to be seen with you.

We'll see about that.

Ruby

I'm out of my depth.

Lacrosse is a fast-moving sport. The ball shoots from one stick to another, and I can't keep up—either with the camera or the naked eye. I should have known from the start that I couldn't report on the game without Lin. We normally split our articles, whatever the sport, so that one of us takes notes on the match and the other takes the photos. But Lin's mum ordered her up to London again today, and at such short notice that we didn't have time to get anyone else on the events team to step in.

But posts about the lacrosse team get way more clicks on the events team blog than anything else, so we can't miss this. The problem is, I can't write a report on "Maxton vs. Eastview—Battle of the Titans" without understanding what's happening on the field. But with everyone yelling at once—players, swearing coaches, and cheers and boos from the crowd—it's hard to follow the action, let alone get photos of the key moments. Especially seeing that I'm working with a camera that is well over ten years old.

"Shit!" Mr. Freeman roars beside me, so loud that I jump a mile. I look up from the camera in my hand to find that I've missed Eastview's second goal. Rats. Lin's going to kill me.

I take a step closer to the coach. There are no action replays when you're watching live, but maybe he can explain what's happening. But before I can open my mouth, he's shouting again.

"Pass, for God's sake, Ellington!"

I whirl back toward the field. Alistair Ellington is sprinting into the other half, so fast that I don't even bother raising the camera—I'd never catch that on film. He tries to dodge between two defenders, but suddenly a third man is blocking his way. Ellington is bloody fast but much smaller than the others. Even I can see he has no chance against three of them.

One defender crashes his shoulder into him hard. Ellington tries to hold his ground but is pushed back at least a foot.

"Pass!" the coach roars again.

Alistair continues to press against the player, and even from here, I can hear the two of them goading each other. Suddenly, Alistair's stance stiffens even further, and for a second, he and the other guy seem frozen to the spot. Mr. Freeman takes a deep breath, presumably to yell further instructions, but then Alistair pulls back his stick, swings, and hits his opponent in the side with full force.

I gasp, horrified. Alistair hits him again, in his belly this time. The other player bellows with pain and drops to his knees. Meanwhile, the second defender lands on top of Alistair, wrestles him to the ground, and rains punches on him with his gloved fists.

Alistair whacks him with his stick too. A shrill blast of the whistle sounds, but it takes several players to pull them apart. I hear James Beaufort's dark voice. He's screaming at Ellington, and I can imagine that, as captain, he'd like to rip his head off right now.

Next to me, Mr. Freeman is swearing freely. Most of his choice of words is certainly not family friendly, "fucking shit" being about the most printable. He's taken his cap off and is clutching his hair so hard I think he actually pulls some of it out. A moment later, the referee sends Alistair off.

He comes over to us, pulls off his helmet, and takes out his mouth guard. He throws them both carelessly to the ground.

"What the hell, Ellington?" growls the coach.

I take a cautious step back so I don't get caught in the crossfire.

"He had it coming," he replies. His voice is so calm you'd never think he was just in a fight.

"You are . . ."

"Suspended for three games?" Alistair shrugs. "If you think the team can do without me, then fine."

He strolls casually away from the coach, drops his stick too, and pulls off his gloves. When he catches sight of me staring, he pauses.

"What?" he asks aggressively.

I shake my head.

Luckily, the referee blows his whistle, and I don't have to answer. I hurry back to my original position. It takes me a few seconds to see the ball—in the net on Wren Fitzgerald's stick. Wren isn't as fast as Alistair, but he's stronger. He rams an Eastview player out of the way with his shoulder, but the ball is soon tackled off him. But Beaufort's on it and catches the ball back when the other player goes to pass.

I pull a face. Beaufort's good. Bloody good. His movement is agile and silky, he keeps in step with his opposition, and if anyone gets in his way, he's brutal. I can't see his face under the helmet, but I'm sure he loves to be on the field. When he plays, it looks like he's spent his entire life running around with a lacrosse stick.

"What are you doing?" Alistair's voice sounds next to me. I jump guiltily as I remember why I'm actually here. I hurriedly open my notebook again.

"I'm writing the game up for the Maxton blog," I explain, not looking up. "Who's the defender who just took the ball off Wren?"

"Harrington," Alistair replies. I can feel his eyes on me as Freeman lets fly another string of curses. Apparently, Beaufort lost the ball while I was writing my notes. Eastview has possession again.

"Come on, Kesh," Alistair mutters.

The Eastview attacker jumps a foot and a half in the air to catch the ball. He lands, takes two quick steps, and then fires it rapidly ahead of him. It all happens so fast that at first, I'm not sure whether it hit the back of the net. But then the Maxton stand cheers loudly as Keshav holds up his stick. Seems like Alistair's muttering did the trick—he's caught it.

"Make me look good when you write your article," Alistair says as I make a note: *Keshav's last-second save.*

I eye him dubiously. It's the first time I've seen him this close, and I realize that his eyes are the color of whisky. "You attacked another player for no reason. How am I meant to make that look good?"

A shadow flits over his face and his eyes rest on Keshav again. "Who says there was no reason?"

I shrug. "From here, it didn't look like you'd put much thought into it."

Alistair raises his eyebrows at me. "I've been waiting for months for the chance to land one on McCormack. And once he mouthed off about me and a friend of mine, I finally had official grounds."

One of his blond curls falls into his face, and he pushes it out of the way. Then he catches sight of my notes. He wrinkles his nose. "How are you going to read that to write it up? It's illegible."

I wish I could protest, but he's right. Normally, my handwriting is neat, and if I try, it can be really nice. But at the speed I'm scribbling here, it's nothing but a scrawl.

"There are usually two of us," I defend myself, when I really shouldn't care what Alistair Ellington thinks about my writing. "And it's not that easy to take photos and watch the game at the same time, let alone know what moves I should be writing about."

"Why didn't you just film the match?" he asks. He sounds genuinely interested, not like he's looking for reasons to laugh at me.

I hold up my camera with no further comment.

Alistair winces. "How old is that thing then?"

"I think my mum bought it before my sister was born," I reply.

"And how old is your sister? Five?"

"Sixteen."

Alistair blinks a few times, then a grin spreads over his face. Now he doesn't look like the tough lacrosse player who was beating another guy with his stick a moment ago. He looks more like . . . an angel. His features are handsome and even, and together with the blond curls, he looks utterly harmless. But I know that's not true. Alistair is one of James Beaufort's best friends—which makes him anything but harmless.

"Hold on," he says suddenly, then turns and vanishes into the changing room. Before I can ask where he's going, he's back beside me. He's holding a black iPhone in his hand.

"I don't have space to film the whole match, but I can take some photos," he says. He unlocks the screen, opens the camera, and turns the phone to face the field. When he sees that I haven't moved, he raises an eyebrow again. "Watch the game, not me."

I blink, confused. I'm too surprised even to be embarrassed that he caught me staring again. "You're helping me?"

He shrugs. "It's not like I've got anything better to do right now."

"That's . . . kind of you." I try not to sound too suspicious but without much success. This situation is so surreal. I can't believe this is Elaine's brother. Elaine would never have helped me. She'd just have laughed at my camera and made sure everyone else knew about it tomorrow too.

For a while, I watch Alistair out of the corner of my eye, but he does seem to be taking his new task seriously. He snaps photo after photo, only sometimes lowering the phone to yell encouragement at his team or swear at the opposition.

I focus on my notes, which is much easier now. When Mr. Freeman comes over, I think at first that he's going to send Alistair away altogether because of the rude words he's shouting at an Eastview player. But instead, he stands next to me and starts explaining the game and telling me what some of the moves are called.

It starts raining in the last ten minutes of the match, but that doesn't seem to dampen the mood, either on the field or in the stands. Quite the reverse. Maxton Hall wins thanks to a goal from Beaufort and an assist from Cyril Vega, and the fans go wild. The coach throws his arms up in the air, fists clenched, and roars.

I hurriedly shut my notebook and shove it into my bag. My hair is dripping now, and my fringe is plastered onto my face. There's no point trying to sort it out and no way that I want to push it back—sadly, I inherited my dad's high forehead.

One by one, the players jog off the field and high-five Alistair—everyone but Keshav, who walks toward the changing room without looking at him. An emotion I can't identify flits over Alistair's face. His grin slips for a split second, and his eyes go dark, impenetrable. But then he blinks and the moment passes so rapidly that I decide I only imagined it.

Yet again, Alistair catches me looking at him. He raises his eyebrows.

"Thanks again," I say hastily, before he can speak. I don't know if he'll still be nice to me with his friends around, and I don't want to find out. "For the photos."

"No problem." He taps his phone screen and then holds it out to me. He's got the number pad up. "Give me your number, and I'll send them to you."

I take the phone. Before I've typed in the last number, I hear a voice that I know only too well these days.

"What are you two up to?"

I look up.

James Beaufort is facing me. He's soaked to the skin. His reddish-blond hair is much darker than normal and hanging down in his face, making his cheekbones look sharper than ever. He has his stick in one hand and helmet in the other and doesn't seem to care that the water is running off his face, down his shoulders, and over his whole body, mingling with the mud that's crusted his top during the game.

Against my will, I'm staring at his wet body. The sight of him is stirring something very far from suspicion and loathing inside me. It's an unfamiliar emotion, but I'm pretty sure that James Beaufort is the last person I should be feeling like this about.

Firmly, I suppress all thoughts about what it could mean and try to look as unfazed as possible.

Luckily, Alistair answers his question. "She's writing up the game on the Maxton blog." He takes his phone from my hand, looks at the number and the name I've saved it under. I doubt he knew who I was until just now. "I'll send you the photos later, Ruby."

"Great, thanks," I say, although I'm preparing my mind for the fact that he probably won't. However much he's surprised me in the last half hour, he's still Alistair Ellington.

"I'll go and see how angry Kesh is," he tells James.

"Raging," James says, turning his cold eyes on his friend and teammate. "And so am I, and everyone else. I told you not to touch McCormack."

"And I didn't listen." Alistair shrugs his shoulders. "You might be captain, James, but you're not my mother." He sounds like he doesn't care what James thinks of him, but when he claps him on the shoulder, it looks to me like an apology. Then he turns on his heel and walks to the changing room.

James is still watching me. His eyes are colder than before. Whether that's because of me or the brief bust-up with Alistair, I don't know, but I just want to get out of here as soon as possible.

"What was that?" he asks.

The rain feels freezing now.

"I don't know what you mean," I say, sounding braver than I really feel.

He makes a brief sound that's probably meant as a laugh. Or a bark? I'm not quite sure. All I know is that his stance is stiffer and even more unyielding than ever.

"Keep your hands off my friends, Ruby."

Before I can reply, he rushes past me into the changing room as the crowd roars.

6

James

"This party's shit." Wren takes a big gulp from his hip flask and passes it to Cyril, who's standing next to him, leaning on the railing with an equally unimpressed look on his face.

Below us is Weston Hall, a huge ballroom with the Renaissance windows, intricate parquet floor, and stuccoed walls that are typical of Maxton. Like the whole place, the atmosphere in this room makes you feel like you've been transported back to the fifteenth century—or it normally does, anyway.

This evening, it makes you feel like you've wandered into a kiddies' birthday party. There are fussy decorations, and on the buffet table, there's nonalcoholic punch and canapés served in little jam jars, tied up with colorful ribbons. The music is dire. There's a DJ, but what he thinks he's doing is a mystery to me. There's no transition between the songs; it's more like he just picked a Spotify playlist and pressed shuffle. I almost expect to hear irritating adverts between tracks, plugging some dire newcomer. To top it all off, nobody seems to have given the guests a clear dress code. Some people are way overdressed and others have gone to no effort at all.

The whole party is a total disaster. It's like someone was trying to shake things up a bit at Maxton Hall but didn't have the guts to chuck out all the traditions altogether. The end result is a total mishmash of styles that's confusing the hell out of everyone. No wonder there's no atmosphere.

"Hey, it's not that bad." Alistair breaks in on my thoughts. He buries his hands in his pockets and bobs up and down on the balls of his feet, his eyes fixed on the dance floor below us, where a few brave souls are now standing.

"No one but you ever likes these parties." Kesh rolls his eyes.

Alistair shrugs his shoulders. "They're hilarious."

Kesh pulls a face. He takes the hip flask from Cyril and hands it to me without drinking.

"It's about to get a whole lot funnier, believe me." I allow myself a large swig of whisky, enjoying the burn as it slides down my throat.

Wren looks from me to Alistair and back again. Then his eyes widen. "Something up your sleeve?"

I ignore the question and give the merest hint of a shrug, but Alistair never could control his expression. You don't need to know him all that well to spot that he's up to something. His eyes twinkle conspiratorially, and he can't keep still—a total giveaway.

"No way. You planned something and told *him* but not me?" Wren points accusingly at Alistair and then me. "You're my best mate. I consider that a personal insult."

I grin. "An insult?"

He nods. "High treason. Acting against the sacred bonds of brotherhood that have bound us since our childhood days."

"Bullshit."

My dry tone earns me a punch on the shoulder.

"Look at it like this, Wren—it means you'll get a nice surprise," Alistair says, pinching Wren's cheek, who grimaces, but lets it pass.

"I hope for both your sakes that it'll be worth it."

He's already slurring a bit, and this is only the third round of the flask. Even so, when Wren makes another grab for it, I let him. It's a waste of good Bowmore to swig it in secret up here rather than savoring it in a crystal tumbler, but at school parties, the booze is kept for the parents and old-Maxtonians. The likes of us aren't allowed anywhere near the bar. That's never stopped us making our own fun though, and most teachers turn a blind eye if they clock that we've been drinking. The worst we've ever got for it has been a warning.

My parents splash so much cash each year that the school has no choice but to be lenient. They simply can't afford to alienate us or our friends.

"Where's Lydia anyway?" Cyril asks. He's trying to sound casual, but he can't fool us. Cyril's been into my sister forever. And it's been way worse since they got together for a bit two years ago. Lydia was only interested in a bit of fun and split up with him after a couple of weeks—she had no idea that Cyril was head over heels and that she was breaking his heart.

Sometimes I'm genuinely sorry for him. Especially when I remember that he hasn't been involved with anyone since and that he's clearly still mourning her.

"Don't you think it's time to . . . I dunno . . . move on or something?" Alistair asks.

Cyril glares at him from ice-blue eyes.

"Lydia went round to a friend's. I think they're coming later," I reply before things can escalate. You can barely even mention her name without Cyril taking it as a personal provocation.

No way can he find out that my sister's having a fling with that joke of a teacher.

Which reminds me that I really need a word with Mr. Sutton. That wanker needs to keep his hands off my sister, or I'll make the rest of his career at Maxton Hall a misery.

I'm annoyed that I haven't dealt with him already. But my first priority was making sure Ruby keeps her mouth shut. Especially because there's still something fishy about that girl.

A few days ago, Lydia and I bumped into her in the corridor on our way to philosophy. My sister stared firmly at the floor, but I looked Ruby over. Our eyes met, and then she looked right through me, not even batting an eyelid. I did the exact opposite— I stared after her for so long that I had to turn my head to watch her walk away. She had such a proud walk. Gripping her folders, determined steps, chin up. She looked like she was going into battle.

Without thinking about it, I'm keeping an eye out for her. My sensors must be kind of tuned in to her, because although there are over a hundred people in the crowd down there, I spot her in sec-onds. I rest both arms on the banister and lean forward slightly.

Ruby is standing at the edge of the buffet, taking frantic notes on a clipboard. She looks up, glances around, and starts writing again. Then she turns on her heel and heads toward the sound system behind the DJ. She speaks to him and points at her notes.

Something clicks in my head.

Oh, God.

She must be on the events team.

My lips twitch. Well, this will be amusing.

Ruby says something else to the DJ, who nods. Then she walks back across the dance floor to her spot by the buffet, slightly on the edge of things. She reaches into the neckline of her dark green dress and pulls something out. A phone. She types and slips it away again. At the same moment, a guy in a suit walks over to her.

I see who it is and grip the wooden balustrade tighter.

Graham Sutton.

I'd be suspicious of any guy who got too close to my sister, but Sutton's setting off a whole extra series of alarm bells. Especially when I see him speaking earnestly to Ruby. She won't meet his eyes but doesn't seem particularly fazed.

I squint, cursing myself for being up here and not down there, where I could hear what they're saying to each other. They might just be talking about something as banal as this event. Or they could be discussing my sister.

What if they're in it together? What if Sutton's in league with Ruby? I'd never thought of that, and I doubt Lydia's ever considered it either. She never told me exactly why she'd been snogging a teacher, but I know my sister well enough to know that this man is more than a bit of an adrenaline rush for her.

I feel an overwhelming need to protect my twin. Almost without thinking about it, I reach into the inside pocket of my jacket and pull out my phone. I unlock it with my thumb and swipe left to launch the camera.

Ruby and Mr. Sutton are standing in a dark corner. He has one hand on her shoulder, and his lips are fairly close to her face so that he can speak to her. At first glance, you can't tell that Ruby's clipboard is between them and that they're both looking at it. Seems as though they really are talking about the party.

Seeing it in real life, it's totally harmless. But on my phone screen, from a carefully chosen angle, and with a bit of editing, you could read the situation entirely differently. I click on the shutter. Again and again.

"What are you doing?" I hear Alistair say, right behind me. He glances over my shoulder at my phone.

"Taking out a little insurance policy," I reply.

He frowns. "What have you got against her?"

I take a deep breath. I could do with a lot more Bowmore, to switch my brain off altogether. It's been days since I managed that.

"She saw something she shouldn't have."

Alistair gives me a long, thoughtful look, then he nods. "OK."

"If she tells anyone, Lydia will be in deep shit."

He looks down, watching Ruby, who's still talking to Mr. Sutton. "I see."

I take one last photo and put the phone back in my pocket. Then I let my eyes roam back to the door. "My guests have arrived."

A grin spreads over Alistair's face. "Showtime."

Ruby

The party's a total success. By eleven, the guests are thronging to Maxton Hall to eat, drink, chat, and dance. Nothing major has gone wrong, and Mr. Lexington just congratulated Lin and me on a successful evening. I'm so relieved that for a brief moment, I consider stepping onto the dance floor and relaxing for a bit. But I told Doug and Camille that they were free for the rest of the night, and somebody has to keep an eye on the buffet so that nobody gets the idea of spiking the punch.

No one was dancing in the first couple of hours, which got me pretty worried. But Kieran, who was in charge of the music, reckoned that was totally normal. And he was right. In the last half hour, people have been dancing to weird remixes of chart hits that do nothing for me personally, but seem to be going down well.

I look around. I don't recognize a lot of the faces, but that's totally normal too. The whole point of this party is to bring people together—a mix of a reunion and wooing of potential sponsors and new parents. Current pupils having a nice evening is only the second priority, as Lexie explained back when I joined the events committee.

Suddenly, the lights go off. And so does the music.

For a second, I freeze, then I hastily fumble in my bra for my phone. "Shit, shit, shit," I mutter, trying to get the flashlight to turn on.

I hear the murmur of annoyance from around the room echoing in my head. This party *has* to go well. Nothing can go wrong. It might be a fuse that's blown, but Lin and I will still get the blame—I can already imagine the head's disappointed lecture on planning and thinking ahead, and the damage we've done to the school's reputation.

There's no point looking for Lin. I have to find Mr. Jones, the caretaker, and head down with him into the cellars, to the fuse box . . .

As I'm making a beeline past the buffet table, the lights come back on. I breathe a sigh of relief and press my hand to my hammering heart. But then I turn around, and the sight of James Beaufort at the DJ booth sends it plummeting down again.

He's talking to the DJ and pressing something into his hand.

Money, probably. I grind my teeth. I'm too far away to get there in time. I eye the dance floor. People are exchanging curious glances, presumably wondering what's happened to the music. Others are heading for the buffet or the bar.

Some of them look nothing like Maxton Hall regulars, but I don't realize that until it's already too late.

"Ladies and gentlemen," the DJ is saying, "I've just heard that a very special surprise has been arranged for you all. Are you ready?" My stomach flips again. Opposite me, across the dance floor, I spot Lin and Kieran, standing like statues with chalk-white faces. "Have fun!"

The lights are dimmed until the room is in semidarkness. The crowd murmurs with surprise as the music comes on again. This track has a thumping bass and a slow beat that sets the chandeliers jangling. I stare at the dance floor. The dancing now is practically obscene with men and women grinding against each other. The mood in the hall has switched in an instant. Just a few minutes ago, it was still dignified and elegant. Now it's dirty and smutty. I'm about to head over to give James Beaufort an earful when somebody touches me on the arm.

"Are you Ruby Bell?" asks the guy who's just turned up. I nod absentmindedly. At the other end of the room, one of the young women has grabbed Mr. Sutton and Mr. Cabot and pulled them into the center of the dance floor.

"This is a present from your friend James Beaufort," he continues, pushing a chair into the backs of my knees so that I fall onto it. Confused, I look up at him.

He's probably in his early twenties, with fair, gelled-back hair and light blue eyes. He steps in front of me and . . . starts dancing. My mouth goes dry. My mind has switched off. I can't believe this is actually happening. But it is. The bloke slowly slips his jacket off his shoulders and then starts to undo his black bow tie. He pulls it right off and throws it over his shoulder, setting a few of the women shrieking with delight. Then he plays with his suspenders, sliding one off his shoulder and smiling alluringly at me. He gets to the second strap; gives a slow, silky twirl; and then snaps it provocatively back onto his chest. Then he leans down to me, moving his hips to the slow beat of the song.

"Don't you want to give me a hand, Ruby?" he whispers, taking my hand in his, which is surprisingly warm, and carrying it to his suspenders.

"Come on, undress him!" someone calls out.

That snaps me out of my state of shock.

I jump up. The guy flinches. For a moment, he looks unsettled, then the inviting smile reappears on his lips. He slides the strap of his suspenders down himself and goes on with the show as if nothing had ever happened.

My heart stands still, my eyes go past him to the dance floor. Two of the young women are dancing in front of Mr. Cabot, wearing nothing but glittering thongs and thin lacy bras.

This has to be a nightmare, and any moment I'm going to wake up, dripping with sweat. But then I catch sight of Alistair Ellington. A man is sitting in his lap, having also divested himself of his suspenders, and now he's starting—with Alistair's help—to unbutton his shirt. I can't kid myself any longer. This is reality.

Furiously, I whirl around. I see him at once. James Beaufort is leaning against the wall, watching the show. There's a glass of amber liquid in his hand and an almost blissful look on his face. The next second, our eyes meet. Smiling, he raises his drink in a toast to me. The rational part of my brain is telling me to start by finding Lin, and then to go to the teachers to put a stop to this non-sense. The irrational part wants to cause James a great deal of pain. That part is considerably louder, but I think better of it and turn away.

I can get my revenge on James Beaufort later. I know exactly how to hurt him.

James

On Monday morning, the party is all anybody's talking about. The
school's web forum practically melted down over the weekend because everyone was sharing photos and videos and commenting on
them. Now we walk down the corridors and people high-five us,
thanking us for the amazing evening. Our little event didn't just
hit the headlines locally, it's the talk of other English schools too.

Obviously, I assured my parents that it was nothing to do with
me, and obviously they didn't believe a word of it, but in the end,
they were angrier with Lydia for not putting in an appearance
at all.

So, all in all, a total success.

That is, until the loudspeakers crackle in the hallway and an
announcement echoes around the school.

"James Beaufort to Mr. Lexington's office immediately."

I'd been expecting that. Every Monday morning, there's an
assembly in Boyd Hall before lessons begin, so Lexie's already
expressed his disappointment over the incident and reminded everyone of the Maxton Hall code of conduct, his voice laden with

significance. It's always the same—we pull a prank, he tells the whole school how shocked he is, summons us to his office to give us a warning, and five minutes later, off we go.

"Let's see if he gives the same lecture as ever," Wren says, draping his arm over my shoulder. He gives me a quick squeeze. "Don't let the bastards get you down."

"I never do," I reply, saying goodbye to him and the others and strolling toward the head's office. When I arrive, his assistant points silently toward the door.

Without hesitating, I knock twice.

"Come in."

I walk in and shut the door behind me. As I turn around, I freeze. Mr. Freeman is standing by the head teacher's desk, and sitting directly in front of it is . . . Ruby. She throws a quick glance at me over her shoulder, then turns her eyes back straight ahead.

"You wanted to speak to me?" I ask. I'm slightly surprised to have an audience.

Lexington waves me toward the chair next to Ruby. "Have a seat." His tone is different from normal. He generally sounds irritated and annoyed in equal measure when he speaks to me, as if the whole thing is a massive pain in the arse and he'd rather turn his attention back to the more important aspects of his work. This time, his voice is worryingly quiet. The furrows in his brow look deeper than normal too. Seems like I didn't pick a good day for a lecture.

I drop into the chair in front of his desk.

"Is it correct that it was you who hired certain . . ." He clears his throat, evidently searching for a suitable word to use in these hallowed rooms. ". . . entertainers, and that it was they who caused the commotion at our party at the weekend?"

I have to suppress a laugh at the word "entertainers."

"That depends who you mean by that, sir," I say slowly. "I swear the DJ was nothing to do with me."

Ruby gasps with outrage. I look at her, but she won't meet my eye.

Mr. Lexington leans across his dark mahogany desk. The light shining into the room from outside is illuminating only half his face. The hush in here suddenly strikes me as almost ghostly.

"Tell me, Mr. Beaufort. How do you think this incident will reflect on the reputation of our school?"

I take a moment to think about my answer. "I think it might do us some good. This place is way too uptight. There's no harm in relaxing a little now and then."

"You must be out of your mind," Ruby breathes.

"Miss Bell!" Mr. Lexington snaps. "It's not your turn to speak."

Ruby's face drains of color. She presses her lips hard together and lowers her gaze to the green backpack in her lap. It looks like it might fall apart at any moment.

"Mr. Beaufort, your actions have crossed a line. I cannot tolerate such actions at Maxton Hall."

. . . and so I'm giving you an official warning. If there is any repeat of this kind of behavior, you will find yourself facing the consequences.

I know Lexington's sermon by heart. I'd love to join in with the words, just to see his face.

"You are a grown adult now, and this is your last year of school. It is high time you finally learn to accept responsibility, and to realize that your actions have an effect on others," Lexington goes on.

Oh. This bit is new.

"Seeing that you ruined the first party of this academic year, I think it's only fair for you to share the work of the school events committee for the rest of term. We can call it community service, under the supervision of Miss Bell."

A second of silence. Then . . .

"What?" Ruby and I exclaim at the same time.

Now we're staring at each other.

"Absolutely no way," I say, and Ruby mumbles, "Sir, I don't know . . ."

Lexington raises a hand for quiet. He looks at me over the top of his rimless glasses, and his eyes seem to bore into mine.

"Mr. Beaufort, over the course of the six years you have been at this school, you have considered yourself at liberty to act in the most outrageous manner," he continues. "And you have never once been called to account. I turned a blind eye when you held a motor race on the school grounds. I let it slide when you and your friends thought it would be amusing to dress the statue of the school's founder in a wig and cheerleader's outfit. And then there was the time you set up online dating profiles for me and other teaching staff here. And when you held an unauthorized party in Boyd Hall. Not to mention the many times you have arrived drunk at the *official* parties. But you have to finally learn that your actions have consequences. Maxton Hall has built up a certain reputation over the last two centuries. We are known for discipline and excellence, and I cannot permit your youthful exuberance to repeatedly call that into question." His eyes are on me again. I'm starting to feel sick. "Mr. Beaufort, you are suspended from the lacrosse team, effective immediately, for the rest of the term."

The blood rushes in my ears. I see Lexington open his mouth and carry on speaking, but not another word gets through to me.

During a match last season, an opposition player tackled me so hard that we both crashed to the ground—and he landed on top of me with his full body weight. I'd never felt pain like it, and for thirty seconds, I couldn't breathe.

That's exactly how I feel right now.

"You . . . You can't do that," I croak, hating how pathetic I sound. I clear my throat, take a deep breath, and summon the mask of impenetrability back onto my face, the way my father taught me.

"Yes, Mr. Beaufort, I can," the head continues calmly, folding his hands over his belly. "And before you threaten me with your parents, let me inform you that I have already spoken to your father this morning. He assured me of his backing in whatever punishment I see fit to impose upon you."

I certainly wasn't expecting that. "Sir, with all due respect, this is our last season together. I'm the team captain, my lads need me." I look up at the coach, appealing for help.

The regret in his eyes feels like a punch in the gut. "This is entirely self-inflicted, Beaufort."

"Alistair's out for the next three games. Without me . . ."

"Cyril will take over as full captain, and there is plenty of fresh blood to fill your role."

My throat goes dry. I feel the heat of rage flood my cheeks, and my hands start to shake. I clench my fists, digging my nails into my palms until it hurts and my knuckles crack.

"Please, coach." Out of the corner of my eye, I can see Ruby shifting back and forth on her chair. She seems to find the whole situation horribly embarrassing, but at this moment, I don't give a fuck what she thinks.

This is my upper sixth. The last few months before my whole life is ruined. I'd do anything to play lacrosse for these few months with my friends. Even if that means I have to beg in front of Ruby Bell.

To my horror, the coach is not budging. He just shakes his head, his arms crossed over his chest.

"Miss Bell, I'm relying on you to show Mr. Beaufort the ropes on the events team," Lexington goes on, as if he hadn't just wrecked my life. "He is to attend every meeting and be involved in every party until the end of term. Should he refuse or cause you any kind of difficulty, come to me immediately, do you hear?"

"Yes, sir," says Ruby, her voice soft yet firm.

"When is the next meeting to be? Mr. Beaufort can make a note of it in his planner right away."

Ruby clears her throat, and, very much against my will, I turn to face her.

Her eyes are hard. Mine are harder.

"Our next meeting is this afternoon, after lunch, in library meeting room eleven," she says, no trace of emotion in her voice.

I grind my teeth. I'm desperately seeking a way out of this situation, but it's impossible. On top of which, I have absolutely no idea how I'm going to explain this whole thing to my parents.

OK, this time I've really fucked up.

Ruby

"What?"

We're in one of the little group-work rooms, but Lin's yell is so loud that probably everyone in the library could hear it too. The rest of the team just stare blankly as I make my announcement.

"As of now, James Beaufort is a member of the events team," I repeat, my voice just as neutral as it was the first time.

Lin bursts into loud laughter. Once she's semi-composed herself, I start again. "So, let's not make a fuss when he arrives in a bit." I'm looking at Jessalyn Keswick as I add that last bit. She's in the middle of topping up her lip gloss. The pale pink flatters her Black skin, just as all her makeup does. Jessalyn is a beautiful person with so much charisma that everyone adores her. Me included. I could spend hours just looking at her.

"What?" she asks with an innocent smile. "I just want to look my best when Beaufort gets here." She blows me a kiss. I roll my eyes but still pretend to catch the kiss and slip it into my pencil case for safekeeping. The rest of the team laughs.

"What does Lexie think this is going to achieve?" Kieran Rutherford asks. He's a year below us, and his pale skin, perceptive onyx eyes, and longish hair make him look like a vampire—a young Count Dracula with chiseled features. He's a scholarship student too, and the most reliable and hardest working member of the team after Lin and me. "Does he want us to convert him and set him back on the straight and narrow?"

Lin snorts. "Believe me, that one's beyond converting."

There it is. The reason Lin's my best friend at Maxton Hall.

"Hey!" Camille objects. No surprise there—she's one of Elaine Ellington's best friends and therefore part of James's gang. On top of that, she can't stand Lin and me and loathes the fact that we're in charge of the committee now. I don't know why she's still on the team, but I suspect it's mainly because she thinks it'll look good on her uni application. She's not exactly passionate about the work.

"Either way," I say hastily, as I see Lin open her mouth to reply.

"He's going to come to our meetings whether we like it or not. I just wanted to warn you in advance. And he's been suspended from the lacrosse team for the rest of term."

Jessalyn whistles. "Wow, that's a bit drastic from Lexington."

A murmur of agreement fills the room. "It's Beaufort's own fault," says Lin. "We spent half our summer holidays planning the Back-to-School party, and he just came along and smashed it up. Plus, Ruby got a solid half-hour lecture from Lexington."

"Seriously?" Kieran asks in disbelief.

I nod, and he exclaims in outrage: "But it's not your fault that Beaufort smuggled those people into the party!"

I give a hesitant shrug. "We were in charge of the event, so Lin and I are responsible. And we should have kept a better watch on the doors. So, if you look at it like that, we're a bit to blame. He wants us to issue an apology on the Maxton blog so that everyone knows we didn't plan it."

This is all adding to my fury at Beaufort. I've never once been in trouble since I started at Maxton Hall, not even with a teacher, let alone the head himself. I need a perfect record to have the least glimmer of a chance of getting into Oxford, and James's childish behavior has jeopardized that. I'm not letting some idiot ruin my future just because he's got more time and money on his hands than he knows what to do with.

"That's insane—it makes no sense. You're the last person who should be taking responsibility for this crap." Kieran frowns with annoyance.

I smile gratefully at him and ignore Lin's meaningful stare. Ever since the end of last term, she's been trying to convince me that Kieran's got a major crush on me. That's nuts though. He's just a nice guy.

I clear my throat. "Anyway, shall we get started?"

The others nod, and I point to the whiteboard, where Lin has already written up the agenda for today's meeting. "First, we need to report back on the party—what went well, what didn't. Not including Beaufort, obviously. Camille, can you take notes?"

Camille glares at me but opens a pad and picks up a pen. Lin starts to give us her impressions of the party, and I glance at the clock. It's just after two. Lunch break is over. Beaufort ought to be here any minute. An uneasy feeling spreads through my stomach. It's fluttery and queasy, like I'm . . . excited.

I immediately push the thought down and get involved in the discussion. We take so long going over the feedback and things to do next time that we have to postpone everything else till the end of the week. We divide up a few jobs between us, and the meeting's over. Lin and I stay in the room to work out how to phrase our apology.

James Beaufort doesn't show up for the whole two and a half hours.

Once we've sent our text to Lexington, we say our goodbyes. Lin heads to her car. She doesn't live far from the school, but there's no bus out that way, so her mum bought her a little second-hand car last summer.

As for me, I live half an hour from Pemwick, the closest town to Maxton Hall. Gormsey is kind of run-down with shabby houses and potholed streets, and totally unglamorous, but I like it there. I don't even mind taking the bus here and back every day. Far from it. On the bus, I can chill. I don't have to be either the Ruby who doesn't talk about home or the Ruby who can't share her school life with her family. I can just be . . . me.

As I walk to the bus stop, I pass the playing fields, where the lacrosse team is training. I watch them sprint up and down the field in full gear.

Then I spot the player with the number seventeen on his shirt.

I stop dead. Then I step closer to the fence and hook my fingers into the mesh.

I can't believe that guy.

I stare open-mouthed at Beaufort, who passes the ball to Cyril Vega as he runs. I can hear his braying laugh from here.

That . . . that . . . *arsehole*!

At that very moment, Beaufort turns and spots me. I can't see his face through the helmet, but his body changes. He stiffens and juts out his chin, kind of defiantly. Bloody idiot! Behind me, I hear the bus arriving. I ignore the hot rage in my belly, turn away from James, and walk the rest of the way to the stop.

Let him do what he likes.

Ruby

As Ember reads my personal statement for my university application form, I circle her name (written in purple pen) in gold. Now *Ask Ember to proofread my statement* looks both more official and more important.

My sister is lying on her back, on her bed, reading aloud. "My passionate interest in politics, from its philosophical principles to the practical application of its economic aspects makes Philosophy, Politics, and Economics the ideal course for me. It links the areas I am most interested in, and I would be thrilled to have the chance to study areas of vital importance to today's society in a depth that only Oxford can offer." She pauses, takes her pen in her mouth, and rolls over onto her front to look at me.

I hold my breath.

Ember grins. I pick up one of the wedge sandals she's dropped on the floor and throw it at her.

"Come on, Ember," I whisper. It's two in the morning, and we should have been in bed hours ago. But I was tweaking my statement until just now, and my sister is practically nocturnal anyway, often working on her blog posts into the early hours, so I crept over to her room and asked her to read it.

"It's a bit waffly," she replies, equally quietly, but I can hardly understand her through the pen in her mouth.

"It's meant to be."

"And it sounds kind of show-offy. Like you're boasting about your knowledge and all the stuff you've already read."

"I'm meant to do that too." I stand up and go over to her bed.

She hums thoughtfully and circles a few lines on the page. "I'd cut these bits anyway," she says, holding it out to me. "You don't have to suck up to the college and keep on mentioning where you're applying to. They know they're Oxford. You don't need to tell them so twenty times."

I blush. "That's true." I take back the paper and put it on her desk with my journal. "You're a sweetheart, thanks."

Ember smiles. "No problem. And I know exactly how you can pay me back."

That's how things have always been between Ember and me. One of us does something for the other and then gets to ask the other one a favor, after which she owes her one again, and so on. A kind of barter economy, a constant trading of favors. But to be honest, Ember and I just like helping each other out.

"Shoot."

"You could finally take me to one of your Maxton Hall parties," she suggests, as casually as possible.

I stiffen.

It's not the first time Ember's asked, and every time I have to disappoint her, it hurts the same. Because it's the only favor she can ask me that I won't do.

I'll never forget the one parents' evening when Mum and Dad

went to Maxton Hall to introduce themselves to my teachers and get to know my classmates' parents. It was awful. Not just the fact that the buildings are hundreds of years old and totally inaccessible. People's expressions couldn't have been more condescending. Mum and Dad had got dressed up for the occasion—but that day, I learned that the Bells and Maxton Hall have very different ideas of "smart." The other parents were wearing suits—Beaufort brand for the men, obviously—while Dad was in jeans and a jacket. Mum's dress was lovely but dusted with flour from the bakery, which we didn't notice until an older lady looked down her nose at us and then turned away to pass comment on it to her friends.

The memory of the pain on Mum's face, which she tried to hide behind a fake smile, still breaks my heart. Same as Dad's proudly jutting chin every time his wheelchair caught in a doorway and Mum and I had to help him. They tried not to show how hurt they were by the wrinkled noses and turned backs of the other parents. But they couldn't fool me.

That day only reinforced my decision that there were two worlds for me—my family and Maxton Hall—and that I would keep them carefully apart. My parents will never be part of the elite, and that's fine. I never want to put them in another situation where they feel so uncomfortable. They've been through enough since Dad's boating accident, and the last thing they need is Maxton Hall shit on top of that.

And the same goes for Ember. My sister is like a glowworm: Her bubbly personality and free-and-easy manner always attract attention. I know exactly what can happen at Maxton, and I have personal experience of what people there are capable of when they think they rule the world. Some of the stories I've overheard in the girls' loos over the last few years have turned my stomach. That's *not* happening to Ember.

I only want the best for my sister. And that does not involve my school, or the guys in it.

"You know we're not allowed to bring people who don't go to the school," I say in the end.

"Maisie was at the Back-to-School party over the weekend," Ember retorts. "She says it was epic."

"Then she must have sneaked past security. Besides, I already told you that the party was a disaster."

"Didn't sound like one, the way Maisie told it."

I press my lips together and shut my planner.

"Come on, Ruby! How long are you going to hold out on me? I promise I'll behave. Truly. I'll act like I belong there."

Her words hit hard. I hate that she thinks I don't want her there for fear that she'd embarrass me. The hopeful way she looks at me makes my throat constrict.

"I'm sorry, I just can't," I say quietly.

In a split second, the hope gives way to fury. "You're so full of shit."

"Ember . . ."

"Just admit that you don't want me at your stupid parties!" she says reproachfully.

I can't reply. I can't lie to her, but I want to protect her.

"If you knew what Maxton Hall was really like, you wouldn't keep asking to come," I whisper.

"If you ever need anything in the middle of the night again, ask your fancy school friends," she hisses. Then she pulls the duvet over her head and turns her face to the wall.

I try to ignore the throbbing ache in my chest. In silence, I pick my journal and the statement off her desk, turn off the light, and leave the room.

━━━

The next morning, I feel like I've been hit by a truck, and I slap on concealer to hide the bags under my eyes. I couldn't fall asleep after the row with Ember, and I spent most of the night lying awake. As always, Lin spots right away that something's wrong, but she assumes it's still linked to Beaufort and the catastrophe over the weekend, and I'm happy to let her.

After class, I head straight for the library. I've got half an hour before our next meeting, and I want to take my books back and get a few out that weren't available last time.

I love the library more than anywhere else at Maxton Hall, and it's where I spend most of my time. It has a vaulted ceiling and open galleries, so despite the dark wood of the shelves, it looks inviting, not gloomy. The moment you walk through the door, you can sense the welcoming, productive atmosphere, and it can't help but boost your mood. Not to mention the staggering array of literature we have access to here. None of the books in Gormsey's tiny library would have been any help with my personal statement, whereas here, I was overwhelmed by choice when I first started looking.

I've spent entire days in my favorite spot by the window, partly because I feel so at home here and partly because you're not allowed to take the reference books home with you—some of them are over a hundred years old. Sometimes when I'm here, I wish there were more hours in my day. Or that I could stay on longer after school. It's like a foretaste of what will await me at Oxford.

Except that the libraries there are bigger and—according to the website—open round the clock.

It's nerve-racking to work through the introductory reading list in the course information. A lot of the books are complex, with paragraphs that I have to read several times before I understand them. But that's fun too, and I've got into the habit of making a little booklet on each of them, summarizing the contents and adding my own thoughts and notes.

I'm in luck, and the three books I'm dying to read are on the shelves again. Once I've checked them out, I head straight for our meeting room. I'm a bit early, but that gives me time to put the agenda up on the whiteboard and go through my notes. We spent so long rehashing the party on Monday that we've got some catching up to do today.

I push the door with one hand, clutching the pile of books to my chest with the other. I put the little stack down on a table. Even before I've put down my backpack, I run my fingers over the cover of Arend Lijphart's *Patterns of Democracy.*

"You and I have a date this weekend," I whisper.

Someone snorts quietly.

I whirl around. At the same moment, my bag slips off my arm and crashes to the floor.

James is at the far end of the room, leaning on the windowsill, arms folded over his chest. He raises his eyebrows at me. "That's kind of sad," he says.

It takes me a moment to pull myself together. "What is?" I ask, picking up my backpack and setting it on the table beside the books. One of the holes in the bottom has ripped even more in the crash, and I swear to myself. I'll have to ask Ember if she'll help me sew it up.

"Wasting your weekends on school shit." He strolls over. "I can think of better things to do with my time."

"What are you doing here?" I reply, unimpressed, and ignoring his remark.

"Didn't you hear Lexie? I have to start taking responsibility and realize that my actions have consequences." He parrots the head's words with a mocking smile.

I open my bag and pull out my planner, my pencil case, and my committee folder. "And you suddenly decided to take notice of that, did you?"

I can't read James's expression as he stands in front of me. At that moment I have no idea what to make of him.

"It's not like I have any choice, is it?"

I give him a skeptical glance. "You seemed to have a choice the other day."

He just shrugs. Presumably, the coach had a go at him for turning up at training. Serves him right.

"I'm here. Just count yourself lucky." Then he bends down and picks something off the floor—a pen. It must have fallen out of my backpack. James holds it out to me. It's an almost-friendly gesture, so I clear my throat and try to think of something to say.

"It's only for a term, James." It's the first time I've said his first name aloud.

His face changes. Suddenly, he doesn't seem to be looking through me anymore—he's looking into my soul. There's a fire in his eyes that burns me and makes me shiver. There are butterflies in my stomach. He looks abruptly away and turns on his heel to return to the back. "That doesn't alter the fact that I hate all this."

My heart is hammering, and I swallow hard as he sits down, arms folded, and stares out of the window.

I don't know what he means by "all this." Not being allowed to play lacrosse. Or having to spend his time here. Or maybe he just means me. But I can live with that.

There's too much at stake to let a spoiled rich boy mess with my head. We both have to get through this, whether we like it or not, and the sooner we face up to that, the easier this time will be.

Without another word, I turn to the whiteboard and write up the agenda for today's meeting. I don't know whether or not James is watching me, and that's making me antsy, but I'm too proud to turn around. Luckily, the door soon opens. "Sorry I'm late, our printer at home went haywire, so I had to find somewhere here to print out my statement, but I've got it done now and . . ." Lin stops mid-sentence as she spots James.

"Hey," he says.

I wonder if that's how he greets everyone. I bet he'll say "hey" to all the panels at his university interviews.

"What's he doing here?" Lin asks me, not taking her eyes off him.

"Community service," I answer truthfully.

James says nothing. He bends down, opens his bag, and pulls out a notebook. He puts it on the table in front of him. It has a black leather cover, embossed with the elaborate "B" of the Beaufort logo. I bet it's worth a fortune. Dad and I went into a branch of Beaufort's in London once, looking for a new suit for him. It was a few years ago when he had to spend a lot of time in court after his accident. I have a very clear memory of the four-figure price tags that made us turn tail after no more than two minutes and creep out of the shop as unobtrusively as possible.

Next to me, Lin coughs. Guiltily, I tear my eyes away from James and curse the way my cheeks are flushing yet again. Thankfully, Lin has the tact not to mention it.

"Here," she says, holding out a clear plastic folder that contains several sheets of paper. "My statement."

I fish mine out of my folder and hand it to her. "Here's mine, but it's not perfect yet."

"Neither is mine," says Lin. "That's why we're reading them for each other. Do you think you'll have a chance to look at it this evening?"

"No can do, sorry. We can go through them tomorrow in the free period after maths." I pull out my gold pen and jot down *Read Lin's statement* in my planner.

"I'm honored to have my name written in your top-tier pen," Lin whispers with a grin. I smile back at her then finish putting the agenda on the board as the rest of the team gradually drifts in. Everyone sneaks sideways glances at James, apart from Camille, who kisses him on either cheek.

Once we're all here, we start the discussion.

"The most important thing today is planning the second big event of this term," Lin opens, her face glowing. "Halloween."

Kieran makes a quiet, spooky "oh-ooooh" noise, and everyone laughs.

"Last year's masked ball was really popular," Lin continues, opening a slideshow of pictures on her laptop. She turns the screen so that we can all see.

"Can't we just do the same thing again? I mean, if it was so popular?" Camille suggests. "That would save a ton of work."

"Certainly not," Lin snaps, and Camille just shrugs. I walk over to the whiteboard and write *Halloween* in the middle of the right-hand side. Then I put a circle around it.

"We need to come up with a theme," Lin says. "Let's just brainstorm, OK?"

For a moment, there's silence.

"I know what I don't want," Jessalyn says in the end.

"What's that? Then we can rule it out from the start," I say, gesturing to her to go on.

"I don't want orange. Black-and-orange decorations are so childish; it's not the look we want for Maxton Hall."

I nod and write *stylish décor* in the top right-hand corner.

"How about black-and-white?" Doug asks. He's the quietest person on the team and hardly ever speaks, so I'm pleasantly surprised that he's made a suggestion. I smile at him and turn back to the board.

"It's been done."

Suddenly, you could hear a pin drop.

I slowly turn around. James is lounging in his chair, in stark contrast to the tension that's now filling the room.

"I'm sorry?" Lin says what I'm thinking.

"Black-and-white's been done," James repeats, just as dryly as the first time.

"I heard what you said," Lin hisses.

He frowns at her. "Then I don't understand your question."

"We're brainstorming, Beaufort. We throw out ideas and write them all down *without* comment so that our spontaneous suggestions can lead to the answer," I explain as quietly as possible.

"I know what brainstorming is, Bell," he replies, jutting his chin at the whiteboard. "And I'm telling you, we won't get anywhere like that."

"Says the guy who thinks you need strippers to create atmosphere," mutters Kieran.

"I wouldn't have had to if I hadn't known how lame your party was going to be."

Nobody speaks, but I can feel the mood in the room going from bad to worse. Everyone but Camille is glaring at James with furious eyes, but he doesn't seem remotely bothered. Eyebrows raised, he looks around. "Oh, come on. Don't tell me you didn't notice."

"You're not all there," says Kieran, and Jessalyn nods.

"Guys," I say. I look at them all in concern. "Pull yourselves together." James's lips twitch suspiciously, and I point my pen at him like it's a gun. "Stop grinning like that. We spent most of the holidays planning that party. It wasn't lame."

James leans forward in his chair, resting both arms on the table. "That's a matter of opinion."

It feels as though there's a vein throbbing at my temple. "Oh, really."

He nods.

"Why's that, if I may ask?" Lin's voice is sickly sweet. I know that tone. It bodes ill, and now I've got goose bumps, and not in a good way.

James lifts a hand and counts on his fingers. "The buffet looked cheap. The music was shit. The dress code was unclear. And it was totally dead for hours."

I can feel Lin shaking beside me. If we were alone, I could wring James's neck for his unconstructive criticism. Everyone in this room put so much work into that party, it's not fair to say it was all a total flop. And not true either. But as team leader, I have to keep my cool. And there *were* things that didn't go entirely to plan; we agreed on that on Monday.

"I agree with you about the music," I say. "It wasn't great. But people danced anyway, so I wouldn't call it a total write-off."

"Because that's what you do at a party. But decent music would have made for a way better atmosphere."

Three years ago, at my old school, I did a course on conflict resolution. It ran over five afternoons and taught us ways to avoid arguments. I don't remember everything, but one thing that did stick in my head is that you have to make everyone feel heard and that you should divert energy away from a row and into what matters.

With this aim in mind, I take a deep breath and look at James. "I hear your criticism, and I'll make note of it. But that doesn't alter the fact that we're still deciding on a theme for Halloween. Doug's suggestion is a good one, and I'll write it down. And I'll write down everyone else's ideas, and in the end, we can have a look through and see what works and what doesn't." I write *Black-and-white* on the board. Then I turn around again. "Anything else?"

"OK, I've got an idea," Jessalyn says, raising her hands like she's seeing a vision. "Classical chic with a ghostly touch. Candles, black flowers. Modernizing the traditional Halloween party."

I make a note.

"Equally dull."

"If you've got nothing to contribute, then shut the fuck up, Beaufort," Lin snarls.

"Black-and-red vampire party," Kieran suggests.

"Still lame," mutters James.

I'm going to get through this. I am not going to stab him in the eye with a pen.

"The truly *lame* thing is the way you keep shooting down our suggestions," Jessalyn retorts. "Come up with your own idea and spare us your negative energy."

James straightens up and glances at his notebook. I doubt there's even a single word in there to do with planning a Halloween party.

"In that case, I suggest a Victorian theme. Weston Hall would be perfect. We could get period plates and cutlery from the time, punch bowls, lace napkins, all that shit. Ideally in black. Have the whole thing lit by candles like they would have then, for a spooky mood. Obviously, we'd have to make sure we didn't burn the school down, but we can take the necessary fire precautions. The dress code would be decadent but classy, in keeping with the era. And the Victorians loved Halloween games. We could include some of them too."

Once he's finished, the room goes silent.

"That's a . . . great idea," I say hesitantly.

His eyes sparkle as he looks at me. "I thought we were just noting down ideas without comment?"

I avoid his gaze and write the suggestion on the board.

"I read that in the nineteenth century, they used to bake cakes with five objects hidden inside them," Kieran says. "Finding one would bring you good luck. We could update that and give prizes to the people who find a charm."

"But we'd have to let them know in advance. In case anyone chokes," Camille points out, wrinkling her nose.

"What kind of music would we play?" asks Jessalyn.

"Classical with a modern twist?" I suggest.

"Not your weird classical-electro-dubstep mashups though," Lin groans.

"Hey! They're cool. And they help me focus." Everyone is giving me a funny look now. Desperately, I turn to Kieran, who generally shares my taste in music. "Come on, Kieran, tell them."

"There are some great remixes of Victorian stuff. I heard something good by Caplet the other day."

I smile gratefully and mouth, "Send me a link."

"So, I'll sort out a band," James says. "And we can work on a dance to get the party started."

A murmur of agreement fills the room, which makes me feel kind of sick. I can't dance a step.

"OK, so it sounds to me almost like we've agreed on a theme," Lin says, her voice as surprised as I feel right now.

She points to the whiteboard. "But all the same, I'd like to put it to the vote. Who's in favor of black-and-white?"

Nobody raises their hand.

"Classic chic?"

No one, again.

"How about a sexy vampire party?"

No hands go up.

"What do you say to a Victorian-style Halloween party?" I ask, and before I've finished the question, four hands are in the air. For a moment, it looks like James considers himself too cool to vote, but in the end, he does too.

I wasn't expecting the meeting to turn out this way. I raise an eyebrow at Lin. "Well then, I'd say we've come up with the theme for this year's Maxton Hall Halloween party."

James

Percy's parked the Rolls right outside the main entrance to the school. He's leaning against the car, phone in one hand, cap in the other. There seems to be more silver in his dark hair every day. As soon as he sees me, he slips his phone away, puts the cap back on again, and straightens up. Not that he needs to, as well he knows.

I run down the steps, and people are only too willing to scatter out of my way. Apparently, I look about as grim as I feel, thanks to the bloody events committee. I should have just kept my mouth shut, kept my Victorian party idea to myself. The thought of the to-do list the others came up with at the end makes me sick. If I were to throw this party at home, I could delegate the whole thing to our staff, and I wouldn't have to lift a finger. But in this instance, I *am* the staff, as Ruby's raised eyebrows made clear.

And there's a whole term of meetings like that to come. On top of which, I'm not even allowed to train with the others on the lacrosse team.

This is definitely not how I planned my last year of school.

By the time I get to the car, all I want to do is throw myself onto the back seat, but before I can get in, Percy takes me by the arm.

"You don't look exactly cheerful, sir."

"Your perceptiveness astounds me, Percy."

He glances uneasily from me to the car door. "You might want to rein your temper in slightly. Miss Beaufort is not in a good way."

At once, I've forgotten the stupid events team altogether.

"What's happened?"

Percy looks uncertain, as if he isn't sure how much he can tell me. In the end he takes a step closer and speaks quietly: "She was having a conversation with someone just now. A young man. It looked more like an argument."

I nod, and Percy opens the door so that I can get into the car.

It's just as well it has tinted windows. Lydia looks awful. Her eyes and nose are bright red, and there are dark gray tearstains down her cheeks. She's never cried as much in her life before as in the last few weeks, and it makes me livid to see her like that while knowing that there's nothing I can do about it.

Lydia and I have always been inseparable. If you have a family like ours, there's nothing for it but to stick together, no matter what. I can barely remember a day when I hadn't seen my twin sister. I get a weird feeling in my chest if she's in trouble, and it's the same the other way around. Our mother says that's not unusual for twins, and, when we were little, she made us promise that we'd treasure that link all our lives and not endanger it lightly.

"What's up?" I say, once Percy's started the engine.

She doesn't reply.

"Lydia . . ."

"None of your business," she snaps.

I raise an eyebrow and look at her until she turns away and stares out of the window. I guess that's the end of our conversation.

I lean back and look out too. The trees flit past us so fast that they just make up a blurry mass of color, and I wish Percy would slow down. Partly because the thought of home makes me feel ill, but mostly because it would give me more time to break Lydia's silence.

I'd like to help her, but I have no idea how. Over the last few weeks, I've done all I could to find out what happened between her and Mr. Sutton, but she always just shut me down. I shouldn't be surprised. We may be inseparable, but we've never discussed our love lives. There are some things you just don't want to know about your sister—and vice versa. But this time, it's different. She's devastated, and the only other time I'd seen her in this kind of state was almost exactly two years ago. And then, it nearly destroyed our entire family.

"Graham's losing his shit," Lydia suddenly whispers, just when I'd stopped expecting it.

I turn back to her and wait for her to go on. My anger at this jerk of a teacher bubbles up yet again, but I push it down. I don't want Lydia to shut me out any more than she's already doing.

"I'm so scared that Ruby will tell Lexington," she croaks.

"She won't."

"How can you be so sure?" I can see the same doubt on her face that I felt about Ruby the first time I met her.

"Because I'm keeping an eye on her," I reply after a while.

Lydia doesn't look convinced. "You can't run around after her the whole time, James."

"I don't have to. She's on the events team."

Lydia looks surprised now, and I give a wry smile.

It's good to see the way the tension seems to drop from her shoulders—not entirely, but a bit, at least. After a while, she says quietly: "I'd totally forgotten about the events team. Exactly how shit is it?"

I just growl.

"Have you spoken to Dad?" she asks cautiously.

I shake my head and look out of the window, just at the moment that the Rolls-Royce comes to a stop. The façade of our house—practically a stately home—towers over us, the dark sky hung with heavy clouds, a reflection of both my mood and what lies ahead of me.

━━━━

"How would you describe me in three words?" Alistair asks over the music thumping from my sound system. He's sitting on the sofa, huddled over his phone, his blond curls falling into his face, and looks up aslant at me over the screen.

I've been mixing us each a gin and tonic and bring the glasses over to the sofa. Not looking up, Alistair holds out his hand and takes one.

We're on our third now, and I'm finally getting the fuzzy feeling in my head that I've been waiting for the whole time. Now I can forget that the others are at lacrosse training. And above all, it suppresses the memory of the last two hours. My father's voice has faded to a dull whisper.

"How about 'highly oversexed bitch'?"

Alistair grins. "Very true. But modesty will probably get better results."

I drop onto the sofa beside him with a laugh. I can't shake off the feeling that he'd had a drink or two already when I texted to ask if he wanted to come over. Apparently, he's not quite as un-fazed about being suspended from the team as he's letting on.

Either way, he burst into my sitting room and announced that he's going to steer clear of Maxton Hall guys from now on and have a closer look at "that online dating shit." His broad grin sug-gested that he didn't mean it entirely seriously and that he's only setting up a profile because he's bored.

But I know him well enough to know that it's more than just a joke. He's had it with Maxton Hall guys because they'll only make out with him in secret. Unlike most of them, Alistair's been out for two years now—much to the displeasure of his arsehole par-ents, who practically cut him off.

If he finds someone online who doesn't make him feel like a guilty secret, I'm all for it. Especially as I could really do with a distraction from my own problems right now.

"Does it have to be exactly three words?" I ask. He shakes his head. "Then . . . 'nice guy, lacrosse, sport, seeking hot dates, blah-blah.'"

He grins crookedly. "Blah-blah, right."

I slide over to him slightly, spilling some of my G&T out of my glass and over my hand. I swear and wipe it off on my jeans, then look at Alistair's phone. His draft profile makes me laugh out loud.

"What?" he demands.

"Liar! You're nowhere near six-foot-one."

He sniffs. "I am."

"I'm a bit over six-foot, and you're at least two inches shorter than me, bro. Take four inches off that and you'll be closer."

He digs his elbow in my ribs and more booze lands on my fingers. "Spoilsport."

"OK, OK." I take three big swigs from my glass and put it down on the table. Then I pick up my laptop off the coffee table, open it, and start searching for vaguely reasonable profiles.

Inviting Alistair over was just what I needed. He got his driver to bring him round right away and since then, he's done nothing but take my mind off things—and not asked a single question.

"Oh, God," I murmur.

Alistair makes an inquiring sound, bending over to look at the screen.

I turn the laptop toward him slightly. "I was looking for inspiration for your profile description, but I wish I'd never clicked on that link now. Seriously, who writes 'In an ideal world, I'd get with my twin, but as I'm an only child, you'll have to do'?"

Alistair hoots with laughter. "I can't be arsed anymore. I'll just put '18, lacrosse, open to everything.'"

"Nah, mate," I say, shaking my head. "'Open to everything' is just asking for dodgy messages."

He just shrugs. A minute or two later, he adds, not looking up from his phone, "Elaine was asking how you were."

I raise an eyebrow but don't answer. This is the first time Alistair's broached the subject since Wren's party, and I can't tell from his voice whether or not this is a serious conversation.

"She's worried about your young, fragile heart and wanted to know if you still think about her often."

OK, definitely not serious then.

"As if," I reply. I doubt that Elaine's wasted a single thought on our night together. More likely, it's Alistair who can't let it go because I've roused his brotherly protective instincts.

"I still can't believe you shagged my sister." He shakes his head and makes gagging noises. "Couldn't you two get engaged at least? Then I could deal with the whole thing better, I think."

I grin and box him on the shoulder. "If I ever get engaged, it certainly won't be to help you sleep better at night."

Alistair sighs in mock despair. Then he holds his phone out to me. "Well, can you at least help me decide which picture to use?"

He shows me two: one where he's topless, lying on a lounger with his arms linked behind his head, and another in black-and-white, of him in a suit, a selfie taken in a mirror.

"The one on the lounger," I say. "You've got too much on in the other one."

"I like your team spirit, Beaufort."

That ticks off the subject of Elaine for a while, and I get us each a fourth G&T. We clink glasses, and Alistair turns his attention back to his new hobby while I scroll half-heartedly through my emails.

I freeze as I see a meeting invitation from Beaufort Offices. I open it reluctantly. All it says is: Business dinner with sales management, Friday week. London, 7pm. Don't be late.

In a flash, my good mood has vanished. An icy shiver runs down my spine as the memories of this afternoon's row with Dad resurface.

You're an embarrassment.

We have a reputation to uphold.

Stupid, childish boy.

I'm annoyed with myself for having flinched as he stepped toward me, hand raised, because I know better than that. Never show either weakness or fear in the presence of Mortimer Beaufort.

This meeting is a further punishment. He is perfectly well aware that it hits me harder than his words or fists could ever do.

We had a deal—while I'm at Maxton Hall, he'll leave me out of everything relating to the business. Making me come to this dinner is his way of telling me, "I'm in charge of your life, and if you don't get your act together, it'll be over before you know it."

Frustratedly, I push the laptop away and head to the bar. I pour a tumbler of whisky and stare into the amber liquid for a moment. Then I turn and take it back to the sofa.

Alistair looks at me. There's no more trace of the grin from earlier on his face. "Everything OK?"

I shrug.

I wanted Alistair to come over to help me forget the stuff with my dad—not to talk about it.

Alistair doesn't insist, just holds out his phone. "I've got a match." On the screen there's a photo of a black-haired guy with plenty of muscle.

I slump down on the sofa until I can rest my head on the back. "What does his profile say?"

"That he needs someone to care for his heart. And his dick."

"How creative."

"Oh. And he's just sent me a dick pic. How about telling me your name *before* you show me your genitals?" Alistair mutters, making me laugh against my will.

That's one of the reasons Alistair's one of my best friends. If I wanted to, I could talk to him about the stuff playing on a loop in my head. I could talk to him about everything—but I don't have to. We've been mates so long that we're in sync with each other, and, while we push each other's limits, we know where they are, and we respect them. I don't think I could build a friendship like this again with anyone else.

"Are you hungry?" I ask after a while.

Alistair nods, and I call down to the kitchen. The encounter with Dad left me with no appetite, so now I'm starving.

While we wait for someone to bring up the food, Alistair looks at more photos of semi-naked guys, and I scroll through my blog roll on my laptop. Apart from a few lacrosse sites and friends' stuff, I've mainly been following travel blogs in the last few months. Reading the posts and looking at pictures of far-flung countries is the perfect way to switch off. I bookmark a few things for later—I'm not quite sober enough to take it in right now.

The school blog is saved on my list too. Only to laugh at really, but when I see the headline in my timeline, Ruby's face pops up in my mind. My stomach gives a lurch, and I don't know whether that's down to my hunger, the booze, or something else entirely.

As if my index finger has a mind of its own, I click on the link.

I flick through the school events (so boring), skim articles (so unoriginal), and look at the photos, searching for Ruby's face. Her name is at the top of a lot of posts, and she's mentioned in relation to all the events, but there isn't a single picture of her. I googled Ruby not long after Lydia told me Ruby had caught her with Sutton, tried to find out as much about her as I could. But there was nothing. She has no social media—no Facebook, no Twitter, no Instagram—or not under her real name, anyway.

Ruby Bell is a phantom.

I keep scrolling. I've now searched the whole of last year and still haven't found what I'm looking for. Whatever that may be. The longer I look, the crosser I feel. Why the hell can't I find anything on her?

"Are you looking at the *school* blog?" Alistair asks suddenly.

I look up, caught in the act. Alistair's looking grossed out. But when he glimpses the word in the little search box on my browser, his face lights up. "Oh, like that, is it?"

"What?"

His grin widens. "Wait till I tell the others."

I slam the laptop shut. "There's nothing to tell."

Alistair's answer is cut off by a knock from Mary, our housekeeper. She steers a little trolley into the room with our dinner, and I stand up, swaying slightly, to refill my glass. Now as well as my dad's voice, I've got Ruby's smug face to wipe out of my brain.

Ruby

Even my pink pen is mocking me. According to my planner, I have to *Ask Beaufort about Victorian clothes*—pretty much the last thing I want to do.

I've had an overdose of James Beaufort this week, and I'm ready for the weekend. Since we agreed on the Halloween party theme, he's been acting like a total dick in our meetings. He either makes one snarky comment after another or ignores us completely. I wouldn't care if we hadn't decided yesterday that the advertising poster for the party ought to feature a couple in authentic Victorian dress. And the simplest, quickest way to get our hands on that kind of costume—for free!—is via the Beauforts and their company archive.

After the meeting, Lin and I drew lots for who'd have to ask James for the favor, and, of course, I lost. Since then, I've been pondering the best way to go about it. Maybe I'll just email him. Then I wouldn't have to speak to him in front of anyone else, which would most probably just earn me some snide remark.

I slam my journal shut and put it in my backpack.

"We can swap," Lin suggests, swinging her own bag onto her shoulder. She picks up her plate, stacks it on top of mine, and takes them both back to the tray station.

I briefly weigh up whether the alternative—an hour listening to Lexie drone on about fire regulations—would be better.

"No, wait," Lin says as we head from the canteen to the study center. "I take that back. I don't want to swap."

"Your loss. I'd have gone for it."

The school is bathed in reddish-gold autumn light, and the first leaves on the oak trees are starting to turn from deep green to delicate yellow or dark red.

"Come on. It's not that bad."

"Says she who yelled 'jackpot!' when she won the talk on fire regulations," I reply dryly.

She gives a sheepish grin. "He's just so arrogant. I mean, he's a full member of the team for the rest of term. So he can bloody well contribute for a change. Especially seeing that the whole thing was his idea."

"Yeah. Shame it was such a good one." I hold my student card to the study center door and wait for the little light in the door handle to turn green. Then I open it and hold it for Lin.

The study center is a small building reserved for the sixth form. You can come here if you want somewhere quiet to write an essay or do some revision. Today, we have the first meeting of a small group for people applying to Oxford.

"Uh-oh," Lin breathes as we enter the tutor room, and I stiffen.

Speak of the devil.

You could fit twenty people in here, but the only occupants besides two girls and a guy I only know by sight are Keshav, Lydia, Alistair, Wren, Cyril, and . . . James. There's also a young woman who is presumably our tutor. She's the only one to say hello.

I take one of the chairs as far as possible from Beaufort's clique. Lin comes to sit next to me. Mechanically, I take out my planner, pens, and the new notebook I bought specially for this group. I arrange everything on the table in front of me—it has to be parallel to the edge—trying hard to act like the rest of them aren't here. I don't want anything to do with James, and certainly not with his friends. The mere thought that the application process means measuring up to people like them—from filthy-rich families who've studied at Oxbridge colleges for generations—makes me feel sick.

I don't know how Lin feels about it all. She was never part of that gang, but she was friends with Elaine Ellington and a couple of other girls in the year above us, so they moved in similar circles. But then her father left her mother for another woman—who soon turned out to be a con artist. She tricked him into marriage, and within a year, he'd lost his entire fortune to her. It was a massive scandal, and as a result, nobody wanted anything to do with the Wangs anymore. Neither in business, nor socially, nor at this school.

Lin's mum had to sell their big place in the country and move to somewhere much smaller, near Pemwick, so that Lin could stay on at Maxton Hall. OK, so it's still about four times the size of our house, but even so, it must have been a major shock for Lin. In one stroke, she'd lost her family and her old life, and all her friends too.

Most of the time, Lin acts like none of it ever happened. Like things have always been the way they are now. But sometimes, I can see a hint of nostalgia in her eyes, a wistfulness that makes me think she does miss her old life. Especially when I catch her looking longingly at the free chair next to Cyril. I've wondered for ages if the two of them ever had something going on, but the moment I even hint at it, Lin changes the subject. I can't blame her; after all, I hardly ever tell her anything about my private life either. But I can't help being curious.

I find my eyes straying to James. His friends are chatting and fidgeting, but he's sat rigid in his chair. Wren's speaking to him, but I'm pretty sure he's not listening. I wonder what thoughts are darkening his face like that.

"Nice that you're all here," the tutor begins, and I tear my eyes away from Beaufort. "My name is Philippa Winfield, but you can call me Pippa. I'm in my second year at Oxford, so I know only too well how you must be feeling at this stage in the application process."

Wren mumbles something that makes Cyril laugh and then try to hide it by clearing his throat. They're probably discussing how pretty Pippa is. She has a dark blond wavy bob and porcelain skin that makes her look almost like a doll. A very pretty, very expensive doll.

"In the weeks ahead, I'll help you prepare for your Thinking Skills Assessments and interviews. The TSA is a two-hour test that you have to take for some courses at Oxford. It helps the colleges to establish whether you have the skills and critical thinking you'll need to study there."

The test is marked on my calendar for just after Halloween, and the thought of everything to come is making me jittery already. Over the next thirty minutes, Pippa tells us how the test is structured, how much time we'll have for each section, and lots of other stuff that I already know. I don't want to know how the test works; I want to learn how to pass it. As if she'd read my mind, Pippa ends by clapping her hands. "So, the best thing to do is simply have a look at some questions of the kind that could come up for the writing task. I personally found it very helpful to discuss particular questions with other candidates because we all have very different ways of thinking, and that can be really eye-opening. So I thought it would be a good idea to do that here." She opens a folder and takes out a pile of papers that she hands out. "You'll find the first question on page two." She points at Wren, who's whispering again. "Would you please read it out?"

"My pleasure," he replies with a cheeky smile, before picking up the sheet and reading. "The first question is: 'If you can give the reasoning behind your actions, does that mean that your actions are rational?'"

Lin's arm shoots up.

"You don't have to put your hands up; this part will be an open discussion," says Pippa, giving her a nod.

"Every action is based on emotions," my friend begins. "Although they say you should think things through and make the intelligent choice rather than listening to your heart, in the end, all decisions are guided by feelings, and so they're irrational."

"That would be a very short essay," says Alistair, and his friends laugh. Everyone but James. He blinks a couple of times like he's just woken from a dream.

"It's a thesis that you could expand on, or one of you can argue against it," says Pippa.

"Before you can answer the question, you have to define what 'rational' even means in this context," Lydia blurts out suddenly. There's a pen jammed behind her ear, and she's holding the sheet of questions. I wonder what course she's applying for.

"Rationality means thinking or acting in a sensible way," mumbles Kesh.

"In this context, 'rational' means 'sensible,'" I say. "But common sense is subjective. How can you define 'sense' or 'reason' when every person has different rules, principles, and values?"

"It seems to me that everyone has more or less the same basic values," Wren puts in.

I hunch my shoulders uncertainly. "I think that depends on your upbringing and the people around you."

"But everybody learns from when they're a little kid that you're not allowed to kill people and all that. If you act according to those values, then that's objectively rational," he replies.

"But you can't trace every action back to those principles," Lin points out.

"So, if I do something that will mess me up, but I know that I'm acting out of a particular principle, does that make it a rational decision?" Lydia asks. I look at her in confusion, but her gaze is fixed on the sheet of questions.

"If it's in keeping with your basic understanding of common sense, then yes," I answer after a brief pause. "And that's exactly what shows us how different other people's principles can be. I'd never choose to do anything that would mess me up."

"So does that mean my basic understanding of common sense is worth less than yours?" Lydia suddenly looks furious. There are spots of red on her pale cheeks.

"What I mean is, in my opinion, an action can't be rational if it results in someone getting hurt. Whether that's myself or some-body else. But those are just my personal standards."

"And your standards are higher than other peoples', right?"

I look at James in surprise. He spoke so quietly that I barely heard him. He no longer looks as though his thoughts are else-where. Now he's right here, in this room, his cold eyes fixed on me.

I grip my pen more tightly. "I'm not talking about me, but in

general, about the fact that everyone has a different way of thinking and acting."

"So let's say I snuck some strippers into a party to liven things
up and give everyone present a nice evening," James says slowly.
"Then, if you look at it your way, that's a thoroughly rational decision."

My pen's going to snap in half any second. "That wasn't a rational decision, it was just immoral, shitty behavior."

"Words like 'shitty' are best avoided, both in your essays and
your interviews," Pippa objects.

"The distinctions you're making aren't what we're dealing with
here," James replies dryly. "For example, if you have two job offers
where one pays better but the other would make you happier, then
the rational decision is to take the job where you earn more."

"If your idea of rationality is based entirely on money, which
wouldn't surprise me, then yes." My body is flooded with energy,
and it feels to me as though nobody but James and me exists any
longer in this room.

Now he raises an eyebrow. "One: You know nothing about me.
Two, the rational action is to take the better-paid job."

"Why is that, if I may ask?"

He looks me straight in the eyes. "Because in this world, nobody is interested in you unless you have money."

His words make me vividly aware of the worn soles on my
shoes and my holey backpack. Rage flames up inside me, flickering and racing. "That shows who you were brought up by."

"What is that supposed to mean?" he asks, his voice dangerously calm.

I shrug my shoulders. "If it's drummed into you from when
you're little that nobody will be interested in you if you don't have

money, then obviously, you're going to act according to an idea of rationality where nothing else matters. And that's what actually makes you poor."

A muscle in his jaw starts to twitch. "You'd better just stop there, Ruby."

"At Oxford, you won't just be able to tell anyone what to say. Maybe you should get used to either people hitting back or being kind of lonely. But even then, you shouldn't have too many problems because hey, you'll still be rich, and so the world will be interested in you."

James flinches like I slapped his face. You could hear a pin drop in the room. The only sound is my own thumping heartbeat and the thunderous roaring in my ears. The next second, he stands up so abruptly that his chair tips over and crashes to the floor. I hold my breath as he strides out of the room and slams the door behind him.

Suddenly, I'm aware of my surroundings again. James's friends are blinking in confusion, as if asking themselves what the hell just happened. Lydia's face is just a picture of incredible shock. A shiver runs down my spine. I'm slowly coming down from the adrenaline spike and realizing what I just said.

So much for staying invisible. Instead of having a professional debate, I got personal because James made me angry. He's right. I really don't know him. And I had no right to accuse him of stuff like that just because he acts like a total jerk. That makes me no better than him.

What on earth got into me?

James

By this point, the pattern spreading over my paper looks pretty impressive. The spiky black zigzags, little spirals, and wild loops look almost three-dimensional. Like you just have to reach out your hand and you'll be sucked into the picture. I'm constantly amazed by what comes out when you're doodling. And how well it can take your mind off things. Such as the fact that the lads are just a few hundred yards away, on the playing field, training for the weekend's match. And the fact that I have another hour and eleven minutes to go before I can leave this room.

"James!"

I look up. Everyone on the events team is watching me. "What?"

"He wasn't even listening!" Jessalyn exclaims, glaring at Ruby in outrage, as if it were her fault that I can't stand these pointless meetings.

"Let me repeat it then," Ruby says calmly, looking at me across the table. "We need costumes to do a photo shoot for the posters. There's a rental shop in Gormsey, but it would be obvious that the clothes aren't original and are made of plastic."

"Gormsey?" I repeat in confusion.

"It's where I live," she explains.

Never heard of it.

I catch myself wondering what Ruby's house is like. What her parents look like. Whether she has brothers or sisters.

Things that shouldn't interest me.

"We agreed last time that we want to make the photos as authentic as possible. But finding good costumes isn't that easy. Beaufort's dates back over a hundred and fifty years though, doesn't it?"

She's making a huge effort to sound friendly, but that doesn't stop an icy chill spreading through my veins.

I can guess what's coming next.

"Do you think you could ask your parents if we could borrow some clothes from the period?"

I wish I could just keep doodling. Or be somewhere else. Playing lacrosse, for instance. Nobody makes any demands of me there. I can just run, tackle, dodge, shoot, be free. On the field, I can forget. Here, I'm constantly reminded of who I am and what lies ahead for me.

I clear my throat. "I'm afraid not."

Ruby looks like she'd been expecting that. "OK. Can I ask why?"

"No, you can't."

"In other words, you don't *want* to help us," she says, exaggeratedly calmly.

"Can't or don't want to. Doesn't change my answer either way."

Her nostrils flare slightly as she tries not to lose her temper. Not with much success, and it's quite funny to watch. I try to ignore how pretty she is. I've never seen a face like hers. Her upturned nose doesn't fit the proud curl of her lips, her catlike eyes don't match the freckles on her nose, and that straight fringe doesn't go with her heart-shaped face. But in a strange way, the whole effect is perfect. And it gets more appealing every time I see her.

I can't explain why I lost it like that yesterday. It wasn't the first time I've been accused of being a spoiled, rich dickhead. It wasn't even the first time *Ruby* has accused me of being one. I don't know why her words got to me so much, but they stirred something inside me, and I didn't like it. Nobody has mentioned the incident, but I was hoping they'd make a joke of it, tease me about how I reacted, and take the sting out of it. Instead, they didn't say a word, gave me meaningful looks, and that just added weight and significance to Ruby's words.

I groan to myself. I wanted to bloody well enjoy my last year of school, didn't want any worries about anyone or anything, wanted to just have fun. Instead, I'm banned from playing lacrosse, I have to sit in this shitty meeting room, which is as stuffy as all hell, and I have to listen to Ruby call me a . . .

She snaps her fingers in my face.

"Sorry," I say, rubbing my face with both hands. "What?"

"We don't need him, guys," says Kieran in irritation.

"I could certainly do without all of you, but unfortunately, I have to lump it until the end of term," I retort, staring coldly at him.

"James!" Ruby snaps.

"What now? I'm just being honest."

"There are times when honesty is out of place."

The words "you're a fine one to talk" are on the tip of my tongue. But I bite them back. It's kind of hot when she tells me off like that. Which probably has to do with it being two weeks since the last party with the boys, so I have excess energy to work off. I desperately need to think about something else. As unobtrusively as possible, I pull my phone from my trouser pocket and message our group. **Party at mine this evening.**

"Look, let's just rent costumes," Lin suggests. "We can photoshop them a bit so that they look less fake."

Kieran snorts.

"That's ridiculous when we have James *Beaufort* on our team."

"Well, in that case, I'll send an inquiry to Beaufort's myself, if James won't help," Ruby says suddenly.

"No, you won't," I say absently, not taking my eyes off my phone. Alistair is typing, the new lads on the team are all rubbish, and the coach is tearing his hair out.

"You can't stop me."

No way do I want her speaking to my parents. I don't want anyone getting anywhere near my parents. Given that their donations go a good way toward financing this whole school and that they're at pretty much every party, that's kind of impossible. But the mere thought of Ruby and my father in the same room turns my stomach.

"Do you seriously want me to tell Mr. Lexington how little effort you're putting in when I meet with him next week?"

Slowly, I raise my eyes and narrow them at Ruby. I can't believe she's actually trying to blackmail me. If I wasn't so angry, I'd be impressed.

"Knock yourself out," I growl.

I spend the rest of the session ignoring her, and nobody else speaks to me. I draw furious patterns in my notebook, circles and spiky objects, which turn into little monsters with sharp teeth, holding lacrosse sticks in their claws. When Ruby declares the meeting over, I stand up so fast it makes Camille jump. I'm almost out of the door when Ruby steps into my path.

"Could you stay a moment?"

"I'm in a hurry," I say through gritted teeth.

I try to step around her, but she moves aside too. "Please."

Her tone is no longer as annoyed as a few minutes ago. Now she sounds tired, like she can't wait to get out of this room at last either. Maybe that's why I nod and let the others past. Or maybe it's thinking about Lexington and how I'd do anything in my power to avoid spending any longer at these team meetings than necessary. Kieran is the last to leave, and as he shuts the door, he gives me a funny look. If I had to guess, I'd say he was jealous. Interesting.

Ruby clears her throat. She's leaning against a table, arms folded. "If you're pissed off with me, don't take it out on the team. It's not their fault, and it's unfair to make their work harder just for that."

The memory of yesterday almost makes me sick. I remember every word she hurled at me. But no way do I want her to know how hard they hit home.

So I avoid her eyes. "I'm not pissed off with you."

"You seem kind of cross though."

I look at her, eyebrows raised. "We had a silly debate in a study group, Ruby Bell. And after a while, I got sick of it. What do you want?"

"I just wanted to apologize. I was unfair and made it personal, and I'm sorry."

OK, that wasn't what I was expecting. It takes me a while to find the right words. "You give yourself way too much credit if you think I'm losing sleep over that."

She blinks several times in a row, clearly confused by my snarky retort. "You know what? Just forget it."

"You don't have to apologize just because you want something from me."

"I'm not apologizing because I want something from you, James," she replies. "But because I'm truly sorry. I was just . . . awful yesterday."

For a while we look at each other, and I hunt for hidden agendas on her face. But I don't see anything. Her expression is honest and open. She seems to genuinely mean that. I weigh up my options for a moment. I could keep giving her the cold shoulder and act like I don't care about what she said. But then I run the risk of her actually blabbing on me to Lexington and him making me stay on this committee for longer. Arguing with Ruby Bell is bloody tiring. It looks like meeting her halfway will make my life a bit easier.

"OK," I say, simply.

Suddenly, the atmosphere between us is considerably less loaded with rage than it was a few minutes ago. I feel like I can breathe again, and Ruby's shoulders look much more relaxed too.

"Good," she says. For a moment, she looks indecisive, like she doesn't know what to do next. Then she nods and turns back to her table.

She picks up her planner, opens it, and ticks something off. I find myself wondering if apologizing to me was genuinely an item on one of her to-do lists. It wouldn't surprise me.

I could leave now. We've said everything that needs to be said. God knows why I don't budge, just keep watching her pack away her stuff. Everything seems to have its place in that godawful backpack of hers, and it's strangely soothing, almost hypnotic the way a folder, a notebook, her pens, a water bottle, and finally her planner disappear into there, one at a time.

"How many costumes do you need for the poster?" I suddenly hear myself asking.

Ruby freezes in mid-movement. She slowly turns her head to look at me. "Two," she says cautiously. "One for a man and one for a woman."

I can see her trying, and failing, not to look too hopeful, and decide not to keep her in suspense any longer.

"I'll ask my parents," I say after a pause.

Ruby's eyes light up, and it's clearly a major effort not to grin. "Honestly?"

I nod. "Happy now?"

Ruby closes her backpack and heaves it onto her shoulder. Then she comes a few steps toward me. "Thanks. That really will help us out."

I shrug, and, for the first time since I've been part of the events team meetings, we leave the room together.

"The plans are coming together, I think? For Halloween?"

She gives me a sideways glance. I'm as surprised as she is that I asked that. Why the hell aren't I out of here?

"Yeah, it looks like it. But I don't think I'll sleep properly until it's over—and been a success."

"Why does it mean so much to you?"

She thinks a moment or two before she answers. "I want to prove that I'm a good team leader. That I'm up to the job. I had to fight to be taken seriously on the team, and then I had to fight not to let Elaine get me down." She glances apologetically at me. "I know you're her friend, but she wasn't a great leader. I don't want all the work and effort that I've put into the committee and everything I'm still doing to have been for nothing."

I mumble thoughtfully, and she looks inquiringly at me.

"I'm just wondering if I'm that passionate about anything."

"Lacrosse?" she asks.

I give a vague shrug. "Maybe."

We walk through the library, down the stairs, and outside, and for the first time, I really understand that the events that seem so pointless and annoying to me are an important part of other people's lives.

"What's the time, anyway?" Ruby asks suddenly.

I look at my watch. "Nearly four."

She swears and starts running. "I'll miss my bus!"

Her green backpack bobs on her back, and her brown hair whirls up as she sprints for the bus stop.

I walk over to the chauffeur waiting for me by our Rolls in the car park. All at once, asking my parents doesn't seem like so much of a big deal.

Ruby

My phone buzzes as my parents, Ember, and I are sitting by the TV watching *The Voice Kids*. I fish it out of my pocket. The button to unlock it has been sticking for a while, and it feels like I have to press it a bit harder every day. Once it's finally unlocked, I'm stunned.

An unknown number has texted me.

> Scored the costumes for the poster. We can pick them up
> in London tomorrow. J.

"I can't believe that girl's only eight." I hear Mum's amazed voice in my ear.

"Why can't you two sing?" Dad asks. "Then I could have sent you on a show like this."

"Our talents lie elsewhere, Dad," Ember replies.

"Oh, really? What can you do then?" A muffled sound makes me look up. Ember just threw a sofa cushion at Dad. He rumbles with laughter.

"My blog has over five hundred followers, Dad. I can sew, and I can show people that a person with a body like mine can wear whatever they want—that's not nothing, is it?"

"You've topped five hundred?" I ask in surprise.

She nods curtly. We haven't been speaking much since the argument. Ember's still angry with me for refusing to take her to the next Maxton Hall party, and so I totally missed her passing that major milestone.

"That's amazing. Well done," I say. I don't know why it sounds so forced, because it's from the heart. Ember's been working on her blog, *Bellbird*, for over a year. She puts so much work and love into it that she deserves to be successful.

"Thanks." Ember turns her attention to the remote and starts fiddling with it.

"D'you reckon Ember could turn up with her sewing machine and audition?" Dad asks. "Or she could give a talk. It would be amazing if you told people the things you've explained to us—that 'fat' is just a descriptive word, with no value judgment, and that's why people should use it!"

Ember snorts with laughter. "I don't think that would work, Dad. It's a singing show."

"Oh. Right. Good point. How about *Britain's Got Talent*? If what you do isn't talented, I don't know what is. If necessary, we could invite your five hundred followers and sneak them into the audience. And then we can all cheer you on."

"Totally!" I agree. "Go and audition with your designs. I'll make banners and hand them out to all five hundred of them."

Ember pulls a face. I stick my tongue out at her. Her eyes begin to sparkle, and a cautious grin spreads over her face. At that moment, I feel like everything's OK again. We've made up without words, same as always. I feel my shoulders slump with relief.

Dad says something else, but at that moment, I'm distracted by the message on my screen. I start to reply but delete it right away. I don't know how to respond. The idea of going up to London with James and spending a day with him outside the boundaries of Maxton Hall feels weird. Weird but . . . exciting, the more I think about it. I type a few more words.

Suddenly, a cushion hits my face.

"Hey!" I shout.

"We hadn't finished our conversation, Ruby," my dad says, deadly serious. "Get involved."

"No, Dad, I can't sing, and no, I'm not auditioning for any show just so you can laugh at me."

"Hmm," he says, looking pensively at me while Mum gushes with delight. "Such a little girl with such a great voice!"

"There are other ways to win a talent show. If the sewing machine isn't an option, you could learn juggling together."

"If you're so keen on the idea, then you can apply yourself," I say dryly.

"You know what? Maybe I will," Dad says, in mock defiance.

"And what would you do?" Mum asks absentmindedly, not taking her eyes off the screen.

"How about . . ."

Danny Jones, one of the jury members, presses his button, and his chair starts to revolve. Mum cheers, and Dad raises his arms euphorically.

Ember and I look at each other and laugh.

"Do we have anything going on tomorrow?" I ask, once the girl has left the stage and things have calmed down a bit.

Dad shakes his head. "No, why?"

"We're planning a Halloween party at the moment and need costumes. One of the boys has come up with some, and he wants to know if we can pick them up in London tomorrow."

"That's a two-hour drive. Is this ominous boy going to drive, or will you go by train?" Mum asks.

I hold up a finger to tell her to wait a moment. Then I type my reply.

OK. How will we get to London? RB

I hope he'll get that my initials are meant as a joke.

My chauffeur will pick you up about 10. OK? JMB

I snort and feel Ember's inquiring eyes on me.

For a moment I consider googling James to find out what the "M" stands for, but I don't. Googling him would also be crossing a line. I don't want to know everything it says about him on the web. There are hundreds of rumors just at school. I could have a lifetime supply of James Beaufort gossip.

"Apparently, this boy has a chauffeur," I reply belatedly.

"A chauffeur?" Ember exclaims. "So he's one of the poshos then?"

"His family owns Beaufort's."

"You're planning to drive to London with the Beaufort boy?" Dad asks. His tone is both surprised and suspicious.

I nod slowly. "Yes. We can borrow some clothes from their archive."

Dad frowns. "And it'll be . . . the two of you?"

"Come on, Angus," Mum says. "Leave Ruby be."

"What? If Ruby has a date, I want to know."

I feel my face go red. "It's not a date, Dad. It's school stuff."

He just growls. But Ember is staring at me wide-eyed. "That's amazing." She drops back onto the sofa and crosses her arms over her chest. "That's so . . . Oh, wow. You don't know what an opportunity this is, Ruby."

"I'll take photos for you," I say placatingly, but Ember's still staring hard at the TV.

"So, is it OK if I go?" I ask Mum. She seems the only sane person in this room.

"Of course," she says at once, giving Dad a warning look when he opens his mouth again. "You're old enough to decide for yourself who you want to do things with."

Inexplicably, her words make my cheeks flush even redder. But without paying much attention, I type a reply:

OK.

Oh and I prefer Ben & Jerry's to champagne. RJB.

P.S. If you add another initial, I'll freak.

I hesitate a moment, wondering if I can really send that. James and I aren't the kind of people to joke around by WhatsApp. Or are we?

See you tomorrow, Ruby.

No, I guess we're not those kind of people.

Ruby

The next morning, I'm on the verge of panic because I have no idea what to wear for this trip to Beaufort's. I don't know if there's a dress code or how nicely I should dress. I'm also wondering if James will wear a suit. We've never set eyes on each other outside school, so we've almost always seen each other in uniform.

In the end, I decide on a black skirt, over-the-knee socks, and an ochre jumper with a white crocheted collar. The black brogues I scored in Gormsey's charity shop a couple of months ago are the finishing touch.

I'm not as brave with fashion as Ember is. I prefer to buy things that make me feel safe and that I know will last. Even so, I like getting dressed up and taking time to look put together—probably another aspect of my love for organization.

Once I'm dressed, I pop into my sister's room, just to be on the safe side. She's awake and sitting at her little desk by the window when I stick my head around the door.

"What?" she asks, without turning around.

"What d'you think?" She turns on her chair, and I open the door fully so she can see my outfit.

"Cute," she says, once she's scanned me over from top to toes.

"Really?" I ask, doing a twirl. When I look back at Ember, she narrows her eyes slightly.

"Not a date, uh-huh?" There's a teasing tone in her voice.

I roll my eyes. "Ember, I can't stand the guy."

"Yeah, right," she replies, standing up. She goes to her tiny built-in wardrobe and opens the door. Then she crouches down until she's half vanished inside it and starts to dig around. I come to stand behind her cautiously and peer over her shoulder. Thirty seconds later, she reemerges and hands me a little burgundy bag.

"My bag!"

"Don't act so shocked. You only ever use your backpack anyway," she says defensively. "But it goes really well with that look."

"I should charge you interest, seeing how long you kept it." I dust off the faux leather. This was another thrift store find. I loved it and used it proudly for a full fortnight before our neighbor, Mrs. Felton, spotted me with it in Mum's bakery and blurted out, loudly, that she'd bought it new fifty years ago. So I was only too happy to lend it to Ember and didn't even want it back at first. But now I'm glad to have it in my hands again.

"I'm not paying interest on something you didn't even know I had," she retorts.

The doorbell rings, and I freeze. I glance at the clock. It's quarter to ten. "He's early," I groan, running back to my room to grab my phone and purse and switch them from one bag to the other.

"Ruby!" Mum calls.

As I go downstairs, I tell myself sternly to keep calm. There's no reason to be worked up. This is just a school trip—Lin and I have done this kind of stuff loads of times, and it won't be any different with James.

I take a deep breath at the last few steps. Mum's opened the door, and as I reach the hall, I see her chatting to a man. I gape.

One: James wasn't lying. He really does have a chauffeur. A uniformed chauffeur at that, with a peaked cap and the whole works. Two: The chauffeur looks like Antonio Banderas. He's tanned, has deep brown eyes, and an expressive, almost sensual mouth. He looks to be in his mid-forties, and he's drop-dead gorgeous. Judging by Mum's pink cheeks, she's of the same opinion.

"Good morning, miss," says the Zorro-chauffeur, raising his cap in greeting.

"Good morning . . ."

"Percy," Mum helps me out, with a beaming smile.

". . . Percy." I smile too and take my jacket from the coat hook. "OK, Mum, see you later."

"Have fun, love. And take lots of photos for us." Mum gives me a kiss on the cheek, and I follow Percy through the door. The next moment, as if by magic, he's opened a huge black umbrella over my head.

"Thank you," I say.

"Not at all. The car is just over here."

I look where he's pointing, and I'm almost rooted to the spot in astonishment. There's a Rolls-Royce in the street outside our house. It's gleaming black, and, even to me, it looks enormous among the rest of the parked cars, like an alien, and I'm used to seeing limos and whatever swish cars these days.

Percy opens the rear door and holds the umbrella over me until I've got in. I thank him, and he nods, then shuts the door behind me. Barely thirty seconds later, the car starts. Nervously, I smooth out my skirt and check it didn't ride up as I sat down.

Only then can I look at James.

He's sitting there, facing me, an unreadable expression on his face. He looks as though even he doesn't know what to think about the fact that I just got into his car. He's wearing a dark gray suit, shot through with fine threads, a white shirt, and a dark silk tie with a pin. He has a glass in his hand, which I hope only contains apple juice, and I notice a silver signet ring on his left hand that I've never seen before. There's a coat of arms on it, presumably his family's crest.

The longer I look at him, the more underdressed I feel in my bodged-together vintage outfit. Everything about James screams money, from the top of his head to his gleaming leather shoes. I try not to let it faze me—after all, I knew what I was getting myself into.

When I look again, I see how tired James seems. His turquoise eyes are bloodshot, and there are bags under them.

"Morning," he says eventually, his voice hoarse.

Maybe he only just woke up. Or partied the night away and hasn't been to bed at all.

"Morning," I reply. "Thanks for the lift."

He doesn't answer but looks me over, like I just did to him, so I stare around the car. There are rows of leather seats, and opposite James there's a bar with glasses and some kind of cupboard or fridge behind a door. There's a dark screen separating us from the driver.

The silence between us is getting unpleasant, so I nod toward Percy: "Your chauffeur could be a Hollywood star. I guess he's in his forties, but he's still one of the handsomest men I've ever seen."

"You flatter me, miss, I'm fifty-two." Percy's voice comes through a speaker in the ceiling.

Embarrassed, I glance at James. He's grinning from ear to ear. My cheeks are burning up.

"If you're going to say things like that, it's a good idea to switch off the intercom, Ruby Bell," James informs me. He's pointing to a flashing red light.

"Oh."

"I'll take care of it, sir," Percy says, and a second later, it's gone.

I bury my face in my hands and shake my head. "In films, the screen just goes up. How am I meant to know you have to press a button too?"

"Don't worry. Percy rarely gets compliments like that from me, so I'm sure he's thrilled."

I shake my head. "I think I'll have to get out."

"Too late for that now. You're trapped here with me for the next two hours." I hear a quiet clatter. "Here, this is for you."

Slowly, I lower my hands. James is holding out a small blue tub.

"Don't say you really brought me ice cream?" I exclaim in disbelief.

"We had some in the house," he says. "If you don't want it, I'll eat it."

Without another word, I take it from him. James bends down to the fridge again, and the next second, he's got another tub of Ben & Jerry's in his hand. Intrigued, I watch him as he pulls off the lid and peels back the foil. The sight of him in that suit with ice cream in his lap seems so surreal that for a moment I wonder if I'm still asleep.

There's condensation coming from the ice cream tub in my hand, and a cold droplet lands in my lap. I look around for a napkin.

"On the right there," says James, nodding toward the bar.

I lean over, take an eggshell-colored napkin off the bar, and spread it over my lap. Then I open the tub and dig my spoon in. I close my eyes with delight. "Mm. Cookie dough."

"I had to guess your favorite flavor," says James. "Was I right?"

"Yeah, definitely," I say with conviction, but then pause. "Mind you, the new salted caramel is really good too. Have you tried it?"

James shakes his head.

For a moment, there's silence between us. Then he says: "This is the best hangover breakfast I've had in ages."

So he *was* out partying yesterday. "Long night?"

I immediately regret the question as he grins suggestively into his ice cream. "You could put it like that."

"Then that part of the dreadful rumors about James Beaufort is true."

"Dreadful rumors about James Beaufort?" he asks in amusement.

I raise an eyebrow. "Come on."

"I have no idea what you're talking about."

"Like you don't know all the stories about you and your friends."

"Such as?"

"That you have caviar for breakfast, go swimming in champagne, you broke a waterbed during sex . . . and so on."

He pauses, spoon halfway to his lips. A second passes, then another. In the end, he pops the spoon into his mouth and eats the ice cream slowly, acting like he's deep in thought. Apparently, he's starting to wake up. His eyes don't have that hazy veil over them anymore.

"OK, then it's time to clear those rumors up," he begins. "I can't stand caviar—the idea of eating fish eggs is just gross. I have a smoothie for breakfast, usually with poached eggs or muesli."

"*In* the smoothie?" I pull a revolted face.

"Not *in* the smoothie. With it."

"Oh, right."

He thinks again. "It's not true about the champagne, either. Or not quite. I did once drop a bloody expensive bottle belonging to Wren's parents in their pool, so I swam in it that way. But that was an accident."

"Wren's parents must love you."

"You have no idea." He grins and keeps on digging into the ice cream.

"And . . . the waterbed?" I ask hesitantly.

James pauses and looks at me, his eyes sparkling. "Does that interest you?"

"To be honest, yes," I admit, not breaking eye contact. "I mean, waterbeds are pretty solid, or so I've heard. Not that easy to break."

"It wasn't a waterbed, just an ordinary one."

I give a dry gulp. There's something in James's eyes I've never seen before. Something dark, heavy, that makes my belly tingle.

"How dull," I croak, my voice betraying the lie.

I don't want to imagine James having sex.

I really don't.

But now I can't stop wondering what he must have been doing to break his bed. And what he looked like at the time. He showed me a flash of skin when he undressed in front of me. I know he's ripped. And I've seen how well he can move playing lacrosse. I bet he makes the women in his bed pretty happy.

At this moment, I'm glad of the ice cream in my hands. I wish I could dunk my face in it to cool down.

"Rumors are mostly untrue or only have a little bit of truth in them." His knowing grin makes me afraid that he knows exactly what I was just thinking, in every detail.

I decide it's time to conclude the subject of waterbeds. "Well, that makes me glad there are no rumors about me."

James puts his tub back in the fridge and the spoon on the bar. Then he leans back in his seat and looks thoughtfully at me. "I tried to find out about you after the business with Lydia."

"I don't think I want to know what people say about me," I say quietly.

"Most of them didn't know who you were. And anything they did say wasn't bad."

I breathe a sigh of relief. "Seriously?"

James nods. "That's why I was so suspicious of you. Anyone with that good a reputation must have a dark secret somewhere."

I pull a face. "I have no dark secrets."

"Of course not." His expression is amused as he leans forward. "Come on, Ruby. Tell me something that no one else at school knows about you."

I shake my head on autopilot. No way am I playing this game. "You tell me something that no one knows about you."

I expect him to protest, but he actually seems to be thinking about it.

"If I don't get into Oxford, my father will kill me." He says it casually, as if he's long come to terms with that fact. But his eyes tell a different story.

"Because he went there?" I ask cautiously.

"Both my parents did. And theirs before them."

I always envied James and his friends for their backgrounds, which give them the best chance of getting into the best unis. But now I realize there's another side to that. So much pressure. And it helps me understand the way James reacted at the study group a bit better. My words must have really hurt.

"I've wanted to go to Oxford since I was little," I say after a while. I suddenly feel like it's OK to trust him with this part of me. He just did, and it helped me get a handle on him a bit. We've done nothing but fight since we first met. It can't do any harm if we try to clear up some of the prejudices we have about each other. "My parents always encouraged me, even if they knew it might just stay a dream. I always got good marks, but there's more to getting into Oxford than that. But then they heard about scholarships to Maxton Hall and applied for me. We didn't expect me to get one, but I must have made a good impression at the interview. Now I feel like it's not just a pipe dream, and I swore I'd do everything I could to make it to Oxford. I want to make my parents proud. And myself."

James says nothing for a moment. He looks at me, and the sudden intensity in his blue-green eyes sends a shiver down my spine. "How long have you been at the school?"

"Two years."

He mumbles.

"What?" I ask.

He shrugs vaguely. "I'm just wondering how I never noticed you before."

My heart skips a beat. At the same time, I'm giving myself a pat on the back. Seems like my just-keep-your-head-down strategy is working perfectly. "I have the ability to glide through corridors like a shadow and blend in with the walls."

His lips twitch slightly. "Sounds like you're the Maxton Hall ghost. Or a chameleon. But anyway, your turn."

"For what?" I look confusedly at him.

"To tell me something about you that nobody else knows."

"I just did!"

He shakes his head. "That doesn't count. You only replied to what I told you."

I take a deep breath and exhale slowly, thinking about what I can tell him. His eyes are alert as they watch me, which doesn't make it any easier. On the contrary.

I shake my head in resignation. "There's nothing to tell."

"I don't believe you." He leans back, crosses his arms over his chest. "Come on. You have to do more than just study."

Oh, no, I don't, I think. But luckily, something comes to mind. "I read manga."

James looks at me like he misheard for a second. Then he smiles. "There, that's something. I wouldn't exactly call it a dark secret, but OK. What's your favorite?"

I'm confused. I didn't expect him to ask questions.

"*Death Note*," I say hesitantly.

"Would you recommend it?"

I have no idea how we got from "James breaks beds during sex" to "Ruby's favorite manga." Not a clue. But I nod slowly. "If you ask me, reading *Death Note* is an important part of anyone's basic education."

James looks startled. "It would be terrible to be lacking that, then."

My lips twitch involuntarily too.

I can't help grinning.

James Beaufort made me grin.

As I realize that, I turn hastily away and look out of the window, but I'm pretty sure he saw it. There was a clear flash of triumph in his eyes.

I wonder why.

Ruby

BEAUFORT'S

James's surname is emblazoned across the front of the flagship store. He gets out of the car and strides purposefully toward the entrance while I stop and stare wide-eyed, first at the sign and then at the huge modern building with—as James told me on the drive here—the largest branch of Beaufort's below, while above that are the offices for the design, sales, and customer services departments and so on, plus, of course, the tailoring workshops. Huge plate-glass windows span all six floors, behind which stand mannequins dressed in the brand's famous classic style.

"Coming?" James calls to me from the door.

We spent the rest of the journey chatting. Not much but more than I'd been expecting. I still can't shake off the feeling that this is all a dream.

I'm in London. With *James Beaufort*.

I just can't believe it.

"Ruby!" James says again, glancing ostentatiously at his watch.

That snaps me out of my trance. Hurriedly, I start moving and join him. He holds the door for me, and I step inside hesitantly. Then I look around.

This is way bigger than the branch I went to with my parents that time. The high ceilings, white walls, and polished hardwood floors give the sales floor an open, inviting air, despite all the furniture being black. Along the far wall are shelves, from floor to ceiling, holding countless shirts. Above them is a brass pole, hanging from which, to the left, is a ladder. As soon as you come through the door, there's a large round table with a bronze statue of a stag in the center. Stacked around that are small piles of perfectly folded trousers. Over the table hangs a chandelier that gives a soft, warm light to the room. There's a unique scent in the air—tangy but not overwhelming, a blend of the natural odors of the fabrics and an aroma that must come from an air freshener.

James nudges me gently with his arm. I look up at him, and he nods toward the back of the shop. I slowly follow him. On our right, there's another wall of shelves. Framed in a gap in its center are photos of men in an array of suits, lit from the sides by two brass lamps. Below that, there's a dark green satin sofa with tartan cushions, a fur-covered futon, and a glass table, standing on which are crystal glasses and a carafe of water.

All around us, I can see robust tweed, fine silk, the softest leather—Beaufort's only uses the best fabrics to guarantee their quality. There's no doubt that I'm in a shop frequented by aristocrats and politicians, and despite myself, I feel a bit out of place.

But that might just be because there seem to be only men around here. Salesmen, men standing on stools in front of huge mirrors toward the back of the shop, and men at their feet taking their measurements, not to mention the man at my side.

Suddenly, one of those men gets up from the floor. He addresses the customer, whose trouser hem he was just adjusting, and then he spots us. At the sight of James, he stiffens. "Mr. Beaufort!" White as chalk, he glances at his watch.

"No worries, Tristan, we've got plenty of time," James replies.

I don't even recognize his voice now. Grand and authoritative. I sneak a peek at him and notice his posture. His hands might be shoved casually into his trouser pockets, but you can see that he's not just any old person around here. I ask myself how he does it. He seems to turn anywhere he sets foot into his own private kingdom. The school, the lacrosse field, this shop. Does it happen if he goes into a café? Maybe I'll have to test that out someday.

Tristan waves another tailor over and hands him his measuring tape. The next moment, he hurries over to us and shakes James's hand. "Apologies for not being here to greet you."

"Don't worry about it, Tristan," James replies. "Can you spare us a few minutes, or are you busy?"

Shocked, the tailor looks up at him. "Of course I have time for you, sir."

James turns to me. "Ruby, this is Tristan MacIntyre, our head tailor. And Tristan, this is Ruby Bell. She's in charge of the Maxton Hall events team."

I raise my eyebrows at James. I'm surprised that he introduced me like that. He could have just said that I'm at school with him. Or added nothing at all beyond my name.

Tristan straightens his jacket, and as his gaze rests on me, he relaxes slightly. A practiced smile crosses his lips. "Mr. Beaufort doesn't often bring school friends here, so I'm very pleased to make your acquaintance, Miss Bell."

I smile back and hold out my hand. He takes it but doesn't shake it as I expected; instead, he turns it and presses a kiss on the back of my hand. Suddenly, I feel like I should curtsy. Fortunately, I stop myself in time and just say: "Pleased to meet you too, Mr. MacIntyre."

"Please call me Tristan."

"Only if you call me Ruby."

His smile broadens, and he turns to James with an expressive look on his face. "We had a few items sent down from the archives. They're up in the workshops. So, if you'd kindly follow me."

He turns on his heel and leads us through the shop to a dark wooden door at the back. It opens onto a staircase.

"I hope you'll like the clothes we picked out," Tristan says as we go up. "They were designed by your great-great-great-grandfather in person, Mr. Beaufort."

I glance at James in surprise, but his face doesn't change as he replies: "I'm sure they'll be fine for the occasion."

"Was that the great-great-great-grandfather who founded the company?" I ask curiously.

Tristan nods. "Exactly, he and his wife, in 1857. Did you know that Beaufort's was originally a fashion house designing for women as well as men? It was only in the early twentieth century that they decided to focus on their core business."

I had known that, ever since Lin had suggested asking James about the costumes. I'd pointed out that it wouldn't be much use because we'd still need a dress for the woman, but she'd explained about the early days of the firm and shown me pictures of the extravagant dresses the brand had sold back then.

"Yes," I say, belatedly. "But I didn't know why."

"We were on shaky ground financially," James says. "My great-grandfather made a few bad decisions, and we were on the edge of going bust. Specializing was the only way out."

"From then on, Beaufort's became the brand it is today," Tristan explains, as if he'd been there at the time. "Nobody else makes a suit like we do. We can provide anything your heart desires, from business suits to full evening dress. The quality of the workmanship is vastly superior to anything you can buy off the rack, quite apart from the fact that we personalize every suit with the customer's initials. Could you demonstrate, Mr. Beaufort?"

I stop and turn to face James, who's standing a step below me. Now we're face-to-face. My eyes meet his for a moment too long, and yet again, I can't read the expression in them. Then I look down to the breast pocket of his dark gray suit, which is embroidered with the initials JMB.

"I've been wondering what the 'M' stands for since yesterday," I admit. I look up again, and suddenly I'm so close to him that I can make out details in his face that I've never noticed before. Such as that his eyelashes are surprisingly dark for his hair color. And the pale freckles adorning his cheeks.

"Mortimer," he replies softly.

"Like your dad?"

He nods and looks past me to Tristan. A clear sign that he has no desire to pursue this conversation any further.

As we climb the rest of the stairs, Tristan tells me about the special fabrics the Beaufort's tailors work with and the vast array of cuff studs they can choose from.

Until now, a suit has just been a . . . suit to me. I could never really tell one from another, let alone have any idea of how many choices have to be made before one can be finished. Or how many ways of making them there are.

"We measure every single check so as to leave nothing to chance," Tristan says as we leave the stairwell and step into a brightly lit corridor. "Attention to detail and the best quality have always been what makes Beaufort's stand out. Which is why we even dress the royal family." He stops near a photograph on the wall. I come closer, and my mouth drops open.

It's the Prince of Wales.

"No way," I breathe.

James says nothing, but Tristan beams proudly. "He is not our only royal client."

We keep walking down the hallway, which is lined the whole way with pictures of celebs, politicians, and aristocrats—all wearing Beaufort's suits. I see Pierce Brosnan, the Beatles, and even the prime minister. There is also a whole row of men whose faces mean nothing to me but whose very bearing tells me that they're both powerful and rich.

"Have you met all these people?" I ask James.

He shrugs. "Some of them."

"That's so cool," I murmur, and I'm almost a bit sad as Tristan opens a door at the end of the corridor, finally leading us into the workroom.

I look around curiously. It's a huge space, almost like a giant warehouse. It's Saturday, but there must be fifty people at work here, either at tailor's dummies or tables laden with cloth.

"This way," says Tristan, leading the way through the room, us in his wake. "The costumes are over here." As we pass, people greet James politely but awkwardly. Glancing back over my shoulder, I see them putting their heads together and whispering. I wrinkle my brow as I look at James. He's put on a mask of nonchalant arrogance, the expression I know from school. I wonder what's going on in his head right now. He doesn't look as though he enjoys the staff here seeming scared of him.

I want to know more about him, I realize suddenly. More about James, about Beaufort's, and about what goes on behind the scenes of this wealthy family.

Tristan stops suddenly, dragging me back to reality. "Voilà," he says, pointing to a dummy beside him, which . . .

. . . takes my breath away.

The tailor's dummy is wearing a Victorian dress. Although it's actually a two-piece, made in pleated green silk, with short sleeves and layered with black lace ruffles. The top is tightly fitted, with a restrained heart-shaped neckline and adorned with black glass beads. The tiered floor-length skirt is ostentatious, and its petticoats make it seem even bigger and heavier. It is by far the most beautiful dress I have ever seen in my life.

I don't know how I'm supposed to take it home, or to school. I'm scared even to touch it in case I make it dirty.

Behind it, there's another dummy dressed in a man's suit that consists of a frock coat, waistcoat, shirt, and trousers. The coat is slightly nipped in at the waist and looks as though it's made of soft wool. The black waistcoat has assorted pockets and sharp points at the bottom. The white shirt has a small collar and a black cravat, which is wider and a different shape from the ties I'm used to.

"A gentleman did nothing by halves in the matter of dress in those days. Every detail had to be perfect," Tristan explains, starting to take the clothes off the mannequin. Once he's finished, he beckons James to follow him behind a screen. "Come on, Mr. Beaufort. Let's see if it fits you."

James follows Tristan behind the screen without looking at me again. He seems more as though he's been left on standby, not fully present. I haven't seen a hint of emotion on his face since we got out of the Rolls. As if his main aim was not to let anyone here have any access to his thoughts or feelings.

I can hear quiet mumbling from Tristan and the rustle of fabric as I venture a step closer to the dress. I wonder what kind of lady might have worn it and what kind of a life she would have led. Did she have dreams, and was she able to fulfill them?

After about five minutes, Tristan comes back around to me. "It fits him perfectly," he declares in triumph.

"You have my measurements, Tristan," James remarks dryly. "I'm sure that helped you out." Then he too emerges from behind the screen.

My mouth goes dry.

James looks as though he's just stepped out of the nineteenth century. The suit fits to a tee, and Tristan has even given him a side-parting and a walking cane. My eyes wander over his body, from top to toe.

James looks *amazing*.

It's not until I look up to his face again that I realize how much I must have been staring, and judging by his filthy grin, James knows exactly what was just going through my head. My cheeks flush hot.

"Your turn, Ruby," Tristan suddenly commands me.

"What?" I look at him in confusion. "What for?"

"To change, of course." He points to the dress. I stare at him and then at James, who is trying, with limited success, to suppress a laugh. It's only then that I realize what the two of them are expecting of me.

"No, no way!" I say in a panicked voice. I was meant to *arrange* the costumes. There was no mention of wearing them.

"Did you think I was the only one going back in time? No

chance." James reaches out to me with the stick and taps me a little too hard on the shin. "So if you would have the goodness to get changed . . ."

"A true gentleman would never hit a lady with a stick, Mr. Beaufort," Tristan reproves him.

James snorts. "Ruby is no lady, Tristan. She's a tyrant."

"You haven't even seen my tyrannical side yet. But I'm happy to show you." I narrow my eyes at James. "You don't happen to have another of those sticks, do you, Tristan?"

"I'm afraid not. But you won't need any such thing once you're wearing this wonderful dress. Come along," says Tristan, looking so hopeful that I no longer have the heart to fight back. I follow him behind the screen; he disappears and returns a moment later with a woman he introduces as his assistant. She helps me put on the bodice and skirt. It soon becomes clear that I could never have managed it alone. Just doing up the array of tiny hooks and eyes is an art in itself, never mind the fact that both garments have metal boning inside them. I have to twist and squirm to get them over my head and hips. Once I'm fully dressed, the hem of the dress is so huge that I barely fit into the small area between the screen and the wall.

"Ready, boss," Tristan's assistant calls out, and he rejoins us. At the sight of me, he claps his hands in delight, and his face lights up. "Beautiful! Now for a few last finishing touches . . ." As if from nowhere, he conjures up a hair clip and steps behind me. By the feel of things, he gathers up the top section of my hair, pulls it back, and fastens it with the clip. Then he comes to stand in front of me again and tweaks at a few more strands until a satisfied expression spreads over his face. After that, I'm finally allowed to turn around to the mirror on the wall behind me.

I catch my breath.

I never knew that I could look like this. Quite apart from the fact that the dress clings to my curves as though it was made for me, I get the feeling that I could be channeling the spirit of the lady who once wore it. I feel beautiful, powerful, and strong. As if the whole world lay at my feet and I could have anything I wanted just at a click of my fingers. I turn slowly to Tristan and smile.

"Thank you for forcing me to put the dress on."

He sketches a bow. "Mr. Beaufort," he says solemnly, "may I present Miss Bell?"

Cautiously, I set myself in motion. One step, two steps, around the screen, four steps, five steps . . . until I stop and dare to look up.

James is chatting with Tristan's assistant, but when he sees me, he breaks off in mid-sentence. His eyebrows shoot up, his lips part slightly. He studies me from top to toe, as if he had all the time in the world, and I swallow hard.

Then he murmurs something I don't quite catch.

"What?"

He clears his throat. "You . . . look very lovely."

My heart skips a beat. It's not the first time I've had a compliment from a boy, but it feels like it. I don't think James says anything like that very often either. His words sound . . . honest. And unmasked.

"It's as though the dress was made for her," Tristan agrees. He pushes me a little closer to James, then whips out his phone. "Now, please look at me as though you're a nineteenth-century lady and gentleman."

Beside me, James snorts almost inaudibly, but when I risk a glance at him, he's facing the camera as though he's done this all his life. I remember the pictures that went around Maxton Hall last year. He and Lydia were modeling their parents' new collection with exactly the same perfectly trained poker face. I turn toward Tristan and try to look elegant and serious. I don't know if I'm doing it right, but he takes photo after photo.

"Now, new pose," he demands after a few minutes. "Bow and hold out your hand to her, so that it looks as though you're inviting her to dance," he suggests.

James follows his instructions like a pro. I doubt many eighteen-year-old boys could bow as elegantly as him—with or without the costume. But James seems to be taking this perfectly seriously. I'm surprised when he suddenly takes my hand and looks up at me. His skin is warm, and although he's barely touching my fingers, a tingle shoots right up my arm.

Now that he's looking at me like that, I can imagine it perfectly. A ballroom full of people in evening dress, tasteful orchestral music, James and me. His hand on my back, leading me across the parquet floor. I'm sure he knows how to move. I can easily imagine letting him lead the dance and just letting go.

I gulp dryly. That's a more pleasant thought than it should be.

"Maybe another picture, with you two face-to-face?" says Tristan, and James straightens up. The silk square in his pocket has slipped slightly, and I automatically reach out to adjust it.

Something flashes in James's eyes. Hastily, I snatch my hand away—and suddenly I don't know what to do with my arms, just let them hang limp at my sides.

Then James takes my hand again. His other hand is on my waist, and I hold my breath. My heart starts racing, and I don't know why, but it feels so good to be touched by him. At that moment, I can't even remember why I can't stand this guy.

What is he doing to me?

James avoids my eyes, his expression that same mix of alert admiration that I'm feeling.

The sounds around us fade away the longer we look at each other. All I can do is sense. His fingers on my waist, moving slightly, his hand holding mine tightly. His eyes are almost like a dare that I'd do anything to accept.

"James." A deep voice rings out behind us.

The fire in his eyes goes out in a split second. His relaxed stance is gone too. Suddenly, he's stiff as a board and drops my hand like it's burned him.

An instant. No longer, and he's back to the James Beaufort I know. All at once, the arrogant twist to his lips and the coldness in his eyes make him look pretty threatening.

"Mum, Dad, I didn't know you were going to be here today."

Oh, God. I start to turn around in the weighty dress, and once I've managed it, my heart sinks down to my toes.

Standing in front of me are Mortimer and Cordelia Beaufort. James and Lydia's parents. Heads of one of the most successful firms in the country. Suddenly, I no longer feel as strong and powerful as I did a moment or two back—especially not in comparison to Cordelia Beaufort. Everything about her is stylish, elegant, and grand. She has a slender face and the same arrogant mouth as James, except for her dark red lipstick. Her skin is like porcelain, and she's wearing a fitted white shift dress, clearly by an expensive designer. Her glossy rust-red hair sits just above her shoulders and is perfectly waved, as if she's come straight from the salon.

James's father has sandy hair, ice-blue eyes, and a mouth that turns down slightly at the corners. His stance is proud and erect, and in his Beaufort suit, he looks like he's on his way to an important business meeting.

His face doesn't change as he looks me over from top to bottom.

Now I know where James inherited his impenetrable mask from.

"We were here for a meeting about China," his mother explains. She steps forward to kiss her son on the cheek, and I catch a waft of her perfume. It seems powdery, like a bouquet of fresh roses.

"Percy told us that he'd driven you and your"—she glances at me—"school friend here."

James doesn't reply. He's making no moves to introduce me to his parents, so I step forward, cheeks burning, and hold out my hand to his mother. "I'm Ruby Bell. Pleased to meet you, Mrs. Beaufort."

She looks at me a moment too long before she strikes. "The pleasure is all mine." She smiles, revealing a row of pearly white teeth.

I want to be like her, I catch myself thinking. I want to walk into a room the way she does, my very aura instantly causing everyone present to see me as a strong woman to be respected.

What I don't want is for my mere presence to strike fear and trembling into people, as seems to be the case with Mr. Beaufort. He gives me a curt nod as we shake hands, then looks around the workshop as if he's already had enough of me.

"I see you've ordered a couple of pieces from the archives," Mrs. Beaufort says, looking at us slightly aslant. She takes a step forward and twitches my skirt. There's a crease between her brows. "The skirt is too long. Kindly alter it, Mr. MacIntyre."

Tristan hasn't uttered a word since the Beauforts arrived, but he nods hastily. "Of course, madam."

Now Mrs. Beaufort gestures to me to turn around. I feel queasy as I do so. "What do you need them for again?"

"The Victorian party at the end of October," James answers. He's like a different person, his voice as monotonous as a robot.

"By which he means the party that he has to organize because he acted like a badly behaved little boy," says Mr. Beaufort.

Mrs. Beaufort clicks her tongue. It wasn't so easy to turn in the dress, but I face the front again and glance subtly from each of them to the next. James doesn't react to his father's words. Mrs. Beaufort looks crossly at her husband for a moment.

Then she turns back to me. She puts her hand on the short sleeves, twitches them, and then says to Tristan: "It needs letting out a little here at the front, Tristan. It's pinching so that, er . . ." She looks questioningly at me.

"Ruby," I say.

"Ruby won't be able to breathe properly," she concludes.

Tristan nods and pulls me and his assistant back behind the screen. I glance back over my shoulder again to James, but he doesn't look my way; he's focused entirely on his parents. His father seems to be nagging him, his eyes fixed on me. He sounds annoyed, but I can't hear what he's saying to James.

I look away, turning back to Tristan. "They seem very . . . important." It's only at the last second that I manage to substitute a more positive word for "terrifying." Tristan has a pincushion on his wrist, and he is already busy, cautiously pinning up the hem of the dress.

"You're right there, Miss." That's all he says.

It's spooky how quiet it's been in this vast room since the Beauforts walked in. Nobody seems to be chatting anymore; even Tristan merely flashes me a brief smile before disappearing and leaving his assistant to help me undress. It's much easier to take the dress off than it was to put it on. In less than ten minutes, I've got my own clothes on again, and I can go back round to the front.

I come to stand next to James, who has taken the frock coat off and draped it lightly over his arm.

Mrs. Beaufort looks me over, then lays her hand on her son's arm. "I'll see you downstairs."

James nods curtly.

She turns to me. "It was nice to meet you, Miss Bell."

James's father doesn't say a word. The pair of them turn and walk out of the workshop. I can't breathe until the door has shut behind them.

"You could have warned me, you know," I say quietly.

Stiffly, James turns toward me. I wish I could read the look in his eyes, but all I can see is an icy turquoise. "Percy is waiting for you downstairs."

"Well, I'm ready. You're the one still stuck in the nineteenth century." I give him a cautious smile.

He doesn't smile back. "Our day trip is over," he begins, his voice sounding just the way he looks. Cool and distant. "You'd better get going."

I frown. "What?"

"You have to go now, Ruby." He says it slowly, emphasizing every syllable, as if I'm stupid. "See you at school."

He turns and walks behind the screen to change. For a moment, all I can do is stare. The next second, I realize what he's just done. The way he spoke to me.

Rage floods through me, and I step forward to give him a piece of my mind. But I don't get far. Tristan catches me by the arm and holds me back. The look in his eyes is regretful but stern. "Come on, Ruby, I'll take you back down."

He tugs gently on my arm. Reluctantly, I let him lead me away. As we cross the workshop, I can feel the sympathetic eyes of all the staff resting on me.

Ruby

My cloak of invisibility has slipped.

Everyone's heard that I was in London with James at the weekend. Apparently, there are even photos of us going into the shop together. Suddenly, people at Maxton Hall whose faces I've never even seen before know my name. Some are friendly and say hi in the hallways, others—the majority—whisper behind my back. It's at its worst in lessons, where I can't concentrate at all because of my classmates staring at me the whole time. Like they're expecting me to stand up any second and blurt out a loud explanation of what Beaufort and I got up to on Saturday.

But it was a day I'd rather forget as soon as possible. I still feel so humiliated, and my anger with James grows every time I think about the horrible way he acted.

When the bell rings, I seriously consider skipping lunch, but I'm too hungry for that to be a realistic option. Besides, Lin promises to act as a human shield for me and to tell me the latest about her dad.

"He's got a new girlfriend already," she announces, once we've eaten in silence for a while.

I look up from my udon noodles. "But not another con artist or anything?" I ask through a mouthful.

"No." She pulls a face. "Or at least I hope not."

"And?" I inquire cautiously.

Lin gives a shrug. She pushes away her half-eaten sandwich and wipes her fingers on a napkin. "I don't know. I just think he could give dating a break for a bit, seeing that it went so wrong the last time."

Lin meets up with her dad once a month so that they don't totally lose contact, and I admire her for the pragmatic way she deals with the whole situation. I don't know if I could even look Dad in the eye if he treated me and Mum that badly.

"Was she nice?" I ask after a while.

She shrugs again. "Yeah. A bit too nice, maybe."

"What do you mean?"

"Oh, I don't know. We just didn't click somehow." She starts to shred the napkin. "But that's OK. You can't get along with everyone."

I think a moment. "Sometimes, surprisingly, you do click with a person after a while." I find my eyes wandering over to James and his pals. They've got one of the good tables by the high windows, and their conversation seems pretty lively. Whatever James just said makes Wren laugh so much he chokes, and Kesh has to whack him on the back.

"Sounds like you're speaking from experience," Lin says, looking pointedly at James.

I shake my head and stare at my noodles again.

"Hey, are you ever going to tell me what happened?"

"I did."

Lin raises an eyebrow. "All you said was 'we got the costumes,' but I'm not an idiot."

I take a deep breath. "It was OK. More than OK, actually. Until his parents suddenly turned up."

Lin inhales sharply. "You met the Beauforts?"

I nod pensively. "They were . . . very impressive. Especially his mother," I begin. "I didn't get to talk to them much because they weren't there long. After that, James went back to normal."

"What did he do?" Lin asks, apparently remembering that I'm not the only one with a tray of food in front of her. She bites into her sandwich and gazes intently at me.

"He chucked me out. I was escorted out of the shop."

She stops chewing and stares.

My shoulders twitch helplessly. I really don't want to think about the horrible drive back on Saturday, where I had to force myself to take deep breaths in and out to calm down.

"It was the most embarrassing thing I've ever experienced," I mumble, risking another glance at James.

At this exact moment, he looks over to me. As our eyes meet, the rage bubbles up again, and I'm on the verge of standing up and whacking him with my tray.

But he blinks, breaks off the connection, and turns his attention back to his friends.

"But why did he throw you out?" Lin asks.

That's exactly what was baffling me the whole rest of the weekend. And there was only one vaguely plausible sounding explanation that I could come up with.

"I think he was embarrassed by me. You should have seen the way his father looked at me. Like I was dirt on the bottom of his shoe." I pull over my little bowl of pudding: chocolate mousse with whipped cream, topped with a strawberry and a sprig of mint. At least there's going to be one nice thing in my day.

"That's rubbish. You mustn't let anyone make you feel that way," Lin says, sounding so angry that I look up.

"It's the truth," I reply. "Even you would never have looked twice at me if it hadn't been for the stuff with your parents."

Lin flinches like I've thrown my dessert in her face. The color drains from her skin, and it's only then that I realize what I just said. I immediately open my mouth to apologize, but she jumps up.

"Nice to know you have such a good opinion of me," she snaps, grabbing her tray even though she hasn't finished eating. She dumps it back at the tray station and leaves the dining hall without looking back at me.

I stare into my mousse and realize that I've lost my appetite. What a shitty day.

By the time I head to the library in the afternoon, I've almost got used to whispers and funny looks in the corridors. I'm finding it easier to ignore them, although their voices still echo in my ears. It never occurred to me before we went that a single day with James could have such an effect on my life at Maxton Hall. What was I thinking? James is the king of this school—of course people are interested in who he spends his free time with. Getting into that car with him was a massive mistake. And now I'm paying for it with my invisibility.

The events meeting is a nightmare. Lin won't look at me, and I can't look at James. It's hard even to tell the others about the costumes without letting on how hurt and angry I feel. But it must have worked because once I'm done, everyone seems thrilled with the photos. Then Camille says that her parents know the people who own a big cutlery factory and that they'll let us have whatever we need for the party. Jessalyn has been getting quotes for decoration rentals, which she goes through with us, and Kieran's been finding music that he plays for us on his laptop.

I only take about half of it in.

Once we've sorted out the jobs for next time and I've closed the meeting, I catch hold of Lin's arm. She's still avoiding eye contact but waits for the rest of the team to leave the room. I shut the door behind them and turn to my friend.

"I didn't mean it like that," I begin. "I'm sorry for what I said. All I meant was . . . you used to be friends with completely different people. I just wonder if we'd have got to know each other this well if things had been different with your parents."

Lin looks at me for a while. Eventually, she sighs and whispers: "You're right."

I'm startled. "Am I?"

She nods. "If you hadn't spoken to me in the loos that day, we'd never have been friends like this," she says, looking me properly in the eye for the first time since lunch. "I was so grateful that you came over to me."

Her voice catches, and she gulps hard. I still remember the day eighteen months ago when I went into the toilets on the first floor and heard someone sobbing. I had no idea who it was in there, only that they seemed extremely upset. So, cautiously, I asked if everything was OK, and Lin just said to leave her alone. I didn't listen, just sat on the floor, opposite the cubicle, passed tissues under the door, and waited till she was ready to come out. That was the start of our friendship.

"I'm so glad I spoke to you too. And I really am sorry."

"Me too. I didn't mean to be bitchy."

"This is just one of those days," I sigh. I pull out my phone and take a photo of the notes we made on the whiteboard during the meeting. Then I sit at my laptop and send the picture plus the minutes Lin took to the others. Meanwhile, Lin starts to wipe the board down.

"Beaufort was looking at you the whole time," she says, out of the blue.

I snort. "I was at the front. Everyone was looking at me."

"Not like that. His eyes were practically begging you to look back at him."

"Bullshit."

Lin shrugs her shoulders. "Whatever. Either way, it was great the way you gave him the brush-off. He deserved it."

I shut the laptop and put it away in my backpack. "I just want everything to go back to how it was," I say as we switch off the lights in the room. "The way people stare at me now, it's like we got up to God-knows-what on Saturday. But none of them have a clue what really happened. Which is nothing."

She hums thoughtfully. "I know. But you know what they're like here. The smallest thing, and they're on it like wolves. Especially if it involves James Beaufort."

I give her a grumpy look. "Hmm."

She digs her elbow gently into my ribs and holds the door for me. "Come on. They'll have forgotten just as soon as the next rumor does the rounds."

We step into the corridor, and I'm about to answer when I see somebody leaning against the wall.

James.

I stare at him.

I'm about to ask what the hell he's doing here still, but I remember just in time that I'm ignoring him. So I look away and walk on.

He levers himself up and comes toward me.

"Do you have a minute?" he asks. His soft tone confuses me. It doesn't fit the James who treated me like shit forty-eight hours ago.

You have to walk away, Ruby.

I'd love to scream my opinion of him in his face, but I'm too fond of my library pass and keycard to the group rooms for that. "No, I don't have a minute," I retort instead. I'm proud of myself for keeping my voice calm but firm. He needs to know that he doesn't get to act like that to me.

"We need to talk," James continues, glancing at Lin a moment. "Alone."

I shake my head. "We don't *need* to do anything, James."

Lin touches my arm—a gesture of encouragement that shows me I'm not on my own here.

Suddenly, I just feel weary. "You know what?" I say, looking James square in the eyes. "Maybe it would be better if we just went back to the old days."

He frowns. "The old days?"

I have to cough. There's a lump in my throat, and it's getting bigger. "I mean the days when you didn't even know I existed. Maybe it would be better if we could go back to that. Because I was much better off then."

He opens his mouth to reply, then shuts it, and the furrows on his brow deepen. In the end, he nods slowly. "Got you."

This is good. He gets what my problem is. So in the future, I won't have to deal with him anymore.

Even so, it hurts as I turn around and walk with Lin toward the exit.

15

Ruby

"What's wrong with you?" Ember asks, making me jump a mile.

I'm stirring a pan of jam, so deep in thought that I didn't even notice her creep up behind me to stare over my shoulder.

"Nothing," I say, a moment too late.

Dad points an unopened packet of preserving sugar at me. "Your sister's right; something's up."

I roll my eyes. "You're bugging me, that's all." I stir a bit too vigorously, and the hot apple mush splashes onto my hand. I inhale with a sharp hiss.

"Get that under cold water now," Mum says, taking the spoon from me. She pushes it into Ember's hand and me over to the sink, where she runs the tap.

"Can't you just leave me in peace?" I mutter.

"Gladly," says Dad. "But you've been like this since that trip on Saturday, and I'd like to know why."

I just mumble. There's no escape, even at home.

I've never understood why everyone complains about Mondays. For me, every Monday symbolizes a new beginning, when you can get things on track for a great week. Normally, I love Mondays. But today, absolutely everything is rubbing me the wrong way. People at school, memories of Saturday, Ember's curious eyes. Even the little splash on my hand that burns like hell. Stupid jam.

I wish I could just shut myself away in my room and focus on the next three months' worth of homework, but my family forced me to help cook up the apples. Even though I'm pretty sure the jam's just an excuse to get me to talk.

A moment later, Ember confirms my suspicions. "Why don't you just tell us what happened?"

"Because you don't really want to know how I am," I retort. "You're only asking because you want all the details about Beaufort's."

"That's not true!"

"No?" I say provokingly. "So you're not interested in what it was like then?"

Now she shifts her weight awkwardly to her other foot. "Yeah, I am. But both things can be true. I can be interested in one of the biggest gentlemen's outfitters in the country and in how you are at the same time. There's room in my heart for both, sis."

"That's sweet," says Dad, rolling past the two of us in his wheelchair to get to the stove. He takes a clean spoon and dunks it in the simmering jam. I always find it fascinating to watch him taste things. When I try a dish, I look . . . normal. With Dad, you can tell at once that he's a professional. His expression changes, like he's mentally taking apart every ingredient and considering whether there's anything missing, and if so, what it could be.

Just like now. He's put his head to one side, and we're watching, intrigued. The next second, his face brightens, and he wheels back slightly to the little metal trolley with all his spices. He reaches for the mixed spice and adds a pinch or two to the pan. The cinnamon smell reminds me of Christmas—my favorite holiday.

"There's nothing to tell, Ember," I say belatedly, making my sister groan with frustration. "You already know everything there is to know about Beaufort's."

"I'd love to see inside the workshop though," she sighs, resting her chin on her hand.

"Would that interest you? You want to specialize in ladies' clothes, don't you?" Dad asks.

The doorbell rings, and we look at each other in surprise.

"Who could that be?" Mum says, heading toward the hall.

"It's about the atmosphere, Dad. Seeing the way people there work, the materials they use, how they cut out. It would have been so interesting." Ember's wistful face makes me feel guilty. I get that she considers it unfair that I had the chance, just out of no-where, to visit a major designer's head office and she didn't. But on the other hand, look how that ended up for me. There's no way I want my sister to ever feel as humiliated as I did at that moment.

"I've got an idea. Couldn't you ask your friend to give me a tour too?" Ember asks. She's only half joking, which unsettles me.

"You can ask him yourself, Ember," says Mum unexpectedly.

I turn around with a frown. "What?"

"The lad's on the doorstep," she explains, jerking her thumb over her shoulder. "You didn't tell me what a looker he is."

I stare at her, my protective instinct going from zero to sixty in nothing flat. "You didn't let him in, did you?"

"Of course not. That's up to you to do that—or not, if you don't want to." Mum comes over and presses a kiss on the top of my head. I can feel my family's nosy eyes on my back as I cross the kitchen and step into the hallway. I feel numb as I walk to the door.

James is on the front steps. It's the first time I've seen him in such casual clothes. His dark jeans and white T-shirt make him look like a perfectly ordinary boy. If I'd bumped into him on the street, I probably wouldn't even have recognized him.

Hanging over his arm is a large black protective cover with the Beaufort's logo on it. I stare at the swirly "B" for a second, suddenly filled with unbearable rage.

He shouldn't be here. I don't want him anywhere near my family. My life here has nothing to do with my life at Maxton Hall, and I can't deal with the fact that he's standing here in front of me, erasing the boundary I drew years ago, just like that—least of all after Saturday.

The moment I open my mouth to give him a piece of my mind, he takes his eyes off our rosebushes and spots me in the doorway. An emotion I can't interpret flickers in his eyes—I never can manage to read him—and then he takes a step up, making our eyes level. He clears his throat and eventually holds the bag out to me.

"I wanted to bring the dress round for you. Tristan has altered it. It should fit you perfectly now."

I make no moves to take it from him. "And you had to come to my house for that?"

He takes a deep breath and exhales violently, then rubs the back of his head with his hand. "I wanted to speak to you about Saturday too. I acted like an arse, and I'm sorry."

For a moment, all I can do is stare at him.

It's the first time I've ever heard him say anything like that, and I can't help wondering how often in his life he's apologized. When I think of every liberty he's taken at school in the last few years, his moral boundaries must generally be set considerably lower than mine.

But now he looks truly sorry.

"I don't understand why you did that," I say quietly.

Especially not after he held my hand and we definitely had a moment. I saw exactly how warm his gaze was, and I clearly felt the chemistry between us. I wasn't just imagining it.

He gulps hard. He doesn't speak for a whole minute, just looks at me with inscrutable eyes. Then he mumbles so quietly that I can barely hear his words: "I don't understand myself sometimes, Ruby Bell."

I open my mouth to reply but shut it again. I get the feeling that he's being honest with me for the first time, and I don't want to ruin it by throwing his apology back in his face. So I say nothing. I'm quiet for so long that with anyone else, it would have got awkward, but I sense that James and I could look at each other in silence for hours—each of us just trying to get a glimpse behind the other one's façade.

"Why did you really come?" I ask finally.

"What you said this afternoon . . ." He hesitates. "What if I don't want to go back to the old days?"

I laugh tonelessly. "You threw me out. And before that, you embarrassed me in front of your parents. You acted like I wasn't good enough to be introduced to them."

He shakes his head. "I didn't mean it like that."

I see him rock back and forward ever so slightly on his feet. It's almost like he's nervous. "It was fun on Saturday. Until . . . my parents turned up." He clears his throat. "I think it would be a shame if we suddenly acted like we don't know each other. You're not invisible to me anymore. And I don't want to pretend that you are."

Although the bitter aftertaste of the weekend is still there, his words make something contract inside me in tingling excitement. "I don't know what you expect from me now, James," I say quietly.

"I don't expect anything from you. I just don't want to go back to how things were before. Can't we just . . . know each other from now on?"

I stare speechlessly at him.

He's not being serious. The thought flashes through my head. He *can't* be being serious. I'm not stupid. I know that James can't stand me—even though we genuinely did have a nice time together on Saturday. I'm the reason he got barred from lacrosse, and I know one of his sister's biggest secrets, which makes me a risk to him and his family. I bet he just wants to keep an eye on me.

"If this is just another of your schemes—" I begin skeptically, but James interrupts me.

"It's not," he says, coming up the last step.

I can't believe his words; I know that perfectly well. I can't get a handle on him—I doubt that anyone can. But at this moment, there's something in his eyes, something honest and remorseful, that takes my breath away for a second.

How has this happened? How did we go, in less than a month, from total strangers to bribery to hatred to here?

The door opens behind me. "Ruby? Everything OK?"

I stiffen. Standing in front of me is James Beaufort with a hundred-and-fifty-year-old dress over his arm and a look on his face that makes me go weak at the knees. Standing behind me is my sister, who I was fighting with over Dad's jam only a few minutes ago. My two worlds have collided head-on, and I don't know how to react. I go hot and cold all over, nod to Ember with a forced smile, and try to tell her, without words, to back off. She looks from James to me and back again, curious and skeptical at the same time, but does eventually draw back, leaving the door ajar.

Only then can I turn back to James. It takes me a couple of breaths to get myself together. Then I realize that I owe him an answer. "I don't know," I say truthfully.

James nods. "OK. Actually, I only really came to apologize for Saturday."

"Only for Saturday?"

Now he smiles wryly. "I'm certainly not going to apologize for treating you to a lap dance."

No clue whether I can accept his apology if he's going to say stuff like that.

I don't know if he means it or if he just wants to pour oil on troubled waters so that I don't tell anyone about Lydia. Even so, it would make my life easier not to be constantly annoyed at him. Or if I could occasionally speak to him about school stuff. I noticed at the weekend that he's got more than just a quick tongue; he's intelligent. He was fun to talk to. And there was that certain something that gave me pins and needles and made me curious for more.

I know it's unwise and that I shouldn't trust him an inch. But the longer I think about it, the more I realize that I don't actually want to go back to the old days.

I look him straight in the eyes so that he'll understand that I'm deadly serious as I say: "I'm not letting you treat me that way again."

"Understood," he replies quietly, holding out the dress to me again.

At that moment, it starts to rain. Not much, but enough that, despite the bag, I'm scared for the dress. Hastily, I take it from James and hang it safely in our hallway.

By the time I get back, James's hair is full of water droplets that are now making their way down his cheeks. He wipes his face with the back of his hand, then runs it through his hair without taking his eyes off me. The polite thing to do would be to invite him in before he gets soaked through, but I simply can't. It doesn't feel right. I can't introduce him to my parents and sister. Maybe I never will be able to.

"I accept your apology," I say in the end.

His eyes light up. It's the first time I've seen an expression like that on his face.

So we stand there in the rain, him on my parents' front steps, me in the doorway, not prepared to let him in.

But it's a start.

James

Watching lacrosse without being allowed to play truly sucks.

My team is pumped with adrenaline as they emerge from the changing rooms, and player after player high-fives me as I stand like a spectator on the edge of the field between the stands. I let the misery wash over me, but at this moment, I regret everything, especially my decision to liven up the Back-to-School party a bit.

The worst part is that Roger Cree, the new guy who's taken my position, is so good that he's developing into a genuine rival. If he'd been crap, my place on the team would be safe, but now? How can I be sure the coach will want to keep me once my suspension is over? Especially seeing how well Cree's getting on with Cyril and the rest of the guys lately.

Speaking of the devil, he comes and holds out his fist to me, and I bump it reluctantly with my own, then join the subs on the bench. I cross my ankles and watch the other team run out onto the field and take their positions against my boys. They're a good team. I recognize a lot of the players from last season. One of their attackers is particularly hard to pin down, and lightning fast. I hope Cyril's got an eye on him.

"Hey, Beaufort. Sorry you don't get to play," one of the guys on the bench says out of nowhere. His name's Matthew, but I doubt that we've ever spoken a word to each other before now.

"Yeah, bro, gotta be shit," someone else agrees.

"I don't get why they banned you anyway. It was a great prank."

"And it's your last year. Can't be great to spend the season on the bench."

OK, that's enough. I jump up without a word and walk to the edge of the field. I'm glad I'm wearing shades. Not just because the sun is bloody bright for October, but also so that nobody can see how I'm feeling.

I stand a little distance from Freeman and cross my arms, looking over the field. I hate watching my team when there's nothing I can do. It takes less than five minutes from the whistle for the opposition to score.

Suddenly, I hear footsteps behind me. I glance over my shoulder and see Ruby and her friend Lin running toward us. They're both bright red in the face with windblown hair. As they come to a halt, Ruby swears loudly. She hasn't spotted me yet, so I get the chance to study her unobtrusively.

She's wearing her uniform even though most people come to watch our games in their own clothes or sports kit. She's got a tripod in one hand and a notebook in the other, and on her back, she has that same tatty backpack that always looks like it's about to fall apart. It's almost exactly the color of puke but makes her look kind of cute all the same. Like a Ninja Turtle. A Ninja Turtle with messed-up hair and a bright red face.

I take my time strolling over to them, watching her set up the tripod and an expensive-looking camera.

"Can I help?" I ask.

Ruby whirls round and stares at me, wide-eyed. Clearly, she still hasn't got used to my efforts to be friendly. I spent the week saying hello when I bumped into her, and she jumped every time, like she just doesn't expect anyone to speak to her outside lessons.

"Have we missed anything?" she asks frantically. Her eyes dart over the field and then back to Mr. Freeman. But he's so deep in the game that he hasn't even noticed that Ruby and Lin are late.

"Ridgeview scored. Right at the whistle," I say.

Ruby nods and scribbles something in her pad. "Great, thanks."

Meanwhile, Lin is getting the camera set up and checking the settings before she starts taking photos.

After that, they're both engrossed in documenting the match.

I realize that I would much rather watch Ruby than my team. The sight of her is way less painful. We regained the lead ages ago, and we're now thumping Ridgeview, but I can't feel as happy as I should. Cree sets up two goals, and in the second half, he scores himself, which makes it crystal clear that the lads don't even need me. I'd rather be anywhere but here, so I don't know why I'm hanging around.

Even so, I stand stony-faced at the edge of the field, letting the game pass me by, clapping when anyone scores, swearing when the other side gets one over on us, while answering all of Ruby and Lin's questions.

After the ninety minutes, I don't feel like we've conquered the world, as I usually do after a win. I'm knackered and can't stand it here a second longer. The idea of spending tonight at Cyril's party amid all the sympathy of everyone who saw me standing here on the edge of the pitch today makes me ill. I turn away without a word before the teams leave the field and run back toward the school. I pull out my phone and get Percy on speed dial to come and pick me up.

"James!"

I glance back over my shoulder.

Ruby is running after me. Her fringe and the wind are not best friends; some of it is sticking straight up in the air. She sees my look and flattens it down against her forehead again. It's one of her quirks that I've really noticed in the last few weeks. Now I know about the little comb she carries around in her pencil case, which she uses when she doesn't think anyone's looking.

"What's up?" I ask.

"Are you OK?"

Why is she asking? Nobody asks me stuff like that—because absolutely nobody cares how I am. And even if that isn't true, most of them have too much respect for me, or are too scared of me, to ask that question.

"It can't be nice to watch the others play, right?" she asks gently.

"Nope."

She shifts her weight from one foot to the other. "Would you rather be alone?"

Uncertainly, I rub the back of my neck and shrug. Thank God for Alistair, who saves me from having to answer. He jogs, red-faced, over the grass and stops in front of us.

"Beaufort! Whither goest thou, my friend?"

OK, that's an even fucking stupider question than Ruby's. "Home."

"Uh, it's Cy's party. Forgotten?"

No, I hadn't forgotten, but Cyril's party is the last thing I'm in the mood for. Not that I can say so to Alistair. The team won, and I'm still co-captain, even if I'm currently suspended. It wouldn't be fair to duck the celebrations with the lads. Not to mention the fact that I can't face the questions that would definitely be asked if I didn't show.

"Sure, I'll be there." Out of the corner of my eye, I see Ruby's expression change. I avoid looking directly at her.

"Don't look like that, mate. It's going to be amazing. We'll have the house to ourselves."

I just growl.

"Hey, why don't you come too, Ruby?" I give Alistair a warning look, but he just grins and looks at us both in turn.

"You don't have to," I say hastily. Cyril's party is definitely not the place for a person like Ruby. "I don't think you'd enjoy it."

I realize that was the wrong thing to say when Ruby frowns. She's looking as though she took it as a challenge—the exact opposite of what I intended.

"What makes you think you know what I like and what I don't?"

Alistair hides a cough, and I glare at him. He did that on purpose. He knows exactly what happens at these parties and what everyone there is like.

"I'd love to come, Alistair. Thanks for asking me," Ruby says with a smile that's way too charming to be real. "When and where?"

Alistair is opening his mouth to reply when I step in.

"I'll give you a lift."

Ruby's shoulders tense.

"There's no need for that, James."

"It's no problem to pick you up on the way."

She raises her eyebrows. "Can you even drive?"

Alistair whistles appreciatively. Apparently, he's enjoying me taking a verbal beating. I shake my head.

"Percy will drive us if that's OK with you."

Now she's grinning from ear to ear. "That's very much OK with me."

"Percy, hmm? Yeah, I could be into him too. Looks a bit like Antonio Banderas," Alistair remarks.

Bloody hell. Why can't I keep my head straight when she's around? I promised Lydia that I'd keep an eye on her—and that's all there is between us. I just have to keep reminding myself of that.

"Great. Percy will be at your place at eight."

Ruby nods. "Fab."

Ruby

Cyril Vega lives in the biggest, poshest house I've ever seen in my life. I'm not even sure that "house" is the right word for what I'm facing here. The grounds—which we were only allowed onto once Percy's number plate had been checked by a security camera— seem endless. Wherever I look, there's nothing but manicured lawns and symmetrically planted shrubs and trees.

As James and I get out of the car, I stop for a moment, stare up, and take in the impressive façade. There are high pillars on either side of the entrance and a huge balcony above it, making the place look like a stately home from a different age.

At my side, James seems entirely unfazed as we climb the broad stone steps to the massive front door. But that's hardly surprising. For one thing, Cyril's one of his best friends, and for another, I bet his own house is at least this big. I feel my palms grow cold and clammy.

What am I doing here?

I swore never to go to one of their crazy parties. But a single stupid comment from James was enough to get my hackles up. I simply had to do the opposite of what he wanted, and in retrospect, that was just plain silly. It's been annoying me all week that the trip to London with James was enough to blow my anonymity at Maxton Hall, and now I'm going to this party with him, where a lot of my year group will be too. I didn't think for a second this afternoon about what that would mean. People will definitely be talking about us again—probably more so this time.

We can hear the music and loud voices even from outside. For a split second I consider faking a sudden illness and getting out of here. But I don't want to give James the satisfaction. So I just rub my hands on my skirt and clear my throat. James gives me a sideways glance that I ignore. Then he opens the front door with a key that, weirdly, he has on his key ring.

We walk into such an imposing entrance hall that it distracts me from my nerves for a moment. It has a marble floor and magnificent furniture in subtle tones, accented in gold and white. There's a huge chandelier hanging from the ceiling, and on either side, a double staircase curving up to a gallery.

At first glance, you'd think the party filled the entire house. The music seems to be coming from another room, but there are guests here in the hall too. None of them pays us any attention. I give a sigh of relief.

"What are they doing up there?" I ask James, pointing to twenty or so girls and boys standing on the gallery.

"Playing a game that only works at Cyril's," he replies. "Kind of a version of beer pong."

I watch as a guy drops something that turns out to be a bunch of table tennis balls over the railing. Some of them fall straight into a row of glasses down here in the foyer, but most miss. That makes the blokes cheer and a couple of girls screech, and it seems like all of them then have a drink.

"I don't get it."

"Me either," he says.

"You made it!" someone yells from upstairs. I look up just in time to see Cyril swing himself onto one of the banisters. He holds on tight, then slides down to us. Just watching him makes me feel sick. Wren pops up beside him but seems to prefer the safer option and takes the stairs. As he walks, he tips back his head and drains his glass.

Cyril gets to us first and greets James with a half hug, slapping him on the back. "I hope we made you proud today."

I feel James tense beside me. "Yup," he says in a neutral tone that's not exactly overflowing with joy, yet without betraying the frustration he must have felt at not being allowed to play himself.

Cyril's gaze lands on me. "And you are . . . ?" he asks, as his ice-blue eyes scan me from top to bottom. He eyes my white blouse with blue vertical stripes and black pleated skirt, looking like he's about to turn up his nose.

Arsehole. Like he's better looking just because his black shirt probably cost more than my entire outfit.

"Ruby." James jumps in to introduce us. "Ruby, this is Cyril."

"Ruby! Alistair told us he'd invited you." Wren grins as he comes toward us. I fight back the urge to look away.

"Hi," I reply, forcing a smile onto my lips.

He says a quick hello to James, then returns his gaze to me. His leering, supercilious smile is sending me a clear message: *This is my realm. I pull the strings here.*

The next moment, James puts his hand on my back. "Cy, be a good host and offer us a drink."

He's speaking in that I'm-James-Beaufort tone, and although I'd never let him boss me around like that, it doesn't seem to bother his friends. They just laugh and lead us past the stairs to the back of the hall. In passing, Cyril picks up a couple of the balls and throws them back upstairs, then he opens a door that leads to a large room.

It's a sitting room, smaller than the entrance hall, but there must still be at least fifty people in here, chatting or dancing. The music is deafening, and smoke gets up my nose and makes my eyes water.

I've only been to a handful of parties before. Small get-togethers in the park in Gormsey and—once—a classmate's fif-teenth birthday party. She invited me out of fake politeness, and I went because Mum insisted on me at least trying to make more friends. I ended up spending half the evening standing in a corner kind of bobbing weirdly to bad music and counting the minutes until I could go home.

The sight that meets my eyes here is a million miles from that. Instead of cheap beer in plastic cups, people are drinking expen-sive spirits from crystal glasses. The music comes not from a cheap Bluetooth speaker but from a sound system with speakers built into the walls. And I can see acres of bare skin.

So, this is what a posh party's like.

I look around, trying to take everything in. The bass is so loud, the floor is shaking under my feet.

When I look around again, I see a conservatory joining onto the room. It houses a huge brightly lit swimming pool—not that I'm going anywhere near that.

There are a couple of people swimming in their underwear, splashing anyone standing near the edge. Others are sitting, smoking, on velvet-covered sofas that look like antiques and must be worth a fortune.

I'm so overwhelmed by the situation that I don't take in what James is asking me at first. "Sorry?"

James leans down a little so that his mouth is level with my ear. "I asked what you'd like to drink, Ruby Bell."

A shiver runs down my spine and goose bumps spread over my arms. I ignore both. "Coke, if there is any. Or water."

James leans back slightly and looks me in the eye. "Do you mind me drinking?"

I shake my head. "No."

"Great. I'll be right back."

The next moment, he and Cyril have vanished. Wren stays put, looking at me with that knowing smile on his face again.

"You don't drink?" His voice is pure provocation.

It's only sheer willpower that stops me turning on my heel and walking away from him. Or yelling at him in front of everyone. But I've managed to ignore him for two years—I'm not going to let a few silly comments rattle me now.

"No," I answer curtly.

Wren comes a step closer. I step back.

"Why not, Ruby?" he asks, taking another step toward me,

until I feel the wall at my back. "Had a bad experience with alcohol?"

I can smell the booze on his breath and see how wide his pupils are. I'm wondering if he's off his face on more than just whisky.

"You know exactly why I don't drink, Wren," I reply coldly, straightening my shoulders. If he doesn't leave me alone, I seriously will hurt him. Out of the corner of my eye, I can see, on my left, a dark wooden sideboard dotted with assorted statues and lamps.

I know how to defend myself.

"I have lovely memories of that evening," Wren answers. He raises his left arm and rests it on the wall beside my head.

"I don't," I hiss between gritted teeth. Until now, he's always left me alone at school. Never even hinted at what happened that night two years ago—so why suddenly here?

"Are you sure?" he whispers, coming closer.

I can't take it anymore. I thrust out both hands and push him hard away from me. "I have no interest in repeating it, Wren."

He takes my hands and links our fingers together. I look around in panic. "I can still hear every word you whispered to me."

"That was only because you got me drunk."

"Oh, really?" He's got that dirty grin on his face again. "Alcohol brings your secret thoughts to the surface, Ruby. You wanted it just as much as I did."

I freeze as the memory of that night now comes back to me: Wren's panting breath, his restless hands all over my body. The thought makes me burn up. Partly with shame and partly because I was actually enjoying it. But the *way* it happened bothers me to this day.

Wren has opened his mouth again when a voice speaks behind us, sounding firm yet bored. "Leave her alone, Fitzgerald."

His eyes widen, and I look past him in surprise. Lydia has joined us. She gives Wren an irritated glare, then takes my hand without another word and pulls me away from him, out into the room a little. It's not until we're out of earshot that she looks at me, eyebrows raised.

"Who'd have thought that *you* of all people had a dirty little secret?"

Panic floods through me, and I clench my fists. But before I can say a word, she lifts her hands. An amused smile plays around her lips. "Don't worry, I won't tell anyone."

I stare at her, and it takes me a moment to grasp what she said. "I don't care who knows about it," I say defiantly, even though we both know that's a barefaced lie.

If I could, I'd wipe that whole evening right out of my memory. I had just started at Maxton Hall. It was the first event I got to go to, and I was so jittery and nervous that I happily drank every cup of punch that Wren brought me. I didn't know he'd spiked it from his hip flask. And when he pulled me into a corridor and kissed me, I was euphoric. Wren was one of the most attractive boys I'd ever seen. And he wanted me. Having my first kiss with him was such a rush.

It wasn't until the next morning that I realized how wrong it had been of him to get me drunk without my knowledge, or how naïve I'd been. Since then, I haven't touched a drop.

Opposite me, Lydia raises an eyebrow. "Seriously? I'd have thought you were more bothered about your reputation than that."

"Snogging someone once two years ago after he spiked my drink won't do much damage to my reputation. It's not like having an affair with a teacher."

I regret the words the moment I've said them. Lydia goes as

white as a sheet. The next second, she takes a threatening step toward me. "You said you'd keep your mouth shut. I—" She falls abruptly silent and moves away again.

"*There* you are." James comes over and hands me a glass of Coke with ice and a slice of lemon. He's holding an expensive-looking crystal glass of something brown in his other hand.

He looks slowly from me to Lydia. "Everything OK?"

"Could you get me a drink too, brother dear? My glass is empty," Lydia says, batting her eyelashes exaggeratedly.

James rolls his eyes but takes her glass and heads off to the bar again. Almost the moment he's gone, Lydia's smile vanishes again. She looks at me with chilly eyes, and I swallow hard. I wish I'd never come. I don't want to be in this room; I want to be at home, where I feel safe and secure. This is the exact opposite of that—an adventure that's too much for me.

"Listen," I say before she can threaten me again. "I'm sorry for what I just said."

Her mouth opens and shuts. Then she gives me a skeptical look. "What?"

"I'm not your enemy," I continue. "And I don't care what you and Mr. Sutton get up to. I won't give you away."

She presses her lips tightly together.

"I just want to be left in peace," I try again.

"Why should I believe you?" she asks, eyes narrowed. "I don't know you."

"True," I say. "But James knows me. And I promised him."

"You promised him," she repeats as if she doesn't quite get the significance of the words.

"Yes," I say hesitantly.

For a moment, she says nothing, just eyes me mistrustfully. But then her expression changes. Suddenly, she looks more as though a few puzzle pieces have just slotted together in her head. Her eyes wander from my face to a point somewhere above my shoulder. "Oh, so that's how it is," she says.

Confused, I look around, trying to work out what she means. I see James standing at the bar. He's picking up one bottle after another, studying the labels.

"That's how what is?" I ask.

She gives me a reassuring smile. "Don't worry, you're not the first."

I have no idea what she's on about.

"Most girls don't take so long to succumb to his charms."

Then it clicks. I can't help myself. I burst out laughing.

Lydia looks startled. "What's so funny?"

"I don't know if anyone's ever told you this, but your brother is pretty much the opposite of charming."

She stares at me, and it's like she doesn't know whether to laugh or go for my throat. James relieves her of the decision by choosing this moment to return.

"Here," he says, holding a drink out to Lydia. "For you, *sister dear.*"

She glances briefly at it, then looks back at me. "I'm watching you, Ruby." She turns and disappears into the crowd.

"What was all that?" James asks in confusion, watching her strawberry-blond ponytail as it moves out of sight.

I just shrug, which makes him frown.

"What did she say?"

"Nothing. She doesn't trust me and doesn't believe I'll keep my mouth shut."

James lets his gaze roam across the room. It seems like he has to think about his next words, like he isn't sure what he can and can't say to me. "It's hard for her to trust anyone."

I look questioningly at him.

"Very few people would keep a secret like that to themselves, Ruby." He gives a shrug. "On the contrary. Ninety percent of them would sell it to the press or try to blackmail us with it. It wouldn't be the first time someone's spent time with us just so they can find out family secrets." He avoids my eyes as he speaks and watches the crowd dancing in the center of the room instead.

"Sounds pretty shit."

One side of his mouth twitches slightly. "It is."

I'd never thought of that. It doesn't excuse James's behavior, but this piece of information has helped me to understand him—and Lydia—a bit better.

"I can't help wondering what I'm even doing here if everyone trusts me so little."

Thoughtfully, his eyes scan my face. He lifts a hand as if to touch me but lowers it again and takes a sip from the glass that was actually meant for Lydia. His second drink. "You're here because Alistair invited you," he says in the end.

"True," I mumble, sticking an annoyingly tickly strand of hair back behind my ear. "Alistair. If it had been up to you, I wouldn't be here now."

"It's not that."

"What then?" I have no idea why the idea that he didn't want me here bothers me so much.

"You just don't belong here, Ruby."

It feels like he's stabbed me. With a sharp little knife or something. It's a huge effort not to let the pain show.

"I . . . I didn't mean it like that," he says at once. Apparently, I didn't do such a good job of not showing the pain as I thought.

"Right." I turn away and look through the huge windows to the pool, which someone just jumped into fully dressed. A few seconds later, James pushes his way in front of me, filling my whole vision.

"Hey, come on. I only meant that I get a bad feeling about you being around certain people. They'll end up messing with you. I feel responsible for you."

"I'm quite capable of looking after myself, thank you very much," I snap back.

He gives me another piercing look, and I take a tiny sip of my Coke so as to break eye contact. Him looking at me like that makes me hot, and it's warm enough in here already.

"I don't want to be a drag. Just act the way you normally do," I say in the end, with a wave of my hand to take in the entire room. Let James get up to whatever it is he usually does at these parties. I don't want him acting like my babysitter.

He nods and downs his second drink. Then he takes my glass and puts it next to his on a little side table. The next moment, he's taken my hand. He pulls me back into the middle of the room, right in the heart of the dancing crowd. My heart hammers wildly, and I wonder what the hell he's up to as he pulls me closer. His chest touches mine and he squeezes my hand, then lets go and starts to move to the music.

James Beaufort is dancing with me. He smiles down at me and circles his hips.

"What are you doing?" I ask in confusion. I'm the only person standing stock-still on the dance floor.

"I'm doing what I normally do at parties," James replies.

Yet again, the look in his eyes seems like a dare that I have to accept. I try to copy his movements. Someone crashes into me from behind and I stumble against him, so he puts a hand on my waist to stop me falling. My throat goes dry and my heart beats faster. An intense heat floods through me as I look up at him again. We're pressed together so tight that not even a sheet of paper would fit between us.

Next to us, someone cheers. I tear my eyes off James's face and look around. At least five pairs of eyes are fixed on us.

I must be out of my mind. James and I might be living in friendly coexistence now, but this is something else entirely. And if I don't want stories about us going around the school like wildfire, I urgently need to get off this dance floor.

"I need the loo," I gasp. James pulls back right away. His eyes glitter knowingly, and at this moment, I'm too confused to understand what that means. He nods to the left-hand corner of the room, where an archway leads out to a corridor. "First right, second door on the left."

I slip between the dancing bodies and then walk down the hall. There are oil paintings of the Vega family on the wall, and the wallpaper shimmers green and gold in the lamplight. The carpet beneath my feet is dark red with an intricate pattern of abstract shapes that somehow resemble animals. I turn right as James said. This part of the hallway is empty, and I lean against the wall for a moment.

I really do not have a clue what I'm doing here. Quite apart from the fact that I feel totally out of place, James unsettles me. The way he touches me, looks at me, his whispered words—if I didn't know better, I'd say he was flirting with me.

On Monday, when he stood at my front door and said he didn't want to go back to the old days, I didn't expect us to end up here. Does he dance like that with everyone he knows? Probably.

Maybe I should just see it as a task to complete. I'm at school with these people, whether I like it or not. And if I make it to Oxford, I might have to deal with some of them, and there'll certainly be plenty of other rich kids.

I take a deep breath, clench my fists, and push myself firmly away from the wall. I'll freshen up and then I'll go back into that sitting room, drink up my Coke, and dance with James. What can go wrong? People are going to talk about me anyway now, and that way, at least I can have a bit of fun.

Having made up my mind, I walk to the door a few feet further down the hall and open it, expecting to find a bathroom. It's dark apart from the light shining in from the hallway. My eyes take a moment to adjust, but then I make out the outline of an antique desk, a collection of plush chairs, and . . . loads of bookcases.

This is definitely not the bathroom—this is a library! After a tiny hesitation, I step curiously inside and look around. Just the first bookcase contains more books than our entire house. A smile spreads over my face, and I venture another step . . . and then I hear it.

Heavy breathing. And muffled sighs.

Turn and leave, a voice is crying in my head, but it's too late. My eyes rest on Alistair, who's standing with his back to another bookcase, further into the room. His head is thrown back, and at that second, he groans loudly.

I hear a quiet smacking sound. "If you keep making that much noise, I'll stop."

I freeze. I know that voice. It's hushed and deep, a little smoky.

"Don't stop," says Alistair, letting his head drop forward.

The guy kneeling in front of him gets up. "Only if you ask nicely."

Alistair pulls him down by the hair to kiss him. The guy leans against the bookcase, one hand on either side of Alistair's head, and kisses him back. Then I recognize who it is.

Keshav.

I gasp while Keshav's mouth roams from Alistair's face down to his throat.

At that moment, Alistair spots me in the doorway.

"Kesh, stop," he whispers in a panic, pushing his friend away violently.

I turn on my heel and flee out of the library back into the corridor. I look around in a panic and decide to run back to the main room. I squeeze past dancing people, their faces blurred before my eyes, searching the room for James.

I see him with his sister, Cyril, and Wren by the pool. They're talking about something, and Wren's making wild arm gestures.

I need a moment to get my head together.

Why the hell do I have to keep catching people in the act when they definitely don't want an audience? Since when have I been collecting strangers' secrets? This is *not* normal.

It's a big effort to breathe and to calm down slightly. I decide that I have to take back my decision from a moment ago. I can't have fun here, and I'll never get used to these people.

I want to go to James and ask him to take me home, but he's so close to the pool that it makes me hesitate a moment. The sight of the water makes me feel sick. In the end, I pluck up all my courage and cautiously enter the conservatory. I stand by the wall, a few feet from the group.

Wren is the first to spot me. "There she is."

I nod curtly to him and almost sigh with relief as James crosses the two steps that separate us. I'd never have imagined he'd ever be the person I felt safest with at a party, but that's how it is today. He's become my anchor, and I have to stop myself from grabbing his hand.

"You OK?" James asks. He's got another glass in his hand, containing another brown drink. His cheeks are slightly flushed now.

"I'd like to go home soon," I whisper, still out of breath.

James frowns but nods instantly. Apparently, he can see that I'm on the verge of freaking out. He drains his glass and puts it down on the nearest table. "No worries."

"Hey, since when have you left my parties before four, man?" Cyril sounds offended.

"Since I've had someone I need to take home," James replies, looking blankly at his friend. It's back, that impenetrable, arrogant wall.

"Come on, Ruby. Don't be a spoilsport and take our buddy away," Wren says, crouching down to splash me with water from the pool. A few drops land on my throat, and it feels like all the air's been crushed from my lungs.

"Stop it," I squeal, hardly recognizing my own voice, it sounds so shrill.

"Are you going to dissolve?" Cyril laughs. He's topless now, wearing black swimming shorts. His hair is still wet. He comes a step closer. I flinch back and grip onto James's arm. I don't care what the others think.

"C'mon, Cy, leave her alone," James says, but not even his air of authority is any good now. Cyril is grinning like a predatory animal. The next moment, he leaps, grabs my bag, and hands it to a grinning Lydia.

"Cyril, don't you dare—" I gasp—but it's too late. He wraps me in an embrace that's anything but loving and pulls me with him into the pool. I scream as I hit the water with full force and thrash my arms and legs in panic.

Then we go under, and my heart stops beating for a second. Suddenly, I'm no longer in the Vegas' house, I'm in a murky, yellowish-green sea. I'm no longer seventeen, I'm eight. And I can't remember how to swim. I'm at the mercy of the bitterly cold water.

I can't breathe.

The seaweed is pulling me down, and I can't move. My arms won't work, my legs are out of action. I have no control over my body.

The pressure on my chest is overwhelming. And then I have no choice but to breathe in the water.

James

Wren and my sister laugh out loud as Cyril reemerges, splashing us with water, but I stare at Ruby, a dark, hazy blotch beneath the water. At first, she was thrashing like crazy, but now she isn't moving.

Something's wrong.

"If she knew we know the playing-dead trick, she wouldn't bother," Wren says, holding his hand out to Cyril to help him out of the pool.

Ruby still hasn't surfaced. Deep inside me, I know that something is very, very wrong. My heart hammers, and I take a run-up.

"James, I don't think she seriously needs—" I don't even hear the rest of Lydia's sentence as I dive headfirst into the pool. I swim with long strokes to Ruby and wrap an arm around her body to pull her up.

She isn't moving.

"Ruby," I pant, once we've surfaced. I shake her. "Ruby!"

Suddenly, her arms flail out. She coughs and gasps for air, and I hold her tight to my chest to stop her going under again.

She's totally freaked out. "Get me out of here!" she demands shrilly. "I need to get out of here!"

I nod and swim her over to the edge. Then I lift her by the hips and set her on the side of the pool. She coughs and splutters again for a long time to get rid of all the water she inhaled in that brief period. I push myself up onto the edge and sit beside her, hold her while she chokes.

"Get me out of here." Ruby's voice is a broken croak that shatters something deep inside me. I help her up. She keeps her eyes down, but I can see the tears mixed with the water on her face. Once she's back on her feet, she staggers sideways. I feel her whole body trembling and crouch down slightly to pick her up. She doesn't even protest, just buries her face in my neck so that nobody can see her cry.

I turn furiously on Cyril, whose smile has vanished.

"You fucking wanker," I say quietly. I'd rather have screamed it in his face, but I don't want to scare Ruby any further.

With her in my arms, I turn and walk out into the garden through the back door of the conservatory.

———

Percy doesn't get here right away, but when he does, he's brought towels and dry clothes. Ruby avoids my eyes as I wrap her in several towels and start to rub her dry. She's still shaking all over. Percy silently hands me another towel, which I spread over her head. Then I squeeze the water from her hair. It might be over-the-top, but I'm not stopping until she stops trembling. Even if it takes all night.

Suddenly, a silent sob shakes her body. I freeze. It's surprisingly painful to see someone as strong as her crying, and I have no idea what to do. I can only keep on drying her, stroking her back in small circles, and then ask Percy to hand me the Maxton Hall sweatshirt he's brought.

"Can you unbutton your blouse?" I ask cautiously.

Ruby doesn't give any indication of having heard me. In any case, I doubt if her trembling fingers are up to much, so I simply pull the hoodie over her head. I pull it down over her body and then, without looking, get to work on her buttons. Once the blouse is open, I push it carefully from her shoulders and then help her to get her arms through the sleeves of the sweatshirt. Just as I'm about to pull the hood up for her, she lifts her hands and grabs my forearms. Her fingers are still ice-cold.

The next moment, she lets her head sink into my chest and takes a deep breath. It's as shaky as the rest of her. It's horrible seeing her like this.

"This is all my fault," I whisper.

Ruby lifts her head and looks up at me. Her eyes are still suspiciously shiny, but I get the feeling she's starting to get herself under control again. She looks like Ruby again. The stubborn, combative Ruby who won't take anything from anyone. A huge weight falls from my heart and a feeling that's heavy and light all at once spreads through my chest.

I turn away from her and unbutton my own shirt to pull on the second hoodie that Percy has brought.

"Come on. Let's get you home," I say after a while, opening the door of the Rolls for her.

She gets in, and I slip onto the seat beside her. As Percy drives off, I let my head sink back against the cushion. Suddenly, the alcohol makes its presence felt and the world spins a little faster than it should.

Ruby stirs beside me, and I glance at her. She's pulled the cuffs of my blue sweatshirt down over her fingers, covering her hands entirely. I feel a desperate need to reach for her. Instead, I look hastily away.

"I'm so scared of water," Ruby whispers into the silence.

I have to keep it together, not look at her. I think she'll feel safer if I keep on looking out of the window, not at her. "Why is that?"

It takes a moment for her to answer. "My dad likes fishing. He always used to take me out in his boat, and we spent weekends out on the water in various places. When I was eight, we were in an accident."

Her body tenses beside me, and I can sense that she's reliving a terrible memory. Her breathing is jagged. Now I do reach for her hand and hold it, beneath my jumper, in my fingers.

It feels small and vulnerable, but I'm sure that Ruby is anything but fragile.

"What happened?"

"We were rammed by a bigger boat that didn't see us. Ours was smashed to bits and Dad hit the water hard. His neck was overextended and one of his vertebrae got shattered."

I squeeze her hand.

"Since then, he's been in a wheelchair. And I've been terrified of water," she concludes hastily.

I don't believe that's the whole story, but I don't ask questions. What she's told me is enough to get a glimpse of what she must have felt when Cyril pulled her into the pool.

"I'm sorry," I say, feeling like an idiot. She's just told me about one of her most traumatic experiences and all I can offer is a lame apology.

"It's OK. You're not like your friends." Her hand emerges from the sleeve and cautiously reaches for mine. I link fingers with her and hesitantly stroke the back of her hand with my thumb.

"That's not true," I mumble, shaking my head. "I'm just like my friends. Worse, even."

She gives an almost imperceptible shake of her head. "Not right now, you're not."

For the rest of the drive, we sink into an amicable silence while I chew over what she just shared with me. After a while, Ruby nods off and her head slips onto my shoulder. Her hand doesn't let go of mine for a second, and I keep running my thumb pensively over her skin, which, luckily, is warm again now.

After twenty minutes, we arrive at Ruby's house. There's a light on, and I should wake her. But I don't have the heart to, not when she looks so peaceful now.

"She's a sweet girl, Mr. Beaufort." Percy's voice suddenly comes through the loudspeaker over my head. "Don't mess this up."

"I have no idea what you mean," I reply.

But I don't let go of Ruby's hand.

18

Ruby

Ember and I spend the whole of Saturday in our pajamas. Mum and Dad are out with friends, so we take advantage of having the kitchen to ourselves to bake chocolate chip cookies. We're in the middle of making sure the bowl is properly cleaned out when the doorbell rings. Both of us jump and stare at each other. Then I tap the side of my nose as fast as lightning. Ember groans as she realizes her defeat and trots off toward the door.

A moment later, I hear a gruff, familiar voice. "Hi, are you Ember? I'm Lin. Where's your sister? I need to speak to her!"

Before I've had time to blink, Lin's standing in front of me, holding out her phone. "Say that's not actually you."

For a while, I can only stare at her. It's the first time Lin's been in our house. Until now, she's only picked me up a few times, and has always waited in the car. Having her here ought to make me nervous. After all, she goes to Maxton Hall too, and so she's a part of my life that I want to keep as far as possible from my family. But the longer I see her standing in our kitchen, the more I realize that the opposite is true. I'm glad she came. Our argument the other day showed me that we could have a real friendship that goes beyond school. Maybe it's time to be brave and open up a little.

I deliberately pop the spatula into my mouth again so as not to have to answer. Unimpressed, Lin comes a few steps closer until she's right in front of me, holding her phone so close to my nose that I have to lean back before I can make anything out in the dark photo.

It's of James from behind, and he's carrying someone who has her arms wrapped tight around his neck and her face buried in his throat. You can't recognize me, but I still blush hotly. I wonder exactly how many other photos there are of that moment. And exactly who's seen them all.

"Ruby?" Lin asks, her tone suddenly a bit less harsh. "What happened yesterday?"

"I went to Cyril's party," I say at last. "Like I told you."

"Yes, you did. What I want to know is what's happening *here*."

"What's happening where?" asks Ember, snatching the phone from Lin's hand. Her mouth drops open as she stares at the photo. "Is that really you?"

"Yes," I admit, gulping hard. Spending today with Ember was meant to take my mind off things. I wanted to suppress the thoughts of last night and stop my head from whirling. What happened yesterday . . . Even I don't know what that was. Let alone how to put it into words or to deal with it.

"Tell me right now what happened yesterday," my sister demands, in an I'm-not-taking-no-for-an-answer voice that she definitely gets from Mum.

I lean down to the oven again to check on the cookies. Sadly, they're not ready yet and can't protect me from Lin and Ember or their questioning looks. I sigh quietly, drop the scraper back in the bowl, and nod toward the dining room. Once we've sat down, I start talking.

By the end of my story, they have very different expressions on their faces. Lin looks mainly skeptical. Ember, by contrast, has rested her chin on her hand and is smiling dreamily at me.

"This Beaufort boy sounds lovely," she sighs.

"He is not!" Lin exclaims in disbelief. "There's no way the bloke you were just talking about is James Beaufort."

All I can do is shrug my shoulders. Looking back at it now, it feels unreal that he actually went so far as to protect me from his friends, but . . . he did. More than that. He took care of me. Got me dressed while acting like a gentleman. He held my hand when I told him about Dad.

Last night has changed things between us. I can feel it distinctly. My whole body tingles when I think about the way he looked at me and the touch of his fingers on my bare skin. The time my body shivered, and James thought I was still cold—which very much wasn't the case. The way he held me as if I was made of thin, fragile glass.

"That's exactly what I meant when I told you to be careful," Lin says, shaking her head and bringing me back to the present.

"I know," I mumble. I wish I could forget the way it felt when I went under the water.

"I can't believe Cyril did that," she continues. "When I see him, I'll wring his neck."

She looks so stunned and disappointed that, yet again, I wonder if Cyril is more to her than just a classmate. Whether there was something between them, and if so, what happened. She's always shut down when the subject of her love life has come up.

Maybe now is a good time to try again, cautiously—after all, I just opened up to her.

But Ember's next words break off my train of thought.

"Lucky James was there." Her eyes look as though they're about to turn into little red hearts. "I can't believe he actually carried you out of that party. *In his arms!*"

Me either. Especially when I think how cold and arrogant he was to me at the start. I can't reconcile that version of him with the James who wrapped me up in heaps of towels and stroked my back until I stopped shaking. The James who messes with my head and haunted my dreams last night, with his warm hands on my bare skin.

Not good. Not good. Not. Good.

"If I didn't have photographic proof, I wouldn't believe it," Lin says, staring back at the picture. "How can a guy be such an arsehole most of the time and then act like a knight in shining armor?"

"Seems like he realized that Cyril crossed the line with Ruby and stepped in. Which shows that he has a good heart," Ember declares. She looks at me, and suddenly, something in her face changes. "Uh-oh."

Lin looks up. "What?" When she sets eyes on me, she groans. "Ruby!"

Evidently, my emotional chaos is right there on my face. "I don't know either, OK?" I say. "I can't stand him, but . . ." I break off with a helpless shrug.

For a moment, Ember looks like she wants to say something more, but then she suddenly stands up. "We should check on the cookies."

The three of us walk into the kitchen, which now smells delicious. As Ember and I get the cookies out of the oven, Lin arranges them symmetrically on a large plate. We then take them into the living room, and she digs me abruptly in the ribs. "It's OK to be attracted to someone even when you know they're an idiot."

I'd love to ask her if she's speaking from experience. But Lin is so cagey about her personal life that I chicken out and just ask: "Do you think?"

She nods.

Of their own accord, my thoughts turn back to James. The back of my hand gets pins and needles where he was stroking it, and, at the memory of him getting undressed in front of me, a sensation of heat wells up in my belly.

"I still can't believe it though. It had to be Beaufort. King of the bloody school," Lin murmurs, dropping onto the sofa.

"Even I don't know how it happened," I admit, reaching for a cookie. It's way too hot still, but I take a huge bite anyway, so as not to have to say anything more.

"If he really looked after you that well, then he's all right by me," Ember concedes, snapping up a cookie of her own. Then she puts her feet up on the coffee table, ankles crossed. "So, what are you going to do now? Have you two spoken since yesterday?"

I shake my head. "My only plan for today was to chill with my sister."

Ember sits bolt upright, like a meerkat. "You have to text him!"

I shake my head, looking from her to Lin. "There's nothing there, girls. We're just . . . friends." It sounds weird to call James a friend, but it's the best I can do at the moment.

"Obviously. Message him now," Lin insists, and I pull my phone from my jeans pocket with a sigh.

I briefly wonder what to say and then settle on the basics.

Thanks. RJB

Having sent the message, I shove my phone into the crack between the sofa cushions so as not to have to look at it.

"What did you say?" asks Ember.

"Just thank you."

Lin wrinkles her nose and finally reaches for a cookie. She breaks it in four and takes one of the quarters. It's rare for her to let herself have anything sweet. Lin is mega strict about healthy eating, which means she basically bans herself anything tasty. I find that a shame but haven't yet succeeded in convincing her that life is way more fun with chocolate in it.

My phone buzzes. It's a serious effort of will not to grab it at once. It would be embarrassing to look that keen in front of Lin and Ember.

Luckily, they can't hear how hard my heart is thumping as I eventually unlock the screen and read the message.

You never did tell me what the J stands for. JMB

I answer right away.

Guess. RJB

James. JMB

Pretty egocentric, don't you think? RJB

Jenna. JMB

Nope. RJB

Jemima. JMB

I'm kind of impressed you only needed 3 guesses. RJB

Then he doesn't answer for a while. I stare at the dark screen, aware of Ember and Lin watching me expectantly. But I don't know myself exactly what I'm waiting for until my phone buzzes again a few minutes later.

Are you feeling better?

No initials. Not joking now. My throat suddenly feels very dry. I don't want to remember yesterday, don't want to think about the water or the fact that I had hysterics in front of loads of people from school and made a total fool of myself. And I really don't want to think about Monday and what I might be in for then.

I'm scared of Monday. There are photos of us.

Lin and Ember start chatting about stuff that's nothing to do with James or yesterday's party, and Ember switches on the TV. She pulls out a DVD from the cupboard and slots it into the machine.

I'm grateful to them for giving me a bit of space, especially when I read James's next text.

Don't stress. All you can see in the pic is my wet back.

I hold my breath. Can I take that at face value, or is he flirting with me indirectly? I haven't the faintest idea. I only know that I want to stay on an equal footing with him.

Well, that's one good part of the photo for me.

I have to wait a long time for him to reply. So long that I'm regretting having typed those words. We're halfway through the film before my phone next buzzes.

Ruby Bell, are you trying to flirt with me?

A smile spreads over my face. I hide it beneath the collar of my PJ top. Then I switch off my phone and do my best to focus my entire attention on the film.

Ruby

When I get off the bus at school on Monday, James is leaning against the playing field fence, and he greets me with a crooked grin.

Given what happened a week ago at his parents' shop, I'd never ever have believed I'd be pleased to see him waiting for me some morning.

"Hi," I say, somewhat breathlessly, coming to a standstill in front of him.

His smile broadens. Apparently, he's happy to see me too. "Hey."

His eyes roam over my face, and again, there's that unfamiliar feeling in my stomach. I wonder if my skin would tingle if he touched me the way he did on Friday. I hastily push the thought away to a dark corner of my brain. "Are you my escort for the day?"

His smile doesn't slip. "I thought we could go in to assembly together so you don't have to answer anyone's questions."

The next moment, he nods toward the school and starts walking. I hook my fingers through the straps on my backpack and follow him.

"How . . . How was the rest of your weekend?" I ask hesitantly.

"We had a family dinner yesterday."

That's all he says. I give him an inquiring sideways glance. He spots it, and his smile slowly fades.

"My aunt Ophelia was visiting. She and my dad don't get on particularly well."

For a moment, the fact that he's told me something so personal leaves me speechless. I wasn't expecting that, especially since he told me how badly he and his sister have been let down after trusting people in the past. On the other hand, I did tell him something about me on Friday. He must have noticed how hard that was for me. And maybe he feels the same as me. Maybe he can sense that something has changed and doesn't want to go back to the stilted way we've acted around each other till now.

Hope blossoms inside me. I have no idea what to call this thing between James and me—friendship? More? Less?—but I'd like to find out, little by little.

"Was there trouble?"

He digs his hands in his pockets. "Family get-togethers are never exactly peaceful. The Beaufort companies actually belong to my mother and her sister. But after my parents married, my dad took control of a lot of stuff and made a lot of changes too, some of which were pretty unpopular—especially with Ophelia," he explains.

"Does she work for the firm too?" I ask curiously.

James grunts. "Yeah, but she has no say in relation to the main company. She's five years younger than Mum, and so she's always been a bit left out. She's more involved in the subsidiaries and other companies my parents have a stake in."

I wonder what Ember would think if our parents left us a firm but gave her no voice in it just because she's younger. No wonder things get tense at Beaufort family dinners.

"There've been loads of decisions she's disagreed with lately, so the mood was pretty crap. But . . . it was OK. I've had worse evenings with my family," he says with a shrug, and the two of us turn left onto the path to Boyd Hall.

A girl in my history class comes past us. Her eyes widen at the sight of James and me together. I wrap my fingers a bit tighter around my backpack straps and gulp. But I put my chin up and stare back at her until she turns and walks off.

"Hey, easy there," says James, nudging me slightly with his shoulder.

"What am I meant to do? If she stares, I'm going to stare back."

He stands in front of me, blocking my path. "You're letting it get to you too much. It doesn't have to matter. Let them say whatever they like."

"But it does matter."

"So? They don't have to know that. You just have to look like none of it interests you. Then they'll leave you alone."

Suddenly, his face changes—his eyelids droop a fraction, his eyebrows relax, his mouth turns up slightly the corners. It's his I-don't-give-a-shit look, the one where he comes across as so arrogant that I want to shake him. "You look like you need a good beating."

"I look like I'd enjoy a good beating. That's the difference," he replies, jerking his chin at me. "Your turn."

I try to copy his expression. Not very successfully, if James's twitching lips are anything to go by.

"OK. Well, maybe you could start by just *not* looking as though you're imagining everyone around you being shot down in flames."

We walk on, and I try to take his advice. Even so, the closer we get to the school, the sicker I feel. Just outside the door to Boyd Hall, James rests his hand on the back of my head and gives it a stroke. Only for a second. It's probably meant to be encouraging, but suddenly, I'm nervous for a whole different reason. I don't know how James does it, but a single touch from him is enough to throw my world off course. It's a brand-new feeling for me, strange and weird. But kind of nice.

"Beaufort!" someone calls behind us, making me jump. People stream past us into assembly, dodging James and me as we stop again.

Wren and Alistair come up the stairs toward us. "Hey, Ruby." Wren rubs the back of his head, almost shyly. "Sorry about Friday."

I'm not sure if he's only apologizing for what happened at the pool or for the way he hassled me at the start of the party. I can't ask without James hearing about Wren and me. I'm sure he's only saying sorry for James's sake, but I'm glad anyway.

So I just nod and say: "That's OK, it wasn't you who threw me in the pool."

Wren gives me a surprised grin, like that wasn't the reaction he'd been expecting.

I find my eyes wandering automatically to Alistair, who is watching me in silence. One look at his face makes me quite certain that he knows. He knows it was me who walked in on him and Kesh in the library.

I smile cautiously at him. He doesn't smile back. His lips are thin and bloodless.

"Can we go in?" James asks, looking around the group. We grunt in agreement and walk up the last few steps.

Assembly has just begun as we arrive in Boyd Hall, and we try to sneak into seats in the back row. Even so, I feel eyes on me as word of who's sitting next to James Beaufort this morning gets around. One head after another turns toward us as Mr. Lexington stands at the front and praises the lacrosse team for their outstanding performance on Friday.

I steal a glimpse at James, but his face shows no emotion, no hint that the situation or the murmuring around us could be unpleasant for him. So I gulp, press my lips together, and follow suit.

After assembly, James and Wren have maths, while Alistair and I are heading to the east wing for art. Before we say goodbye, James murmurs to me: "Remember the good beating."

His words are entirely innocent, but I feel my cheeks burning hot. I ignore it and follow Alistair, who has already walked away. Things between us are still tense, but I feel the need to say something. But I have no idea what.

Alistair saves me the decision, taking my arm just before the classroom door. He pulls me aside and looks seriously at me.

"What you saw on Friday," he begins quietly, then pauses. His eyes flit to a couple of people who've just come around the corner. He nods to them with a fake smile and waits for them to go past, into the room. Then he turns back to me. "You can't tell a soul about it."

"Of course not," I answer, equally quietly.

"No, Ruby, you don't understand. You have to promise me. Swear you won't tell anyone," Alistair whispers urgently.

"What makes you think I'd do such a thing?" I retort.

"I . . . It's just . . ." He has to pause again as more students say hi to him in passing. "Keshav doesn't want anyone to know." I can see by his eyes how hard it is for him to say those words. Suddenly, he's no longer the arrogant, posh boy who beats people up on the lacrosse field. Now he looks incredibly young. And vulnerable.

No wonder. It can't feel good to be with someone who keeps you hidden, like you're a dirty secret.

"I won't tell a soul, Alistair. I promise."

He nods, and for a moment I can see the relief in his face. Then his expression changes, and he seems to be weighing me up. "If I ever find out that you did tell anyone, I'll make your life hell."

He then walks into the classroom without a backward glance.

———

I get through the rest of the day better than I expected. A few people give me funny looks or whisper behind my back, but nobody has the guts to speak to me or mention what happened on Friday. Looks like James's protection this morning actually did the trick.

I eat lunch with Lin as usual. Or as usual until someone comes up to our table.

"Is this seat free?" asks Lydia Beaufort.

Lin and I turn our heads and stare at her. She gestures to the chair next to Lin with her tray.

"Yes?" I answer, although it sounds more like a question.

Lydia sits opposite me without hesitation, spreads a napkin over her lap, and starts to eat her pasta. Lin glances inquiringly at me, but I shrug helplessly. I have no idea what Lydia's doing here. Maybe James has passed the job of escort duty on to her? Or maybe she's decided to follow through with what she said on Friday and keep an eye on me herself?

I look at James, who is sitting at the other end of the dining hall with his friends. I might be mistaken, but the atmosphere between them seems less relaxed than normal today. James and Alistair seem to be having an animated discussion while Keshav's staring at his phone and Wren's reading a book. There's no sign of Cyril.

"He doesn't know I've joined you," Lydia says suddenly. She dabs at her mouth and sips from her water bottle. "I'm here because I wanted to apologize for Friday."

"But you didn't do anything," I reply in confusion.

She shakes her head. "My friends and I were all out of order."

"So you're having lunch with us?" Lin asks skeptically.

Lydia just shrugs. "I've seen what vultures people can be. If I sit here, no one will dare come over." She nods toward a group of kids who are staring at us. When they notice that I've looked around, they look away and stick their heads together, whispering.

"And I wanted to check on how you're doing," Lydia adds.

I can't hide my surprise. Thinking back on our last conversation, all I can see is her distrustful gaze. She didn't give me the impression of being interested in my well-being, and I can't help wondering if my dip in the pool is really the only reason she's sitting here at our table.

I decide to answer her question honestly all the same. "I'd prefer it if that hadn't happened on Friday. But I'm OK."

"Cy really doesn't know when to stop sometimes," she says.

I shrug my shoulders.

"But I've known him all my life," she continues. "That genuinely was his idea of funny."

"What he did was anything but funny," Lin objects, looking surprised when Lydia nods.

"He crossed the line. And I've told him so."

I glance up from my soup in surprise. "Really?"

"Yes. Of course."

For a moment I don't know what to say. In the end I settle on: "That was kind. Thank you."

Lydia smiles and turns back to her penne.

I look at Lin at the same moment that she looks at me. I give another almost imperceptible shrug, and we both focus on our lunch.

After a while, Lin tells me about her morning, which began badly when her car wouldn't start. It feels weird to make small talk with Lydia there, but she joins in on our conversation as if it was the most natural thing in the world, and in the end, I stop asking myself what her ulterior motive might be. Maybe she's just being nice and genuinely wanted to apologize. She wouldn't be the first member of her family to surprise me.

Once we've finished eating, I heave my backpack onto my lap and pull out a little tin that I put in the middle of the table.

"There were some cookies left from the weekend," I say, taking off the lid. "Anyone up for dessert?"

Lydia's eyes light up. "Did you make them yourself?"

"With Lin and my sister," I say. "On Saturday, in our PJs."

"That sounds amazing," she says, taking a cookie. "Way better than my Saturday." She bites into it and chews pensively. "Oh, wow, this is delicious."

"Thanks." I smile. "James said you had family visiting."

"Yeah, that's always . . . something else. I'd way rather have spent the day in my pajamas."

I can't imagine someone like Lydia in pajamas at all, and the attempt makes me grin.

After lunch, Lin and I head for the group room to get ready for today's meeting. While I write the agenda on the board, Lin puts the handouts we just got printed at the school office at everyone's places. Then we wait for the others, who gradually drift in. James takes the window seat, same as always. He puts the black notebook on the table in front of him and crosses his arms over his chest. The familiar sight gives me a twinge because it makes me realize that whether or not James and I are getting on better, he's not here voluntarily. Being here means he isn't at lacrosse training—it's a punishment that he hates.

"Ruby?" Kieran came up to me without me noticing.

"Hmm?" I say, looking at him. Kieran's only a fraction taller than me. His black hair falls over his face and he shakes it aside.

"I wondered if you had a minute after the meeting? I've got quite a range of bands, and I thought I'd rather discuss them with you before narrowing them down to three."

"Hang on," I mumble, looking in my planner. All it says is *Birthday plans with Mum & Dad*. "Yeah, no problem."

Kieran smiles with relief. "Great."

He goes back to his seat, which is diagonally opposite James. Our eyes meet, and a mocking smile crosses his lips as he looks from me to Kieran and back again.

"What?" I mouth.

James picks up his phone. A moment later, mine lights up on the table in front of me.

He's into you.

I roll my eyes and ignore him.

"OK, everyone. Let's see where things stand now," Lin opens the meeting, pointing to Jessalyn on her right.

"I've got lots of quotes for the décor. One of them is offering us a really good discount." Jessa passes around the printed portfolio. "Thanks again for the tip, Beaufort."

I look at James in surprise as he gives Jessa a nod. Given how often his eyes stray over to the playing fields, I'd never have expected him to put himself out unasked. And without telling me either.

"I've come up with a few designs for the invites," says Doug next, handing Lin a USB stick. She plugs it in and starts the presentation. "The first one is more traditional, based on last year's," he explains.

I study the swirling gold letters on the black background, but before I can express an opinion, Camille says: "I thought we were trying to move away from last year's party?"

The others mumble in agreement.

"OK, then here's the next idea," Doug continues, nodding to Lin to click on.

The next invitation is in gaudy colors, typical Halloween.

"That doesn't look as elegant as I'd imagine a Victorian party to be," Kieran says hesitantly.

I nod. "Yeah, I agree, to be honest."

Doug nods, and Lin clicks to the next slide. A whisper runs through the room, and I sit bolt upright. The next moment, I lean in closer to the screen and narrow my eyes at the invitation.

It's designed to look like old paper. The event is announced in fancy but legible lettering at the top, right under which I see . . . me. With James, who's bowing and holding my hand gently in his, as if he's inviting me to dance.

It's one of the photos Tristan took that Saturday in London. I can't believe it was forwarded to Doug without me knowing about it. I look up from the laptop screen to James across the room. His eyes are dancing, but he won't meet my gaze.

"It looks amazing," says Jessa after a while. A murmur of agreement fills the room. "That dress is dreamy. You don't happen to have another couple, do you?" she asks James.

He shakes his head. "Be glad I got anything at all."

"The invitation is great, Doug." Lin turns to the screen to look at it on a bigger scale. Then she stands up and takes a few steps back. "I think the details could be in a different font though, something a bit more modern."

"Yeah, I agree," I say, trying not to let anyone see how uncertain I am about the picture. If we go with this invitation, my face will be all over the school—all over Pemwick! I don't know if I'm ready for that level of attention. Unfortunately, that's not up for debate—obviously, the team are thrilled and are already discussing whether to use the same printers as last time.

I study the picture again. James in his Victorian suit, my hand in his. The memory of how it felt to be so close to him, how electric that moment was, fills me with warmth. I don't dare even glance in his direction for the entire rest of the meeting.

Once we're done, Jessa, Camille, and Doug say goodbye. Kieran comes over so that we can check the bands out on Lin's laptop, and I see her walk over to James. She sits down beside him and starts talking. I watch with a frown as he nods and makes a note of something in his pad. I don't realize that Kieran's speaking to me until it's too late.

"Sorry, what were you saying?" I ask.

"That I think this is going to be the best party Maxton Hall has ever seen," he repeats, smiling at me.

"That would be great. We've been planning it for so long, I can hardly wait for the night."

"Me either. I really hope you'll save a dance for me." Kieran's still smiling, looking at me through his black lashes. I give a dry gulp.

He's into you.

Lin's been telling me that for months. Could she be right? Until now, I've always seen Kieran as this ambitious little vampire in the year below us. I thought he was being nice to me in the hope that I might suggest him as team leader next year. I never believed that he might have a crush on me.

Suddenly, I realize how close Kieran's sitting to me and that our knees are almost touching under the table. I budge to the side and then feel cross with myself. This situation is entirely innocent. Why am I letting James's words faze me like this?

I glare at him at the exact moment that he looks at me. Unlike me, he's not hiding anything, it's all public. I long to stick my tongue out at him. But that would be childish, so I beam at Kieran and nod. "Of course. But I'll have to take some lessons first."

"I can show you during the rehearsals," he says, and I could swear I can see a slight blush on his cheeks. *Oh boy.*

"Good. OK," I say, louder than I intended. I cough. "Shall we listen to the music then?"

We pull out our headphones and go through the samples that Kieran's collected. After that, we check out reviews online and shortlist them.

"I think I'd suggest these three to the others. Why don't you ask them their fees and then we'll decide on Wednesday or Friday which is best," I say in the end.

Kieran nods. "Fine."

"Great." I smile, taking off the headphones. I open my planner and grab my pink pen to note down today's tasks.

"You're turning eighteen on Saturday?" he asks in surprise.

I instantly slam my journal shut. I'm trying not to show it, but it bothers me that Kieran peeked inside it. This is kind of my diary and definitely not meant for others' eyes to see.

"Yeah," I say after a brief pause.

"So, what are your plans?"

Lin picks this moment to turn around from her conversation with James. "We're . . ." She falls silent as I glare warningly at her. It's nobody's business at Maxton Hall what I'm doing for my birthday. That's my private life, and I don't want anyone knowing about it. "Nothing much," she says in the end, pressing her lips firmly together.

"You didn't say you're almost an adult," says James, standing up. He raises both arms over his head and stretches. "Why aren't I invited?"

"Because you don't know how to behave," I retort.

"I'll show you exactly how well I can behave," he says, sounding like the exact opposite. Suddenly, I'm remembering the party again. Not the pool and everything that came after that. The moment on the dance floor when I stumbled into James and felt his body against mine. He was looking at me exactly like this, with a shameless glitter in his eyes that makes my stomach tingle.

I have to pull myself together and remember where we are before I reply. "You're not invited, James."

"OK." Again, it sounds more like he's saying *We'll see about that*.

Kieran gets up and shoulders his bag. "I'll call you then, OK?"

I nod, and he leaves the room with a hand gesture that's halfway between a wave and a high five.

I stash my planner in my backpack and shut Lin's laptop down. I slip it into its case and stand up. "Are you hanging around, or shall I lock up?"

James and Lin shake their heads. "We're done."

The two of them pack up their stuff too, and I eye them suspiciously. I want to know what they were talking about. I hope Lin didn't let him in on my birthday plans. I might have shared an important part of me with James on Friday, but there are things he doesn't need to know. And the fact that I'm planning to spend the evening of my eighteenth birthday playing board games with Lin and my family is one of them.

"Rutherford is so into you," James says once we've left the library.

"Rubbish," I say, shaking my head.

"I think he likes you," Lin agrees with James, entirely unnecessarily.

I glance at her.

"What? I've been telling you for years. He can read your every wish in your eyes, and he's so nice. It's really, really obvious."

"What's obvious about it? Nothing's obvious. He's nice to me because I'm team leader. He *has* to be nice to me."

Lin smiles at me and strokes my arm. "OK, let me correct that. It's obvious to everyone but you."

James laughs quietly, and I glare at him. I wish I knew what's made the two of them pal up like this. I can't remember them ever agreeing about anything before, let alone sending each other amused glances over the top of my head. I'm not sure I approve of this development.

I'm almost relieved when Lin hugs me goodbye and heads off to the car park.

James insists on walking me to the bus. "You're giving the poor boy hope," he says out of nowhere.

"What's your problem, James? Jealous?" It's the best I can do in the spur of the moment. But he doesn't answer, and when I glance at him, I see that he's dug his hands in his trouser pockets and is frowning, staring straight ahead.

"If you need anyone to give you dancing lessons," he says, after a brief pause, "I'm your man."

"You can't be serious," I exclaim in disbelief. "Are you really jealous of *Kieran*?"

"No." He's still not looking at me. "But I don't want that guy getting the wrong idea."

"What idea?" I ask.

"That sucking up to you is all it takes to make you smile. That's pathetic."

I stop abruptly. "Excuse me? I can smile perfectly well without anyone sucking up to me!"

He finally turns to me, but I can't read the expression in his dark eyes. "Really? You never smiled at me like that."

"You've never given me much reason to smile."

For a moment, he just stares at me. I don't get why he's suddenly being like this. He seems worked up, and I can't follow his argument. I decide to change the subject before the atmosphere gets any worse. "Thanks for looking out for me today."

He just nods.

"Honestly. Nobody made any stupid remarks. I know it would have been different if you hadn't walked into school or assembly with me."

He still doesn't reply, so I add: "Your sister sat with us in the dining hall today, and . . ."

Suddenly, James takes my arm and stands in front of me. I hold my breath and look up at him in surprise. His eyes are deadly serious.

"I'm sorry," he says.

"What for?" I ask quietly.

"For never having given you any reason to look at me the way you just looked at Kieran."

"James . . ."

"I'm going to change that," he goes on, looking me deep in the eyes.

I swallow. My stomach suddenly feels wobbly, my knees weak. I'm aware of his hand on my arm, can feel his gentle touch through my blazer. I get goose bumps down my arm. The sudden feeling that I need to touch him too takes me entirely unawares. I don't want much. It would be enough to put my hands on his hips, to hold him tight. But I can't. It's not an option. Any more than this horrible breathlessness when he's this close, or the butterflies in my tummy when he looks at me like that.

"My bus is coming," I exclaim, pulling back.

The intensity doesn't fade from his eyes. I turn and sprint away so that I'm no longer entirely at his mercy. I've never been so glad in my life to get on the bus.

20

Ruby

On Saturday morning I wake up at six—with no alarm clock. I'm always like this on my birthday. I find it hard to sleep for the sheer anticipation of what Mum and Dad will have come up with for me. On special occasions, Mum brings home the world's most delicious cakes from the bakery where she works, while Dad cooks us a special meal and gets either Ember or me to help him decorate the whole of downstairs. By seven, I can hear them getting stuff ready, and I'm looking forward to what it's all going to be. After all, you only turn eighteen once.

I listen to my heart, trying to see if I feel any different, but I don't. It was the same for Lin back in August. Or at least, that's what she said as we lay side by side in the grass after her barbecue, staring up at the stars.

I roll onto my side and reach for my phone. Jessa's sent me a lovely text, and Lin left me a voice note just after half past one, singing quietly and then wishing me a gorgeous day. She ends the message by saying how certain she is that we'll both get into Oxford and that she can hardly wait.

After that, I get dressed, sit down at my desk, and flick through my planner as a distraction. The Halloween party is a week from today. It seems like forever that I've been totally focused on this event. On Friday morning, the posters arrived from the print shop, and we put them up around the school during that day's meeting. My fears were unfounded. Nobody said anything about the photo of James and me, or teased me about it. In fact, I only got positive reactions, and Mr. Lexington emailed me to say that the guests from outside the school had been very complimentary about the design too.

I still haven't got used to pretty much everyone at Maxton Hall knowing my name now though. It's weird when people say hi or pull out a chair for me in the dining hall. But I'm trying not to let them see that it bothers me, just to act the same as normal, like I don't mind all the attention. That's what James does. He acts like he doesn't give a shit about anything. But these days, I know that that's not true.

My thoughts drift automatically back to that moment last Monday. *I'm going to change that.* He sounded so determined and gave me such an insistent look. As though there was nothing that mattered to him more in the world just then than to convince me that he was serious.

I shake myself to get thoughts of James out of my head. But as my sight clears, I jump.

James

I've written his name in my diary. And I didn't even notice! My cheeks burn up, and I reach straight for the white-out in my pencil case. I hold it over the first couple of letters, but then pause. Slowly, I put the little tube down again and run my fingers gently over his name. My fingertips tingle. Not a good sign. I've spent days asking myself what that's all about. After all, he's still . . . him. But I can't deny the fact that something's changed. For ages now, the sight of him has filled me not with rage and suspicion but with something else. Something warm and exciting.

I can't help smiling. Because I'm pleased to see him. Because I enjoy his company. Because he's quick and intelligent and I find him interesting. Because he's like a puzzle that I'm desperate to solve.

I'd never have thought it possible, but I don't hate James Beaufort anymore. Far from it.

Suddenly, my door opens, and Ember walks in. Guiltily, I slam my bullet journal shut.

Ember's dubious gaze is fixed on me, and then her eyes turn to my planner as if she knows perfectly well that it's hiding some cringeworthy secret. But she grins and bounces toward me, taking my hand to pull me up from my chair. "I'm surprised you haven't tried to come down yet," she says. She keeps on pulling at my arm, but there's really no need. I'm more than willing to follow.

We leave my room, and I wrap my arms around her waist to give her a hug. "You have to fulfill my every wish today."

At this moment, I realize that there's a hint of sadness mingling with my pleasure. This is the last birthday I'll spend here with my family and Ember. Who knows where I'll be this time next year? Will I actually be in Oxford? With Lin at my side? Or all alone? And what if they don't want me after all—where will I be then?

Ember breaks into my thoughts as we go through the door on our right to the living room. "Here's the birthday girl!" she exclaims.

"Surprise!" shout my family.

I squeal and clap my hands to my mouth and feel my eyes

starting to sting. I don't often cry, and if I do, it's alone in my room where no one can see me. But as I see my grandparents, aunt, uncle, and cousin here with my parents, and they all start to sing "Happy Birthday," it's impossible to control my emotions.

The room is beautifully decorated. Dad and Ember have excelled themselves this year. There are white and mint-green pompoms hanging from the ceiling, the dining table is bedecked with a garland in the same colors, and all my presents are piled at the back on the coffee table, with two metallic mint-green balloons shimmering above them, shaped like the numbers that make up my age.

The next half hour goes by as if in a dream. Everyone hugs me, wishes me a happy birthday, asks how I'm feeling, and then they give me their presents. From Uncle Tom, Aunt Trudy, and my cousin Max, there's the box set of *My Hero Academia*, a manga series I've had my eye on for months; Ember gives me new pens and pretty stickers for my planner; my grandparents have bought two textbooks from the Oxford reading list. My parents give me an external hard drive for my laptop, which I've been wanting since the start of the year when it just gave up the ghost for no apparent reason, wiping out pretty much all my files.

"So, who's that from?" I ask, pointing to a large parcel that's still on the table.

"A secret admirer," says Mum, waggling her eyebrows. I look suspiciously from her to Dad. He just shrugs.

"It came in the post," Ember explains.

"No address on it?" I ask, studying the black cardboard box and blue bow curiously.

"I don't think that's necessary—we all know who it's from," Ember says.

"Oh my God, you've got a boyfriend!" Max is looking at me wide-eyed.

Ember says "Yes" at the same moment that I shout "No!"

"Open it," Trudy demands, peering over my shoulder. She reaches out a hand and acts like she's about to pull open the bow. I just about manage to push the parcel away in time. I pick it up and sit down on the sofa.

Slowly, I undo the bow. I feel horribly watched and glare at my family in an attempt to stop them staring at me like this. Not that it does any good. You could hear a pin drop. I sigh and take off the lid.

The box contains a bag. I hold my breath as I pull it out and set it down in my lap. It's in dark brown waxed leather with an adjustable strap and two little front pockets beneath a flap that fastens with snaps. Cautiously, I open it. The satchel has a lining in blue and green checks and an array of sections that strikes me as perfect. There's a laptop pocket, lots of little ones on the side that you can close with zips, and a main central pocket with a smaller side section.

With this bag at my side, I could conquer the world. There's no doubt about that. I close it gently and stroke the leather. Then I notice something I didn't spot at first. There are three letters on the bottom right-hand corner of the flap. My initials. RJB.

It takes my breath away. I feel like I'm in a dream, and I hardly even hear my family's oohs and aahs. I peek into the box, and on the bottom, amid the black tissue paper, there's a card. It's creamy white and edged in gold, with a message in black ink.

Happy Birthday, Ruby! J

That's all. But it's enough for an explosion of feelings in my belly to set my entire body tingling. I don't know how to react, can only stare at the bag until zeros and pound signs start dancing in front of my eyes. This is undoubtedly the most expensive gift I've ever been given. But I don't want to think about that.

And I don't want to wonder what it means that James was thinking of me enough to give me this kind of a present. Did he notice that my backpack was about to fall apart at the seams? Did he know that I've been saving up for months to buy a new bag for next year? Did he feel sorry for me?

I don't know, and thinking about it makes my head swim.

"The boy has style, that's for sure," sighs Trudy.

"And money," Max adds helpfully.

"I don't think it'll have cost him anything, seeing that his parents own the company that made the bag," Ember suggests.

"Everyone!" Mum interrupts them, pointing to the lavish breakfast laid out on the table. "Leave Ruby in peace and sit down." She comes over to me, lifts the bag from my lap, puts it carefully back in the box, and takes my hand to pull me up. She puts an arm around my shoulder and gives me a squeeze. "It's not nice to talk about a present like that. The young man has put a lot of thought into it, and it's a wonderful gesture that we should be thankful for." She taps her finger against my nose. "Now go and blow out your candles."

We head to the table together. Every time I've blown out my birthday candles in the last ten years, I've made the same wish. *Oxford.* But this year, another name pops up in my head, and I have to stop for a moment and concentrate.

"You get to wish for two things on your eighteenth," says Dad gently. I hadn't noticed him wheeling over to my side, but now he strokes my back softly. Evidently, my inner struggle was visible on my face.

"That's true," says Mum. "It's the birthday law."

My cheeks flush, and I turn away from them. I refuse to analyze why James's name was the first thing I thought of. Or why I take my parents at their words as I shut my eyes and blow hard.

It's the nicest birthday party we've ever had. After our brunch, we go out for a walk and take a new family photo in Gormsey Park, although it's only on the tenth shot that nobody has their eyes shut. Lin comes over in the afternoon, and we play board games and charades, which Lin and I narrowly win over Max and Aunt Trudy. In the evening, Ember and I help Dad to serve up a three-course dinner, a lot of which he made in advance yesterday. We sit around the table until late, and it surprises me how effortlessly Lin fits into our family circle. She doesn't seem to mind not getting the odd in-joke, she asks Mum loads of questions about her work at the bakery, and has a long conversation with Dad about his injury. It turns out that Lin has an uncle who uses a wheelchair too, which was total news to me. I admire how naturally she talks about the subject and the way she isn't fazed by Dad's disability.

By the time everyone leaves, I'm so full and content that I could drop off to sleep right away. But once I'm in my pajamas, I catch sight of the black cardboard box on my desk. I get up and walk over to it. Hesitantly, I lift the lid and pull out the satchel. I open the two catches with a soft click. Carefully, I take the things I need for school on Monday and begin to pack them, one by one, into the pockets. It takes me a few attempts to be satisfied with my arrangement. This is heaven on earth compared to my old bag, where everything had to go in together. There are even little pen loops at the front, which I fill with the colors I use most often in my bullet journal.

I don't know whether James could guess how thrilled I am with this gift. But now that I look at the bag filled up like this, I realize that there's no way I could give it back. I bend down and reach into the left-hand front pocket for my phone, which I slipped in there experimentally. I hesitate only a second, then find and dial James's number. I hold the handset to my ear and wait for it to ring. It rings. And rings. I'm about to hang up when he answers.

"Ruby Bell." It almost sounds as though he was expecting me to call.

"James Beaufort." If he's going to say my full name, well, two can play at that game. Once upon a time, the syllables sounded like swear words as I spat them from my mouth, but now they feel different on my tongue. Better.

"How's it going?" he asks, although I can hardly hear him. There's music in the background, getting gradually quieter. I wonder where he is and what he's doing.

"It's going great. I've just packed up my new bag," I reply, running my fingers over the seam of the middle pocket. The stitching feels perfectly even.

"Do you like it?" he asks, and I wish I knew what he looks like right now. What he's wearing. In my head, he's in uniform because I've rarely seen him wear anything else, but I try to conjure up the image of James in black jeans and a white shirt. Standing on our doorstep that day, he looked like a perfectly ordinary guy. Not the heir to a company worth billions. More human. Tangible.

"It's beautiful. You know you didn't have to do that, don't you?" I add after a while. I close the bag and sit on my chair, feet up on the desk, ankles crossed.

"I wanted to give you something. And I thought the James would be a good choice for a person as organized as you."

"The James?"

"That's what the bag's called."

"You gave me a bag named after you?"

"I didn't choose the name, that was Mum. There's a Lydia too. And others named after my parents. But the Lydia would be too small for you, and the Mortimer's too big. Besides, I thought it would be funny to see you around school with the James."

I can't help grinning. "Do you give all your friends Beaufort stuff?" I ask.

He goes quiet for a bit, and all I can hear is the music playing quietly in the background. "No," he answers in the end.

That's all he says.

I don't know what that means. I just don't know what this is between us, let alone what I want it to be. All I know is that it makes me really happy to hear his voice.

"When you own the company, you'll have to name a bag after me one day," I say to break the silence.

"Can I let you in on a secret, Ruby?" His voice is hoarse now, and rough. I wonder who he's out with. And whether he's ditched them to speak to me.

"You can tell me anything you like," I whisper.

There's a brief pause when all I can hear are his footsteps. It sounds as though he's walking on gravel. The crunching sound fades away, and I can't hear the music at all anymore.

"I . . . don't want to take the company over at all."

If he were here, I'd be staring at him in amazement. As it is, my only option is to press my phone more firmly to my ear.

"To be honest, I don't even want to go to Oxford," he continues.

My heart is beating so hard, I can hear it thumping in my ears. "What do you want to do then?"

He inhales with a laugh. "That's the first time in ages anyone's asked me that."

"But it's such an important question."

"And I don't know how to answer it." For a moment he says nothing. "It's always been set in stone, you know? Never mind that Lydia would much rather take Beaufort's over or that she'd be much better at it too. She loves the company, but I'll be the one Dad will take onto the board next year. I've known it all my life, and I deal with it. But it isn't what I want." Another pause, then: "Doesn't look as though I'll ever get the chance to figure out what that is. I don't get to plan my own life, it's always been planned for me: Maxton Hall, Oxford, Beaufort's. That's all there is for me."

I grip my phone tighter, hold it to my ear, holding James as close to me as I can. That must be the most truthful thing I've ever heard him say. I can't believe he's trusted me with it. That he'll let me keep this secret for him.

"My parents have always told me that the world's my oyster. That it doesn't matter where I'm from or where I want to go. Mum and Dad have always said I can go my own way and that no dream is too big. I think everybody deserves a world full of possibilities."

He makes a quiet, desperate sound. "Some days . . ." he begins, then stops as if he doesn't know whether he's already said too much. But then he goes on, plucks up the courage for more honesty. "Some days I feel like it's crushing me so that I can't breathe."

"Oh, James," I whisper. My heart aches for him. I never realized all the pressure on him, that his family responsibilities are such a burden to him. He always gave the impression of enjoying the power his surname gives him. But bit by bit, the jigsaw pieces fit together in my head: the way he tenses at the mention of Oxford, his stoic expression when his parents turned up in London, the way his eyes darken whenever anyone talks about the firm.

Suddenly, I get it. I understand why he acted the way he did at the start of term. What his childish pranks and don't-give-a-shit pose are all about.

"This is your last year where you don't have any responsibilities," I murmur.

"It's my last chance to be free," he agrees quietly.

I wish I could contradict him, but I can't. No more than I can offer him a solution to his problems—there isn't one. An inheritance like that isn't the kind of thing where you can just sit down around a table with your parents and talk it over. Besides, I'm sure he's already weighed all the options. And if I'm right about James, he'll do what his parents demand anyway. He'd never let his family down.

"I wish I was with you." The words are out of my mouth before I can think about what they mean.

"What would you do if you were?" he replies. Suddenly, there's a whole new undertone to his voice. He no longer sounds despairing, he sounds . . . teasing. Like he's hoping for an indecent proposal.

"I'd give you a hug." Not so indecent, but heartfelt.

"I think I'd like that."

We've never hugged each other properly, and if we were face-to-face, I'd never dare say a thing like that. But now, with his dark voice in my ear and not having to look him in the eye, suddenly nothing feels impossible to me. I feel brave and sad and nervous and happy—all at once.

"Did you have a nice birthday?" James asks after a while.

"Yes," I reply, starting to tell him about my day, my presents, and that Lin and I won at charades this evening. James laughs at the right moments, clearly relieved at the change of subject. Then we talk about all kinds of things: how his weekend's been (crap), the English test he's got next week (hard but doable), our favorite singers and bands (Iron & Wine, me; Death Cab for Cutie, him), and films (*Rise of the Guardians*, me; *The Secret Life of Walter Mitty*, him). I learn so much about him. Such as his fondness for blogs, same as Ember. He tells me about a travel blog he's just discovered—he'd only intended to read one post on it but ended up going down a rabbit hole and missing a business meeting with his parents because he spent hours engrossed in the author's travels around the world and didn't notice the time. Which is me right now. Before I know it, it's three a.m., and I'm lying wide-awake on my bed, James's voice still in my ear. I stare at the folded lacrosse jumper on my bedside table.

And all I can think of is James.

Ruby

Mr. Lexington's steely gaze bores into me as I try to keep still and not squirm about in my chair. It never feels any less weird to sit in his office. His stance is the same as ever: hands loosely folded on the desk but looking at me with a razor-sharp air, as if he'd stop at nothing if it would benefit our school. I wouldn't want him as an enemy.

I doubt that I'll ever get used to this weekly meeting with him. Especially not when Lin leaves me in the lurch like she's done today because she's had to go to London to help her mum with a reception at the gallery.

But there's one upside to being alone in front of the head's desk right now, facing his eagle eyes. I got to make my suggestion without Lin eyeing me askance or kicking me under the table.

"Do I understand you correctly, Miss Bell?" Lexington asks, leaning a little closer. He furrows his brow at me. "You want me to lift Mr. Beaufort's punishment?"

I nod slowly. "Yes, sir."

He narrows his eyes further still. "Why should I share your opinion? It isn't even half-term yet."

"He's really put a lot of work in, sir," I say, "in a way I never expected. He has good ideas, and it's thanks to him that we've been able to raise the bar for Maxton Hall events with the Halloween party."

Lexington leans back, exhaling audibly.

The thought seems to please him. He reacts to anything that makes Maxton Hall look good like a magpie that's found a glittering jewel. I decide to go the extra mile. "I think James can serve the school better on the lacrosse team. They need him. Roger Cree is good, but he doesn't have as much experience. Mr. Freeman said so when we interviewed him for the Maxton blog on Friday."

Lexington's frown deepens. I can see that he's weighing up the pros and cons in his mind.

"And you're not just saying that because the boy is causing trouble, and you want to get rid of him?" he insists dubiously.

I wonder what Lexington would say if he knew that the opposite was true. I don't want to get rid of James. If I had the choice, I'd spend every moment of my time with him.

But after he confided in me and I realized what the upper sixth means to him, I couldn't help myself. I just had to speak to Mr. Lexington. It was the only thing I could think of that would genuinely help James and take a tiny bit of the weight off his shoulders—however briefly. I'm not just doing it as a favor to him though, but because it's true. James really has put the effort in, and that should be rewarded. At least this way he gets to spend the rest of the season playing lacrosse with his friends and enjoy the year.

I can't suppress the question of what this means for us though. We're friends now, aren't we? Or something like that. Will he spend time with me after this? Probably not. The thought makes something clench painfully in my chest, but I put all my strength into ignoring it. I'm doing this for James, not for me.

"Miss Bell?" Lexington's voice snaps me out of my thoughts, and it takes me a moment to remember what his question was.

I shake my head. "Not at all, sir. I'm just thinking about the good of the school. He's helped us, and now he should go back to helping his team. We can't afford another thumping like Friday if we want to defend our title."

Bull's-eye. Lexington's gray eyes flash, his shoulders suddenly tense.

"I see." He nods, and I find myself holding my breath. "Very well. Mr. Beaufort may end his work on the events committee and get back to playing lacrosse." Relief floods through me, and I start looking forward to how James will react when I tell him the news. I smile gratefully, but Lexington holds up a warning finger. "But not until next week, after the party. I'm not taking the risk of him coming up with some new way to embarrass the school."

My smile only slips slightly. "Of course, sir."

"And keep this to yourself for the time being." He picks up his telephone receiver, presses a button, and growls: "Ask Mr. Freeman to come to my office, would you?"

I sit uncertainly on my chair. I don't know whether I'm free to go or whether the head wants to discuss something else with me, but when he looks up, frowns, and waves vaguely with his hand, I take it as my cue to leave the room.

━━━━

I wasn't exaggerating when I told Lexie that we'd raised the bar with the Halloween party. Once the day finally dawns, we tick off the last few preparations; then, it's as though a huge boulder falls from my heart as the first guests start to arrive. The party is a success. More than that. It's beyond my wildest dreams.

Jessalyn's and Camille's decorations look amazing. They've hung fancy vintage picture frames in the entrance to Weston Hall—old family portraits and huge mirrors, lit up from all angles. There are black lace tablecloths and napkins on the buffet and the little tables around the edge of the dance floor. They have spanned thin cobwebs all around the room, plus dozens of chains of fairy lights—at least fifty—flickering with a candle effect. We decided not to use the chandelier, and there are large silver candlesticks on the tables and windowsills instead; they don't give much light, but that only adds to the ghostly, mysterious atmosphere.

The room is filling up now, and nearly all the tables are in use. Mr. Lexington is giving his official welcoming speech, watched by Lin, me, and the rest of the events team from the side of the buffet. He praises our organizational skills, at which Camille takes a step forward and waves to the audience like a queen. Lin and I look at each other, failing to suppress our grins.

I have to admit though that we all look like royalty today. I'm wearing the dress from the Beaufort archive, and Camille's apricot gown is perfect against her pale skin. Jessalyn's expansive dress is pale pink, while Lin's is the same shade of royal blue as the school colors. I wonder if that's deliberate. The boys look amazing too. Doug's simple sand-colored suit is cut like the one James is wearing on the poster. And Kieran . . . Kieran's top hat, black suit, jacquard waistcoat, and beige neckcloth make him look like he's genuinely from a different age.

The head teacher brings his thanks to a close and bows with a flourish of his top hat. I don't dare look at Lin this time—I'd be sure to burst out laughing.

I feel jittery. I don't know whether that's because everything's gone to plan so far and the party is going to be a success or because I'm scared of some unforeseen disaster. My eyes flit nervously around the room.

"He'll be here soon," Lin whispers in my ear.

"I have no idea what you mean," I retort, equally quietly.

That's a lie. I know exactly who she means.

There's no sign of James yet. His friends and Lydia aren't here either, although his parents are, as they're on the PTA. I'm painfully aware of his absence; although I don't want to let it distract me, it feels like an important part of the party is missing—after all, he worked as hard as the rest of us to make it a success.

Everyone claps after Lexington's speech, and we move apart to take up our positions. I join Lin and the caterers in keeping an eye on the buffet, watching as Jessalyn, Camille, Doug, and Kieran move onto the dance floor with some of the theater group. The music begins, and the five couples dance in formation, going through an array of steps that look incredibly complicated to me. I'm so glad they bought my argument that someone has to look out for the guests, meaning that I don't have to join in.

Kieran and a girl I don't know lead the other dancers across the floor, moving apart so that girls and boys line up opposite each other. They run past each other on the diagonal, circling around and meeting in the middle, face-to-face once more. All eyes in the room are on them, the guests watching the dance spellbound.

At that moment, the huge double doors to Weston Hall fly open. One by one, people turn to look, making Kieran and his partner pause in their dance for a moment. I frown at the door. My heart leaps.

James and his gang walk in, each smarter than the next. James is wearing the antique Beaufort suit, but the others have dressed extravagantly too—perfect down to every silk square, every button. Lydia is wearing a gorgeous silver silk dress, and her fantastic hairdo must have taken hours. They all look as though they've stepped out of a Victorian film. As they pass the dance floor and head for the buffet, you can see on their faces what they think of this party. Cyril turns up his nose, while Wren's flushed cheeks suggest that he's had a drink or two already. Kesh's black eyes flit unimpressed around the room and over the guests. At the sight of me, his expression darkens, and he puts more distance between himself and Alistair. It seems like a reflex action, which makes Alistair frown in annoyance.

James comes over to me, and I virtually drink in his appearance. I've seen him wearing that suit on hundreds of posters in the last few weeks, but, in the flesh, it takes my breath away—as it did that day in London. By the time he stops in front of me, my heart is pounding rapidly and unevenly.

"So? How's it going?" he asks, a mocking smile on his lips. He acts like he didn't just crash our party late.

"Brilliantly," Lin answers for me. Apparently, I spent a bit too long staring at James.

He nods. "That's good."

"Hope it's going to be better than the last one, or we're out of here," grumbles Cyril.

"Don't act like you're too good for our parties," Lin says through gritted teeth. I look at her in surprise.

"It's not an act."

His words make Lin's cheeks flush an angry red. "You really are—"

"Hey, peace, people." James's voice is quiet but firm. He glances at Cyril, at which he turns away from Lin and heads over to Wren, who is nearby, helping himself to a glass of punch.

One word from James, and a guy like Cyril Vega shuts up. Sometimes the power James has at this school freaks me out.

As if nothing ever happened, he turns to the buffet and takes an hors d'oeuvre. He lifts it to his nose and studies it carefully before popping it into his mouth. Once he's swallowed, he says to me: "Way better than last time."

I roll my eyes. "You suggested the caterers yourself."

He grins, then lets his eyes roam over me. I feel warm as I see his expression change and the mocking smile turn into something gentler, more honest—a smile that seems to be meant only for me. "You look beautiful."

Something flutters in my stomach, and I gulp hard. "You've seen me in this dress before."

"That doesn't change the fact that you look beautiful in it."

"Thank you. You look very handsome too." I smooth the dress, although there's nothing to smooth, and James suddenly faces me, bowing slightly, holding out his hand. I turn to his friends, but they seem more concerned with tipping booze from a flask into their glasses without being seen. Only Lydia is watching her brother, a peculiar expression in her eyes. I turn back to James.

"What are you doing?" I ask, cheeks burning.

"Would you do me the honor of dancing with me?"

I bite back a laugh. "There's a reason I didn't join in with the opening performance or any of the rehearsals, James. I can't dance. Or not like this."

"In Victorian times, it was considered very rude to turn down the offer of a dance, Ruby Bell."

"Then I must ask you to forgive me. Sadly, I have to keep an eye on the buffet."

James straightens up and takes two steps toward Lin. He whispers in her ear, making her laugh. Then she nods and shoos him away. James comes back to me, offering me his arm. "Lin says she'll take charge for a while."

I hesitate a moment longer but then take his arm. I glare over my shoulder at Lin, which she answers with an apologetic shrug, and James leads me toward the dance floor. I barely even noticed that since the first dance came to an end, it's been filling up with more and more couples in Victorian dress. Looking around now, I really could have gone back in time.

Quietly, the band strikes up a new tune, soft but rhythmical, which slowly fills the whole hall. James takes my hand in his and lays his other hand on my back. He leads me a few steps to the side, sways us forward and back, takes two steps back and one to the left, while I follow him, staring at our feet the whole time—or rather at the huge hem of the dress.

"Don't look down," he says quietly.

I raise my eyes with a heavy heart. James seems as though he's spent his life dancing at balls. Which might even be true. I wish I had gone to the rehearsals now, or at least watched a few online tutorials and practiced with Ember.

Suddenly, James lowers his head until his mouth is close to my ear. "Relax," he whispers.

Easier said than done. But I try. I try to ease the tension in my arms and not to focus so desperately on getting the steps right. I let myself fall—the way I imagined it the first time we tried on these costumes.

James catches me. He leads me gently over the floor, and I feel as if I'm floating. I wonder if I'll ever get the chance to dance like this again. What would happen if I told him that, as of now, he's not forced to take part in our meetings?

I don't want to, but I suddenly feel a weight on my chest. I try to ignore it, but it gets more crushing every time I think about what will happen between James and me after tonight.

"What's wrong?" he asks suddenly, narrowing his eyes as he checks out my face.

"I have to tell you something."

James's turquoise eyes are on me, expectant and patient, although there's a spark of suspicion in them too.

"I thought about what you told me on my birthday. That you only have one year of school left and then . . ." I clear my throat, feeling James suddenly tense. "Well, anyway, I spoke to Lexie. He thinks it's about time you got back to training."

His movements catch for a second, then he dances on as if he's learned the choreography by heart.

"What?" he croaks. His voice is hoarse. That's always what gives him away. His eyes stay hard, he stands up straight, moves confidently—but his voice doesn't play along. You can always tell if something has got to James. Like now.

"I think you've done a great job on the team. Lexie can definitely reward that." I'm trying to keep my voice calm, to relax the atmosphere between us, but the opposite happens. James's eyes darken, and the next moment he holds me tight—closer than would have been acceptable in Victorian times. But the dance floor is full, and everyone seems too preoccupied with themselves to take any notice of us. Of us and the fact that James's intense stare is taking my breath away.

His voice lightens again. "You . . ."

Suddenly, the fairy lights go out. All at once. A few musicians play wrong notes, the sound echoing around the hall. The only light now is from the candles.

"James, I swear to you, if this is one of your tricks—" I hiss.

"It's not," he interrupts. I can barely make out his face, but he seems as surprised as me. Then he swears quietly. "We need to get to the power. They can't play like this. And it'll kill the mood."

I nod, and James grips my hand tighter. We fight our way through the confused people on the dance floor, and I almost step on the hem of my dress. Once we get out into the corridor, I sigh with relief. James lets go of my hand as we take the stairs down to the cellar, and I grip onto the banister. I try not to think about why I instantly deeply miss the feeling of his warm skin. It's pitch-black down here. James pulls out his phone and switches on the flashlight to light the corridor.

"So cold," I murmur, rubbing my arms. "And spooky." I feel like a clown or a monster or a mutant mix of the two could jump out at us around a corner any second.

James doesn't reply, heads straight to a large box to the left-hand side.

"I ought to be worried by the fact that you know exactly where the fuse box is."

He gives an embarrassed smile and opens the box with the master key on his key ring, then steps aside so that we can both see in. Two fuses have blown, and as James trips the switches back up again, we hear the distant relieved cheers from upstairs. The next second, the neon lights turn on down here too with a quiet click. I sigh with relief. James shuts the fuse box again, and I turn on my heel. I can't get out of this cellar soon enough.

I gather up my skirts and climb the stairs. I'm almost at the top when James stops right behind me and says, "Wait." I turn and look inquiringly at him.

"Did you really think I'd do a thing like that again?" He sounds genuinely surprised, like he can't believe I'd suspect him.

But, to be honest . . . I did.

I don't know what there is between James and me. And even though we've got closer in the last few weeks, that doesn't mean I trust him. There's too much history for that, and I can still hear his warning, and Lydia's, clearly in my head. I promised Lin I'd be careful, and I'm sticking to that.

"For a millisecond, maybe," I admit in a small voice.

He stares hard at me. "I'd never pull a trick like that again, Ruby. Not now that I know how much work you put into these events and how much they mean to you."

It feels as though someone is pressing both their hands onto my rib cage, making it hard to breathe. "Sorry," I say quietly. "I think I was just scared. That it might be a repeat of the start of term."

James shakes his head. "No."

He comes up another step, and now our eyes are level. His face is so close to mine that I can see little blue flecks in his eyes and a dark ring around his iris.

I can't imagine what it'll be like when I don't see James in meetings every other day. Just the thought of it makes my throat constrict. Will he have any reason to spend time with me after that? He'll be training and have more time for his friends than he has done lately. Will he realize how much he's missed them? How much more fun he has spending his Saturday evenings drinking and partying instead of texting me about UK politics or my new favorite manga?

Will he notice how little our worlds fit together?

I've enjoyed these last few weeks so much, and I don't want to lose him. But I'm afraid I have no claim on him. We both know which world he'll choose in the end.

The pressure on my chest is growing more and more. Maybe it would be easier if I make the decision for him, before he gets the chance to hurt me.

"So this is our last job on the team together," I say, looking him straight in the eye. My heart is pounding wildly. If he comes closer, I'm sure he'll hear it.

"True," James replies quietly.

For a while, we just look at each other. Then we both breathe in as if to say something, but pause. The air between us is crackling, and my pulse is racing so fast that I can't bear it a second longer. I do the first thing that comes into my head. I hold out my hand to James.

"It's been really nice working with you," I say, as formally as possible.

At first, James looks surprised. Then his turquoise eyes fill with an emotion I've seen before but couldn't place. Now I know what it is: yearning.

He takes my hand and holds it gently but firmly. "That sounds as though you're saying goodbye to me."

At the moment I hear those words, I understand that he's right. And yet I realize that it's the last thing I want. I don't want to say goodbye to him. I want to hold on to the chance to talk to James. To tell him more about me and to listen when he confides in me.

I want to know everything about you.

The thought overwhelms me suddenly, and the same yearning I can see in his eyes fills my stomach. It's burning hot, downright desperate, flows through my veins, and makes my fingers grip his more tightly. I don't know what's happening, but . . . my knees feel weak, and his hand is so warm in mine. I wonder what it would feel like on other parts of my body. I want more than just this touch. More of *him*.

"James . . ."

"Yes," he murmurs again. He sounds just as confused, as breathless as me.

The next second, he pulls me so that I fall into him.

He looks me in the eyes for a split second. Then he takes the back of my neck in his hand and holds it fast.

The next moment, he presses his lips onto mine.

I can't think. My head switches off, there are no more rational thoughts, only the glowing heat flooding my body. I wrap both arms around his neck and bury my hands in his hair. He starts to move his mouth against mine.

James kisses the way he moves and acts: proud and self-assured. He knows exactly what to do, knows exactly how to touch me to fan the heat into flames. He presses his tongue into my mouth without hesitation and without any shyness and plays with mine until I feel like my knees might give way any moment. But even if they did, he'd be there to catch me. His arm is tight around me, and he's holding me close. I can feel his body through the weighty fabric of my dress, but it's not enough. I need more.

I groan quietly and let my hands slide to his shoulders, then back to his throat and the front of his collar. His skin is warm and velvety, and everything within me shouts more, more, *more*.

I want more of him. To undress him, here on this staircase, in the middle of the school. I wouldn't care if anyone came along and caught us. All that matters to me is James, his mouth on my lips, my jaw, my throat. He takes my skin between his teeth, pinches slightly, but I wish he'd bite harder. I want him to leave marks on my body, so that in a few hours I'll be able to see that this really happened, that it wasn't my imagination.

"Ruby . . ." I thought I knew every color of his voice. But this is new. That's what he sounds like once he's kissed me out of my mind. He takes my face and looks at me. His thumbs run over my cheeks. My jaw. My lips. My cheeks again. "Ruby."

I lean forward and lay my mouth on his. A painful ache tugs at my belly and works its way up until it's hard to breathe. Now I understand why he keeps whispering my name. I want to do the same. James, *James*. Always James.

"James." A commanding voice speaks above us.

We spring apart. I step on the hem of my skirt and lose my balance, but James reaches out and grabs my waist. He waits until I'm holding safely onto the banister again. Then he lets go of me at once and looks up. I follow his gaze.

Mortimer Beaufort is standing at the top of the stairs, hands linked behind his back, watching us with dark eyes. My heart pounds.

"Your mother is looking for you."

James stretches his back and nods briefly. "I'll be there in a minute."

Mr. Beaufort raises an eyebrow slightly. "She wants you now, not in a minute."

James stiffens. I hold out my hand and gently stroke his arm in the hope that his father can't see us. James takes my hand in his and looks at our intertwined fingers. I hear him sigh quietly. Then he lifts my hand to his lips and presses a soft kiss onto it.

"I'm sorry," he whispers, and I can feel the words on my wrist. The next moment, he pushes carefully past me and goes up the stairs toward his father, who is waiting for him with stiff shoulders and eyes like ice. When James reaches him, he grabs him by the shoulder and steers him back into the hall while I stand on the steps, feeling my burning cheeks and wondering exactly what he was apologizing for.

James

"I told you to stay away from that girl."

I stare out of the window. The dark fields blur into one with the trees, almost completely bare now, a single, dark mass. Which is pretty much how my insides feel too, at this moment. I'm hot and cold all at once, the palms of my hands are clammy, and my throat is dry. I feel sick when the opposite ought to be true.

I wish I could be back with Ruby, her beautiful lips and the feeling she gave me. In my mind, she's still in my arms; I'm enjoying her burying her hands in my hair and gently biting my lips.

If we hadn't been interrupted, I'd have done much more than just kiss her.

"I'm speaking to you," my father repeats. I feel sure that he's about to throw his glass across the car. Telling Percy I'd go home with my parents was the stupidest idea I've had in a long time.

"James, darling, we only want the best for you," my mother adds more diplomatically. I can't look at either of them. If I did, the rage would boil over inside me, and I don't know if I'd be able to tune out after that.

Why did this have to happen today, of all days? Why did Dad have to catch me with Ruby at exactly that moment?

"A scholarship girl from a working-class background with a tragic family history is not quite what we had in mind for you," Mum continues. I yank my head around to stare at her. I want to ask her how the hell she knows so much about Ruby, but it doesn't actually surprise me. Nothing about my family surprises me anymore.

"You can do better than that, darling. Someone like Elaine Ellington, maybe. I hear that you two get on well—why not invite her to the house one of these days?" My mother's voice is calm and soothing. I know she wants to patch up the mood between Dad and me, but it's way too late for that.

"There will never be anything between Elaine and me, Mum." Besides that, I'm pretty sure she's dropped out of uni and is desperate to hide that fact. Being from a blue-blooded family doesn't make her a better person than Ruby. Ruby works harder than anyone to get what she wants. She's intelligent, good-hearted, and . . . gorgeous. A great kisser. And an even better listener.

Instantly, the image of her pops up in my head again. Remembering her mouth is the only thing getting me through this drive. I wish we'd had more time. The few minutes with her were definitely not enough.

"Don't embarrass the family by getting involved with a little gold digger like that," my father continues. "I find your behavior distasteful. We brought you up better than that."

Despite my best efforts, I can't ignore him any longer. Not when he talks about Ruby like that. Seething rage bubbles over inside me, and my eyes are filled with fury as I turn on him. "Shut it."

My mother gasps in outrage; beside me, Lydia stiffens. She reaches for my hand, but I snatch it away. She gets to sleep with her teacher, but I'm not even allowed to spend time with someone I like without a lecture?

The car stops, and we undo our seat belts. I wait for Lydia and Mum to get out, then I follow them. My father is close behind me, and before I've even taken two steps, he takes my shoulder and pulls me back, turning me to face him. He grabs my collar and shakes me.

"How dare you speak to me like that?" he growls, pushing me away so hard that I stumble back. The next moment, he lashes out, slapping my face with the back of his hand. Pain shoots through my cheek, and for a second, all I can see are the bright dots dancing in front of my eyes. A metallic taste spreads through my mouth.

"For God's sake, Dad!" Lydia cries, running to me. She puts an arm around my back and holds me tight before I can do anything so stupid as to hit back. I'd love that so much—just to hit back. To cause him the same pain that he's caused me since I was a kid.

Mum takes Dad by the arm. He tears himself away from her, turns, and stomps into the house. Once he's gone, she looks sorrowfully at me. "This is what comes of spending time with the wrong sort of people, James." Then she lifts her huge skirts to hurry after my father. I watch them walk away and try to suppress the rage that is slowly but surely developing into a hatred that I don't want to feel. I wipe my mouth with the back of my hand and then study the blood on my skin as if it belonged to someone else.

Lydia stands in front of me and takes me by the shoulders. "Is she really worth the stress, James?" she asks urgently.

I look at her, way too worked up to really think about her question. "Mind your own shit," I growl, pulling away from her hands. I turn tail and walk across the courtyard back to the main gates. As I go, I dig my phone out of my pocket and dial Wren's number.

I'm in urgent need of a distraction.

═══

It takes three drinks before the anger starts to ebb away. I'm leaning against the wall in Wren's parents' sitting room, drinking whisky from a crystal glass and allowing the thumping music to gradually numb my thoughts.

"Well, look at that. The prodigal returns." Cyril's voice sounds behind me. I turn and face him as he walks toward me, arms outstretched, a mocking grin on his face.

"To what do we owe the honor?" he continues. He's about to say something else, but then he sees my mouth and whistles through his teeth instead. "That looks bad, mate."

I don't answer, just down the rest of my drink. I can hold my booze, but my cheeks already feel numb.

"Leave him alone, Cy," Wren calls from the sofa. There's a blond girl snuggled up with him, running her hand up and down his thigh. She looks familiar, and when she lifts her head from her shoulder, I see why. Camille. Last I knew, she was with Kesh, not Wren, but these things change quite frequently.

"What's wrong with you, Beaufort?" Cyril asks again, putting an arm around my shoulders and steering me onto another sofa. I let myself fall onto it and rub my sore face while Cyril pours another glass for me and holds it out. "The James I grew up with doesn't let anyone push him around. He doesn't get suspended from the team, and he won't do anyone's dirty work for them."

Cyril calling everything I've done with the events team in the last few weeks "dirty work" makes new rage build up inside me, but I restrain myself. He is what he is, and I've had enough stress this evening already. All I want is to get drunk, to drink until I can't feel a thing. Not Dad's hand and not Ruby's lips either. "I had no choice. You know that."

"Bullshit," says Wren. His eyes flicker with amusement. "Ruby just makes you horny."

I don't answer, just take a sip and close my eyes. Whatever Cyril's mixed me, it's strong enough to burn its way down my throat to my stomach.

"Are you serious? You put up with all that shit because you're into Ruby Bell?" Cyril asks in surprise.

"That's why he's changed." Wren's not looking at me as he says that, but at Camille, whose hair he's stroking pensively.

"He's been sucking right up to her. You should have seen him at the last few meetings," she puts in. She looks sympathetically at me. "Or did you just do that so you could get back to lacrosse quicker?"

Glass halfway to my lips, I pause. "Where did you hear that?"

"Ruby told us before the party."

I frown and look at Wren, who is still stroking Camille's hair. Is that why he brought her home this evening? So he could question her about me?

"I haven't changed." My tongue feels heavy as I say that, and the words are hushed and slurred.

"Yes, you have." Alistair drops onto the sofa to my left. His golden hair is a mess, and his cheeks are flushed. Either he's had a few already, or he left the party with some guy, and he's come straight from Wren's spare bedroom.

"How have I changed, if you please?" I ask, deliberately calmly, trying to kid myself that I don't care what they think of me.

Alistair lifts a hand and ticks the points off on his fingers. "One, you don't party with us anymore, or if you do you leave before dawn, which the old James Beaufort would never have done. Two, you're happy to spend your free time with the geeks on the events team—nothing personal, Camille." She sticks her middle finger up at him. "Three, you suddenly don't give a fuck about our deal."

"I didn't come here to listen to this bullshit."

Alistair raises an eyebrow. "It's not bullshit, and you know it."

"Alistair's right. We want to enjoy our last year of school and really live it up," Wren says. "That was the deal. Carpe fucking diem, mate. Every day, so long as we're together. The sad part is that somewhere along the way, you seem to have lost the James who got every party started."

I lean back and take another swig, although it burns. The truth of his words gets through to me, and my stomach knots.

They're right.

The plan was to make the upper sixth the best year of my life and enjoy the time with my mates. The lads who've been a second family to me. The plan was not to develop feelings for someone I can have no future with.

I can still taste Ruby on my lips and feel her hands on my body. Unfortunately, all that means is that I'm still way too sober.

Ruby gave me a feeling I've never known before. Which is that, with her at my side, everything is possible. A beautiful, ugly lie. Because the truth is that, for me, nothing is possible. Unlike her, the world is not my oyster. The course of my life is preset.

Maybe that was exactly what attracted me to Ruby in the first place. She takes her life in her own hands while I'm just a puppet, pulled this way and that. She can live while I just exist.

We don't fit together.

I only wish I'd realized that before I kissed her.

23

Ruby

How do you speak to someone after you've made out?

The only other boy I'd kissed before James was Wren, and I just ignored him, acted like it never happened. That's not an option with James. I spend most of Sunday lying on my bed and staring at his hoodie, which is still on my desk. I'd like to message him, or call him, but I don't know what to say—apart from *Can we do that again, please?* and *What does this mean for us?*—and I'm too scared. Besides which, he and his parents disappeared so abruptly that I didn't even get a chance to say goodbye.

In the end, my musings get so much on my own nerves that I decide to start working on our post-party jobs to take my mind off them. Apart from the brief power outage at the start, everything went to plan, and I had an email from Mr. Lexington in my inbox this morning, praising our team for all their hard work. I forward it on to everyone with my own warm words. Then I pick up one of the books my grandparents gave me and read the first few chapters. Marking key passages and sticking in colorful Post-its has always helped me clear my head. As I take notes, I'm filling my brain with information and trying to chase away the memories of James's firm grip on the back of my neck, and his lips on mine.

I can't help wondering how many girls he must have kissed to be that good at it.

I can't help wondering how far we would have gone if his dad hadn't interrupted us.

I can't help wondering if I'll ever get the chance to kiss him like that again.

OK, so maybe the book isn't doing as much to push out the memory as I hoped. But I won't let James mess with my head. And I certainly won't let him drive me out of my mind. That's my own and it isn't going anywhere just because James has released a few butterflies in my stomach.

This afternoon, I read almost half the book, which is kind of extreme. By the evening, I'm so tired that I fall into bed half dead. Unfortunately, all I dream of is James, his dark eyes and his hoarse voice whispering my name, over and over and over again.

━━━━

The next morning feels like my first day of school. I'm nervous and jittery, and my stomach somersaults as the bus pulls up at the stop. I'm wondering what it'll be like to see James again. Will he come over to me? Or should I go to him? Is that too blatant? Will we act like nothing ever happened? Or have we been considerably more than just friends since Saturday? The thoughts whirl in my head, and I'm annoyed with myself for not having just rung him yesterday. Then at least I'd know where we stand and how I should act. I hate being so unsure of myself.

Once I've got off the bus, I pay particular attention to straightening out my school uniform. I don't want a single pleat out of place; my tie has to be straight. I'm carrying the bag James gave me over my shoulder. The weight of it gives me a strange sense of security. Like it's confirmation that there really is something between James and me. I run my fingers over the initials on the flap as I look up at the huge iron gates to Maxton Hall.

I can do this. Just act normal. Nothing has changed, I reassure myself in my thoughts, then I stand up straight and walk into the school grounds.

There's no sign of James in assembly. His friends are sitting on the back row, and as I walk past them, I hear Cyril snort. I don't know if it's aimed at me, but it makes me feel queasy all the same. I turn round and he gives me a cold stare. I ignore him.

My day starts with history, and however hard I try, I just can't focus. All I can think of is that after this, I have maths in the room that James is sitting in now. We often bump into each other in the corridor because Mrs. Wakefield practically always runs late.

When the bell rings, I try not to stand up too quickly but, judging by the look Alistair gives me from across the room, without much success. I walk toward the main building. The closer I get to the classroom, the faster my heart beats. Just before I have to turn into the corridor, I stop to adjust my black over-knee socks so that they're exactly level. Then I take a deep breath and turn the corner.

In my mind, I'm prepared to meet James, but the sight of him next to Lydia in the hallway still makes my heart skip for a moment. He looks strange yet familiar in uniform. After a short pause, while I try to settle my pulse, I walk on. I can just say hi to them. Just hello, nothing more. There's nothing weird about that. I really don't want things to get weird. I just need to look into his eyes to know what's what. Will I see the same nervousness in them that tormented me all Sunday?

Lydia sees me first. She gives James an almost imperceptible nudge with her arm. He mumbles a few words and nods to her. Then he walks over to me. My smile turns of its own accord into a grin. He's only a few steps away, and I open my mouth to greet him when . . .

. . . he walks past me.

"Hey," I hear him say behind me. I turn and see that he's speaking to Cyril. They have a brief chat, James makes hand gestures, and Cyril laughs. Then the two of them walk the few feet to their classroom and go in without a backward glance.

Intense pain spreads through my rib cage. I freeze, rooted to the spot, right there in the middle of the corridor. I swallow. When I look up, the only other person still in sight is Lydia. For a moment, it looks as though she wants to say something, but then she too turns on her heel and disappears without a word into another classroom. Meanwhile, I can't even put one foot in front of another. It's simply impossible to move.

———

I spend the rest of the day in a daze. Every lesson seems longer than the last. I hear the words our teachers say but don't understand them, don't take a single thing in. I can't even manage to walk into the dining hall at lunchtime. The mere thought of seeing James there with his friends, firmly anchored back in his own world, turns my stomach. Instead, I sit in the library and stare out of the window.

I just don't know what I've done wrong. I can't explain why

he'd act like that. I'm racking my brain over it, but I don't think I made a mistake. And even if I did, I didn't deserve to be treated that way. I spend the whole of maths trying to kid myself that he simply hadn't seen me. But we bumped into each other in the hall after class, and he walked straight past me without even looking at me. An unmistakable signal.

Of course, Lin notices that something's wrong, but I never even told her about the kiss, and there's no way I can do that now. It feels like there's a gaping wound in my chest. Everything hurts—breathing, moving, speaking.

Lin has to take charge of the team meeting on her own as I just sit beside her, doodling in my planner. I see the place where I erased James's name. Nobody but me knows what's under that white mark, but I run my finger over it and swallow hard.

I didn't imagine our kiss. The way James said my name. The way he looked at me. The desperate way he touched me. There was something between us. Something huge. And even if he's decided, for whatever reason, that the whole thing was a mistake, he could have just told me that today. I'm a rational human being and know that sometimes there are things that simply can't work out. That would have hurt too, but I could have lived with that.

The thing I can't deal with is him acting so horribly. The longer I sit here in this meeting, staring at his empty place, the angrier I feel. Was it all just a game for him? Did he want to see how far he could take me? Maybe it was just a dare from his mates. Or he wanted to wrap me round his little finger so that I'd put in a good word for him with Lexington. The mere thought makes me sick. Was everything I've learned about him in the last few weeks a big, fat lie? Was he actually the James Beaufort I knew first of all the whole time? Calculating, sly, and arrogant?

I look out of the window and see, at a distance, the lacrosse team on the playing field. My rage shoots through the roof. It eats away at me from inside out, and my skin feels hot and cold all at once. Unconsciously, I'm grinding my teeth so hard that they squeak. It's a massive effort not to show the muddled emotions washing around inside me during the meeting. Once it's over, I turn to Lin.

"Do you mind if I go home? I don't feel well."

She looks thoughtfully at me and then nods slowly. "Of course not. I'll look after everything here. I'll give you a call later, if you like." It sounds like a cautious offer, and I squeeze her shoulder gratefully.

I leave the room without saying goodbye to the others. Suddenly, the bag over my shoulder feels less like a gift from a friend and more like a bribe. All I can focus on, as I stamp through the library and head out toward the sports grounds, are my disappointment and anger.

I can hear the shouts and yells from miles away. Bloody lacrosse.

I stop abruptly on the edge of the field, looking around, arms crossed. It doesn't take me long to spot the royal blue shirt with the white seventeen on it.

"Beaufort, your girlfriend's here," Wren yells out, barely a second later. I can't see his grin through his helmet, but I can clearly hear it in his voice.

James turns and sees me standing at the sideline. I'm almost expecting him to ghost me again, but then he waves a hand.

"Carry on," he calls, then jogs over to me. Now he looks at me for the first time today—or I think he does. I can't really tell because of the helmet.

"So." My voice is trembling with rage. I don't know myself. I'm always calm, never this churned up, never out of control. Since when do I act like this? Since when can't I take a rational approach to things, like I used to?

Since James came into my life. That's the answer. I've only been like this since I've known him.

He doesn't speak. I wait for him to show any kind of reaction, but he doesn't.

"Could you take that thing off maybe?" I ask, pointing to his helmet.

He sighs with annoyance but does as I request. His hair is sweaty and messed up, his cheeks are red. Now that he's standing in front of me, I can see that his mouth is wounded. He looks like he's been in a fight. Cautiously, I lift my hand—it happens entirely on autopilot—to touch him, but he flinches back. I clench my fist, then drop my hand again, discouraged.

"What's wrong with you?" I ask, angrily.

His face is entirely emotionless as he looks at me. "Why would anything be wrong?"

I'm sure my cheeks are just as red as his, but only because he makes me absolutely furious. "You're acting like an arsehole, that's what's wrong."

His eyebrows contract, low over his eyes. "Am I?"

"Stop being such an idiot and tell me why you're ignoring me," I insist, more quietly but no less firmly.

He still doesn't speak, just looks at me as though this conversation is boring him to death. I take a step toward him.

"Was this all part of your plan?" I ask him. "Were you just so nice to me so that you could get back to training?"

He gives a snort that sounds almost like a laugh, but suddenly, he can't meet my eyes. Instead, he stares at the ground, at the spot where our toes are almost touching.

"In case I have to remind you, you kissed me *after* I let you off the events team. So by that point, it really wasn't necessary."

He still isn't replying.

"Why are you acting like this?" I ask him, hating myself for the way my voice is shaking. "Is it because of your dad? Did he do something?"

James looks up, and now my anger seems to be reflected in his eyes. "If it makes you feel any better, feel free to think that."

It feels like he's thumped me in the chest. "*You* kissed *me*. Not the other way around. You didn't need to do that if you were going to be this ashamed of it afterward."

The frown deepens on his forehead. "Don't read so much into it. You gave me something, I was pleased. End of conversation."

"You were pleased—end of conversation?" I repeat in disbelief. It's hard to accept that the boy standing in front of me now is the same one who kissed me on the stairs on Saturday. That it was his tongue that parted my lips, his touch that made me go weak at the knees.

Now he simply shrugs his shoulders.

"For God's sake, James, what's wrong with you?" I mutter, shaking my head.

Despite my anger, I can't help wondering what happened to his mouth. Who he was fighting. Whether there was any way I could have stopped it.

"You could have just told me that the kiss was a mistake," I say, as calmly as possible.

"Fine, then I'll tell you that now," he replies coolly. "We had a nice time, but now things need to get back to the old days."

I can't believe he actually just said that. I feel like I don't know the script anymore. Something is really wrong here, but I can't stop it going off track. It feels like an unstoppable avalanche, sweeping away everything in its path.

"You don't have to destroy our friendship in this mean way just because your friends said something or your parents are guilt-tripping you, you know?"

He smiles, but it's more of a grimace, nothing like the way he's looked at me in recent weeks. I barely recognize him. "It's like you're obsessed with controlling everything around you, correcting every mistake you find in other people—but it doesn't work like that, Ruby. This has nothing to do with my friends or my family. This is me." He lays the palm of his hand on his chest protector. "Horrible and twisted and wrong. It's time you faced up to that idea."

The anger fades away and despair takes its place. It's the same feeling that washed over me at the party when I imagined having to say goodbye to him. But it's deeper this time, and much more painful. Because he's saying goodbye to me, and it seems final.

I give it one last try, lifting my hand and laying it on his cheek. I stroke his skin gently with my thumb. "You are not horrible or twisted or wrong."

He gives a bitter laugh and shakes his head.

"I don't want to lose you," I whisper, plucking up every last ounce of courage I can find inside me.

He puts his hand on top of mine on his cheek. He shuts his eyes, and it almost looks as though this moment is causing him physical pain. His fingers gently stroke the back of my hand, and the tingle spreads through me. "You can't lose a thing that isn't yours in the first place, Ruby Bell."

He pulls my hand from his face. Then he opens his eyes again and looks at me. It's the way he used to look two months ago—cold and distant. Suddenly, I feel hollowed out. Icy cold floods through me as the meaning of his words hits home.

"Beaufort!" Wren calls across the field. "You're missing your first training session in weeks. Come on, man!"

He wants to turn around; I can see it in the way his body tenses. It's as though there's an invisible wire linking him to his friends.

"Are we done here? The boys are waiting," he says emotionlessly, gesturing with his thumb over his shoulder.

I've never felt so humiliated in my life. Adrenaline pumps through my body, mingled with pain, despair, and rage. I have to clench my fists to stop myself from shoving him in the chest. I want to, more than anything, but when he's this cold and distant, I'm not giving him the satisfaction of losing it in front of his friends.

"Yes. We're done," I say, with as much dignity as I can muster.

James takes no interest in my words. He turns away before I've finished speaking and runs back to the team. My pride dwindles with every step he takes until I can barely stand upright.

24

Ruby

Green—*Important!*

   Turquoise—*School*

   Pink—*Maxton Hall Events Committee*

   Purple—*Family*

   Orange—*Diet and Exercise*

If I divided my afternoon up by colors, it would look like this:

Purple—*Cry my eyes out with Ember*

Purple—*Cry my eyes out with Mum*

Purple—*Avoid Dad so he can't ask me too many questions*

Orange—*Go for a run with Ember to clear my head*

Green—*Give James Beaufort the bag back and inform him exactly how far he can take a jump off a cliff*

A good list, in my opinion. And if it actually existed, I'd already have ticked off every item except the last.

I spent an hour with my hair in a towel, trying to write him a letter. Now I'm still sitting here surrounded by crumpled sheets of paper as I decide to call it a day. I wanted to write something that expressed my anger and disappointment, but on paper, the words suddenly seemed totally irrational. I wish I'd said all this to him on the sports field, but at the time, I was too shocked to have a ready reply.

Pinned to my noticeboard in front of me is the card James sent me for my birthday. The words meant so much to me back then. I genuinely believed he meant them. Now it feels as though I imagined everything that happened between us. Like all the phone calls, the times we laughed together, our kiss, all of it, were just figments of my imagination.

Suddenly, I can't look at the card a moment longer. I snatch it off the pinboard, pick up a black pen, and write the first and most meaningful words that come to mind:

James,
Fuck you.
Ruby

I tilt my head to one side and study my handiwork. I wrote the words directly beneath his, and it hurts to see them and to realize that we've actually reached this point.

"Ruby?" Ember pokes her head around my door. "Dad's cooked dinner. Coming?"

I nod, unable to take my eyes off the card.

Ember walks in and looks over my shoulder. She sighs and strokes my arm. Then, without another word, she fetches the box from behind the door and helps me to stow the bag away in it again. My heart bleeds as I put the card on top and tape the box up.

"I can take it to the post office on my way to school tomorrow," she says quietly.

There's a lump in my throat, getting bigger by the second. "Thanks," I croak as Ember takes me in her arms.

My sister takes the parcel into her room so that I don't have to look at it. I'm grateful to her for not mentioning James's jumper, even though I clearly saw her eyes rest on it for a moment. I didn't have the heart to pack it away in the box too. And I refuse to think about what that means.

After dinner, I lie on my bed and stare at the ceiling. I'm giving myself this one evening and night to mourn for what there was between James and me. To grieve for the friend I've lost without knowing why.

But no longer than that. I'm still me, and I've sworn to myself that I won't let anything or anyone get in my way. As of tomorrow, everything will be back to normal, the way it's been these last two years. I'll concentrate on school and go to events meetings. I'll have lunch in the dining hall with Lin. I'll prepare for the Oxford interviews.

I'll go back to living in a world where James Beaufort, like the rest of Maxton Hall, doesn't even know my name.

James

Ruby is scarily good at avoiding me. It's like she's memorized my timetable by heart so that she doesn't bump into me anywhere. When our paths cross, she walks firmly past me without deigning to look at me, both hands gripping the straps of her green backpack. Every time I see her, I remember her card, which is folded up in my wallet, and which I sometimes pull out when my yearning for Ruby is too strong.

Like now, for example.

When will this finally stop? When will I be able to think about anything apart from Ruby? Especially seeing that this is about the worst possible time to be distracted. The Thinking Skills Assessment is on Thursday, and if I'm going to stand the slightest chance, I need to really shine.

Unfortunately, I can't remember a single one of the things Lydia and I have been talking about in the last half hour. We printed out every practice exercise we could find, spread them out in her room, and worked through them one by one, until there was smoke coming out of our ears. Lydia shuts the book she was scanning for an answer and props herself up on her elbows. She's lying on her stomach, knees bent, and she's kicking her feet in time with the music that's playing quietly in the background. When she holds out her hand, I silently pass her the bag of crisps we've been helping ourselves from this last hour.

Then I run my fingers around the edge of Ruby's card, yet again. It's lost its edge now; the corners are crumpled. I'm about to put it away again when Lydia commando crawls a little way toward me.

"What's that?" she asks, suddenly, grabbing the card faster than I can react. I want to snatch it back, but Lydia's unfolded it and is reading my words, and Ruby's. Her eyes darken, and when she looks up, I can see sympathy in them. "James . . ."

I snatch the card from her hand and slip it back in my wallet, which I then slide into my trouser pocket. After that, I reopen the book that Lydia had finished with and start to read. The letters make no sense, however hard I focus.

Why the fuck is my heart racing like this? And why do I feel like I just got caught?

"James."

I look up from the book. "What?"

Lydia sits up, cross-legged, and starts to wind her hair up into a messy bun, which she then holds in place with a hair elastic. "What's that card all about?"

I shrug my shoulders. "Nothing."

Lydia raises one eyebrow and glances eloquently at the pocket into which the wallet, card and all, just disappeared. Then she looks at me again, more warmly this time. "What happened between you and Ruby?"

My shoulders tense. "I have no idea what you're talking about."

Lydia snorts quietly and shakes her head. "I know exactly how you're feeling," she says after a few moments of awkward silence. "You don't have to act unbothered by the thing with Ruby around me. I've got eyes in my head, James. I know when you're feeling shit."

I stare at the book again. Lydia's right. I'm miserable. My entire life is a disaster, and there's nothing I can do about it.

"The one thing bothering me," I say, "is this fucking family, and the fact that I can't face my own future."

I feel Lydia's empathetic eyes on me, but I can't look at her. I'm afraid that if I do, I'll lose my last ounce of self-control, and I can't allow that to happen. Not in this house, where my father's eyes and ears are everywhere, and where I've never felt truly safe.

"Ruby isn't doing well either. Why . . ."

"I was only keeping an eye on Ruby for *your* sake," I interrupt her. "That's all there is to it." The words scratch in my throat and feel so wrong as I say them. I can't breathe, and Lydia is watching me so intently that the weight on my chest is getting heavier by the second. The unfamiliar sting in my eyes makes me blink and swallow hard.

"Oh, James," she whispers, taking my cold hand and rubbing her thumb over the back of it. I can't remember the last time we held hands like this. I watch her pale fingers for a while, as they wrap around mine. Somehow, this simple gesture of hers has helped me breathe a bit more easily.

"I know what it's like when you can't have a person, even though you know they're the only thing that would make this life more bearable," Lydia says out of the blue, squeezing my hand. "When I met Graham, I knew at once that we had something special."

Suddenly, I look up. Lydia returns my gaze calmly. She's never spoken to me about the business with Sutton before, and every time I've tried to get her to talk, she's vehemently shut me down. The fact that she's doing it now shows me how crap I am at hiding my desperation from her, and how sorry she must feel for me. Even so, I'm glad she's changed the subject.

"How did you even meet? Was it at school?"

She shakes her head. For a moment, it looks like she's hunting for the right words. I can see what an effort it is for her to tell this story. After all, it's a secret she's been keeping for ages.

"It was over two years ago, just after I broke up with Gregg," Lydia begins, and the hot rage immediately fires up my stomach. Gregg Fletcher spent months posing as Lydia's boyfriend when he was actually a hack on a national newspaper. He used Lydia and broke her heart just to get the gossip on our family and the firm.

I squeeze her hand back. "I was so tired then," she continues. "Of . . . everything. I was like a zombie."

"I remember." After Fletcher's tell-all story, the press was on us like hyenas. It was a difficult time, and we all had to find our own ways of dealing with it. Mine were doing coke and getting drunk, hers were a deathly silence and a wall that nobody could break down.

"One evening, I was just desperate. I had nobody to talk to, but

I really needed someone. I was fifteen years old, and I'd fallen into a relationship with a journalist because I was naïve enough to believe that there might be someone out there who was actually interested in *me*. Not just Beaufort's. I was in a bad way. I was beating myself up, asking how I could have been so stupid."

She pauses for a moment and takes a deep breath.

"That evening, I set up an anonymous profile on Tumblr. I just wanted to let everything out, without consequences. My first post was just a pile of messed-up words. I just wrote out how I felt and that I wished I could be a completely different person. A day later, I got a really sweet message."

I stare at her. "From Sutton?"

She nods. "It wasn't much, just kind words, sympathy, but right then, they meant the world to me." A slight smile plays around her lips. "After that, we started messaging each other regularly. We talked about all kinds of stuff; told each other things we'd never told anyone else. He wrote to me about Oxford and the competitive atmosphere, the pressure that was starting to get to him. I told him about my broken heart and my fears for the future. We gave each other hope. I never gave him my real name, obviously, and I didn't know his either. But the things I shared with him felt more real than anything else in my life."

"That's insane."

She nods again. "I know."

"Then what?" I ask.

"Six months later, we talked for the first time. On the phone. For five hours. My ear hurt all night because I'd pressed it to the phone so hard. After that, we kept on calling."

I remember the night of Ruby's birthday and the eternity we'd talked for. I left Wren's party and came home just so I could keep listening to her voice.

"So that's why you kept chucking me out of your room," I say with a grin. "And eventually you met in person?"

"It was over a year until I dared meet up with Graham. We went for coffee once he'd finished his degree."

"And when did you . . . get together?" I ask, realizing as I say it that I sound like I'm in year seven.

Lydia flushes. "We were never really a couple, but we spent a lot of the summer holidays together." She clears her throat. "When Graham got a training post at Maxton Hall, he broke up with me. Right away. He said we could still be friends online, but no more than that." Her eyes start to glitter suspiciously. "I was OK with that, you know? Better than losing him completely. At the end of the school year, his placement was coming to an end, so I started to hope again. But we were back to square one in the middle of the summer when he got a permanent job there after all. The same heartache as before. But this time he didn't even want to message me. He cut me right out of his life because he said that was better for both of us."

I think for a moment about everything she's just told me. "So what happened at the start of term?" I ask. "The day Ruby saw you together?"

She gulps. "Some kind of slipup."

I nod slowly. I knew Sutton meant more to Lydia than just a nice way to pass the time. She'd been too upset in the last few weeks and leaped to his defense too quickly if I made any remark about him. But I'd had no idea that they'd known each other for two years. Or that it had been that serious.

"Just one more year, then maybe you could . . ." I don't even know what I'm trying to suggest. Even once Lydia's left Maxton Hall, a relationship with her ex-teacher would shatter her reputation forever. I can just imagine what our parents would say to that.

"I'm not stupid, James. I know that Graham and I have no chance." She pulls her hand away and reaches for the crisps as if she hadn't just confessed her deepest secret to me. She shoves a handful into her mouth, eyes fixed on her duvet case.

It hurts to see her like this. And it hurts even more that I can't help her. Because she's right. There's no future for her and Sutton, any more than there is for Ruby and me.

"Thank you for telling me," I say in the end.

Lydia swallows the crisps and takes a big swig from her water bottle. "Maybe one day you can tell me about Ruby."

The pressure on my chest, which had slowly faded as she spoke, is suddenly back. I ignore Lydia's searching gaze and pull the next question sheet off the pile. "There's nothing to tell."

I hear Lydia's sigh as if it's from miles away. The words on the paper blur with the memory of Ruby walking toward me over the sports grounds and the mean words I hurled at her. It keeps replaying on a grisly loop in my mind's eye until I stop even trying to concentrate on the question and just stare at the wall.

The TSA goes well. Everyone in my family is so certain I'll have passed that I don't even want to think about what will happen if I don't.

The week after that, we have one of the last meetings of the Oxford study group. Ruby sits with Lin at the far end of the room. She still won't look at me but doesn't give any indication of anything having happened between us either. She acts just the same as ever, running rings around us with her sharp-witted arguments and once even manages to leave the tutor speechless.

It's hard for me not to watch her the entire time. Bloody hard. The moment she opens her mouth, I hang on to her every word, and I feel the urge to kiss her lips.

At times like this, I conjure up the image of my father and remember the back of his hand hitting my cheek and the pain that throbbed in my jaw for days. It wasn't the first time he'd hit me. It's not like he does it all the time, but often enough—especially when he thinks I'm not living up to the family name.

It hurts that Ruby doesn't measure up to his standards, but I have to live with it. I was born into a family that I can't cut myself off from, however much I'd love to. I'll go to Oxford, and I'll inherit Beaufort's.

It's time to accept that and stop feeling sorry for myself.

"Let's have a look at the second question. James, would you like to share your thoughts with us, please?" Pippa asks. I have no idea what she was just saying. The only word that got through to me was my own name.

"Not really," I reply, leaning back in my chair. To be honest, all I really want to do is go home. And to be entirely honest, all I want is Ruby, and that's not an option.

It's like torture to have her sitting in this room, not looking at me. She was the only thing that motivated me. Now there's just lacrosse. Nothing else matters. Not even parties with my friends can distract me from how pointless everything in my life feels at the moment. The time until my exams is ticking away faster, and I just don't know if I can hold it all together. How I can stop my existence from feeling this superfluous.

"If you are invited for an interview, you have to have an answer prepared for every question," Pippa says sternly, making an encouraging gesture.

I pick up the paper so that I can read the italicized text better.

When, if ever, is forgiveness wrong?

I look at the question. Ten seconds pass. Another ten, then my silence gets uncomfortable, and someone clears their throat. A cold shiver runs up my arms and down my spine. The paper in my hands is getting heavier and heavier, and after a while, I have to put it down on the table. It feels as though I'm swallowing cement, but my mouth is empty. Apart from my useless tongue, which is incapable of forming words.

"Forgiveness generally follows a harmful act," says Ruby's voice suddenly. "But forgiving someone for the pain they've caused you doesn't make it just go away. As long as you can still feel the pain, forgiveness is wrong."

I look up. Ruby's face is blank as she looks at me, and I wish I could stretch my hands out to her. There are only a few yards between us, but the distance feels so unbridgeable that it's hard to breathe.

Pull yourself the fuck together, Beaufort.

"If you forgive people too easily, they get the feeling they can do whatever they like. That means that the anger of the person who had something bad done to them is the punishment for the guilty person, who desperately wants to be forgiven," Lin adds.

Yes, Ruby's anger feels like a punishment that I deserve. But I still wish she wouldn't spend the rest of the school year hating me. She should be looking forward to getting to live her dream in Oxford.

If anyone deserves that, it's her.

"Forgiveness can never be wrong," I retort quietly. Something flashes in Ruby's piercing green eyes. "Forgiveness is a sign of greatness and strength. If you spend years losing yourself in anger and destroying yourself, then you're no better than the person who did you wrong."

Ruby gives a scornful snort. "Only a person who's always doing other people wrong could say that."

"Isn't there a saying? 'Forgive but don't forget'?" Alistair looks around the room, and Keshav and Wren mumble agreement. "You can forgive someone for what they did, but that doesn't mean the thing didn't happen. Forgiveness is necessary to draw a line under a thing. Forgetting can take a long time, or never happen at all, and that's OK. Forgiveness helps you to let go and move on."

Lydia straightens up beside me. "That sounds like you can forgive someone with a click of your fingers, and forgetting is the only difficult part. But you shouldn't forgive everything that's done to you. If it's really bad, you can't set yourself free just like that."

"That's what I think too," says Ruby. "If you forgive too quickly, that means you don't take yourself seriously and push your own pain aside too casually. Which is self-sabotaging behavior. It takes time to recognize when you have to let go, that's true, but it's wrong to see the decision to forgive just as a simple means to an end."

"Maybe we could make a distinction between healthy and unhealthy forgiveness," Lydia suggests, and Ruby nods. "Unhealthy forgiveness comes too fast and means there might be circumstances where you let yourself get hurt again. But healthy forgiveness has to come after time to think. In that case, you respect yourself enough not to let yourself be treated badly again."

"But forgiveness isn't the same as reconciliation," muses Wren, who's sitting next to Lydia. I lean forward slightly to see him. He's got his hands linked behind his head and is slumped deep in his chair. "If the original meaning of forgiveness is letting go of anger, it's intended more for the victim than for the perpetrator, so they can decide for themselves the measure by which they forgive."

"But there are unforgivable crimes." Kesh spoke quietly. Everyone turns to him, but he's crossed his arms and looks like that's all he wants to say.

"Can you expand on that a little, Keshav?" Pippa asks encouragingly.

"I mean murder and stuff like that—I think it's totally OK if the victim's family don't forgive. I mean, why should they?"

The nape of my neck tingles slightly, and I glance almost imperceptibly back at Ruby. Her eyes meet mine, and the pins and needles strengthen. There are two tables between us, and all that space, but I want to jump across the gap, take her face in my hands, and kiss her again.

"But that brings us back to individual moral standards. Everyone's threshold for what they consider unforgivable is different," says Lydia.

Kesh is replying, but I'm not listening. In Ruby's eyes, I can see exactly where her moral threshold is set. The things I said to her are unforgivable. Her lips are set into a hard line, and there are dark circles under her eyes, which must be my fault. She will never forgive me, and even though I knew we had no future together, it's only in this moment that I grasp what that really means. I will never have the chance to touch her again. I'll never truly talk to her again. Laugh with her. Kiss her.

The realization shakes me to the core. It's as though a deep black hole has opened up beneath me, and I'm falling into it. Falling and falling and falling.

I try with all my might to take deep, even breaths, while the rest of the discussion rushes on around me. Just like everything else.

25

Ruby

I always used to love dreaming. In my dreams, the impossible became possible. I could fly and sometimes do magic; I went to Oxford and traveled the world as an ambassador. Most of the time, my dreams were vivid and so realistic that the next day, I'd go to school super motivated, trying to give more than a hundred percent.

Now I hate my dreams. In most of them, James plays the leading role, and I just want that to stop. I wake up in the middle of the night—not because they're nightmares, but from the throbbing between my legs because I dreamed about him taking hold of me and kissing me. I dream that he offers me payment in kind for my silence, and this time, I don't stop him unbuttoning his shirt. I dream of him leading me into a world where he hasn't wiped me from his life.

This is yet another morning when I wake up with hot cheeks and the duvet between my legs. I groan and roll onto my back, laying an arm over my eyes. This can't go on. I somehow have to succeed in driving James out of my subconscious, or else I'll go mad. How am I meant to forget him if my dreams every night show me everything that could have happened between us?

I rub my eyes and reach for my phone on my bedside table. It's just before six, so my alarm will go off in ten minutes anyway. Wearily, I sit up and open my inbox. I've had eight new emails since last night. I scroll slowly through them to see if there's anything important.

As I see the sender's name on the last message, I sit up in bed so hastily that I feel dizzy.

It's from the admissions officer at St. Hilda's.

I hold my breath as I open it.

Dear Ruby,

I am very happy to invite you for an interview at St. Hilda's College, Oxford. Many congratulations on successfully reaching this stage in the application process.

I don't take in any of the rest of the text. I squeal so loudly that it echoes around the entire house. Ember comes running into my room, and I jump out of bed. It takes me a moment to regain my balance, but once I've done so, I jam my phone under her nose. Meanwhile, I start jumping up and down.

"Oh my God!" she screams, grabbing my hands and dancing around in circles with me. "Oh my God, Ruby!"

After that, I run downstairs so fast that I almost land flat on my face. Dad is wheeling out into the hallway; Mum's coming wide-eyed out of the kitchen. I hold up my phone triumphantly.

"I got an interview!"

Mum claps her hands to her mouth, and Dad cheers. Ember

wraps her arms around my waist and hugs me tight. "I'm so happy for you! But I don't want you to move out."

"I've only been invited for an interview; it doesn't mean I'll get in. And if I do, Oxford's only a couple of hours away anyway." I'm so excited that I can't stand still. My dream seemed so distant for years, but now it's come a whole lot closer. It suddenly feels so real that I can almost touch it. My whole body is tingling with energy.

"We all know you're going to rock the interview," says Dad, his choice of words making Ember and me laugh. "They'll have no choice but to accept you."

I'm grinning so widely that the corners of my mouth are starting to ache. But I can't stop. It's been ages since I've looked forward to anything this much.

"I'm so proud of you, love." Mum drops a kiss on the top of my head and gives me a hug. Once she lets go, I bend down to Dad, who hugs me too.

"So what exactly does this mean for now?" he asks, once I've straightened up again.

I read the email through to the end this time. "It says here to arrive by eight on Sunday evening. The interviews then run on Monday and Tuesday. The journey home again is on Wednesday morning."

"Four days in Oxford," Mum whispers with a shake of her head. "I knew they'd invite you."

I beam at her again. "It says here that I get free accommodation and meals."

"There, I knew you'd picked the right college," says Dad, his eyes sparkling happily.

"I know exactly what you need to wear." Ember grabs my hand and pulls me toward the stairs.

"I picked my Oxford outfits back before the summer holidays."
Longer than that, really, if you take into account the Oxford Style
Pinterest board I've had for over a year, which Ember and I constantly pin inspirations to. I wave to Mum and Dad as Ember
drags me along behind her. From the stairs, I hear my parents.

"Oxford," whispers Mum.

"Oxford," Dad replies equally quietly.

They sound so happy. I hope with all my heart that I'll do well
in the interviews. I want to keep making them proud, being their
reason to be so pleased. When my family is happy, I am too.

I let Ember pull me into my bedroom and over to my wardrobe. As she pulls out heaps of clothes and lays them in outfits on
my bed, I fill in the reply form and confirm that I will be attend-
ing. Then I send Lin a screenshot of the message and wait nervously for her to answer.

I still can't quite believe it.

It might only be for four days, but: I'm going to Oxford.

———

It's dark by the time we arrive on Sunday evening. Even so, my
parents, Ember, and I decide to take a stroll. St. Hilda's is at the
eastern end of the High, and we walk along the Cherwell, its
water glittering moodily in the light of the streetlamps, and between the imposing buildings in weathered but far from weather-
beaten stone. The bay windows with white frames and little
balustrades exude the charm of old stories, and I long to hear them
all one day.

St. Hilda's is just beautiful. I push Dad over the paved paths in
the college grounds with Mum and Ember on either side of us,
and it feels like I'm walking straight into a fairy tale. The grin

that's been permanently fixed to my face since last week broadens further still.

"Next year, you'll be sitting right there," says Dad out of nowhere, pointing to the lawn on our left. "With a pile of textbooks under your nose. On a tartan blanket."

"That's a very precise image, Dad," I say with a smile.

"It is." He nods solemnly.

Apart from its prettiness, I like St. Hilda's for its diversity, sense of community, and the respect its students have for one another. Everyone's welcome here, no matter where they're from or what their background is. After my time at Maxton Hall, that's what I need. I want to feel at home and not to have to hide away again. I can't imagine spending the next three years at one of the more conservative colleges, like Balliol.

Besides, St. Hilda's has unicorns on its coat of arms.

"I can't believe I'm really here," I whisper. "I'm so lucky."

Ember clicks her tongue. "It's not luck. You worked hard for this."

She's right. But the thought of the interviews over the next couple of days still makes me feel sick. I have to do a bit of last-minute preparation tonight and look through the notes I made during Pippa's sessions. I know them off by heart, but I know it'll make me feel better all the same.

Once we've been to the porter's lodge to get my key for the room I'll be staying in for the next few days, I say goodbye to my family with a heavy heart, take my little blue holdall, and step inside. The building is nothing special indoors—blue carpet, pale white walls—but I still have butterflies in my stomach as I climb the stairs to the first floor. This might soon be my new home.

My room is at the end of the corridor on the left. I pull out my key, and I'm about to stick it in the lock when I hear someone's footsteps behind me. I turn around with a smile.

It dies on my lips.

I'd assumed it would be a student, but the person standing there has red-blond, wind-tousled hair and is wearing a black, tailored coat.

It's James.

"You have got to be kidding me," I exclaim. I thought he had applied to Balliol.

He looks just as surprised as me. His expression darkens, and he looks at the key in his hand. He takes three long strides, small suitcase in tow, and reaches the door opposite mine.

It feels like fate is playing an unkind trick on me.

Without a word, he opens the door and steps into his room. His glowering eyes rest on me a moment longer, then he shuts the door behind me, leaving me out in the hall.

I've had myself so firmly under control in the last few weeks. I've ignored him, even when it hurt, and acted like the whole thing had washed over me without a trace. I didn't want to give him the satisfaction of seeing how angry and upset I am. And how much I miss him. But now I feel the rage rising up within me again. I'd love to go and kick his door in. I want to hurl all the pent-up words of the last few weeks at his head.

But I know there's nothing more to say. He is the way he is. I was a little interlude for him, and it was unrealistic to think James could ever be any kind of friend to me, let alone something more.

I can't let the fact that he's here get to me. I have a goal, and I'm not losing sight of it. I've come too far for that. Maybe I should just see it as another challenge that I have to overcome on my way to Oxford. And so long as James doesn't get in my way, I can live with him staying opposite me. I'll act the same as I do at school: pretend he doesn't exist.

With that resolve, I open the door and enter my room. It's minimalist—a small wooden desk, a white built-in wardrobe, and a simple bed. From the window, there's a view of the quad with a huge beech tree in the center. I step closer to get a better look. The copper leaves have fallen; the lawn is covered with them. There's a path leading all the way around the edge, with lampposts and benches. I copy Dad—I imagine myself sitting out there in a few months' time, a pile of books beside me, my head full of the new things I'm learning, in simply perfect grounds.

The whole thing with James hurts like hell, but suddenly it doesn't feel so bad. I'm going to do this.

26

Ruby

For a moment when I wake up the next morning, I'm confused by the stark white bedcovers lying over me. The mattress feels weird too as I turn over in bed. And it smells very different from my room.

You're at St. Hilda's.

I sit bolt upright and look around. Then I give a quiet squeal. I snatch my phone off the bedside table and skim through my notifications. Mum and Dad are reminding me to eat a good breakfast, because they know that nerves sometimes take my appetite away, and Ember has sent me a motivational quote that I'd love to copy straight into my journal. Kieran is wishing me luck and says he's sure I've got this. The last message is from Lin. She's taken a photo of her room at St. John's, which doesn't look very different from mine. I text back that I'm looking forward to seeing her in the pub this evening—that's one of the dates on the timetable the office emailed me in advance—and wishing her good luck for her own interviews.

After that, I get up and slowly get ready. My hands are shaking with excitement as I do my makeup and slip into my clothes.

I picked out the cognac-colored cord skirt and white blouse embroidered with subtle flowers months ago and hung them up in my wardrobe, waiting for this day. I've also got my burgundy bag, and I put on the plaited leather bracelet that Ember gave me too.

It doesn't go with the rest of the outfit, but you can hardly see it under my long sleeves, and the moment I fasten it, I feel like there's a part of my sister and my family here with me.

In the breakfast room, you can tell at a glance who the real students are and who's only here for the interviews. The former group head straight for the serving hatch, laughing and chatting casually, and I feel a burning desire to be like them this time next year. I want to get my coffee without going twice round in a circle because I can't find the machine, to sit at a table with my friends and talk about the weekend with them. And I want to give the sixth-formers here for interviews an encouraging smile in the hope that it'll make them feel better.

Yesterday evening, this all felt so unreal. Now, Oxford is becoming a reality. I listen to the two girls next to me as they talk about a seminar, and at first, I don't even notice that they've caught me eavesdropping. I hastily lower my head and stare at my toast; I've only taken two bites, but it feels like a lump of lead in my stomach.

According to my schedule, I should go to the common room after breakfast. When I open the door, I'm surprised by how loud it is in there until I see that there are older students here too, lounging around on the battered sofas and talking at top volume, clearly trying to lighten the mood a little.

I find a free chair next to one of the sofas and sit down on it.

There's a boy my age beside me, a book and a pile of flash cards in his lap. He smiles at me, but it strikes me as more of a grimace. He looks as tense as I feel. My fingers tremble as I pull out my own notes and start to look through them one last time.

Suddenly, I feel pins and needles in the back of my neck, spreading over my whole body. I lift my head and look over to the door. The next moment, I wish I hadn't. James is standing there, hands deep in his pockets, an impenetrable expression on his face.

Please don't see me, please don't see me, please don't see me . . .

He spots me on the chair. His eyes stray slowly over my face, take in my outfit, and land on the cards in my hand. The corners of his lips twitch almost imperceptibly, but then, as if he's reminded himself not to smile, his face hardens again, and he looks around the common room for an empty seat.

"Ruby Bell?" says a voice I don't know. One of the older students has got up from the sofa. He's huge—must be at least six-foot-three—has wavy brown hair, slicked back slightly with gel, and a beaming white smile. He's one of the guys who was trying to cheer things up just now, and that makes me like him right away.

"That's me," I croak, getting up. My hands are cold and clammy. I wipe them on the hem of my skirt to warm them up—I want to be able to shake hands with him without it being unpleasant. I put the flash cards back in my bag and stand up to walk to the door where he's waiting for me.

As I pass James, I straighten my chin, determined just to ignore him. But he takes my hand. His warm fingers wrap gently around my wrist. His thumb strokes the sensitive skin there.

"Good luck," he whispers. Then he lets me go and walks to the chair that I just vacated.

It takes me a few seconds to pull myself together again. My heart is racing, and this time it's got nothing to do with my excitement.

The boy who called my name smiles at me and beckons me over. "Hi. I'm Jude Sherington. I'll show you where to go for your interview," he says, nodding toward a corridor. I walk out of the common room without looking back. A few minutes to determine everything. In a few minutes, I might know whether or not I get to study here.

I touch the spot where James's thumb stroked my wrist. I should focus, but I can't forget the feeling of his fingers on my skin, all the way to my interview.

=====

I wish I could pace up and down to get rid of the nerves. But Jude is still there, smiling at me every minute or two. He led me through a maze of corridors and is now leaning silently against the wall while I sit on a chair opposite the professor's office, waiting for her to open it. Any second now, surely.

I exhale audibly.

"Nervous?" asks Jude.

What a question. "So nervous. How did you feel when you did it?"

"Kind of like this." He lifts a hand and shakes it exaggeratedly. I love how honest he is.

"But you got through it."

"Yep." He smiles encouragingly again. "It's not rocket science. You'll be fine."

I nod, shrug, and shake my head, all at once. Jude laughs, and I pull a face. At that moment, the door opens, and a girl walks out of the office. Her cheeks are red and her lips are bloodless. Apparently, I'm not the only person to be eaten up by nerves. Unfortunately, I don't get a chance to ask her what it was like as she disappears without a word. The office door shuts again, and I look questioningly at Jude, who still has that reassuring look on his face.

"Don't worry, she'll tell you when to go in."

So now the waiting starts again. By this point, it feels as though I've used up all my jitters on just sitting here this long. After five more minutes, my left foot has fallen asleep, and I move it unobtrusively to stop the pins and needles. It feels like there's a whole anthill dancing around in my ankle boot. I shake my foot out again—and at that exact moment, the door creaks open. The professor comes into sight, and I freeze, my foot hanging in the air at a funny angle.

"Ruby, come in please." She has a pleasant, calm voice, which acts like a fire blanket on my anxious nerves. I hear Jude behind me say, "Good luck," but I don't have the head space to thank him. She holds the door for me, and, as we walk together into the room where my interview will take place, she introduces herself to me as Prudence.

The office is about the size of our living room, but it's so cluttered that it seems kind of cozy. The furniture looks antique, like it's been there since the college was founded, and the air smells of old books. The walls are lined with shelves, stacked high with towers of books. There's another professor sitting at a writing desk on the other side of the room. She's busily making notes and only looks up when Prudence leads me to a table. I smooth my skirt again and sit up straight on the chair. The two women settle down across the desk from me, open their notebooks, and then lean back.

My heart is pounding in my throat, but I try not to let that show, to look confident. I'm certain that I can do well here. I'm prepared, and I've done everything I could to be ready.

I take a deep breath and let the air out again slowly.

"We're very pleased to meet you, Ruby." The second academic opens proceedings. "My name is Ada Jenson, and, like Prudence, I teach politics here at St. Hilda's." Her voice also has a soothing effect on me, and I wonder how it's possible for some of the cleverest women in the country also to have the skill of making people feel at ease in a situation like this.

"Thank you for inviting me," I answer, then clear my throat. My voice sounds like I've swallowed something sticky that's got caught on the way down.

"We'll get started right away," Prudence continues. "Can you tell me why you'd like to study here?"

I stare at her. I wasn't expecting that. Everything I've read about these interviews suggested that the opening question would be directly related to the course. I can't help myself—a grin spreads over my face. So I tell them. Everything. I tell them how I got interested in politics when I was little and that I've dreamed of studying at Oxford since I was seven. I tell them that my twelfth birthday present from my dad was subscriptions to *The Spectator* and *The New Statesman* and that he spent hours watching televised debates in parliament with me. I tell them about my passion for organization and debating and my longing to change things for the better. I try not to suck up too much while emphasizing that Oxford is the best university for me, the place I can learn what I need to get to my goals.

I'm almost out of breath when I finish, and I can't tell whether or not they're satisfied with my answer. I wasn't exactly expecting them to high-five me or whatever, so that doesn't worry me. After that, they do ask me questions about politics. I try to make good arguments and not be fazed by their follow-up questions. The whole interview is over in no more than about fifteen minutes.

"Thank you for the conversation," I say, but Ada is already deep in her notes and doesn't hear me. Prudence brings me to the door and smiles again as she says goodbye. I follow suit, then walk outside. The door closes behind me, and, all of a sudden, I feel utterly exhausted.

Sitting on the chair opposite me is the same boy who smiled at me in the common room earlier on. I remember the girl with pale lips who vanished before I could even speak to her. I'd have loved a few encouraging words from her, but now I understand why she fled so fast. Now that the adrenaline is ebbing away, I just want to get out of this building, into the fresh air. Even so, I force myself to speak. "You've got this, good luck," I say honestly, then head outside, trying to find my way back to my room.

Ruby

I spend the rest of the day exploring the college. I get a takeaway coffee, stroll around the lawns and extensive grounds, and look inside the buildings where my student guide tells me PPE is taught. I'm thrilled to mingle with the real students, and, at one point, I'm so deep in thought that I accidentally wander into a lecture theater. Nobody seems to notice me, so I sit cautiously down in the back row and spend the next hour and a half listening to a lecture on the work of Immanuel Kant.

The best ninety minutes of my life.

In the evening, applicants to all Oxford colleges are invited to the Turf Tavern, a legendary pub frequented by all kinds of famous people, including Oscar Wilde, Thomas Hardy, Elizabeth Taylor, Margaret Thatcher, and the cast of *Harry Potter*. I get to the meeting place given on my timetable way too early, but I'm not the only one. There are some of the people I recognize from the common room this morning among the little chattering groups, and Jude is here too. He greets me with his beaming smile and immediately starts to ask me about my interview. Once everyone's arrived, we set off. The pub is about a mile and a half from St. Hilda's. Our route takes us over Magdalen Bridge, beneath which the River Cherwell glitters in the orange-red light of the setting sun. We pass a deer park, and a few of the animals look up curiously, twitching their ears at the sound of us. Like most of the others, I stretch out my hand to them, but they clearly aren't tame enough to stroke. They all turn tail and bolt away across the Grove. After that, we walk between old buildings, sometimes on paths that are only just wide enough for two people to go side by side.

It's starting to get dark. If I'd been alone, I'd have been scared in these alleyways, but Jude is at my side, telling me about his studies and taking my mind off things. I'm hanging on his every word. Everything I've seen today, and what he's telling me now, is deepening my longing to study here. I've never wanted anything in my life as much as I do Oxford. Now that I've had a taste, I'd be crushed if I didn't make it. Can I do this? I don't know. I really don't want to have to fall back onto plan B.

Suddenly, the path opens out. There are streetlights shining up ahead, while scraps of conversation and music fill my ears. A few minutes later, we emerge into a courtyard crammed with people. Most of them look like students, and they're chatting and drinking pints of beer.

Our group weaves between them to the Turf Tavern door. It's an ancient, half-timbered building, with dark beams running diagonally across the white plaster. The roof is wonky, and in places, it's overgrown with moss. Some people have managed to get seats under umbrellas outside the pub. It's cold enough that I can see my misty breath in the air, so it's hardly surprising that most of them are wrapped up in thick coats, scarves, and woolly blankets.

There's a chain of colorful lights running along beneath the sign and above the front door, which is dark green with peeling paint. Jude holds it open for me, and I step inside the pub.

It feels practically medieval in here. The Turf has a low ceiling and rough, bare stone walls. There are little wall sconces, while the lamps over the tables have shades like dinner plates. We're led down a narrow corridor to an area behind and to one side of the noisy main bar.

Given Jude's height—in here, it feels like he's about six-six—I can't see much apart from his back in front of me.

But then I hear it. A laugh I know very well.

Jude walks over to one of the tables reserved for us and pulls out a chair. The others all start looking for seats while I stand there, staring at the group who've bagged the table next to ours. Sitting there are Wren, Alistair, Cyril, Camille, Keshav, Lydia, and . . . James.

James, who wished me luck this morning, and stroked my wrist.

James, who freezes, his beer halfway to his lips, as he spots me, only to turn back to Cyril a second later and act like nothing ever happened.

I gulp hard.

I don't know why I'm so surprised to bump into him and his mates here. I knew they were applying to Oxford, and this evening in the pub is a fixed point of several colleges' programs for anyone invited to interview. Even so, it dampens my euphoria, and I have to admit that Oxford won't be the entirely fresh start I've so often painted it as in my mind. I'll have to live with seeing some of them again.

If I even get in, that is.

"Ruby!"

I whirl around and see Lin coming toward me, arms outstretched. Her cheeks are flushed from the cold air outside, and she's got a chunky gray scarf around her neck, which covers half her face. The next moment, she flings her arms around me, and I hug her back, just as hard.

"Tell me everything," I say excitedly, once we've let each other go.

"Come on, sit down," says Jude, pointing to a bench facing him. Lin drops onto it first, and I follow suit once I've slipped off my coat. Somehow, I manage not to glance in James's direction again.

"This is so cool," Lin says, once we've sat down and looked at the menus. "Almost like we've gone back in time."

"Yeah, there's a real sense of history here," I agree. "But spill! Your text was so cryptic. How did it go?"

"You first!" Lin replies, and I give her the short version of my interview this morning.

"They had total poker faces—I had no clue whether what I was saying was right or wrong. I bet they were confused by the way I grinned at them after the first question," I say.

"Well, at least they weren't glaring at you. I got a tutor with a unibrow, and he frowned so hard it made me lose my train of thought a couple of times. I was so glad when it was over." She sighs, scowls, and props her chin on her hand. "It really didn't go well."

"But there's another interview," I say encouragingly, squeezing her arm for a moment. "You've got this."

"Two more, actually. One each for economics and philosophy. Lucky you to have both combined."

"But that means you have two more chances to prove yourself. That's a good thing, trust me."

"In my interview, they asked me if I could retrieve a pen that had gone under the armchair," Jude pipes up unexpectedly.

"What?" asks Lin.

"I thought it was part of the interview and started to work out the economic grounds for the question and build an answer based on that." He grins. "But in the end, they really did just want me to pick up the pen."

Lin and I start to laugh.

Then a barman comes to take our orders. Jude says drinking in the Turf is an absolute must, at least once, so Lin and I both get pints and a few nibbles. As we wait for our food, I tell her about my afternoon and the lecture I snuck into. After that, we make the most of the opportunity to bombard Jude with questions about seminars, tutorials, fellow students, and life in Oxford.

Our drinks arrive after a while. I've never had beer before. The only other alcohol I've drunk was the sweet stuff Wren plied me with at that party. I know what I'm doing this time as we clink glasses. This is my decision. It's my own choice to drink because it's part of the experience. It feels grown-up and exciting to do a thing I've never allowed myself in the past.

I lift the glass and take a sip. Then I pull a revolted face. "Ugh, that's *vile*!" I exclaim.

Jude and Lin burst out laughing, and I look from one of them to the other, genuinely confused. "Why would anyone drink this of their own free will?"

"Your first beer?" Jude asks.

I nod. "And my last."

"You say that *now*," he replies, waggling his eyebrows, and Lin nods.

"It's like coffee. It's disgusting when you're a child, but the older you get, the better it tastes." Lin points to my mouth. "You've got a foam mustache, by the way."

Startled, I wipe my lips with the back of my hand. "I've always liked coffee. This is . . . It tastes . . . like licking a tree."

They explode with laughter again.

"I don't want to know how you know what licking a tree tastes like," Jude jokes.

I push the beer away to the middle of the table. "Help yourselves. I'm going to get myself a Coke."

I slip off the bench, squeeze between two tables and down the narrow corridor to the bar. It's even more crowded than before—after all, the Turf Tavern's a tourist trap as well as a student hangout. It takes almost ten minutes to get the barman's attention. I smile as he finally hands me a Coke and turn away.

At that moment, I spot Lydia. She's pushing her way hastily through the throng to the loos and doesn't seem to see me. Her cheeks are pale, and I see her hand shake as she pushes a man out of her way. Puzzled, I watch her vanish into the ladies'.

I guess she's had too much to drink. But it's not even eight. I shake my head and walk back to our table, where Jude and Lin are deep in conversation with some of the others we came here with. I plunge into the chat, sipping my drink occasionally. I keep squinting over to where Lydia was sitting, but she still hasn't come back from the toilet. Thinking about it, she didn't look well. Looked really bad, in fact.

Cautiously, I watch her friends. James and Wren are talking; Camille's practically in Keshav's lap, and whatever she's whispering into his ear is making him smile. Opposite them, Alistair downs half his pint in one. His eyes are bitter, his brows frowning. He might be answering the question Wren just asked him, but he doesn't take his eyes off Camille and Keshav, who are flirting right in front of him. It's bad enough that Keshav won't admit to being with Alistair, but on top of that, he's smooching with a girl in public, and that sinks him totally beneath respect in my eyes.

None of the boys seems to have noticed that Lydia hasn't come back. I hesitate a moment but then excuse myself and stand up. It's obvious that alcohol levels around here have risen in the last hour. People are yelling at each other so loudly it's almost drowning out the music, and hardly anyone gets out of my way as I squeeze past. Once I've finally made it across the room, I sigh with relief. I head into the ladies' loos and look around cautiously. There are several cubicles, and miraculously, all but one are open.

I hear a quiet sniff through the door. And then . . . a loud choking.

I knock hesitantly and then realize that it isn't locked. It opens a little, but I don't have the nerve to just walk in. "Lydia?"

"Leave me alone," she croaks.

I remember the Monday after the party when she sat with me at lunch and apologized to me. She was nice to me, just because. Now I have the chance to repay that. "Can I do anything to help?" I ask quietly.

No answer. Instead, I hear Lydia gag, followed by an unappealing splashing sound. I hurry to the sinks, pull a few paper towels from the dispenser, and run them under the tap. Then I cough gently before holding them under the toilet door to Lydia. "Here."

The towels vanish from my hand.

I crouch there, unsure what to do. I don't want to leave Lydia on her own in this state, but I don't know how to help her either.

The toilet flushes, and, after a while, the door opens a crack. I can see a tiny bit of Lydia's face. It's just not fair. Despite her watery eyes and flushed cheeks, she still looks so pretty. I can see so much of her brother in her face.

But this is definitely neither the time nor the place for thinking about James.

"Should I get you a glass of water or something?"

"No, that's OK. I just need a few minutes for the walls to stop spinning." She leans her back against the wall. Then she shuts her eyes, and her head drops forward.

"Too much to drink?" I ask.

Lydia shakes her head almost imperceptibly. "I haven't been drinking at all," she whispers.

"Are you ill?" I try again. "There must be an emergency pharmacy around here somewhere. If you aren't feeling better."

Lydia doesn't reply.

"Or . . ." I suggest hesitantly, ". . . is it nerves? Are you anxious about tomorrow?"

Now she does look at me. She looks kind of amused but deeply sad at the same time. "No," she says. "It's not nerves. I had both my interviews today, and they went fine."

"That's great," I say cautiously, seeing that Lydia doesn't look all that thrilled. On the contrary, suddenly her eyes fill with tears again. "Why aren't you happy?"

She shrugs and lays a hand on her stomach. "It doesn't matter how they went. I'm not going to study here."

"Why not? Don't you want to?"

Lydia gulps. "I do, actually."

"So what's the problem? If the interviews went well, then I'm sure you'll get in."

"That's not what I mean. I just don't think . . . I'll be able to study here."

I don't get it. "Why not?" I ask in confusion.

She doesn't reply. She looks down and stares at the hand on her stomach. She starts to slowly run it over her blouse—or rather, over the little bulge beneath it.

I wouldn't normally have thought twice about it. Everyone has a roll or two on their belly when they sit down. But most people don't stroke those little bulges. And they don't look at them with the loving expression that is currently spreading over Lydia's face.

It suddenly clicks, and I inhale sharply. "You really weren't drinking," I whisper.

A tear runs slowly down her cheek. "Haven't for months."

I remember the drink she asked James for at Cyril's party but then left. And of course, I'm remembering the day I caught her with Mr. Sutton. There's a lump in my throat.

"Is it . . . ?" I don't dare finish the question, but there's no need. Lydia knows what I'm asking and nods.

"I don't know what to say," I admit.

"That makes two of us." She dabs at the corners of her eyes with her fingers.

"How far along are you?" I whisper.

Lydia gently strokes her belly. "Twelve weeks."

"Who else knows?" I ask.

"Nobody."

"Not even James?"

She shakes her head. "No. And I want to keep it that way."

"Why did you tell me then?"

"Because you wouldn't stop asking questions," she says at once. Then she sighs. "Besides, James trusts you. And he never trusts anyone."

I bite my lips together and try not to think about what that means. "At some point, in the not too far distant future, it's going to be less easy to hide," I say, nodding at her belly.

"I know." Her words sound so broken, so sad, that I'm engulfed by a wave of sympathy.

"You can always talk to me anytime you want. Even over the next few weeks and months. If you don't have anyone else, I mean."

Lydia eyes me skeptically. "Why should I?"

I tentatively stroke her arm. "Seriously, Lydia, I mean it. This is a big deal. I get it if you don't want to talk, but . . ." I look at her stomach. "You're going to have a baby."

She follows my gaze. "It's weird to hear you say that. I mean, I know that, but nobody's said it out loud before. That made it feel a bit more real."

I totally understand what she means. Once you say a thing, you give it space to unfold and become real.

"Do you want me to walk you back?" I ask after a long while.

Lydia hesitates, and for a few seconds, she just looks at me without a word. Then she nods and smiles carefully—for the first time this evening. I don't know whether she genuinely trusts me, but if she doesn't, that might change in the future. I know the two biggest secrets in her life, and I have every intention of keeping them. I'm not going to go behind Lydia's back. Anything but. I can imagine that she might need a friend in such a tough time.

I get to my feet and hold out my hand to help her up.

"You know I was just puking over the toilet bowl, right?" she asks.

I screw up my nose. "Thanks for reminding me," I reply, but don't pull my hand back.

With a smile, Lydia takes it.

28

Ruby

The interview the next day is horrendous. That's partly because I spent half the night lying awake, thinking about Lydia's situation, and partly because I don't hit it off with either of the instructors. They start by making jokes that I don't understand, and then once we finally get going, they're dissatisfied with my answers. I'm asked how many people there are in the room, and I reply that nobody can say for certain. After all, I could be dreaming, or the two tutors might just be in my head. It's one of the exercises we went through with Pippa, but they really don't like my approach to the question. The philosophy tutor describes it as "pseudo-intellectual," then invites me to challenge my answer and work out why it's fallacious. Then he asks me for a logical response, and, in a small voice, I say, "Three."

As a result, I'm totally unsure of myself, and I overthink everything else I say. It's an utter disaster, and, half an hour later, when it's finally over, my head is spinning.

I bid them a polite goodbye and leave the room like I'm on autopilot. Once I get outside, I realize how dizzy I am, and I have to lean on the wall for a moment so as not to lose my balance.

My eyes rest on the next applicant.

James, obviously.

His habit of turning up at every low point in my life and experiencing them live is driving me nuts. He's chatting with the student who showed him the way here—or rather, she's chatting him up while he stares at the toes of his shoes. It's not until one of the instructors shuts the door behind me that he lifts his head.

He looks great. He's wearing black trousers and a dark green shirt that flatters his broad shoulders and upper body. I hate that they suit him so well. I also hate the fact that he's so formally dressed without coming across as a try-hard. I basically hate everything about him.

Especially the way he broke my heart. Every time he looks at me, the pain that I've been repressing so successfully in the last few weeks comes flooding back. My heart pounds in my throat, my mouth goes dry, and a queasy feeling spreads through my stomach. And then there's that bloody yearning. The need to go over to him and take his hand in mine, just to touch him and to feel his warm skin on mine. I'd like to wish him luck, like he did for me yesterday, but I just can't bring myself to speak to him. If I open my mouth—just now, when I'm on the brink of tears—my voice will break.

Suddenly, James gets up and takes a step toward me. Before he can say anything, I look away and hurry off down the corridor.

━━━━

The rest of the day stretches out like chewing gum. After the interview, all I want to do is go back to my room and curl up under the sheets, but I bump into a couple of other sixth-formers who are just about to be given a tour of the college by two current students. I saw a lot yesterday, but given how bad that interview was, I'm not sure if I'll ever get the chance to spend time in St. Hilda's again, so I join the group. It's bittersweet to look around a college and university I might not get into, but Tom and Liz put so much effort into the tour that I decide to push those dark thoughts down for a while and focus on what they're telling us.

St. Hilda's was the last women-only college to be established in Oxford, and men have only been allowed to study here for nine years. I already knew about its reputation for friendliness, but as we walk through the grounds, I sense that it isn't unjustified. Students say hi to one another in passing, and even people sitting in the library, looking super stressed amid stacks of books, take a moment to answer our questions. The atmosphere here seems like the total opposite of Maxton Hall. There's no subdivision into rich and poor, cool and uncool, worthy and unworthy—everyone here seems to be equal.

The thought that I might have seriously screwed up makes something clench wistfully inside me.

Lin messages me at lunchtime, asking how my interview went, but I can't find the energy to answer her, or my parents and Ember either. I'm disappointed in myself and have to come to terms with what happened before I can face them. I know exactly how they'll react: understanding, loving, and comforting. And at the moment, I just couldn't bear that.

We head back to the common room in the early evening. I'm really looking forward to crawling back to my room, but there's one last item on the program—a get-together with Jude and a couple of others, who are there to answer any questions we still have about studying here and life in Oxford. I try my hardest to rediscover my positive energy, but I just can't. So I bag one of the comfy-looking wingback chairs, curl up in it, and decide that I'll just sit here and listen.

The room gradually fills up. After a while, James puts in an appearance too. He walks in with the girl who was showing him around this afternoon and who was waiting with him ahead of his interview. The two of them are chatting, and, however hard I try, I can't take my eyes off him.

I never did understand why it's called heartache, and now I get that even less. It's not just my heart that hurts when I look at James—every part of me aches. It's hard even to breathe. It should be called whole-body-blocked-airways-ache. That sounds way less romantic and, in my opinion, a lot more fitting.

Just at the moment that I succeed in tearing my eyes off him, James spots me in my armchair. Our eyes meet for the tiniest fraction of a second, but it still sets my skin tingling.

I'm too tired and frustrated to fight it.

"OK, everyone!" Jude begins, clapping his hands. "Are we all here? Then let's get started. There are still some seats back there," he adds, gesturing vaguely in my direction. Most of us have settled comfortably into the sofas and armchairs, but there are a couple of dining chairs beside me, with embroidered seats. From the corner of my eye, I spot James and two other boys coming toward me. I venture a cautious sideways glance. James returns it, his eyes dark.

I budge over a little to the right in my chair. I don't care what he thinks of me. I just don't want to sit too close to him. I don't even want to be in the same room as him. The pain in my chest is bad enough as it is.

"Feel free to ask us anything," Liz explains. "About study, private life, career aspirations."

"Absolutely anything?" the guy sitting next to James asks.

"You can *ask* us anything, but it's up to us whether we answer." Jude grins at him, and a couple of people laugh shyly.

"OK, who wants to start?" asks the student who came in with James. She's really pretty, with black hair and dark skin. I don't think she's wearing makeup, but her cheeks are glowing slightly. I'd like to ask her how she managed that, but I'm afraid it would be too off-topic for our Q&A.

"Honestly, how stressful is it to study here? Do you have time for a personal life?" asks a girl I haven't even seen before.

Jude, Liz, and the pretty girl look at each other, and Jude gestures to Liz to go first with her answer.

"The academic side is more intense than other universities, obviously, and then you're living in college, and it takes a while to settle into that too. But there is still plenty of time for other stuff."

People around the room murmur quietly, most of them looking pretty relieved by that answer.

"Next question!" Jude announces, looking round expectantly. Short silence. Then . . .

"Is it true what people say, that the teaching here is a joke compared to Balliol?"

My head flies around to look at James. He's looking straight ahead, apparently genuinely interested, to where the three students are sitting, returning his gaze rather perplexed.

"The courses are the same," Jude begins hesitantly, his brow furrowed slightly. "But as I study here and not there, I can't be the judge of that. I can only tell you what things are like at St. Hilda's."

"A 'yes' would have done."

I stare at James. I can't believe he just said that. And in that vile tone he's learned from his father, the one that sets off a chain of furious reactions deep within me.

The urge to open my mouth is growing by the second, and my defenses are crumbling little by little.

Don't do it, don't do it, don't do it . . .

I ignore my common sense.

"You're so obvious," I burst out.

James turns slowly toward me. "Obvious, how?"

"The only reason St. Hilda's isn't good enough for you is that your dad didn't study here." I try to keep my voice calm, but not with much success. Not after the day I've had. Not when he's acting like this.

Something like pain flickers in James's eyes. "That's not true," he says.

At such a barefaced lie, all the fury I've been holding back with all my strength in recent weeks bursts out of me like a storm. I can't keep it in a second longer, and the words just well up out of me, loud and unfiltered. "What isn't true? That St. Hilda's isn't good enough for you, just like I'm not good enough for you, because your parents want something else for you? That you only ever do what they want instead of actually thinking for once about what *you* want from life? You're such a coward!"

Suddenly, the common room is eerily quiet. I'm breathing hard, my chest is rising and falling like crazy, and I feel a dangerous prickling behind my eyes.

Oh no. *No.*

No way am I crying in front of all these people and embarrassing myself even more than I've already just done.

I jump up abruptly and leave the room without another word.

I run down the hall and make it to the stairs before I hear equally hasty footsteps behind me. I take the steps two at a time until I get to the top and turn down the landing. James is right behind me. He overtakes me and stands in my way, so that I have to stop too.

"That's not true," he repeats breathlessly. His cheeks are red, his hair's a mess. Whenever I see him, I feel like my body is tied to his in some irrational way. The need to touch him grows the closer he comes, regardless of how livid I am with him. This is impossible. How can I still want him when he hurts me this badly?

"What isn't true?" I can barely get the words out for all the pent-up emotion inside me.

I'm totally unprepared for the pain in his eyes. "That you're not good enough for me."

For a moment, I stare at him in confusion. Then I clench my fists, so hard that my nails dig into my skin.

"Fucking hell," I breathe.

He takes another step toward me. "Ruby—"

"No!" I interrupt him. "You don't get to do this to me. You don't get to break up with me and humiliate me in front of all your friends and then just stroke my wrist and whisper 'good luck' to me. You showed me more than clearly that you don't want me in your oh-so-perfect life."

"That wasn't . . . I . . ."

First he comes running after me, and now he can't even get out a coherent sentence. I want to grab him by the shoulders and shake him. "That wasn't you?" My voice is dripping with mockery.

"I'm sorry for how I acted. I'm so sorry, Ruby. But I . . . just can't. It's impossible."

I throw my arms up in the air. "So why the fuck are you here then? Why are you even talking to me?"

"Because I . . ." He breaks off again. He contracts his eyebrows as if he doesn't know the answer to that himself. He opens his mouth and shuts it again. It looks like he's trying to stop himself saying the words on the tip of his tongue.

"You don't know what you want from me. You don't know what you want from life. I don't think you know a damn thing."

His cheeks redden even more. Now his stance is the mirror image of mine—stiff shoulders, clenched fists. I've never seen him like this. He takes a furious step toward me, and I feel the heat radiating off him.

"I know exactly what I want." The stutter has vanished, and he suddenly sounds composed.

"So why not take it then?"

"Because what *I* want has never had anything to do with anything."

The last remnants of my self-control have been hanging by a silken thread, and his words now cut through it.

"For me it has! For me, what you want has *always* had everything to do with it!" I yell, shoving his chest with both hands.

James reacts lightning fast, grabbing my wrists. He holds my hands firmly to his ribs.

We're breathing. Fast and jerky. I can feel his pounding heartbeat beneath my fingers. It's beating so fast. Because of me. Because of what there is between us. The thing that's been growing between us for months now.

We move at the same time. James pulls me to him, and I leap toward him. Our mouths meet. Furiously, I shove my hands into his hair, pull at it, and he grabs my hips, digs his fingers into my skin. I bite his bottom lip because I'm so angry. He groans deeply and slips a hand down to my bum. His other hand runs up my spine to the nape of my neck. All the weeks I've spent ignoring him with all my might, fighting against my own feelings, break over me like a tornado.

Our kiss is a continuation of our row, a fight that transforms the rage inside me into something else and drags a sound from me that I've never made in my life before. A despairing groan that sounds almost like a sob. I run my tongue over his lower lip and enjoy the taste of him.

The next moment, James pulls me up and kisses me deeply and intently. Now his kiss suddenly feels like an apology. I can tell from his shaking fingers how long he's been wanting to do that and what an effort it must have been for him to hold himself back. He kisses me like he wants to drown in me; it's a mixture of desire, despair, hatred, and the full gamut of emotion in between, and it makes me *mad*, but at the same time, I haven't felt this alive in weeks. I don't understand how this is possible. I don't understand how a person you actually want to hate can do this to you.

James grabs me by the waist, picks me up, and stumbles down the corridor with me in his arms, without our lips breaking contact even once. My back slams into the door to James's room, and I gasp sharply. Furiously, I scratch his neck. James groans into my mouth and presses against me; his firm body is the only thing stopping me from falling to the floor. His hand runs from my waist to my thigh, then moves away, and I hear the clink of keys. The next moment, he's holding me tighter again, and the door opens behind me. James carries me over the threshold and kicks it shut. I only vaguely notice the bang. Nothing seems to matter anymore; in this moment there is only him and me and the feelings we're letting carry us. This time, nobody is going to interrupt us. Nobody is going to ruin the thing between us.

Only the two of us have any power over what's going to happen next.

My movements are gentler now but no less passionate. In a few steps, we're by the bed, and James lets himself fall onto it. He presses an arm behind my back to soften the impact and, the next moment, squeezes up against me, so perfectly that I groan and wrap my legs around his hips.

His mouth roams tenderly over every inch of my face. He kisses my cheeks and the corners of my lips. The tip of my nose. His lips graze my jaw. I hold tight to his shoulders and shut my eyes. Stars burst behind my eyelids as he sucks on my throat and presses his lips against the place where my pulse always beats faster.

"Ruby . . ." He whispers my name exactly the way he did that night, over a month ago, when we kissed on the school cellar stairs. The memory suddenly washes violently over me, bringing my despair and pain with it. I can't hold the burning behind my eyes back any longer. Hot tears form in my eyes and run down my face.

James freezes. He leans away from me a little and watches me from under heavy eyelids. With his dilated pupils and flushed cheeks, he looks like he's on drugs. He tenderly strokes my cheeks and keeps on whispering my name.

I cover my face with an arm so that he can't see my tears, but James takes my hand and lifts it carefully. He interlinks our fingers and brings our hands down to the bed, beside my head. With his other hand, he brushes a stray strand of hair off my forehead. Then he slowly runs his index finger over the sensitive skin beneath my eyes to wipe my cheeks dry.

"I'm sorry," he whispers into my temple, pressing a kiss onto my hairline.

He doesn't stop caressing my face. It's like his arms have formed a protected space, just for the two of us. When I look up, I see how swollen his bottom lip is. You can clearly see where I bit it, and I start to feel guilty. Gently, I stroke the reddened skin, and James shuts his eyes. I touch his jaw, run my finger over his frowning eyebrows, and trace the individual freckles on his cheeks. Now, in winter, they're so pale that you can only see them from close-up.

"I'm so sorry," he breathes, and it sounds as though his voice might break any second.

"That's not enough for me," I reply, equally quietly.

He leans forward and presses his hot brow against mine. "Me either."

For a long time, we hold that position. His weight feels so good on me, and I wrap my arms around his back, dig my fingers into his shirt, and just hold him tight. I can feel his heartbeat, as fast and irregular as my own, and enjoy the all-encompassing feeling of being this close to him.

But this doesn't change everything that's happened between us. The things he yelled at me, and the way he treated me. I can't forget that. Not if I want more from him than a whispered apology. I want an explanation, and I think he owes me one.

"We can't go on like this, James."

He smiles. The corners of his lips only twitch slightly, but I see it very clearly. And the tension in his body is easing too. The furrows on his brow smooth, and everything about him seems to soften.

"What is there to smile about?"

He pulls back a little and looks at me. His expression is hopeful. "It's so long since you said my name. It feels good."

Shaking my head, I take his face in my hand, lean forward, and kiss him carefully. It feels like a dream just to be able to do this when I was so sure I'd never have the opportunity again. His mouth fits mine perfectly. It feels right, like a puzzle piece slotting into place. James's hand strays from my face over my neck and shoulders. A hot tingle runs down my spine as he strokes my side and then grasps my waist. His body trembles above me. I want to carry on from exactly where we left off just now, but I can't do that without knowing exactly where we stand.

James seems to sense that and pulls away from me carefully. "By the lacrosse field . . . I told you that you can't lose a thing that doesn't belong to you."

The memory of his words stabs me. I want to look away, but I can't. Too many of the emotions I'm feeling at this moment are reflected in James's eyes.

"That was a lie. I've belonged to you since you threw my money back in my face, Ruby Bell."

29

James

Her eyes widen at my words. I roll off her, pulling her with me so that we end up both lying on our sides, able to look at each other. I leave my hand on her waist, stroking her there. I want to touch her everywhere, right now, forever. I've missed her so much it's almost killed me, and now it feels as though there's air in my lungs for the first time in weeks.

But I have to do this right. I'm not taking the risk of losing Ruby just because I can't bring myself to tell her what's wrong with me. Why I am the way I am, and why I make decisions that hurt us both so much. It's hard to find the right words, especially as the fear that she'll never forgive me is constricting my throat. I don't know what I'd do then.

Ruby looks at me calmly, waits. Her hair is messed up, and her cheeks and lips are red. She's so beautiful that, when I eventually clear my throat, I have to look away and stare at my hand on her waist.

"I told you that I'm joining the company after my A levels. And . . . it's important to my parents to have a wife at my side—the right kind of partner. To them, it's part of the deal. They'd ideally like to get me engaged to someone right away, so that nothing can go wrong."

Ruby makes an indefinable sound, and as I look up, she screws up her nose. It's good to know that she doesn't like that idea—after all, I can't imagine what I'd do if Ruby's parents wanted to get her linked up with someone who wasn't me.

"Right from the start, you've been so special to me. I've changed. I didn't even notice it myself, but my friends and family certainly did. I've had weeks of them asking me what's wrong, why I'm miles away the whole time and all that. When my dad saw us together in the workshop, he had an inkling. And then he caught us on Halloween . . ." I gulp, hard. "Then he was sure of it."

"Is that why you had a split lip? Did he hit you?" she asks, cautiously lifting her fingers to my mouth. The place where she bit me is still throbbing—but not in a bad way.

"Yes," I say quietly. I've never spoken to anyone about my father before. Not even Lydia; she sees a lot, but even she doesn't know everything. I'm sure my friends guess what our home life is like, but they never mentioned it if I turn up at theirs with a black eye or a fat lip. It's as though there came a point when we decided that the subject doesn't exist for us, and everyone sticks to that. Which I often find very convenient.

"Does he often hit you, James?" Ruby whispers.

I can't answer her, especially not when she's looking at me with that much sympathy in her eyes. This isn't what this is all about. All I want is to explain to her why I treated her like shit—which is one hundred percent my own fault, however hard my situation might be.

"That's not the point," I answer belatedly. My voice has taken on a raw edge, and I have to cough again. "Anyway, my parents saw you as a threat. They noticed how much you matter to me. Way more than the fucking company."

Something in Ruby's eyes changes. She looks so intense and penetrating that I get the feeling she can see right into my soul. There's no possibility of hiding from her—and at this moment, I realize that I don't even want to. My parents were right to be worried. Ruby is dangerous to them, and to everything they've planned for me and my future.

I can't believe I'm only just realizing this.

I'm in love with Ruby Jemima Bell.

My feelings for her are all-encompassing and overwhelming and not going away, no matter how I try to ignore them—that's been only too clear to me in the last few weeks. Ruby crept into my life, wreaked total havoc, and now she deserves a place amid the chaos she's created.

I don't care who I have to fight, and I don't care if my father kicks me out onto the street. Lydia once asked me if Ruby was worth all the stress. I let everyone and everything around me influence me into believing that she wasn't. That was the stupidest decision I ever made, and I hate myself for having pushed Ruby away like that. I know that I can't take it back, but I have to at least try.

"You're right—I really don't know what I want from life. Everything has always been preordained for me—what I have to do, what I'm not allowed. Sometimes it feels like I'm an extra in a script that's been written for me, one where I can't change a thing."

Ruby grumbles quietly.

"After my dad caught us, he lost it. In his eyes, there's no question of me spending time with anyone who doesn't match up to his ideas about my life."

My words make her flinch almost imperceptibly, and I immediately take her hands in mine and hold them tight.

"That made me think about what life would be like for us in the future, and all I could see were problems. My parents act like dictators when it comes to their kids' lives. And you . . . you told me back then that you were planning for a successful career. I couldn't bear the idea of my dad getting in your way just because it didn't suit him for you to be with his son. I was shit-scared because I knew that I wouldn't be able to do anything about it. I'd never be able to protect you from him."

My heart is pounding in my throat. I know perfectly well that I sound pathetic and idiotic, but I want to be honest with her. At any cost.

"You're going to conquer the world, Ruby. And you need to be with someone who'll support you along the way and whose family welcomes you with open arms. But I can't offer you that. I can't offer you anything but a heap of problems that I have no idea how to solve."

Ruby looks at me in silence, and I don't even dare breathe. I'm expecting her to get up and walk out of the room without a word. I'd deserve that, I know. But she makes no moves to leave. Instead, she leans forward and presses her lips onto mine.

I'm so stunned that I don't kiss her back.

"Ah, James," she murmurs. She frees her hand from mine and runs it over my chest until it's lying on my heart. "You stupid, bloody idiot . . ."

OK, I wasn't expecting that.

"Why are you wasting time worrying about the future when we have the present?" she asks quietly.

"Because you deserve better. My future is going to be shit. Yours doesn't have to be."

She squeezes my cheeks. "That's not true," she whispers fiercely. "You have just as many options as everyone else. You only have to take them, James."

I love it when she says my name. Her voice wraps gently around the letters, and I wish I could shut my eyes and ask her to say it again.

"Why didn't you just tell me all this?" she asks, shaking her head. "Instead of pushing me away with no explanation."

I can see pain in her eyes, the pain my behavior must have caused her. I lay my hand on top of hers and link our fingers on my chest. "I'm so sorry, Ruby. I really thought we were better off without each other."

"It didn't feel *better*," she whispers hoarsely. "You ghosted me, and then gave me the biggest brush-off in the history of the world."

"I know. God, Ruby. I'm so sorry."

I shut my eyes. I don't know what I'll do if she won't forgive me. If she decides that the stress I've brought into her life is too much. If I can never be as close to her again as I am now.

I hold her hand tight, press it to my heart, which is pounding like crazy, and I don't have the guts to look at her.

"James," Ruby says. She starts to pull her hand away, and I want to cling on to it, but I know that I don't have the right. If Ruby wants to leave, I have to let her. But then I feel her fingers in my hair. She runs her hand gently over my head, again and again.

I don't know how long we lie there like this, but I'm scared to move, afraid of destroying the moment. Seeing Ruby this close is the best feeling in the world. I'd give up everything for it. I don't know why it took me this long to realize that.

"James," Ruby murmurs again, after a long time. She kisses my temple. "It's OK. I forgive you."

I take a deep breath to mumble another apology but freeze as the meaning of her words gets through to me. I open my eyes. Ruby has leaned back slightly and is looking at me with steady eyes.

"What?" I ask, my voice rough.

"It's OK. I forgive you," she repeats slowly, stroking my ribs. "That doesn't mean I'll forget the way you behaved. If you ever do a thing like that again . . ." She shrugs vaguely. When I take in what she just said and see her cautious smile, the relief that I feel is almost overwhelming. I wrap my arms around her, pull her close to my body, and murmur breathlessly into her lips, "I won't. I won't, I promise."

Then I kiss her.

I try to use the kiss to show her how grateful I am and to share all the whirling emotions inside me. Ruby rolls on top of me, and I hold her tight. She teases me with her tongue and strokes it over my still-throbbing lower lip. A growl sounds from deep in my chest and I suck on her tongue, so that now it's she who gasps.

I have no idea how we got here, but in this second, I feel like I'm flying, not falling. Ruby forgives me. She forgives me, and she'll stay in my life.

The next moment, she pulls her lips away from me and starts to unbutton my shirt.

"What are you doing?" I ask hoarsely.

"Undressing you."

She carries on until the last button is undone and she has a full view of my naked torso. She bites her lip and touches my stomach, hesitantly at first and then a bit more boldly. The look with which she's devouring my body makes me glad of the many hours of extra training I've put in over the last month.

Ruby leans down and kisses a trail over my stomach, and I inhale sharply. Then I can suddenly feel her tongue against my waistband, and I lean up on my elbows. "What are you doing?"

She looks up at me through half-closed eyes. "Isn't this what couples do when they make up?"

"Are we a couple?"

"Well, I'm not having you as a friend with benefits. I don't want that."

I grin. "Friend with benefits?"

"You know what I mean."

"How can anyone have an IQ like yours and then come out in all seriousness with a phrase like 'friend with benefits'?" I murmur in amusement, which earns me a punch in the guts. I groan with pain. "I preferred it when you were using your tongue."

Another punch, then she works her way back up again until her face is only a hand's width from mine. "Do you really think it's wise to be that cheeky this soon?"

I feel as though my pounding heart is going to burst my rib cage any second. Ruby is straddling me, her upper body pressed against mine, the buttons on her blouse scratching my skin slightly. My hard-on presses almost painfully against the cloth of my trousers, and I shut my eyes for a moment as Ruby shifts her hips.

I want her.

I want her more than I've ever wanted anything.

"I'm whatever you want," I croak, meaning every word. "Friend, boyfriend, friend with benefits, anything." I don't care what my parents say or what lies ahead in the future. Ruby's right—we have the present. And I can't deny what I feel for her a second longer.

"Anything? Really?" she whispers.

"Anything," I repeat, running my hands up her thighs. Something glitters in Ruby's moss-green eyes. As I run my thumb over the inside of her thigh, I hear her gasp for breath. A triumphant smile spreads over my lips. She's incredibly sensitive. I repeat the movement, but higher up this time. Ruby shuts her eyes. She looks gorgeous with her wavy hair; long, dark lashes; and her cute blouse with its bow at the collar. I'd love to pull on the black ribbon, but I don't dare. If we're really going to the next level, then it's for her to take the next step.

As if she'd read my thoughts, Ruby leans forward until her mouth is close to my ear. The next moment, her lips run along the rim of it and down, and she takes my earlobe between her teeth. My body reacts violently to her. I have goose bumps all over, and the arousal is making me almost dizzy. She keeps on teasing me, trailing kisses down my throat and sucking at the crook of my neck.

I swear under my breath.

Ruby pushes away from me, looking at me seriously. "Don't you like that?"

"Yes." My voice is rough and scratchy with desire. "Yes, I like it."

I wanted to give her time and not rush her, I wanted to be patient and act like a gentleman, but . . . I can't any longer. I want to show her what she does to me. My hands tremble as I take hold of her face and press my lips against hers. Ruby groans with surprise as I roll over and pin her firmly beneath me. The moment I press my erection against her, she gasps in my mouth and clings on to my back. If she's like this already, I can hardly wait to be inside her.

The next second, she strokes the shirt off my arms until it falls to the floor beside the bed. Her hands wander over my back, hesitantly at first, and then she gently scratches her nails along my spine until she reaches my bum and squeezes it.

"Shit, Ruby," I growl.

"I've wanted to do that for so long," she replies, giving me a slap. I laugh breathlessly into her neck and bite her gently in revenge. She reacts by wrapping her legs around my hips and pressing herself more firmly against me. Fuck's sake, is she trying to kill me?

I lean back a little, then take the ribbon at her collar between my fingers. I look her in the eyes as I slowly pull on it. Ruby gulps hard and watches, as if in a trance, while I undo the buttons. She sits up so that I can slip the blouse off her shoulders. I don't know where I throw it; I only have eyes for Ruby. The light of the lantern outside casts pale stripes over her skin and the skin-tone bra she's wearing. Ruby's body is beautiful—curvaceous and soft in all the right places. It's obvious at school that Ruby knows exactly what she wants—apparently, she's the same in bed, and that's making my throat dry out.

I lean down and dot a row of kisses over her cleavage. I put my hands around her breasts and stroke them, which makes Ruby gasp with surprise. I'm longing to rip the rest of her clothes off her body and sink into her, but I hold back.

This is our first time. I want us both to remember—years from now—how good it was.

So I take it slowly as I explore her upper body. I run my lips and teeth over every inch of skin, lick across her breasts, and hold her tighter. I move further down and run my teeth over the arch of her ribs. Her hushed gasps and the way she tenses are like a guidebook to her body. As I reach her waistband, she digs her fingers in my hair. Questioningly, I look up at her. She has me in her hand; it's for her alone to decide what happens next.

"Keep going," she whispers, almost inaudibly.

I don't need any further invitation.

First, I pull off her shoes, then her socks. Ruby watches me, a slight smile on her lips. Then I unzip her trousers and help her pull them off her legs. After that, she's lying there in front of me, in her underwear, and I hold my breath. I don't know what I did to deserve this. Not a clue. Perhaps that's what people call karma. Goes something like: *Hey, is your whole life going to shit? Well, to make up for that, here's the most amazing girl in the world. She's forgiven you and likes you and even though you don't deserve it, she's letting you get her undressed.*

Or something.

Whatever Ruby's reason might be for letting me do this—I'm going to show her how highly I value her.

I lean down and kiss my way up her legs. Then there's no more thinking, only feeling. I run both hands over Ruby's hips. I gently stroke her sides, run my hand over her belly, to the top of her knickers. Ruby's breathing faster and heavier.

Keep going. The echo of her words sounds in my head.

I keep going. I hook my finger into her knickers and pull them down. She's in front of me nearly naked, and I can't think straight anymore. I don't hesitate another second, just start to draw a teasing trail along her groin and down. As I press my mouth to her middle, Ruby swears loudly. She buries her hands in my hair again, and for a moment, I don't know whether she wants to push me away or pull me closer. I move my mouth, press a kiss onto her heat. As I let my tongue flicker out, she squirms, and I press a hand onto her belly to hold her firm. I enjoy the way she scratches her fingers over my scalp and shows me where she wants me and how hard. As her breath comes faster and her legs stiffen, I slip a finger into her wet heat. I suck on her and move my finger slowly and regularly. It doesn't take long for Ruby to cry out my name and rear up beneath me.

I keep on licking and kissing her until the waves rolling through her body gradually lessen. She's right out of breath as I eventually let go of her and slide up the bed so that I can look at her. Her hair is tousled, and her cheeks are red. She's staring at the ceiling, and it takes a few minutes for her breathing to get back to normal.

Then she wraps her arms around my neck and grins at me.

"You totally have to do that again," she says.

I grin back at her, resolving in my mind that I'm going to spend an entire night sometime with my head between Ruby's legs.

"Your cheeky mouth comes in very handy down there."

I shake my head and look at her, then press a soft kiss on her lips. Ruby doesn't allow the kiss to stay on the surface. No, she pulls me closer and slips her tongue into my mouth. I'm surprised by the stormy way she kisses me. Apparently, she likes the taste of herself on my lips. She wraps a leg around me and presses against me. A hot tingling shoots through my body, and I groan into her mouth and thrust up with my hips, which makes Ruby give an "oh" of surprise. The next moment, her hands are on my belt. Her movements are clumsy and driven by lust. I can't believe how much I like to see her this way.

After she's undone my fly, she wants to push my trousers down, but I stop her. "Hold on," I say, pulling my wallet from my back pocket. I open it and pull out the condom. I lay it on the pillow, then take off my trousers and socks. I drop everything beside the bed, then I'm on top of Ruby again. I slide my hand behind her back and undo the catch on her bra. I help her to slip it off, and then there isn't even a millimeter of fabric between us. Ruby groans quietly as I take her breast in one hand and start to stroke it.

I love the way she responds to my every movement. I've never been with a girl like her before. Her reactions make me so horny that I can hardly bear it. When she's under my boxers, pulling them over my bottom, I nearly lose my mind.

"How do you want me?" I whisper, kissing my way up to her face again. I stroke her hair off her face and run my fingers over her jaw. I want to show her with every touch how much she means to me.

"Just like that," Ruby breathes, tenderly stroking my back. I nod and reach for the plastic wrapper. My hands are shaking as I roll the condom onto me. Ruby rests on her elbows, watching my every movement with curiosity glittering in her eyes. Without hesitation, I take her hand and wrap it around my shaft. It twitches in her hand, and Ruby looks at me with dark eyes. I cautiously move our hands up and down, pressing firmly. She swallows hard. I let go of her hand, and she starts to move it on her own, doubtfully at first but then with increasing confidence. I pant as she clasps exactly the right spot.

"Ruby . . ." I whisper.

The next moment, she lets go of me and lies down again.

Her dark hair is fanned over the white pillow, and her green eyes are sparkling like something in a dream as I cover her body with mine and take over the place between her legs. It happens almost by itself; I glide my tip inside her and hold my breath as Ruby sighs beneath me. She's incredibly tight but wet enough that I dare to cautiously press forward. I touch her cheek, stroke her bottom lip with my thumb, then press my mouth onto hers. I kiss her slowly and with feeling as I pull out of her a little, then cautiously thrust into her again. At that moment, Ruby shifts the angle of her hips—and the resistance eases. I sink my full length into her, and we both groan. A thought is trying to fight its way through the layers of emotion to the surface of my mind, but I can't quite grasp it. There's no more room in my head. It's full of Ruby, the taste and the heat of her, surrounding me. I thrust again, and Ruby pants breathlessly. She wraps a leg around my hips, and I hold on to her thigh.

It feels so perfect that I wish we'd done this sooner instead of scattering boulders in our path. I dig my fingers into her thighs and hold her still while I try to find something approaching a steady rhythm. Ruby's hands are all over me; she leans down and kisses my chest, presses into me with every stroke, as though she can't get enough of me. I feel the same. She feels so good that it's bloody hard not to lose control of my movements.

"You're shaking," she whispers, running her hand up my back. She holds on to my shoulders while I kiss the spot behind her ear and slowly thrust into her.

"Because I have to control myself."

"Is this the James Beaufort who breaks waterbeds having sex?" she asks breathlessly.

I bite at her throat. "I already told you it wasn't a waterbed."

Ruby ignores my words and wraps her other leg around me too. She moves her hips so that I slip deeper inside her. I groan, and, almost by itself, my body follows her indirect instructions. I put a hand on the nape of Ruby's neck and hold her so that her head doesn't bang into the bed. Then I press into her, harder and faster than before. Ruby scratches my back and with every movement, makes sure that I gradually lose control. It doesn't take long for the headboard to whack audibly into the wall, and I can no longer suppress the sounds coming from deep in my chest. Ruby's breathing faster than ever, her nails digging into my skin. Her eyes are shut, but I just have to see what's happening to her.

"Look at me," I pant.

She does as I say, and our eyes meet. The connection between us is more intense than ever. I can't look away, and Ruby seems to feel the same. We're moving in unison, as if we were made to do this very thing. I thrust into her, again and again, until I find a place inside her that makes her groan loudly. Her muscles contract around me and suddenly it's too much. The bed isn't creaking loudly enough to drown out our noises as we climax together. My world explodes, and all that's left is a universe of colored stars and lights, where there's no room for anything but Ruby.

30

Ruby

"You should have said before." James runs a finger down my spine, and I shudder.

"Why?"

I'm lying with my head on his chest, absent-mindedly stroking his firm stomach. Our legs are interlinked, and we're still naked, although James has pulled the duvet over us now.

"Because I'd have been gentler," he murmurs, pressing his lips against my hairline.

"I think it would have scared you, and you'd have run away."

"I wouldn't. I'd just have been more careful."

I put my head back and look up into his face. There's a crease between his brows—he looks genuinely worried.

"But I didn't want it gentle and careful."

One corner of his mouth twitches slightly, and there's a dark flash in his eyes. It vanishes as fast as it came. "Maybe I should have thought about a change of scene. Nobody should lose their virginity in a college bedroom with a squeaky bed."

I sit up in outrage. For a split second, James's gaze lands on my breasts, then he looks me in the eyes again. "Hello? If I'm going to lose my virginity anyway, then yes please to doing so in Oxford."

He shakes his head with a laugh. The next moment, he takes hold of my elbows and pulls me down until I land on top of him. He wraps his arms around me and holds me firmly to his warm body. "You're crazy, Ruby Bell."

Maybe a little, I admit in my mind.

But it all felt so right. James and me—maybe it will never be simple for us, and maybe James's father will do everything he can to get me out of his son's life, but I'm ready to fight for James. This thing between us is something special. As of today, I know that, and the way he looks at me, and touches me, tells me that he feels the same. We'll do this. I've never been this certain of anything.

"How did it go for you?" I ask after a while, not meeting his eyes.

"Hmm?"

I focus on the pattern I'm drawing on his stomach. "I mean . . . how was your first time?"

He exhales audibly, and his belly sinks under my hand. "Do you really want to know?"

Now I do look at him. "Of course I do."

"It was OK. I was fourteen, drunk, and I made a mess of it."

"Fourteen?" Oh God, then he's had four years' practice. I don't want to think about how many girls he must have been with to be this good.

"Wren bet me I wouldn't, so I did. It took about two minutes and didn't feel great."

"Then you're not exactly entitled to throw opinions about successful first times around the place," I say quietly.

"If you ever tell anyone your story, I hope this will come out of it better."

I press a kiss onto his chest. "Definitely. It was perfect."

I don't understand why, but it feels entirely normal to be lying here with him like this. As if this is right where I belong. I haven't felt this good in weeks, and even the slightly painful throbbing between my legs isn't bothering me. I meant what I said: It was perfect. And I can't imagine a better time or place for it.

"You seemed really upset this afternoon," James says out of nowhere, which does damp my mood a bit.

"The interview was shit," I mumble.

His lips roam over my hairline again and graze my temple. "Those tutors were both dickheads. I think they get off on deliberately unsettling applicants. I'm sure you were great." He says it with such certainty that I almost believe him. Almost.

"I really wasn't. I got one question totally wrong. And I could definitely tell that they didn't think much of what I said."

"In what way?"

I tell him about the morning's debacle.

"Like I said, I swear they get off on it. Don't worry so much. If *you* don't get into Oxford, nobody will." He sounds more confident than I feel, but it's good even to talk to anyone about it. Especially because James knows how much it means to me.

"Thank you for saying that."

He kisses my lips by way of answer. It's an effort not to just lose myself in him, to pull my head back after a while and ask: "How did yours go?"

He makes a rumbling sound that's hard to interpret, and suddenly there's that look on his face, the one that turns up anytime the talk comes around to Beaufort's, Oxford, or his future. And it makes my heart ache.

"Talk to me," I whisper.

James looks darkly back at me. In the end, he gives in and takes a deep breath. "I know that Oxford means the world to you, which is why it's so hard for me to talk to you about it, but . . . to me, I find all the drama a bit silly."

I try not to let that get to me. Not everyone has the same dreams and ambitions. James feeling that way has nothing to do with me and everything to do with him.

"When I was in the interview earlier . . . Everything just moved on around me. Like in a black-and-white film that someone's fast-forwarding, and I'm the only person who doesn't budge."

"If you really don't want to study here, or go into your parents' firm—what would you rather do instead?"

He shakes his head, and I see the panic in his eyes. "Please don't ask me that."

"Why not?" I stroke his cheek and feel how rough his skin is there. There's a bit of stubble coming through, and he'll have shaved it off in the morning. But James looks amazing with a five o'clock shadow.

"You were right when you said that I don't know what I want from life. I don't think about everything I could do, because if I allow myself to dream, it just makes everything all the more depressing afterward."

He still thinks that he has no chance to take control of his own life. But why would he, when there's a legacy like that waiting for him, like a huge burden on his shoulders?

"Dreams are important, James," I whisper.

"Then you're my dream."

For a moment, that takes my breath away, but I quickly realize that that was cheating—that he's just trying to avoid responding to what I just said. "I'm afraid that's not how it works."

He gives me a wonky smile. "Yeah, that would've been too easy."

"So, what do you like? What gives you a buzz?"

He has to think about that for a moment. I feel that he's suddenly tense, and I kiss his chest as if to tell him that it's OK and to take his time.

"I like lacrosse," he begins hesitantly. "And books. Art. Good music. Oh, and spicy food. Spicy Asian food, to be precise. Someday, I'd like to go to Bangkok and try all kinds of things in the street markets there."

I grin into his skin. "What, like deep-fried locusts?"

"Exactly." His tension gradually eases.

"That all sounds in the realm of possibility."

"Those are things you do on holiday, not goals in life."

I run my hand in gentle circles around his stomach. "It's a start. You could do all those things if you stopped getting in your own way."

James says nothing.

I have an idea. Abruptly, I stand up and hunt for my underwear on the floor. I find everything right next to the bed and slip into my knickers first, then my bra. I spot a gray T-shirt of James's on the chair by the desk. I pull it on and then turn my attention to the desk.

"What are you doing?" James asks behind me. I grab his black notebook, the one with the fancy "B," and a pen, then turn to face him. He's pulled his boxer shorts back on too.

"We're going to make a list," I answer, clambering back into bed with the book.

James looks inquiringly at me. I tap the mattress beside me. The bed is still warm, and the scent of James is all around me. Slowly, he comes toward me, his eyes suspicious. The mattress sags beneath his weight as he sits down.

I lean over him to switch on the bedside lamp. Then I open his notebook in my lap.

"Whenever I feel bad, I make lists. Ever since I was little, it's helped me to stay focused and to keep a clear head. Even when things aren't going so well," I explain. "I find inspiring quotes or make notes of things I want to do one day, or want to change about the world, or whatever." I pick up the pen. "I normally make it all a bit more colorful, but this will have to do."

The suspicion vanishes from his face, and he smiles. "You want to make a list like that for me?"

I nod. "Maybe it'll help motivate you too."

He studies the blank page in the notebook and then nods. "OK."

I grin and set the pen to paper. Then I write *To Do* in swirly letters in the middle at the top. I draw a wavy line under the title. Then I write: *1. Travel to Bangkok.* I look expectantly at James. "What next?"

He rubs his chin pensively.

"It can be anything," I remind him.

"I'd like to keep playing lacrosse," he says in the end, quietly.

"Oh, yes," I murmur, making a note of the second point on the list. Then I draw a little lacrosse stick and James's shirt with the seventeen on it. By the time I glance up, his expression is so warm, it makes my belly start to tingle.

"So, what now?"

He needs another moment to think. I don't want to pressure him, so I wait patiently.

"I'd like to read more," he says. "And not just my usual stuff."

"What do you normally read?"

"Nonfiction books my dad gives me. Biographies of successful businessmen." He frowns. "But there's so much more. I'd like to try manga, for example." He gives me a smile that speaks volumes.

"I could give you a list of recommendations," I say, smiling back at him.

"I'd devour them."

I grin and bend over the list. *3. Read more, other genres,* I write. "What else?"

James swallows hard. "Obviously, I'd like a job where I feel fulfilled. I don't know what, or if it's even possible, but . . ." He shrugs his shoulders. It seems like he wants to say more but won't let himself. I put the pen down and hold his face. I tenderly run my thumb over his warm cheek and then lean in to kiss him. He shuts his eyes and sighs softly.

"Everything is possible, James," I whisper, leaning back again. I pick up the pen and jot down: *4. Find a fulfilling career.* After that, I eye my handiwork thoughtfully.

"There's something missing," James says suddenly, grabbing for the notebook. He takes the pen from me and writes something down.

"Finished," he murmurs, holding the book out. I slide over next to him until my bare thigh is touching his and read what he's added.

5. Ruby

I hold my breath and look from the list to James and back again.

"If you're with me, I feel as though I can do anything," he says hoarsely. "So that's why you definitely belong on a list that's there to make me happy."

I don't know what to say. So I climb onto his lap and fling my arms around his neck. He puts his hand on the back of my head and kisses me. Together, we sink back into the pillow, with molten lips and his dreams in our hands.

James

Sadly, the best night of my life by miles has to come to an end eventually. Ruby and I tried to pull an all-nighter, but around four a.m., we fell asleep, only to wake up again with a jump about three hours later because we thought we'd overslept, and her parents might already be waiting at the door. Luckily it was a false alarm, but we don't have long left.

I find it incredibly hard to let Ruby go back to her room. I don't want to say goodbye to her and keep pulling her back to me and kissing her, as if it's going to be at least a month before I see her again. But we're going to be in school together again tomorrow, and I might even see her before that if I can sneak out of the house. My chances are pretty good. My father considered it a personal insult that I was invited to St. Hilda's for an interview. He even offered to pull some strings so I could swap places with Lydia, who—unlike me—did get an interview from Balliol. I can still hear words like "useless" and "waste of space" swirling around my head. I don't think he'll be interested in how it went.

Percy picks me up in the early morning. He takes my suitcase from me and stows it in the boot of the Rolls before he gets in again and we go to meet Lydia. The screen is up and the intercom is off, so apparently, he's not in the mood to chat. That suits me fine as it gives me another chance to look at Ruby's list. I don't know how realistic the items on it really are, but at least it will always remind me of last night.

I'm now wearing the gray T-shirt that Ruby had on until this morning, and her scent clings to me. I feel as though I can still taste her on my tongue, and I get goose bumps every time I remember the way she groaned my name. I want to do that again. Right away, ideally.

When Lydia joins me in the car, she can immediately see that something's changed. She narrows her eyes at me, looks me up and down, then into my face again. A knowing grin spreads across her features. "You look like you had a good night." She knows me too well.

I fold the list up again and slip it back into my wallet. It can replace the fuck-you card that I ripped up and threw in the college bin.

"Do I get any details?"

The question surprises me. Lydia might have opened up to me about her and Sutton, but we're not usually willing to discuss our love lives with each other.

I eye her dubiously. "Since when have you been interested in what I get up to at night?"

She shrugs her shoulders. "Since it's been Ruby you're messing around with."

The words "messing around" feel absolutely insufficient for what Ruby and I have. "One, who says it was Ruby I spent the night with? And two, I thought you couldn't stand her."

Lydia rolls her eyes. "One, I'm not stupid. And two, if you like her, I do too. Simple."

"That's good. Because I think you're going to be seeing more of her, and not just at school."

Lydia's mouth drops open. "Are you serious about her?"

I can't help the smile that spreads over my face. The next moment, Lydia whacks me on the arm. "I can't believe it! James!"

"What?"

"If Dad finds out, he'll freak," she says, shaking her head. Her hand is still on my arm. She gives it a quick squeeze. "But you look very happy. I'm pleased for you both."

I didn't know it would be like this. I didn't know what it felt like to be in love or that the mere thought of Ruby would set my heart racing. I wish I could tell Percy to drive straight round to hers because I'm afraid I can't survive a second longer without her.

"What's up with Percy?" Lydia asks, out of the blue, as if she's read my mind. She's speaking quieter now and nods toward the driver's area.

"No idea."

"He didn't even ask me how it went," she murmurs.

"You can tell me," I offer, but Lydia wrinkles her nose.

"You're weird when you're in love."

I just pull a face.

We spend the rest of the journey in companionable silence. Lydia taps on her phone, and I stare out of the window, thinking about last night. When we reach the house, I walk around the car to help Percy with the cases. He holds out a hand to stop me and looks seriously at me.

"You should go in, Mr. Beaufort." He hasn't spoken that sternly to me since I was seven and spilled Coke on the back seat of a new car. Percy looks from me to Lydia and back again, then gives a gulp and turns his attention to the bags. Lydia and I look at each other in confusion and walk up the steps to the door.

"What's wrong with him?" she whispers, even though we're well out of earshot.

"No idea. Have you spoken to Dad since yesterday?"

She shakes her head, I open the door, and we walk into the house together. Lydia puts her bag down on the little table next to the front door as Mary, our housekeeper, comes into the front hall. At the sight of us, she goes as white as chalk. I'm about to say hello when she turns and heads for the sitting room. Lydia and I exchange glances again. Together, we walk across the hall and into the room Mary just entered.

Dad is standing at the fireplace. He has his back to us, but I can tell that there's a glass of pale brown liquor in his hand—and it's not even midday. The fire in the hearth crackles quietly, and Mary murmurs something to him, then hastily vanishes.

"Dad?" I ask.

He turns, his face expressionless as usual. Even so, the dark rings under his eyes make me feel uneasy.

"Sit down." He waves toward the green satin sofa and settles himself in the armchair beside it.

I don't want to sit down. I want to know what the hell is going on here. Lydia takes a seat, but I stay standing in the doorway, staring at my father. He lifts his glass to his lips and drains the rest of the whisky. Then he puts it down on a small table.

"Sit down, James." It's an order now, not a request. But I can't move from the spot. The tension is too much. Something's happened, I sensed it the moment I walked into the house.

"Where's Mum?" Lydia asks. Her voice sounds fake, like she's trying to be cheerful, to lift the mood between Dad and me. But she must know that there's something wrong here.

"Your mother had a stroke."

My father leans back in the chair, arms on the armrests, legs crossed with one ankle resting on the other knee. His face is steely. Impassive. Exactly the same as always.

"Wh-what . . . What do you mean?" Lydia stammers.

"Your mother had a stroke." He repeats the words as if he's learned them by heart. "She's dead."

Lydia claps her hands to her mouth and sobs. I feel like I'm not really here. My soul has detached from my body, and I'm watching the scene from somewhere else entirely.

Dad keeps talking, but I only take in the occasional scrap.

. . . vessel burst . . . came too late . . . hospital . . . nothing more they could do for her . . .

His mouth is moving, but his words are mingled with the wailing sound from Lydia's throat. I can hear something else too. Gasping. Loud, hasty panting.

I think it's me.

I press my hand to my chest to try to make it stop. It doesn't work. I'm breathing faster and faster but can't seem to get any air. None of the tips I've read on the internet about panic attacks are any use to me now. My body switches onto autopilot, making me break out in a cold sweat.

Mum is dead.

She's *dead*.

My father's face doesn't change. Maybe this is all just a bad joke. Maybe it's my punishment for not getting an interview at Balliol.

"When?" I'm still breathing hard, but I get the word out. I feel dizzy. The ground is swaying under my feet. I have to hold on to something but don't remember how to tell my arms they need to move.

My father looks at me, his expression unreadable. "On Monday afternoon."

My heart. It's going to stop any moment, or else explode in my chest. At first, I don't take in what my dad just said because I'm too busy getting air into my lungs. But after a few choppy breaths, the meaning of his words dawns on me.

On Monday afternoon.

Today is Wednesday.

"Let me get this straight," I say, my voice trembling. "Mum had a stroke two days ago, and you're telling us this now?"

I shouldn't have to ask a question like that. I should go over to my sister and give her a hug. We should be crying together. But it doesn't feel real. It still feels as though this isn't really happening—it's happening to someone else who has temporarily taken control of my body, and I'm just watching on. Powerless and totally stunned.

Dad drums his fingers on the armrests. "I didn't want you to mess up your interviews."

I can't explain what happens next. It's as though a blazing bolt of lightning strikes in my brain. The next moment, I hurl myself at my father and ram my fist into his face. I punch so hard that the chair tips over beneath him, and Dad and I crash to the ground. Lydia screams. Something falls to the ground and shatters. My fist connects with my father's indifferent face yet again. Blood spurts from his nose, and a bone in my hand crunches dangerously. There are shards of glass all around us. My hand is burning and throbbing, but I draw my arm back for another blow.

"James, stop it!" Lydia cries.

Someone grabs me from behind and pulls me away from my father. I fight like a wild animal, trying to shake off their firm grip. I want to make my father pay. For everything.

Dad gets up with Lydia's help. Blood is running from his nose and one corner of his mouth. He touches his face with his fingers and studies the dark redness of it. Then he looks at Percy, who is still holding on to me. "Get him out of here until he's calmed down."

Percy pulls me away and drags me down the hall. His arms are so tight around my ribs that I can't breathe. We crash into a sideboard, and something else falls and breaks. He doesn't let go of me until we're outside. I turn on my heel, ready to march back into the house.

"Mr. Beaufort, you have to stop," Percy says, grabbing me by the shoulders. I push his hands away and shove him in the chest.

"Out of the way, Percy."

"No." His voice is firm, and his fingers dig deep into the fabric of my jacket.

"He kept it a secret from us. *You* kept it a secret from us," I gasp. I push him again. "My mother is dead, and you didn't tell me." The words feel like acid, and suddenly, the burning is everywhere: in my mouth, my throat, my chest, and my eyes. My vision blurs.

"My mother is dead."

A dull ache races through my body. It hurts so much. I don't think I can bear it. It brings me to my knees, and I still can't breathe properly. This has to stop. I have to silence this pain.

My hands are shaking uncontrollably. The next moment, I whirl around and run toward the garage.

"Mr. Beaufort!"

I wave him back. Percy runs after me. My feet carry me to my car. Hands shaking, I dig the key out of my pocket and open the driver's door. My peripheral vision is getting darker, and it feels as though I might faint any moment. Whatever. Nothing matters a fuck. I start the car. Percy stands right in front of it. That doesn't matter either. I step on the accelerator, and he jumps out of the way at the last second. Tires squealing, I drive away, wiping my wet cheeks with the back of my hand.

32

Ruby

The doorbell rings just as I pull a Jenga block out of the stack. I jump, which makes the entire tower collapse. Mum, Dad, and Ember boo, and I swear under my breath.

"You're out for the next round," Mum says, rubbing her hands. She's the best at this game and practically always wins.

Once I'd told my family about the visit and shown them a slideshow of my Oxford photos on my laptop, we had dinner together and decided to have a game night. We're on our third round of Jenga, and I've already lost twice. I admit defeat, and as the others start stacking the little wooden blocks again, I go to answer the door. My eyes widen as I see who it is standing there.

"Lydia?"

She looks distraught. Her cheeks are red, and her eyes are swollen. I take a step toward her, but she wards me off. "Is James here?"

I shake my head. "No. What's happened?" I ask in alarm.

Lydia doesn't even seem to hear me. She pulls her phone out of her jacket pocket and dials a number, then holds it to her ear. I walk outside in my socks and grab her arm. I stare hard at her. "What's happened?"

She just shakes her head.

"Cy? It's me," she says suddenly into the phone. "Is James with you?"

Cyril says something at the other end of the line, and relief spreads over her face. "Thank God."

I can hear Cyril's voice again but can't make out the words. Whatever he's saying, it makes Lydia's expression darken again.

"OK. No, I'll come." He replies, and Lydia glances briefly at me. "Yes. See you in a bit."

Once she's hung up, she's about to turn and run back to the car, where Percy is waiting. He's leaning against it, looking just as worried, which makes me feel sick.

"Lydia, please tell me what's happened," I say abruptly.

She opens her mouth and shuts it again. "I don't think that's a good idea."

I gesture to her to wait. Then I run back into the house, slip on my boots, grab my coat and the scarf Dad knitted for me. I call out to my family that I have to go out and take my key off the hook by the front door. As I go, I wrap my scarf around my neck. Lydia looks like she wants to stop me but just doesn't have the strength.

She disappears into the car without another word. I say hello to Percy, who just nods to me, then get into the back too. Lydia is sitting in James's usual place. Her eyes are glassy, and she's fiddling with the hem of her red coat. I want to take her hand but don't dare.

"The offer's still open. If you want to talk, I mean," I say quietly.

Lydia flinches as if I'd yelled at her. She looks up, and there are tears swimming in her eyes. Every second in her company makes

me feel queasier. What can have happened to make her this dis-
traught? I suddenly have a horrible thought. I glance at the ceiling.
The little red light isn't on, which means that Percy can't hear us.
I lean forward slightly.

"Is everything OK with the baby?" I whisper.

Lydia gives a panicked glance at the driver's seat, but the screen
is up too. Then she turns back to me. "Yes," she says hoarsely. "At
home, we had a . . ." She pauses and seems to be deciding how far
she can trust me. "There was trouble."

Given what James told me about his father last night, I can get
a picture of what "trouble" might mean in the Beaufort house. I
have goose bumps all over.

"Is James OK, Lydia?" I whisper, not able to suppress the panic
in my voice.

Lydia gives a helpless shrug. "Cyril says so."

The next quarter of an hour feels like eternity. I hold tight to
the hem of my jacket, trying not to freak out with anxiety. I don't
know exactly what's going on, and Lydia won't meet my eyes, just
strokes her belly, lost in thought. Now and then, she blinks hard,
like she's fighting back tears. Once, her phone buzzes. She reads
the message, then presses her lips together. After that, she really
doesn't seem like she wants to talk.

When we get to Cyril's, Lydia jumps out of the car and hurries
toward the house. She slips on the icy steps, and I catch her at the
last moment, grabbing her arm so that she doesn't fall. She mumbles a thank-you.

Cyril's in the doorway. When Lydia reaches him, he greets her
with wide-open arms. "Well, fancy that. See who's gracing our
party with their presence."

He hugs her, but she just stands there, letting it happen, like a lifeless doll. It's a while before Cyril lets her go. Then he sees me. "And you even brought a plus-one. How nice." The tone of his voice makes it perfectly clear that he doesn't mean those last two words. Then he takes a step to the side, and we walk in. The music is thumping out from the back of the house, but it's loud enough from here. Cyril still has an arm around Lydia's shoulders. I wonder if he knows what's happened or whether he just has the tact not to ask her about it.

We cross the hall that I was in the last time. There's nobody up on the gallery tonight; everything seems to be happening in the sitting room. We walk in, the music hits us, and I look around. It's not as crowded as the other time I was here. This party is on a much smaller scale. I don't know why, but that makes me even more worried. There are a few people I don't know dancing around in their underwear in the middle of the room. Alistair is sitting on one of the sofas, making out with some huge guy with tattoos. Further back, I spot Kesh by a drinks trolley. He's glaring at them, narrow-eyed, then downs his drink in one.

The back of my neck starts to tingle . . . and I see James. He's sitting on a sofa near the pool. My shoulders stiffen as my eyes take him in. He looks wrecked. His hair's a mess, his shirtsleeves are rolled up, and I can see spots of something red on the gray T-shirt beneath it—the shirt I was wearing last night. My heart sinks into my boots.

I'm about to go over to him when I see him bend down. He leans his head over the table, presses a finger to one nostril, and inhales a white substance with the other. My mouth drops open. Did he just . . . ?

A blond girl who looks vaguely familiar clambers out of the pool and strolls over to James. She bends a finger and beckons him over. He stands up, head aslant. She walks the last few feet and stops right in front of him. Then she lifts her hands and starts to unbutton his shirt. At that moment, I recognize her. The girl groping my boyfriend is Elaine Ellington. A cold shiver runs down my spine, and I feel a stabbing pain in my stomach. I'm rooted to the spot.

"How long's he been like this?" Lydia asks Cyril.

"All afternoon. He's totally out of it."

Lydia hisses out a curse. The two of them keep talking, but I can't hear them over the roaring in my ears. Elaine pushes the shirt over James's shoulders, and it falls to the floor. Then she starts fiddling with his belt.

That's enough.

At that moment, my anger is greater than my phobia of water. I'm over to them in just a few strides.

"What the hell are you doing?" I snarl.

James turns his head but looks straight through me, not at me.

He's like a total stranger. His face is stony, his pupils are so huge that you can hardly see his irises at all, and I can't make out their unusual turquoise color. His cheeks are pale, and his eyes are lined in red.

This isn't my James. This is the guy he was months ago, the guy who bribes people, gets off his head with his friends every weekend, gets horizontal with one girl after another. He's the guy who doesn't feel a thing, doesn't give a shit about anything.

"James," I whisper, taking his hand. His skin is as cold as ice.

For a second, something flickers in his eyes. It's dark and all-consuming, seems to be eating him up from the inside out. He inhales audibly, shuts his eyes for a moment—and when he opens them, that expression has gone again.

"You shouldn't be here, Ruby."

"But I . . ."

Even as I'm speaking, he turns away and jumps into the pool. The loud splash startles me. Little water droplets land on my face, and I jump back. Elaine and a few other guests, dressed only in their underwear, follow James into the water. Wren's with them too. He resurfaces with a roar and splashes James, who grins and shakes the water out of his hair.

Everything here feels so wrong. I'm longing to talk to James, but there are lots of reasons why that's not possible. I'm too scared to get any closer to the water, and I don't think he's in any fit state to take in anything anyone says to him. James looks impassive. Like the world is rushing past him, and he's just numb, being swept along with it.

Elaine moves closer to James. He swims on his back to the wall, and she smiles and follows him. My heart is beating faster and faster. I don't understand what's going on here. It's like a bad dream. Under the water, I can make out the vague outline of her body pressed into his. She's standing between his legs, leaning in and whispering into his ear. They look comfortable. Like this isn't the first time this has happened. Everything within me is shouting at me to go and tear her away from him, but I can't move. James does nothing as Elaine takes his face in her hands and kisses him.

Something shatters inside me. Little shards of glass penetrate my rib cage and work their way deeper into my soul until I can hardly breathe.

Suddenly, someone puts their hand on my shoulder. "Now that's the James Beaufort I know," Cyril whispers in my ear.

I want to say: *But he's not the James Beaufort that I know. You have no idea what he's really like.*

He's my boyfriend, you stupid arsehole.

But that's not true. If James Beaufort were my boyfriend, he wouldn't be doing this. If he were my boyfriend, he'd have come to me and told me about his problems instead of using drugs and alcohol and his superficial friends to distract himself from the pain. If he were my boyfriend, he wouldn't have another girl's tongue shoved down his throat right now.

I turn on my heel. I slip on the wet floor but just about catch myself in time. I fight my way back through the sitting room as fast as I can. My footsteps echo on the floor of the huge entrance hall as I run to the door. I have to get out of here, right now. But I'm afraid there's nowhere in the entire world where I can forget what just happened.

"Ruby!" Lydia calls behind me. I stop and look back over my shoulder. As I see how desperate she looks, a guilty feeling rises up inside me.

"I'm really sorry your family life is so shit, Lydia," I say, my voice trembling. "But I can't do this. Not like this, not after . . ." After what? After I thought we'd worked through this exact issue? After we spent the night together? There's no way I can say that to her.

"He needs you now," she pleads.

I give a bitter laugh and lean my head right back to stare at the ceiling. This hall is so over-the-top. Gold as far as the eye can see, priceless oil paintings, expensive antique vases—things that suddenly strike me as utterly trivial. I turn and keep walking until I finally reach the exit. Lydia calls something out behind me, but I'm not listening anymore.

When the heavy door slams shut behind me, I see it as symbolic.

For a brief moment, I truly thought that James and I could make this work, if we both wanted it enough. But now one thing is clear to me:

I will never be a part of his world.

Unfortunately, I'm only recognizing that now, when it's far too late.

ACKNOWLEDGMENTS

I would like to thank so many people who have been involved in creating *Save Me*:

My husband, Christian, who is always by my side with his help and encouragement.

Jerome Scheuren, whose experience of applying to Oxford was a great help in plotting.

My beta readers, Laura Janßen, Ivy Bekoe, and Saskia Weyel, for their invaluable suggestions.

Kim Nina Ocker, official book-godmother to Ruby and James, for her infectious enthusiasm and all our writing days together.

My friends Lucie Kallies and Maren Haase, who are always there to listen to me—life is much more fun with them in it.

Gesa Weiß and Kristina Langenbuch, who set *Save Me* firmly on the path, and Christiane Düring, who took it on from there with the greatest dedication.

My editor, Stephanie Bubley, for working out the plot together, for listening to me, for looking into K-pop for me, and for working so closely together on the text. Eternal thanks go to the whole team at LYX, especially Ruza Kelava and Simon Decot, who made it possible for me to write this new series.

And now I need to add a little postscript, seeing that the book has been translated into English:

Huge thanks to Flavia Viotti and Giuseppe Terrano for carrying *Save Me* over the seas and into the hands of English-speaking readers. My heartfelt thanks to Berkley, and especially to Cindy Hwang, for being a joy to work with.

This English translation has largely come about thanks to the people who brought my characters to life. I would like to thank all the actors on *Maxton Hall*, especially the magnificent Harriet Herbig-Matten, who understood both Ruby's depths and her determination, and Damian Hardung, who captured James's emotional life like no other.

Finally, I would like to thank all my readers for picking up this book. You are wonderful, and I'm sorry about the ending . . . Fortunately, Ruby and James will be back soon to pick up their story!

Keep reading for an excerpt from

SAVE
YOU

The next novel in the Maxton Hall series
by Mona Kasten

Lydia

James is drunk. Or coked-up. Or both.

It's been three days since anyone could really talk to him. He's just been on one long bender in our sitting room, draining bottle after bottle and acting like nothing's happened. I don't understand how he can be like this. Apparently, he's not even interested in the fact that our family is now in ruins.

"I think it's his way of grieving."

I give Cyril a sideways glance. He's the only other person who knows what's happened. I told him at his party, the night that James got off his face and snogged Elaine in front of Ruby's very eyes. Somebody had to help me get James home without either Percy or Dad spotting the state he was in. Our families are close friends, so Cy and I have known each other since we were kids. And even though Dad made me promise not to tell anyone about Mum before the official press release goes out, I know I can trust him and that he'll keep the secret—even from Wren, Keshav, and Alistair.

I couldn't have got through the last few days without his help.

He convinced Dad to leave James alone for a bit and told the lads not to ask questions for the time being. They're sticking to that, although I get the impression that with every passing day, they're finding it harder and harder to watch James destroying himself.

While my brother is doing his very best to shut off his brain, all I can do is wonder how I'm meant to cope. My mum is dead. Graham's mum died seven years ago. The baby growing inside me isn't going to have a granny.

Seriously. That's the thought running through my head on a perpetual ticker. Instead of grieving, I'm wrestling with the fact that my child will never know the embrace of a loving grandmother. What the hell is wrong with me?

But I can't help it. The thoughts in my head have taken on a life of their own—they escalate until I'm wallowing in catastrophic scenarios and I'm so scared of the future that I can't think about anything else. It's like I've been in a state of shock for three days. I guess something inside me—and James—broke horribly when Dad told us what had happened.

"I don't know how to help him," I whisper, watching James tip back his head and drain yet another glass. It hurts to see him suffering. He can't keep on like this forever. Sooner or later, he's going to have to face reality. And in my view, there's only one person in the world who can help him with that.

I pull out my phone for the squillionth time and call Ruby's number, but she doesn't pick up. I wish I could be angry with her, but I can't. If I'd caught Graham with someone else, I wouldn't want anything to do with him, or anyone associated with him, ever again either.

"Are you calling her again?" Cy asks, glancing skeptically at my phone. I nod, and he frowns disapprovingly. I'm not surprised by his reaction. He thinks Ruby's only interested in James for his money. I know that's not true, but once Cyril's made up his mind about a person, it's very hard to convince him to change it. And I might find it frustrating, but I can't resent him for it. It's his way of taking care of his friends.

"He won't listen to any of us. I think she might be able to get through to him before he has a total breakdown." My voice sounds weird in my own ears. So cold and flat—but inwardly, I'm the total opposite.

The pain makes it almost impossible even to stand up straight. It's like I've been tied up and spent days trying to undo the knots. Like my thoughts are whirling on a never-ending carousel that I can't jump down from. Everything seems pointless, and the harder I struggle against the helplessness rising up within me, the more completely it grips me.

I've lost one of the most important people in my life. I don't know how I can get through this alone. I *need* my twin brother. But all James will do is get shitfaced and smash everything that gets in his way. I haven't seen my dad since Wednesday. He's away, meeting with lawyers and accountants, settling the future of the Beaufort companies. He doesn't even have a second to spare on Mum's funeral—he's hired a woman called Julia to organize it, and she's been strolling in and out of our house for days like she's part of the family now.

The thought of Mum's funeral makes my throat clench. I can't breathe; my eyes start to sting. Hastily, I turn away, but Cyril notices.

"Lydia . . ." he whispers, gently reaching for my hand.

I pull away from him and leave the room without a word. I don't want the boys to see me cry. Sooner or later, they're going to start asking questions, whatever Cyril says; we can't stall them forever. They're not idiots. Even for James, this is out of character. OK, so he gets a bit out of hand sometimes, but he normally knows his limits. And the boys have clocked that right now, he doesn't. Keshav has started hiding bottles of the hard stuff from the bar, and Alistair "accidentally" flushed James's last few grams of cocaine down the loo—and that tells you everything you need to know.

I can't wait to put an end to all this secrecy. It won't be long now. The press release is going out at three on the dot, and then all the boys will know—and it won't be just them, either. The whole world will learn that Mum died. I can already see the headlines and the reporters doorstepping us and hanging around outside the school. I feel sick and stumble down the hall toward the library.

The lamps are on, casting faint light on the rows of shelves full of antique, leather-bound books. I lean on the bookcases as I cross the room, my knees shaking. Right at the back, by the window, there's an armchair upholstered in dark red velvet. It's been my favorite spot in this house ever since I was little. This is where I came to hide away when I wanted some peace—from the boys, from Dad, from the expectations that go with the name Beaufort.

At the sight of this little reading nook, my tears flow all the faster. I curl up in the chair, wrapping my arms around my legs. Then I bury my face in my knees and cry quietly.

Everything around me feels so surreal. Like this is a bad dream that I could wake up from if I just tried hard enough. I wish myself back to the summer, eighteen months ago, when Mum was still alive and Graham could give me a hug when I was having a bad day.

I wipe my eyes with one hand and pull my phone from my jeans pocket with the other. As I unlock the screen, I notice streaks of mascara all over the backs of my hands.

I open my contacts. I haven't spoken to Graham for months, but he's still saved in my favorites, along with James's number. He doesn't even know about our baby, let alone that my mum died. I've honored his wish and haven't called him. It's been the hardest thing I've ever done in my whole life. We were in touch pretty much every day for over two years, and then it suddenly stopped, practically overnight. It felt like going cold turkey.

And now . . . I'm having a relapse. I can't help it. I call his number and hold my breath as I listen to it ring. The ringing stops after a moment. I shut my eyes and listen intently, trying to hear whether or not he's picked up. At this moment, it's like I could actually drown in the lonely helplessness I've been feeling for days.

"Don't call me. We agreed," he says quietly. The sound of his soft, scratchy voice tips me over the edge. My body is shaken by a violent sob. I press my free hand to my mouth so that Graham won't hear.

But it's too late.

"Lydia?"

I notice the panic in his voice, but I can't speak, only shake my head. My breath is out of control, far too fast.

Graham doesn't hang up. He stays on the line, making quiet, soothing sounds. On the one hand, hearing him is churning me up more than ever, but on the other, it feels so safe and familiar that I press my phone even harder to my ear. I think his voice was one of the reasons I fell in love with him—long before I ever saw him in person. I remember the hours we spent on the phone, my ear sore and burning, remember waking up with Graham still on the line. His voice, gentle and quiet, deep, and just as piercing as his golden-brown eyes.

I've always felt safe with Graham. For ages, he was my rock. It's only thanks to him that I was able to move on from the thing with Gregg and start to look ahead again.

And even though I'm devastated, this feeling of security starts trying to fight its way back to the top. Just hearing his voice is helping me calm down ever so slightly. I don't know how long I sit here like this but, gradually, my tears stop.

"What's wrong?" he whispers in the end.

I can't answer. All I can do is utter a helpless sound.

For a minute, he stays quiet. I hear him breathe in a few times like he's going to say something, but at the last moment, he always holds back. When he finally speaks, his voice is hushed and full of pain: "There's nothing I'd rather do than drive over to see you, to be there for you."

I shut my eyes and imagine him sitting in his flat, at the old wooden table that looks about ready to collapse. Graham likes to claim it's an antique, but he actually pulled it out of a skip and revarnished it.

"I know," I whisper.

"But you know that I can't, don't you?"

Something in the sitting room just smashed. I hear breaking glass, then someone yelling. I can't tell whether they're hurt or having fun, but I straighten up all the same. I can't let James add a physical injury to the list.

"Sorry for phoning," I whisper, my voice broken, and I end the call.

I feel a stab in the heart as I get up and leave my little safe haven to go and check on my brother.

Ember

My sister is ill.

I wouldn't normally find that surprising—after all, it's December, it's freezing, and everywhere you look, people are coughing and sneezing. It's only a matter of when, not if, you're going to catch a cold.

But my sister never gets ill. Seriously, never.

When Ruby came home three nights ago and went to bed without a word, I didn't think anything of it. After all, she'd just come through the marathon of applying to Oxford and it must have been mentally and physically exhausting. But the next day, she said she had a cold and couldn't go to school. That made me dubious because anyone who knows Ruby knows that she'd drag herself in, even with a temperature, out of fear of missing something important.

Today is Saturday, and I'm starting to feel really worried. Ruby's barely left her room. She's lying in bed, reading one book after another, and pretending that her eyes are red because she's ill. But she can't fool me. Something bad has happened and she won't tell me what, which is driving me crazy.

Right now, I'm squinting through the crack around her door, watching her stir her soup without eating any of it. I can't remember ever seeing her like this. Her face is pale, and there are bluish circles under her eyes, getting darker with every day. Her hair is greasy and limp, hanging uncombed around her face, and she's wearing the same baggy clothes as yesterday and the day before. Normally, Ruby is the epitome of togetherness. It's not just her planner or her schoolwork—she takes pride in her appearance too. I didn't know she even had any slobby clothes.

"Stop lurking outside my room," she says suddenly, and I jump, caught. I act like I was coming in anyway, and push the door open.

Ruby raises her eyebrows at me. Then she puts the bowl of soup down on her bedside table, on the tray I brought it up on. I suppress a sigh.

"If you don't want it, I'll eat it," I threaten, nodding toward the soup. Not that it has the desired effect. Ruby gestures vaguely.

"Knock yourself out."

I groan with frustration as I lower myself onto the edge of her bed. "It's been hard, but I've left you alone for the last couple of days because I can see you're not exactly in the mood to talk, but . . . I'm genuinely worried about you."

Ruby pulls her duvet up to her chin, so that only her head is peeking out. Her eyes are dull and sad, like whatever happened to her has just this minute hit her with full force. But then she blinks, and she's back—or she's acting like she is. There's been a funny look in her eyes since last Wednesday. It's been like only her body was here, and her mind has been somewhere else entirely.

"It's just a cold. I'll be better soon," she says flatly, sounding like one of those lifeless computerized voices when you're on hold, like she's been replaced by a robot.

Ruby turns her face to the wall and disappears under the duvet again—a clear sign that as far as she's concerned, the conversation is over. I sigh, and I'm about to stand up when her phone lights up on the bedside table, catching my attention. I lean over slightly so that I can see the screen.

"Lin's calling you," I mumble.

All I hear is a muffled "don't care."

I frown and watch as the call ends and, a moment later, the number of missed calls pops up on the screen. It's in the double digits. "She's called you more than ten times, Ruby. Whatever's happened, you won't be able to hide forever."

My sister just growls.

Mum says I should give her time, but every day, it's getting harder to watch Ruby suffer. It doesn't take a genius to come to the conclusion that James Beaufort and his arsehole friends have something to do with this.

But I thought Ruby had got over Beaufort. So, what's happened? And when?

I've tried to analyze the situation the way Ruby would, and I've made a mental list:

1. Ruby was in Oxford for her interviews.
2. When she got back, everything was fine.
3. That evening, Lydia Beaufort turned up on our doorstep, and Ruby went off with her.
4. After that, everything changed. Ruby hid away and has barely spoken since.
5. Why???

OK. So, Ruby's list would probably be way more structured that that, but I've put things in a logical order, and clearly, whatever happened, it happened on Wednesday evening.

But where did she and Lydia go?

My eyes wander from Ruby, or rather the top of her head, which is all I can see poking out of her duvet, to her phone and back again. She won't miss it, I'm pretty sure of that.

"If you need anything, I'm next door," I say, even though I know she won't take me up on the offer. Then I give an extraloud sigh as I stand up and make a lightning-fast grab for her phone. I shove it up one sleeve of my baggy, loose-knit sweater and tiptoe back into my own room.

Once I've shut the door behind me, I exhale with relief—and instantly feel guilty. My gaze is drawn to the wall, as if Ruby can see me from her bed. She'll probably never speak to me again when she finds out that I've invaded her privacy like this. But as her sister, it's my duty to find out how to help. Right?

I walk to my desk and sit down on the creaky chair. Then I pull her phone from my sleeve. My sister makes a massive secret of everything that goes on at Maxton Hall, but obviously I know the kind of people she's at school with: rich kids whose parents are actual aristocrats, actors, politicians, or entrepreneurs. People with power and influence in this country, who quite often hit the headlines. I've been following some of Ruby's year on Insta for a while, so I know the gossip. Just the thought of what some of them might have done to Ruby turns my stomach.

I only hesitate for a tiny moment, then I unlock Ruby's phone and bring up her calls list. Lin isn't the only person who's been ringing. A number she doesn't have saved has called her loads of times too. I make up my mind and find Lin's details—after all, she's the only person from Ruby's horrible school I've ever met in person. Hesitantly, I hold the handset to my ear. She picks up after just one ring.

"Ruby," I hear Lin say breathlessly. "Thank God. How are you?"

"Lin—it's me, Ember," I interrupt her.

"Ember? What . . . ?"

"Ruby's not doing very well."

Lin goes quiet for a moment. Then, slowly, she says: "That's hardly surprising, considering what's happened."

"What *has* happened?" I burst out. "What the hell has happened, Lin? Ruby won't talk to me, and I'm so worried. Did Beaufort hurt her? If he did, the dickhead, I'll . . ."

"Ember." Now it's her cutting me off. "What are you talking about?"

I frown. "What are *you* talking about?"

"I'm talking about the fact that Ruby messaged me on Wednesday to say she'd made up with James Beaufort, and now today, I hear that his mum died last Monday."

MONA KASTEN was born in 1992 and studied Library and Information Management before switching to writing full-time. She lives in Hamburg, Germany, with her family, their cats, and an enormous number of books; she loves caffeine in every form, long forest walks, and days when she can do nothing but write. For more information, visit: monakasten.de.

RACHEL WARD completed the MA in Literary Translation at the University of East Anglia in 2002 and has been working as a freelance translator from German and French to English ever since. She lives in Wymondham, near Norwich, UK, and specializes in works for children and young adults, as well as in crime fiction and contemporary literature. She also loves coffee and cats and can be found on social media as @racheltranslates and at forwardtranslations.co.uk.

Ready to find
your next great read?

Let us help.

Visit prh.com/nextread